We Solve Murders

We Solve Murders

Murders

RICHARD OSMAN

PAMELA DORMAN BOOKS / VIKING

VIKING

An imprint of Penguin Random House LLC
penguinrandomhouse.com

Simultaneously published in hardcover in Great Britain by Viking,
an imprint of Penguin Random House Ltd, London, in 2024

First United States edition published by Pamela Dorman Books, 2024

A Pamela Dorman Book/Viking

ISBN 9780593653227 (hardcover)
ISBN 9780593653234 (ebook)

Library of Congress Control Number: 2024941965

Printed in the United States of America
1   3   5   7   9   10   8   6   4   2

Designed by Cassandra Garruzzo Mueller

To Janet Elizabeth Wright, 1946–2023
With love to fill a lifetime

We Solve Murders

Y ou must leave as few clues as possible. That's the only rule.

You have to talk to people sometimes; it's inevitable. There are orders to be given, shipments to be arranged, people to be killed, etc., etc. You cannot exist in a vacuum, for goodness' sake.

You need to ring François Loubet? In an absolute emergency? You'll get a phone with a voice-changer built in. And, by the way, if it's not an absolute emergency, you'll regret ringing very soon.

But most communication is by message or email. High-end criminals are much like millennials in that way.

Everything is encrypted, naturally, but what if the authorities break the code? It happens. A lot of very good criminals are in prison right now because a nerd with a laptop had too much time on their hands. So you must hide as well as you can.

You can hide your IP address—that is very easy. François Loubet's emails go through a world tour of different locations before being sent. Even a nerd with a laptop would never be able to discover from where they were actually sent.

But everyone's language leaves a unique signature. A particular use of words, a rhythm, a personality. Someone could read an email, and then read a postcard you sent in 2009 and know for a fact they were sent by the same person. Science, you see. So often the enemy of the honest criminal.

That's why ChatGPT has been such a godsend.

After writing an email, a text, anything really, you can simply run the whole thing through ChatGPT and it instantly deletes your personality. It flattens you out, irons your creases, washes you away, quirk by quirk, until you disappear.

"ChatGPT, rewrite in the style of a friendly English gentleman, please." That is always Loubet's prompt.

Handy, because if these emails were written in François Loubet's own language, it would all become much more obvious. Too obvious.

But, as it stands, you might find a thousand emails, but you would still have no way of knowing where François Loubet was, and you would still have no way of knowing who François Loubet is.

You would, of course, know what François Loubet does, but there would be precious little you could do about it.

PART ONE

From the New Forest to South Carolina

1

It had *finally* happened.

Andrew Fairbanks had always known he would be famous one day. And that day—a quiet, sunny Tuesday in early August—had, at last, arrived.

The years of Instagram fitness videos had given him a following, sure, but nothing like this. This was *insane*.

There had been an on-off relationship with a minor pop singer, which had seen his picture in the papers from time to time. But not on the front pages like today.

The notoriety Andrew Fairbanks had chased for so long was finally his. His name on lips around the world. Trending on social media. That selfie on the yacht was everywhere. Andrew, shirtless and tanned, winking into the camera, the warm sun winking along behind him. His bottle of Krusher Energy Drink raised in a happy toast.

And the comments beneath the photo! The heart emojis, the fire emojis, the lust. Everything Andrew had ever dreamed of.

Some of the other comments might have dampened his spirits a little, however. "Gone too soon," "So fit, RIP," "So haunting to see that photo when you knew what was about to happen"—but you couldn't argue with the volume. Impressive traffic. In the offices of the *Love Island* production team, his photograph was passed around, and there were discussions about how perfect he might have been if only, well, *you know.*

Yes, finally, everybody knew Andrew Fairbanks. Or, as he was now more commonly known, "Tragic Instagram influencer, Andrew Fairbanks."

So it wasn't all upside. And, in fact, even that slim upside is starting to dim. It is Wednesday afternoon by now, and his name is already beginning to slip down the rankings. Other things are happening in the world. A baseball star has driven his pickup into his ex-wife's swimming pool. A beauty vlogger has said something inappropriate about Taylor Swift. The conversation, like the tide, is turning.

Andrew Fairbanks had been found dead: shot in the head, tied to a rope, and thrown from a yacht bobbing about in the Atlantic. There was no one else on the yacht, and no sign that anyone had ever been there, with the exception of a leather bag containing nearly one million dollars.

But none of this gives you the right to be famous more than a day or so. One day, perhaps, there might be a podcast about the case or, better still, a Netflix true-crime documentary, but, for now, Andrew's limelight is turning to dusk.

Soon Andrew Fairbanks will be just a figure in a photograph, holding a purple energy drink in front of a blue sea, a corpse in a South Carolina mortuary, and the odd "Remember that guy that died on that yacht with all that money?"

Who killed him? Who knows? Someone or other, certainly, and social media has a lot of opinions on it. Why did they kill him? No idea—someone must have had their reasons, mustn't they? Jealous partner? Instagram fitness rival? Could be all sorts of explanations. Can you *believe* what this vlogger has said about Taylor Swift?

Just for the one day, though, what a ride it had been. If Andrew had still been alive, he would have been looking for a full-time manager. Get me a few more deals, protein bars, teeth-whitening clinics, perhaps I could launch my own vodka?

Yes, just for a day, everybody had wanted a piece of Andrew Fairbanks. Although, after the sharks had finished with him, there weren't that many pieces left.

And that's show business.

2

What don't you like about yourself?" asks Rosie D'Antonio. She sits on an inflatable chair shaped like a throne, in a swimming pool shaped like a swan. "I always ask people."

Amy Wheeler is sitting, bolt upright, on a garden chair at the poolside, the sun in her eyes and her gun within easy reach. She likes South Carolina. This hidden offshoot of it, at least. Early morning and the temperature in the nineties, an Atlantic breeze, and nobody, for the time being, trying to kill her. She hasn't shot at anyone in a while, but you can't have everything.

"My nose, I suppose," says Amy.

"What's wrong with your nose?" asks Rosie, sipping something green through a non-recyclable straw, her trailing hand rippling the water.

"Don't know," says Amy. She is impressed that Rosie D'Antonio is in full, perfect makeup while in the pool. How old is she? Sixty? Eighty? A mystery. The age on her file reads *Refused to disclose*. "It's just wrong, when I look at it. It's off."

"Get it done," says Rosie. "Bigger, smaller, whatever you think you need. Life's too short to not like your nose. Hunger and famine are problems, or no Wi-Fi; noses aren't a problem. What else?"

"Hair," says Amy. She is in danger of relaxing. Feels it creeping up on her. Amy hates relaxing. Too much time to think. She prefers to *do*. "It never does what it's told."

"I see *that*," says Rosie. "But it's easily fixed. There's a hair technician I use. She flies in from somewhere. Chile, I think. Five thousand dollars and your troubles are over. I'll pay."

"And my ears are lopsided," says Amy.

Rosie tilts her head and paddles herself toward Amy, considering her very carefully. "I'm not seeing that. You have great ears. Like Goldie Hawn's."

"I measured them with a ruler once," says Amy, "when I was at school. It's only a millimeter, but I always see it. And my legs are too short for my body."

Rosie nods, pushing herself back into the middle of the pool, where the sun is hitting hardest. "More to the point, though, Amy, what do you *like* about yourself?"

"I'm English," says Amy. "I don't like anything about myself."

"Yawn," says Rosie. "I used to be English too, and I got over it. Pick something."

"I think I'm loyal," says Amy.

"That's a good quality," agrees Rosie. "For a bodyguard."

"And my short legs give me a low center of gravity," says Amy. "So I'm very good at fighting."

"There you go." Rosie nods. "Loyal, and very good at fighting."

Rosie raises her face to the sun.

"If someone does try to shoot me this week, do you have to dive in front of the bullet?"

"That's the idea," says Amy, without conviction. "Though that's mainly in films."

It's hard to dive in front of a bullet, in Amy's experience. They go very fast indeed.

"Or in books, sure," says Rosie. "Would you like a joint? I'm going to have one?"

"Best not," says Amy. "Maximum Impact gives us mandatory blood tests every three months, company policy. A single trace of any drug and I'm fired."

Rosie gives a "fair enough" grunt.

It's not the most exciting job Amy has ever had, but it's sunny, and she likes the client. Rosie D'Antonio, the world's bestselling novelist, "if you don't count Lee Child." Her Spanish-style mansion on her own private island just off the coast of South Carolina. With her own personal chef.

For various operational reasons Amy once had to spend the best part of a month living inside an abandoned oil pipeline in Syria, so this is a step up. The chef brings her a plate of smoked salmon blinis. He's not really a chef—he's a former Navy SEAL called Kevin—but he is learning fast. Last night his boeuf bourguignon was a triumph. Rosie's regular chef has been given two weeks' leave. Amy, Rosie, and Kevin, the Navy SEAL, are the only people on the island, and that's how it's going to stay for now.

"No one's allowed to kill me," says Rosie. She has paddled over to the side of the pool, and is now rolling a cigarette. "Except me."

"And I won't let you," says Amy.

"But someone might try to shoot me," says Rosie. "Given one never knows anymore, the world being as it is and so on. So, if they *do* try, no jumping in front of the bullet, okay? Not on my account. Let them kill the old woman."

Maximum Impact Solutions, Amy's employer, is the world's biggest close-protection agency, possibly the second biggest since Henk van Veen left and took half his clients with him. If someone steals from you, or someone wants to kill you, or if there is discontent among your private army, they are the people to call. Maximum Impact Solutions has many mottos, but "Let them kill the old woman" is not one of them.

"I'm not going to let anybody kill you," says Amy.

Amy remembers watching Rosie on the communal TV when she was growing up. Those shoulder pads, that attitude. It had meant a lot to Amy, seeing how strong a woman could be, while she slept each night curled up in a ball under her bed and dreamed of better days. Rosie will not die on her watch.

"What's that accent?" asks Rosie, taking the first drag on her joint. "It's cute. Is it Manchester?"

"Watford," says Amy.

"Eesh," says Rosie. "I've been gone too long. Tell me about Watford."

"It's a town," says Amy. "In England."

"I know that, Amy. Is it pretty?"

"It's not the first word I'd use," says Amy. She is looking forward to ringing her father-in-law, Steve, later. It's a Friday, so he should be around. He'll get a kick out of hearing about Rosie. Strong women had certainly been his thing. Maybe they will be again one day.

Thinking about strong women makes Amy think about Bella Sanchez. And thinking about Bella Sanchez makes her think about Mark Gooch. And thinking about Mark Gooch makes her . . .

And that's the problem right there, Amy, isn't it! When you relax, you *think*. None of that stuff is her business. Stop thinking: it never works out for you. Hit things, drive fast, defuse explosives, but, for the love of God, don't *think*. Life isn't *school*.

"England is nuts," says Rosie. "In the eighties they loved me, then in the nineties they hated me, in the noughties they forgot me, in the twenty tens they remembered me, and now they love me again. I haven't changed a jot in all that time. You ever read any of my books, Amy the bodyguard?"

"No," lies Amy. Everyone has read one of Rosie D'Antonio's books. Amy has been reading her books since she was a teenager. A social worker once handed one to her, a finger on their lips to warn Amy that this contraband was their little secret. And what a secret. The death, the glamour, the clothes, the blood. Shoulder pads and poison. But it's important not to fangirl a client. A bullet doesn't care how famous you are. Which actually *is* one of Maximum Impact Solutions' mottos.

Amy had been rereading *Death Pulls the Trigger* on the plane up here yesterday. They'd made a film of it with Angelina Jolie, but the book was better. Lots of sex with millionaires, lots of guns. Stuff Amy could relate to.

"You married?" Rosie asks. "Kids?"

"Married, no kids," says Amy.

"He a good guy? The husband?"

"Yeah, he is," says Amy, thinking of Adam. "As good as I am, anyway. I like him."

Rosie nods. "That's a good answer. Does he worry about you?"

"He doesn't like it when I get shot at," says Amy. "And once, in Morocco, I got attacked with a sword, and he cried."

"Did you cry?"

"I haven't cried since I was twelve," says Amy. "I learned not to."

"That sounds healthy," says Rosie. "Can I put you in a book? Five six, blue eyes, blonde, never cries, kills bad guys?"

"No," says Amy. "I don't like publicity."

"I promise not to mention your ears."

Amy and her father-in-law try to talk every day. They've never really discussed it; it's just become a habit important to both of them. Well, it's a habit important to Amy, and she hopes it's important to Steve too. Occasionally they'll miss a day. For example, Amy had to stay completely quiet for twelve hours in that oil pipeline, on account of a hit squad, so on that day she had to make do with texting. Steve understands. The job is the job.

"Do you get to choose what you wear?" Rosie asks. "Or is it a uniform?"

Amy looks down at her combat fatigues and faded Under Armour T-shirt.

"I choose."

Rosie raises a questioning eyebrow. "Well, nobody's perfect."

Amy doesn't like to leave it too long between calls, because you never knew what Steve was eating, if he was looking after himself. It is illogical, in her opinion, to eat poorly.

She should probably ring her husband too, but she worries less about Adam. And, besides, what would they talk about?

"When you came in," says Rosie, "there was a copy of *Death Pulls the Trigger* at the top of your bag. Thumbed through to about halfway."

Amy nods. Busted.

"So you *have* read one of my books? You said you hadn't?"

"Client research."

"Bullshit," says Rosie. "You like it?"

"There was nothing else to read."

"Course you like it, I see you. You read the bit where she shoots the guy on the plane?"

"That's a good bit," says Amy.

"Yeah, that's a good bit," says Rosie, nodding. "A pilot I was seeing let me shoot a gun on his plane for research. Have you ever done that?"

"Shot a gun on a plane? No," lies Amy.

"Nothing really happens," says Rosie. "They had to replace the calfskin on one of the sofas, but that was it."

"If it had pierced the fuselage, the cabin could have depressurized and you could all have died," says Amy. Amy had once parachuted out of a plane after exactly such an incident. She had spent the next five days evading rebel forces in Burkina Faso. Actually a lot of fun in the end. Amy finds adrenaline good for the soul, and very good for the skin. Sometimes she watches skincare tutorials on Instagram, but there's not a single one that will do for your skin what being shot at and then jumping out of a plane will do. Perhaps she should do her own videos? Again, she finds that she is thinking, and so she stops.

"Lucky it didn't, then," says Rosie, knocking back the rest of whatever goop is sitting in her glass. "I'm getting itchy feet, Amy. Can't we go somewhere on the mainland? Have a drink? Raise a bit of hell?"

Rosie's troubles had started when she had included a character in her most recent novel, *Dead Men & Diamonds*, very clearly based on a Russian chemicals oligarch named Vasiliy Karpin. Vasiliy, it seemed, had lacked the sense of humor one usually associates with chemicals billionaires, and, after a bullet in the post and a botched abduction at a Nashville book signing, Rosie had called in the professionals, and was confined to barracks for the foreseeable future.

People are talking to people. Jeff Nolan, Amy's boss, has reached out to some of Vasiliy's colleagues in London. Conversations are ongoing. Vasiliy will be persuaded to drop this particular vendetta soon enough. Maximum Impact Solutions has clients who could do him a few favors. An accommodation will be found, Vasiliy will be placated, and Rosie will be free to go about her business again. And, if not, Amy will be ready.

Until then, Amy and Rosie are stuck on this idyllic island, with their hastily trained executive chef. Amy could definitely use a few days here, probably needs the rest if she's being honest, but she'll have to be back on the move soon. No one is going to kill Rosie D'Antonio, so Amy is essentially just a very expensive babysitter. And where's the fun in that for either of them?

"We're going nowhere for the moment," says Amy. "You might get murdered."

Rosie rolls her eyes and starts to roll another joint. "Oh, Amy, I'd rather be murdered than *bored*."

And on that point, Amy Wheeler, who spent so much of her childhood trying to be as quiet and as small as possible, is inclined to agree.

3

"at, ginger, unapproachable. Haughty even, the little bugger. Mason's Lane. Contact attempted but rebuffed. 3:58 a.m."

Steve puts his Dictaphone back in his pocket. He hears the sound of the ginger cat inexpertly scaling a back fence. It was not often he saw an unfamiliar cat on his walk. It was almost certainly nothing, but almost everything was almost certainly nothing, wasn't it? And yet some things did eventually turn out to be something. He once caught an armed robber because of a Twix wrapper in a blast furnace. One rarely knows the significance of things at the time, and it doesn't cost a penny piece to note things down.

Steve turns left on to the top of the High Street, and sees it stretch out like an unspooling gray ribbon before him, lit by the dim bulb of the moon.

If you were to visit Axley—and you should, you'd like it—you might think you had found the perfect English village. A gently sloping high street, looping around a touch at the bottom where it skirts the bank of the village pond. There are two pubs, The Brass Monkey and The Flagon, identical to the tourists but teeming with subtle and important differences to the locals. For example, one flies a Union Jack and the other the Ukrainian flag. There's a butcher, a baker. No candlestick maker, but you will find a little gift shop selling scented candles and bookmarks. Striped awnings, bicycles leaned against shop fronts, chalkboards promising cream teas or tarot readings or dog treats. There is a church at the top of the village, and a small bookmaker at the bottom of the village, take your pick. Steve used to visit both, and now visits neither.

And, all around, there is the New Forest. The forest is the whole point of the place. The village itself simply found itself a small clearing and settled in. There are walks and trails, the chirrup and buzz of wildlife, and the backpacks and rain macs of the tourists. Stray New Forest ponies some days wander on to the main road and are accorded due reverence. It was their forest long before it was yours, and it will be theirs long afterward too. Axley simply shelters among the trees, curled into a little nutshell.

When Steve first moved here—twelve years ago, was it? Something like that, Debbie would remember, probably fifteen the way time goes—it hadn't fooled him for a second. Steve hadn't been hoodwinked by the hollyhocks and the cupcakes and the cheery "Good morning" greetings. Steve had seen secrets behind every pastel front door, seen corpses in every back alley, and every time the church bells rang in the hour, Steve had heard the chimes of death.

A crisp packet has blown into a hedge. Steve retrieves it and places it in a bin. Monster Munch. They don't sell Monster Munch in the local shop, so that will have been a tourist.

No, Steve had refused to be fooled by Axley. Twenty-five years in the police force had taught him to always think the worst of everyone, and everything. Always expect the worst, and you'll always be prepared. Never let anyone, or anything, take you by surprise.

Ironic, given what soon happened.

Steve stops by the window of the estate agent and peers through the glass. If he was moving to the village today, he wouldn't be able to afford it. The only way anyone can afford to buy a house these days is to have bought it fifteen years ago.

Steve had been wrong about Axley—he'd be the first to admit it. There were no murderers lurking behind the doors, no mutilated corpses in blood-soaked alleys. And, thus, Steve had begun to relax.

Steve had never relaxed as a child; his dad had made sure of that. School? Too bright to fit in but not bright enough to get out. Then joining the Metropolitan Police at the age of eighteen, seeing the worst that London had to offer, day after day. Sometimes this included his own colleagues. Every day a fight.

Steve takes out his Dictaphone once more. "Pale-blue Volkswagen Passat, registration number PN17 DFQ, in car park of The Brass Monkey." Steve walks around the car. "An ancient tax disc." There is the wrapper from a Greggs in the footwell. Where is the nearest Greggs? Southampton? The services on the M27?

He resumes his walk. He will go as far as the pond, sit there for a while, then head back up. Of course he will—that's what Steve does every night.

Axley had transformed Steve. Not all at once, but, smile by smile, favor by favor, and scone by scone, the people and the place had taken down the wall that he had built up over so many years. Debbie had told him it would, and he hadn't believed her. She had been born here, and, when Steve finally left the Met, she had persuaded him to make the move. She knew.

Steve had worried there would be no excitement, no adrenaline, but Debbie had reassured him. "If you get bored, we're only twenty miles from Southampton, and there are plenty of murders there."

But Steve didn't miss the excitement, and he didn't miss the adrenaline.

Steve liked to stay in; he liked to cook for Debbie; he liked to hear birdsong; he found himself a solid pub-quiz team. Good but improvable.

A stray cat, a proper bruiser, came to visit them and refused to leave. After a week or two of snarling and bullying, from both Steve and the cat, they each let down their guard. And now you'll find Steve, reading his paper in an old armchair, Trouble curled up on his lap, purring in his sleep. Two old rascals, safe and sound.

Debbie persuaded him to set up his agency. He was happy not working—she was bringing in enough money from painting—but she was right. He probably needed something to do, and probably needed to contribute something to the community. The name of his agency, "Steve Investigates," was his idea. He remembers a Sunday lunch when his boy, Adam, had come round with his wife, Amy. Amy is a bodyguard, works with billionaires and oligarchs, always on the other side of the world. Adam does something or other with money. Steve speaks to Amy more than he speaks to Adam. She's the one who rings; she's the one who makes sure they visit if she's in England on a job.

Amy had told him to call the company "Maverick Steel International Investigations." Branding is very important in the world of private investigations, she had said, but Steve had countered that his name was Steve, and he investigates things, and if that wasn't a brand, what was?

Amy is working with Rosie D'Antonio, the author, somewhere or other in America. Steve will play it cool when he next talks to Amy, but he will want all the gossip. There's always gossip when she's protecting celebrities. Once Amy was working with a singer in a boy band, and he took heroin on an elephant.

"Google America time difference," says Steve into his Dictaphone.

Steve Investigates keeps him pleasantly busy and adequately afloat. He has a few contacts with insurance companies. If you've ever claimed a year's salary because of a bad back anywhere in the New Forest, Steve has probably sat outside your house at some point, perhaps followed you to the gym. It makes Steve happy to find that people are almost always telling the truth about these things. He'll look into affairs if you really, really want him to. His only rule is that he won't travel any distance. Steve doesn't want to stray too far from Axley. He'll drive up to Brockenhurst if you need him to, couple of nice pubs up there. At a push he'll head over toward Ringwood or down toward Lymington, but ask him to go to Southampton, or Portsmouth, and Steve will politely decline.

Get yourself involved in a murder case, say, and before you know it your time is not your own. Steve never misses the Wednesday-night quiz at The

Brass Monkey now. A murder would almost certainly get in the way of that at some point. No thank you.

Steve reaches the pond and takes his customary seat. Debbie's favorite. The ducks love this bench, but they are all safely asleep now, tucked up, like the rest of the village, Steve keeping watch over them all. Least he can do after everything Axley has done for him.

Steve still remembers that feeling of relaxation, of finally letting life settle around him. Of trusting that people wished him well, and that each day would bring happiness. Of feeling safe. It didn't work out that way, of course. When does it?

In one sense, Debbie's death hadn't taken him by surprise. He'd mentally prepared for it every day since they'd fallen in love. That *something* would surely take her away. Cancer, heart disease, a car hitting her bike on a country road, a stroke, burglars. Something would steal his immense good luck at loving her, and being loved by her.

In the end it had been a train carriage that derailed as it approached a country station. There had been three people on the platform: Debbie and two other poor souls, who left their lives behind that rainy January day.

And, despite his assiduous preparation, it had taken him by surprise. You can think something often enough, but you will never be prepared for your heart disintegrating.

After Debbie's death the village gathered around him, carried him through. Walking through this village, where he knows everyone and everyone knows him, Steve is grateful that at least he feels loved. Because if you don't feel loved, it's difficult to feel anything at all.

A lone pony wanders by the side of the pond, head bobbing as he walks. Steve eyes him suspiciously. Well, Steve eyes him. His looks are always suspicious. He gets in trouble for it at the pub all the time.

"You should be asleep," he tells the pony.

The pony turns his head toward Steve, as if to say, "So should you." Steve accepts that the pony has a point. The pony continues his slow walk, moving across the high street and down the passage alongside the greetings-card shop, stopping to nuzzle something in a dustbin along the way. Axley belongs to Steve once again.

Steve rubs his fingers across the brass plaque on the bench. Debbie's name, the date of her birth, the date of her death. He presses "record" on his Dictaphone, because otherwise he would just be a man on a bench talking to himself.

"Hey, Debs. We came second in the quiz yesterday. Norman from the shop had his brother-in-law staying and he's been on *The Weakest Link*, so we had no chance. The gang was going to lodge a complaint—seemed a bit suspicious, you know—but I took a look at it all when I got back home, and he really is Norman's brother-in-law, so there's not a lot we can do. Trouble killed a vole, first one in a while; nice to know he's still got it in him. And he took it into Margaret's house, not ours, so that was a result. Just saw a new cat on Mason's Lane, ginger, tough guy, you know the sort. Umm . . . Amy's working with Rosie D'Antonio, you know, the writer. Very beautiful, people say, but not my type. I'll send her your love. Amy, not Rosie D'Antonio. I'll get the gossip for you. There's a new pie at the shop, chicken and something. I think you can just heat it up in the microwave; I'll let you know if I feel adventurous. Nothing else this evening. Love you, Debs."

Steve switches off his Dictaphone and puts it back in his pocket. He pats the bench.

"Love you, doll. I'm going to see if that cat is still around."

Steve begins his walk back up the high street. Tomorrow he is resuming the search for a dog that got lost at a local campsite; the owners, down from London, were understandably beside themselves. Steve knows how dogs think—he'll find him in no time. Five hundred pounds they've paid him, up front too, cash. Steve would have done it for fifty pounds. Londoners and their money are soon parted. And there's a local shop that has had money go missing from the till. Steve set up a remote camera last week, and he's going to head over to pick up the footage. It's the daughter of the owner—Steve worked that out almost immediately. Steve knows how people think too; they're surprisingly similar to dogs, in actual fact. But the owner isn't going to believe it was her daughter until she sees the evidence.

Axley is peaceful and quiet, and Steve is grateful for it. Other old coppers he knew, they're all in their late fifties now, are still chasing around on dodgy knees for dodgy bosses, drinking or smoking or stressing themselves to death. But Steve understands how life ends, and he has no intention of raging against it.

You can't have the thrills of life without the pain of life, so Steve has decided to go without the thrills. He chooses to watch the TV, to do his pub quizzes, to help people when he can, but always to return to his armchair with a cat called Trouble.

When you arrest someone, you generally get two different types of reactions. Some people kick and scream all the way to the cells, while others go quietly, knowing the game is up.

Who knows when your own game will be up? When you're standing on that platform and the train derails?

Whenever it might be, Steve intends to go quietly.

4

Jeff Nolan, CEO of Maximum Impact Solutions, is thinking about Andrew Fairbanks.

People have to be killed sometimes; that's just business, and Jeff understands that more than anyone. But eaten by a shark? Sends a message, Jeff supposes, and perhaps that's the point. When Bella Sanchez had been killed, it hadn't really made much of a splash. Mark Gooch had got people talking a little, joining the dots, but this was the first one to really get serious attention. The first one that had people asking questions. The police for one. Jeff doesn't like the police visiting him at work. He had tried to be helpful—after all, a young man was dead—but there is, after all, such a thing as client confidentiality.

Jeff knows the connection between the three deaths. Knows who's behind them all too.

François Loubet.

Jeff has work to do. He's not going to lose his business over three murders, for goodness' sake.

The police aren't the real problem here; they very rarely are. The real problem is the clients. Already this morning he'd had a Premier League footballer and a Dutch cannabis importer canceling their contracts. They no longer had confidence in Maximum Impact Solutions. You couldn't blame them. There would be other calls as news spread. No doubt they'd go to Henk, his former partner, and very former best friend.

And now Max Highfield, of all people, has paid him a visit. You'd think Max Highfield would have better things to do with his time, and yet here he is, shoes off, feet on Jeff's boardroom table, stirring up trouble.

"It makes me look bad, Jeff," says Max, running a hand through his hair like a grizzled veteran who has seen too much war, rather than like a man who has just had breakfast at The Ivy.

"I see that, Max," says Jeff. "I see that."

Jeff knew it. As soon as Andrew Fairbanks had died, he knew that other clients would start putting two and two together. People google. Especially celebrities—they're never off it.

"How much business do I bring you?" asks Max.

"Oh, plenty, plenty," says Jeff. "That's why we pay you three quarters of a million pounds a year, Max."

That's Max Highfield's "consultancy" fee. Plus a ten-grand bonus for each new recruit. Introducing other famous people to the business. Actors mainly, but Max is handsome enough to know everyone.

"Three quarters of a million?" Max laughs. "D'you know what I got for the last Marvel movie?"

"No," says Jeff. "And you don't need to tell me. I'm sure its confid—"

"Eight point five million," says Max. "Eight point five million. And that's pounds, not dollars. You ever been paid eight point five million for a job, Jeff?"

"I have, yes," says Jeff. "A number of times—but that's beside the point. I understand, reputationally, that this is difficult for you."

"Three clients dead," says Max, now drumming out a pattern on his voluminous superhero thighs. "That's a lot of dead clients."

"I mean," says Jeff, "playing devil's advocate here, between us, not big clients, small fry, with all due respect to their souls. It's not like Andrew Fairbanks was going to win an Oscar any day soon. He was a fitness influencer."

Max suddenly turns very serious. He even takes his feet off the board-room table. "Oscars are overrated, Jeff. It's all politics."

"I'm sure," says Jeff. "Now, if—"

"Lot of great actors never won an Oscar," says Max.

"Agreed, agreed. So here's my plan," says Jeff.

"Samuel L. Jackson has never won one. Did you know that?" Max High-field is shaking his head, slowly and sadly.

"I confess I didn't," says Jeff. "I've got an operative on the scene in South Carolina, where Andrew Fairbanks was murdered. She's—"

"Travolta's never won one," says Max. "Johnny Depp. Jason Statham. It's politics. Your face has to fit."

"I'm going to speak to her," says Jeff. "Make discreet inquiries."

"Sorry, you're asking who to do what?" says Max. "We were talking about the Oscars, bro?"

"I'm saying I have an operative in South Carolina," says Jeff again. "Amy Wheeler—she looked after you briefly years ago."

"I remember her," says Max. He stares at Jeff intensely for a while. He has clearly been told at some point that his intense stare is effective. "Tom Cruise, there's another one. Jeff, has anyone ever told you that you look like a black Jason Statham?"

Jeff decides he might as well just plow on.

"It's all delicate, Max, I'm sure you get it," says Jeff. "You know the na-ture of this business. But I want you to know we're taking this very seri-ously."

"I'm thinking of joining Henk," says Max, putting his feet back on the table. "I thought I should let you know. I bet he'd pay more money too."

"Well, I'd be shocked if you weren't thinking about it," says Jeff. Max Highfield would be Henk's highest-profile steal yet. "And we can talk about money."

"Amy Wheeler was the one who stopped me riding my motorbike off that bridge," Max says.

"That was her," says Jeff. "I believe you'd taken too much of your pain-killer medication?"

"They don't tell you not to mix it with whisky," says Max.

"Don't they?" Jeff says. "I'm sure I've heard somewhere that—"

"And she bled all over my denim jacket."

"To be fair," says Jeff, "she broke up a fight you'd started in a bar, and someone attacked her with a piece of broken glass."

"Harry Styles gave me that jacket," says Max.

"Max," says Jeff, looking to wrest back the conversation, "will you trust me, for the next few weeks? Until we can find out what's going on?"

"Course, course," says Max. "Couple of weeks."

Max begins to slip his shoes on, the signal that he is ready to move on to the next stop in Max World. Jeff stands.

"Loved the new film, by the way. *Rampage 7.*"

"Thanks, man," says Max. "I wasn't in love with *Rampage 6*, but we're back on track here. And it's nice to play triplets."

Jeff nods in agreement. As one of the triplets, Max has a mustache, and as one of the other triplets, he has an eye patch and a French, or possibly Dutch, accent.

"Henk said someone needs to teach you to hold a gun properly, but I loved it," says Jeff. "I hold them sideways too sometimes."

"Henk said that?" Max stands to his full height. The full six feet four inches that meant Max wasn't stuck acting in minor British soap operas for long.

"Afraid so."

"Huh," says Max. A man who has been given something to think about.

"Not everyone gets cinema," says Jeff.

"I am misunderstood, as a man," says Max. "And as an artist. And that's Britain all over."

"Terrible country, agreed," says Jeff, his extended hand engulfed in Max's. "I'll get this sorted."

As Max leaves, a heady haze of testosterone and Tom Ford lingering behind him, he passes Susan Knox on her way in to see Jeff. As he passes her, Max gives her a firm pat on the backside.

"There she is," says Max. "My hot cougar."

"She's the head of HR, Max," says Jeff.

"She doesn't mind," says Max over his shoulder, as he leaves the room. "It's a compliment."

"I'm guessing you do mind?" says Jeff, inviting Susan to sit. "That sort of thing?"

"That sort of thing? Yes," says Susan, impassively. "I mind *that sort of thing.*"

"Would you like me to do something?" Jeff asks.

"Dismantle the patriarchy?" suggests Susan.

"I'll talk to them," says Jeff. "They don't really like black guys interfering, but I'll do my best. Is that the François Loubet file?"

Susan nods and places the file on Jeff's desk. "May I ask why you wanted it?"

They had done a job for Loubet around two years ago. Didn't meet him, of course; no one meets François Loubet. He's the world's biggest money-smuggler and, as such, likes to keep himself to himself. They were protecting one of his staff. Henk had objected at the time; he was always a bit more particular than Jeff when it came to their clients. But, as Jeff had said, if you don't protect criminals you very soon run out of clients. Henk will discover this in his new business. Perhaps this row had been the beginning of the end for the two of them?

Jeff opens the file and looks at Susan. "Have you read it?"

"Have I read it?" Susan asks. "No, it's confidential."

Jeff nods. Of course she's read it; that's okay. Susan reads everything, but she knows how to keep quiet.

On top of the file is the printout of an email message Jeff had sent to François Loubet a few months ago, before the killings had started. Evidence, if he ever needs it.

Mssr Loubet,

I trust this email finds you well. You will remember we carried out some work for you around two years ago. Your prompt payment was greatly appreciated. I write with troubling news, however.

If I might express myself plainly, two of my clients have recently been caught carrying large sums of money through international customs.

This leads me to believe that my firm is being targeted by a professional money-smuggling syndicate, and the only money-smuggler who has had any connection with Maximum Impact Solutions is you. Your urgent help is needed in providing information that could assist me. Can we talk?

I'm afraid I cannot let this threat to my company continue, and I will take all the steps necessary to protect my clients and my business. Which also means that if you yourself, François, are behind it, which I believe you are, I will hunt you down.

Yours faithfully,
Jeff Nolan

Jeff looks up from the printout.

"You know what François Loubet does for a living, Susan?"

Susan shakes her head. "Without looking at his file, I would have no way of knowing."

"Perhaps you accidentally glanced at the file one day, though, while making copies, something like that?"

"If I had glanced at it," says Susan, "and such things happen, I would say he was the world's leading money-smuggler, is the number-one name on the FBI's Most Wanted list, and has recently been in email correspondence with you."

"That was a hell of a glance," says Jeff.

"I do a lot of photocopying," replies Susan. "I also understand that no one knows who he is?"

Jeff nods. "You see why I'm looking at his file now?"

"Andrew Fairbanks found with all that money?" Susan suggests.

"On top of everything else you might have accidentally glanced at in the file," says Jeff.

"It's certainly a situation," says Susan. "But you've been in situations before, and you always seem to struggle free. I hope you'll be able to do so on this occasion. It would be useful to identify him, so is there anything I can do to help?"

"Is there anyone with Amy Wheeler?" Jeff asks. "On the Rosie D'Antonio job?"

"An ex–Navy SEAL called Kevin," says Susan. As always, she has the answer at hand. That's why Jeff doesn't mind her looking at documents. Not *all* documents, of course.

"He's not one of ours," says Jeff.

"Booked through a local affiliate," says Susan. "Perfectly adequate, by all accounts, and a clean bill of health from the Lowesport Police Department."

"Amy's recent client history makes for interesting reading," says Jeff. "Given the killings. What would your view be on that, as head of HR?"

"As head of HR, I would say you need to speak to her as a matter of urgency," says Susan. "I would bring her home immediately."

Susan has worked with him since his earliest days in the City. Jeff would say that she's been with him through thick and thin, but, honestly, there hasn't been all that much thin.

Jeff thinks about his next move. Amy will have worked out that the three murders mean big trouble for her. She will have realized that everything is pointing to her. He decides he will message her. Bring her back to London, and see her reaction.

Jeff picks up another piece of paper from his desk. "Thank you for the plot synopsis for *Rampage 7*, by the way."

He had been reading it just before Max Highfield arrived.

"It was a pleasure," says Susan. "Well, it was excruciating, but I live to serve."

Jeff looks at Susan again. He would be lost in this place without her. His eyes and ears. His wise counsel. He owes her.

"I'm going to do something about Max Highfield," he says. "His behavior is unacceptable."

Susan stands. "I just want to do my job, Jeff. Now bring Amy Wheeler home; she might be in danger."

"Mmm," says Jeff.

Susan leans across and puts her hand on Jeff's. "I love you, Jeff, but I don't need you to save me from Max Highfield. I can take care of him myself—do you understand?"

Jeff understands, and is grateful. Max is worth an awful lot of money to him. He would be worth an awful lot of money to Henk too.

Henk van Veen. He and his old friend built this place together. Butch and Sundance, Cagney and Lacey. Then, three months ago, the split. Perhaps it was to do with Loubet? You never could tell with Henk.

Jeff looks over at a long mirror on the far wall of the boardroom. Behind it is Henk's "secret den." He would sit there, deadly quiet, in an armchair, tumbler of brandy in hand, and watch meetings through the mirrored glass. He said it was to add an extra layer of security to their business, but really it was to make sure no one was talking about him. That was Henk. Suspicious, paranoid. Useful skills in their business but irritating in a business partner.

Everyone quickly found out about the secret den, though, largely because Jeff quickly told them about it. Thereafter, whenever anyone wanted to talk about Henk, they would go to the pub instead.

Jeff looks at Susan. "May I ask you one more question?"

"Fire away," says Susan.

Jeff picks up the Loubet file again.

"Do you think Henk has ever looked at this file?"

"Oh, Henk looked at *everything*," says Susan.

5

W hat you up to?" asks Steve. The phone is cradled between his shoulder and his ear, both hands rubbing Trouble's head. If you rubbed his head with only one hand, he let you know you were doing a poor job.

"Sitting by a pool drinking a protein shake," says Amy. "You?"

"Watching *Tipping Point* while eating a Scotch egg," says Steve. "Where's your client? Shouldn't you be with her?"

"She's in an oxygen tent," says Amy. "She's meditating. What's *Tipping Point*?"

"What's *Tipping Point*?" says Steve. "You're serious?"

"I'm guessing it's a game show?" says Amy.

"Too right it's a game show. 'What's *Tipping Point*' indeed." Sometimes Steve wonders what world Amy is living in. Everybody knows *Tipping Point*.

"Couldn't you go for a walk or something?" asks Amy. "Do some tae kwon do? Get some fresh air?"

"I've got the window open," says Steve. "And I've already been for two walks. I walked to the shop to get this Scotch egg, and I walked home again."

"You shouldn't eat Scotch eggs," says Amy. "They're not real food. They're ultra-processed."

"That's why they're so delicious," says Steve.

"You have to eat properly, okay?" Amy says. "How are those organic vegetable boxes I ordered for you?"

Steve looks through to the kitchen and sees a pile of uneaten vegetables. Bob from the bakery comes to get them once a week for his compost heap.

"Terrific," says Steve. "Courgettes, all sorts." He knows he won't get away with that easily. Amy is a trained interrogator.

"And how do you cook courgettes?" Amy asks.

"Well, you know," says Steve. He must have seen this somewhere on a TV show. "Chop them up, whack them in a pan—"

"Uh huh."

"Bit of oil, bit of salt." That sounds convincing. And, anyway, she can't *prove* anything.

"Steve, have you eaten anything from any of the boxes?"

"Not yet," admits Steve. "I've been too busy to cook. I gave Margaret next door some spring onions and an aubergine, though."

"I just don't want you to die," says Amy. "I know that's selfish of me."

"I don't want you to die either, but I don't stop you flying off around the world with guns." Sometimes you need to go on the attack with Amy. That's what she respects.

"I know," says Amy. "But that's different. I'm me."

"Scotch eggs and guns are the same thing, Amy. There's an equivalence. How's Rosie D'Antonio? Diva?"

"Not yet," says Amy. "I quite like her. Would you get a nose job, if you were me?"

"I once got my nose broken," says Steve. "A woman in a pub with a brick. I was trying to arrest her brother on the Old Kent Road. What's an oxygen tent?"

"A tent full of oxygen," says Amy. "Anything interesting on?"

"A lost dog," says Steve. "Londoners. What's the weather like?"

"Sunny," says Amy. "You'd hate it. You'd melt."

"What SPF are you wearing?"

"I don't believe in it," says Amy. "I sweat a lot; it protects me naturally."

"Jesus, Amy," says Steve. "Thirty on the arms, fifty on the face. So no one's shot at her yet?"

"Not yet," says Amy. "Where's the dog, do you reckon?"

"Having fun, I expect," says Steve. "Sniffing trees. I've got a plan, though."

"You've always got a plan."

"When am I going to see you next? Margaret was asking after you. She'd like to see you."

"Straight after this, there's the Diamond Conference in Dubai," says Amy. "I'm going to join Adam there; you should come out."

"To Dubai? Never going to happen in a million years."

"They've rented us a villa," says Amy. "Pack your trunks and fly out."

"I don't have trunks," says Steve.

"I think they sell them in shops," says Amy.

"And I don't fly," says Steve. "Sitting next to people. What if they want to talk to me?"

"No one wants to talk to you, don't worry."

"And there's the pub quiz on the Wednesday," says Steve. "And I've got some shelves arriving. I have to sign for them. So no can do."

"Margaret could sign for the shelves," suggests Amy. He can hear that she knows it's a losing battle, but, bless her, she always tries. "You could fly from Southampton Airport—I've looked into it."

"Southampton?" says Steve. "There's roadworks on the A31—how long's that going to take me? How's Adam?"

"You tell me? He said he rang you at the weekend?"

"Oh, yeah, yeah, of course he did," says Steve. Another lie. He should honestly just answer "no comment" to everything Amy asks. It would save him a lot of trouble. "He's very well. Enjoying himself. Missing you."

"He didn't ring you, did he?"

"Of course he didn't," says Steve. "What would we talk about?"

"Anything. You're his dad. What do we talk about?"

"Dogs. Scotch eggs. Oxygen tents. My failings as a human being?"

"You could talk to him about that?"

"With Adam? Come on, Ames. Those are our things."

"I'll tell him to ring you," says Amy. "He's in Macau."

"Is he?" says Steve, wondering where Macau might be. He'll look it up; it's exactly the sort of thing that comes up at the quiz. "No sign of the Russians, then? No hitmen?"

"We're on a private island, Steve," says Amy. "The only people who could kill me here are Rosie and an ex–Navy SEAL called Kevin. I promise I'm safe."

"Eyes open, though?"

"Eyes open always," says Amy. "Shall we talk again later?"

"Later is good," says Steve. "Just got the dog thing, and a pub lunch, and someone's nicking money from a shop."

"Home in time for *Stopping Point*?"

"*Tipping Point*," says Steve. "Don't talk to strangers."

"What was that thing Debbie used to say?" Amy asks. "A stranger's just a friend you haven't met yet?"

"She nicked that from a film," says Steve.

"She'd fly out to Dubai," says Amy.

"I wouldn't stop her," says Steve. "Let her sit in those roadworks."

"You'd go with her, Steve," says Amy. "You know you would."

"Not with these shelves on their way, I wouldn't," says Steve. "Debbie or no Debbie."

"You'd be powerless," says Amy. "I'm going to raise a glass to her when I get off the phone. She'd have got on with Rosie."

"She'd have loved a private island. If we ever got one of the private booths at Nando's, she was beside herself."

"Take care, Pops," says Amy. "Talk later."

"Love you, Ames. And you're definitely safe?"

"Love you too, and, yes, I promise I've never been safer."

Steve removes a hand from Trouble's head and gets an admonishing look. He switches his phone off. He always cries after a call with Amy. He doesn't know why, but he's learned to accept it. As the tears come, Trouble stretches a paw up to Steve's chest. Probably hungry.

6

Felicity Woollaston knows she should move to a new office, what with all the money coming in now. But she likes it here. Two rooms above a travel agent on Letchworth Garden City High Street. It suits her. Quiet, no passing traffic. No clients eager to hop on a train and experience that bustling Letchworth lifestyle. Just Felicity, a fish tank, and Classic FM.

She should also get staff, she knows that too, but who could she trust? In the current situation? Her setup has been the same for nearly forty years now. Just Felicity herself, taking care of her clients, and Felicity, using a slightly different voice, as her own receptionist. In truth, she'd never been busy enough to need staff, or rich enough to pay them. Two things that have both changed in the last two years, for reasons she has yet to entirely fathom.

She looks out of her window onto Letchworth High Street. A man rides a mobility scooter into the WHSmith opposite; a teenager on a lunch break smokes a cigarette on a bandstand; and a man in a suit—let's assume an estate agent—is leaning on an open car door, talking on a mobile phone. To his wife? To a buyer? Difficult to tell, but, either way, she can see that he is lying.

She had been ready to retire until all these new clients came along. She has never actually met any of them; that's not how this new deal seems to work. It's been explained to her a hundred times, but Felicity is still used to the old ways, the personal touch. If a client is in panto, say, Felicity is there on the first night, front and center. Flowers delivered to the dressing room. If a client is opening a local leisure center, Felicity is there, local press in tow. Felicity's clients don't work all that much, and so, when they do, the least she can do is support them. They used to work a lot: Sue Chambers would do bits of TV, Alan Baxter did the breakfast show on Chiltern FM, Malcolm Carnegie would do after-dinner speaking at rugby clubs. But not so much these days. Sue's hip means she can't travel, Alan had got in trouble for a post about Adolf Hitler on Facebook, and Malcolm Carnegie died at a service station. She still has the odd local radio DJ, as well as Miriam (who had been a regular on *Bergerac* for two series) and a disgraced ventriloquist; but, in all honesty, Felicity had been on the verge of admitting defeat until the woman in the trouser suit had rung her buzzer.

Forty years in the business. Not bad. Never been rich but never gone hungry. A couple of young clients who moved agencies when they made it big (no hard feelings, these things happen), a couple of youngsters who could have gone all the way but didn't. The usual. But she was older now. She came into work because the alternative was to stay at home, and she preferred the phone not ringing in the office to the phone not ringing at home. Preferred having no work to having no family.

So the woman who had visited, green trouser suit, from Whistles, in Felicity's estimation, had caught her on a very good day. While they were having a nice cup of tea—Felicity had had to nip out to buy some milk—the woman had explained to Felicity about the world of "influencers" and "brand management." Felicity had nodded politely and pretended to understand, and tried to drop a few names of people she had known at the BBC, telling a story about once having nearly represented Angela Rippon, at which the woman nodded just as politely. It had seemed that the conversation was heading nowhere until the woman offered her all that money, and, before you knew it, Felicity Woollaston Associates had become Vivid Viral Media Agency. Bills and invoices with lots of different company names started to arrive, and Felicity bundled them up every Friday and took them to the post office to forward on. One of her favorite tasks of the week, because the post office is next to a nice coffee shop.

Felicity wasn't ever quite sure of her role in the whole business, but she was assured that her name and reputation still meant a great deal in the industry, and the partnership had really begun to flourish. Every month Felicity would find a sum of money in her bank account that was most agreeable, enough for everything she needed, and she didn't seem to have to do very much to earn it.

She opens an email, from a Bonnie Gregor, apparently a "home inspiration influencer." Usually she just forwards the emails on to a contact address, but sometimes she reads them. Bonnie is twenty-five, has two kids, Maxie and Mimi, lovely names, and 14K followers on Instagram. She seems very nice—spelling leaves a little to be desired, but Felicity is flexible enough to know that doesn't really matter these days. Maybe her new bosses will like Bonnie? So few emails are actually sent to her that at least she can be helpful by forwarding this one.

She wishes, she supposes, that she had someone to talk to about all this, but her accountant died ten years ago, her husband five years ago, and most of her contemporaries are out of the business now. She tried to read up on "influencers"—you must always do your due diligence—but it seemed a different world from the one she had understood. She even googled "Vivid Viral Media Agency," her own new company, and nothing seemed to come up except for her own postal and email addresses. Which was a funny way of doing business, but times change, don't they?

So she potters along. She has just booked Sue Chambers to do a talking head on a clip show called *Britain's Favourite Biscuits*, which Sue could record on Zoom at home. Felicity will be by her side to ensure the technology works. She has also just booked Alan Baxter for a slot on something called GB News, and they were happy to send a car, although Felicity had been unable to argue them up from a Prius. Alan won't love that, but a car is a car.

So, outwardly, things haven't changed. It's just the money, the odd bit of post, and the free gifts being sent to the office.

Even now she sees, stacked along the far wall of her office, crates and crates of XPlump Collagen Lip Gel, Bomb Squad Protein Balls, and, making the entire wall glow an unearthly purple color, a new delivery this week from a company called Krusher Energy Drink.

What names these products have. What a business she now finds herself in.

Felicity wonders, briefly, if she should be asking a few more questions about it all, before turning her mind, instead, to which Boots Meal Deal she is going to have for her lunch.

7

Steve Wheeler still *reads* about murder, of course he does. Just as a retired center-forward still looks at the football scores on a Saturday afternoon. Takes a professional interest, with his feet up. Likes to imagine he could still do the job if called upon, but is glad no one is ever going to call on him. He doesn't watch a lot of the true-crime programs, because he knows the pain and sadness of murder, and, also, he can always work out who did it in the first episode. But, sure, the odd thing catches his eye now and again; he's not made of stone.

This one, Andrew Fairbanks is the name of the guy, jumped out at him from Friday's paper because he was killed in South Carolina, and that's where Amy is. That, and the fact that the guy was shot, drowned, *and* attacked by sharks. Steve knows from experience that the box on the death certificate won't be big enough to fit all that in.

But Andrew Fairbanks is someone else's business, and, right now, Steve has his own business to attend to.

It was indeed the daughter who had been stealing from the shop, as Steve knew from the moment he took the job. Mollie Bright is her name, and her eyes are currently filling with tears.

"I would never, never steal from my mum," says Mollie. "Never."

"And yet here you are, on camera, stealing from your mum," says Steve, showing the girl the footage from his hidden camera.

The girl watches the footage and tries to think of a way around it. "I was borrowing it."

"That's fair," says Steve. "When are you planning to give it back?"

"Soon," says the girl.

Steve nods. "Three hundred quid, give or take. Over the last month."

"I know," says the girl.

He might ask Amy about the murder when they next chat. He can't just talk about new postmen, can he? Rosie D'Antonio sounds like a nice easy job. Amy deserves one.

He knows Amy can handle herself—he once saw her knock out an MMA fighter with a single punch at a Christmas party—but he also knows the things that can go wrong. Steve worries that Amy will be killed; Amy worries that Steve doesn't eat properly. Steve worries that Amy and Adam don't see enough of each other; Amy worries that Steve is lonely. There is a healthy equivalence of concern, and, also, they make each other laugh.

He looks at Mollie, tears in the corners of her eyes.

"Saving up for something?" he asks her.

Mollie shakes her head.

"Bought something?" Steve asks.

The girl shakes her head again.

"Given it to someone?" The girl does not answer, but, this time, does not shake her head. There we go.

"A boy?" asks Steve. "Or girl?"

Mollie looks away, thinking. She looks back at Steve, then she motions to the floor.

"Is that your dog?"

Steve looks at the dog. He'd half forgotten he was there. "No, some campers lost him. I have to give him back. You want to stroke him? He seems friendly."

Mollie starts to stroke the dog. The dog rolls over on his back. "How did you find him?"

"You know the horses at the back of the Matchwood Campsite?"

Mollie nods.

"I figured he probably followed them all along the fence—you know dogs and horses—and walked too far to find his way back. I took the jacket of one of the owners and placed it on the ground near the stables. When I went back this morning, the dog was sitting on it."

"Shouldn't you have taken him straight back?"

Steve shrugs. "The owners have gone to the Beaulieu National Motor Museum. Asked if I'd hold on to him for the day."

This makes Mollie look at Steve quizzically. Steve shrugs. "They're from London; they're used to being pampered."

"What do you call him?"

"Lucrative."

Mollie nods, and turns her attention back to the dog. After some silent cooing and stroking, she says, "A girl at school told me I had to get the money. She knows I work here in the holidays."

Steve nods. "Threatened to beat you up?"

"Something like that," says Mollie. "Worse."

"Internet bullying?" Steve asks. He's read about it.

Mollie nods.

Well, this won't stand. "Does she have a name? This girl?"

Mollie shakes her head.

"Should be easy to find, then," says Steve. "A girl at your school with no name. That'll stick out."

"Lauren Gough," says Mollie. "But don't speak to her—she'll kill me."

"I won't speak to her," says Steve.

"Promise?"

"Nope," says Steve. He bets that Lauren Gough is Gary Gough's daughter. And every copper in Hampshire knows where Gary Gough lives.

Steve likes fitting things together. Just as a hobby now, you understand. He had pootled about online this morning, reading about Andrew Fairbanks, for an hour or so, Trouble dozing on his lap. Fairbanks was a fitness "guru" on Instagram, though Steve noted that he had only 18K followers, which seemed a little low for an "influencer." Even the Steam Museum in Lyndhurst has 8K followers, and you're not likely to see Ernie Dubbs, life president of the museum, with his shirt off on a yacht anytime soon.

Fairbanks had been in South Carolina to film a short ad for a new energy drink. Again—with 18K followers? Steve looked up the name of the company behind the ad—why not, something to talk to Amy about. Vivid Viral Media Agency. Offices in Letchworth Garden City. Are there really viral video agencies in places like Letchworth Garden City? Seems odd to Steve, gets his detective senses tingling, but, you know, someone else's problem. Someone else's murder.

The door to the office opens, and Mollie's mother, Jenny Bright, walks in. "Any luck?"

"You could say that," says Steve.

"Is that your dog?" asks Jenny. "About time you got a dog, Steve. I don't like to see a man living with a cat. It's off."

"No," says Steve. "Long story. But here's the news. There's nothing on the video."

He sees Mollie's quick glance.

"So, it's no one on your staff."

"I was five minutes away from sacking Mrs. Thompson," says Jenny. "So I suppose that's good news? Where's the money, though?"

"Quite the mystery, this one," says Steve. "Someone slipped this through my letter box this morning."

Steve takes out the envelope of cash the Londoners gave him to find their dog. It has "To Steve Investigates" written on it. He pulls out three hundred pounds and hands it over. They'd paid him way too much to find the dog, so it would be nice to do something useful with it. Steve sees Mollie avert her eyes from the dog for a moment.

"The money?" asks Jenny. "All of it?"

"Three hundred pounds," says Steve. "No note, nothing. Whoever stole it must have felt guilty, or was only borrowing it. I choose to think it was someone terrified of my investigative skills."

"Thank you, Steve," says Jenny. "That's a weight off. What do I owe you?"

"On the house," says Steve. "I didn't have to do anything. Just bent down and picked up an envelope."

"Can I give you a scented candle at least?"

"Don't believe in them, I'm afraid," says Steve. "I'll have one of those notebooks with a New Forest pony on the cover, though. If you've got one going?"

"Coming right up," says Jenny and heads back out into the shop.

Mollie waits until her mother is out of earshot. "Thank you. You're kind."

Steve stands. "I choose to be kind sometimes. I'm not always. I just can't stand a bully."

"I'm sorry," says Mollie. "Do you have any daughters?"

"Yeah," says Steve. "Well, no, a daughter-in-law. I don't suppose that's the same thing, is it? It feels like the same thing. Anyway, if anyone threatened her, I'd kill them. Which isn't kind."

There was no mention in anything Steve read of who was sailing with Fairbanks, or who might have shot him, or where that killer might have disappeared to. The police, quite rightly, are keeping that kind of thing to themselves for now. The public always wanted to know everything straightaway these days.

There was a short clip on Sky News of the sheriff, a man named Justin Scroggie, avoiding the questions of the assembled media in a very professional manner. "We will not rest until the killer of Mr. Fairbanks is found," he said.

You really only say that when you know you're not going to catch the killer. If you know you're going to solve it, you just keep quiet, or you look straight into the camera and say, "We are actively pursuing a lead."

Scroggie didn't seem right to Steve either. Hair and uniform too neat to be a good cop. Perhaps Steve's being too judgmental, but being judgmental is a good thing if you're right.

"I'll pay you back," says Mollie. "It might be a while, though. I get forty quid a week."

"Listen," says Steve, "why don't you take this dog for a walk so I can go to the pub? Then we'll call it quits."

"Deal," says Mollie. "You won't kill Lauren Gough, will you?"

"Ach," says Steve. "We'll see."

The tiniest, tiniest part of Steve is envious of Justin Scroggie, and the case he has in front of him, but a pint and a pub lunch will fix all that.

8

ChatGPT, rewrite in the style of a friendly English gentleman, please.

I do like to write things down from time to time. It's pure vanity, but everyone wants to be understood, don't they? For reasons of privacy and security, and to avoid serious prison time, I have never received credit for my many, many crimes, and it would be nice to receive a bit of credit when I'm gone. For the people who love me to truly understand the scale of my achievements.

Though I promise not to be gone anytime soon!

To wit: a jolly interesting email has arrived. What do you make of this, I wonder?

> Monsieur Loubet,
>
> Please, please, please, Andrew Fairbanks has to be the last death. No more killing. This is not what I asked for. You can have all the money back if you make this stop.
>
> Joe Blow

Goodness gracious me!

First, I should introduce "Joe Blow." My partner in crime. Could be a woman, could be a man. Perhaps Joe is using ChatGPT just like me? "ChatGPT, make me sound like a whiny troublemaker!" I shouldn't mock—this business frightens some people. But my point is that Joe Blow could be a sixty-year-old lorry driver from Inverness, for all I know. That's the joy of ChatGPT. A marvelous invention for the writer and the criminal alike!

Whoever Joe Blow is, they work for Maximum Impact Solutions, I know that. And whoever they might eventually turn out to be, I have been paying them for some time to provide me with couriers to help with my business interests.

And now it seems that my partner in crime is getting cold feet? Sometimes they do. It's a blasted nuisance. Perhaps Joe Blow needs a lesson in manners? Shall we?

> Oh, I quite agree, Joe, I quite agree. No more killing.
>
> Though I note that there have been only three deaths, and in the grand scheme of things I would argue that does not constitute an awful lot. Let us not dwell on semantics, though, we are friends!
>
> And this latest one, Mr. Fairbanks, might finally do the trick and frighten Jeff Nolan away, shouldn't you think? No more blasted trouble from him after this one, is what I surmise.
>
> Believe me when I say I understand the ambit of your queasiness. But you cannot take my money and not expect a little blood on your hands! That would be, with respect, naive. You must keep the money I have paid you; you have earned it with all the information you have sent me. However, we had a deal. I can suggest investments if that would be at all useful?
>
> One mustn't urinate a windfall against a wall, must one?

You will be glad to hear that our arrangement is now over—unless Mr. Jeff Nolan continues to contact me, in which case our connection will resume.

Gosh, Mr. Jeff Nolan is a man who does not seem to take a bally hint!

You do have to accept we have acted as a team, though, Joe, and that these deaths are as much your responsibility as they are mine. Where there is money, people die. You wanted my money, and thus you find yourself here.

Amy Wheeler will be the last one, I promise. Does she need to die? Hmm, to be discussed, but I do believe that her death will tie up any loose ends. I trust I have your cooperation in this matter?

Although perhaps we should dispose of Jeff Nolan too? Would that be overkill? Please forgive my pun, Joe!

With warmest regards,
François Loubet

There, I think I have made myself plain to our friend Joe Blow.

The problem is, people are very happy to make a few pounds sterling off me, but they can get very squeamish when the bullets start flying, and the sharks come out to play.

There are many, many layers between me and these murders, but it always pays to be cautious. That's the lesson I hope I am teaching you here, in this silly voice I am growing to love.

I am not worried about Amy Wheeler—please don't think that—but I admit that I shall sleep a little easier when she is dead. I must get on to that. I shall talk to my man soonest.

Tally-ho!

9

"aten by a shark," says Rosie D'Antonio, throwing a towel over her shoulder and heading for the sauna. "Probably already dead, though, so that would have taken the edge off."

"Yes," agrees Amy, and watches her client go. While Rosie had been reading out the news report, Amy had kept a straight face, not a flicker of emotion. But from the moment Rosie mentioned the name "Andrew Fairbanks" and said he was an "influencer," Amy knew she was in trouble. She opens her laptop and heads straight for the same report.

There he is. Andrew Fairbanks. Smiling his final smile. He must have died fifty miles or so from where she's sitting right now. A painless death if the bullet had killed him. A horrible one if it hadn't. She checks one final detail online. As she suspected: Andrew Fairbanks had been a client of Maximum Impact Solutions.

Something was most definitely up, and Amy was at the heart of it. She messages Jeff Nolan immediately.

Andrew Fairbanks. Am nearby. Advise.

Jeff recruited her personally, ten years ago now. She was the receptionist at a gym in the City. "Concierge," they called her, but Amy didn't think concierges spent as much time as she did unblocking toilets. It's where she had met Adam. She caught him trying to steal one of the towels, and soon they were in love.

A fight had broken out one day in the gym. Two steroid-crazed bankers, huge men both, started hammering each other with free weights. Amy had run into the gym, disarmed one of the men, and tackled him to the ground, while a series of young men in singlets pretended they had been about to rush forward to help her. Meanwhile, another, older, utterly harmless-looking gym member had somehow got the other monster in a choke hold. She knew the older man as Jeff, as he was always forgetting his locker key. When the police arrived to take the two meatheads into custody—good luck, officers—she had asked Jeff if he was okay, and whether he might like a complimentary glass of elderflower tonic. Jeff had replied that he was quite all right, thank you, all in a day's work, and wondered if Amy might like a job?

There is a message on her phone. Jeff.

We need to talk.

You're telling me, thinks Amy.

The day after the fight at the gym, she'd had an interview in a suite on the eightieth floor of a nearby iconic office building, which she has since learned never to mention for reasons of security. After she passed through a series of electronic doors, there stood Jeff Nolan, looking very different in a suit. Jeff proceeded to test her computer skills, and then asked her to punch him as hard as she could. Amy had always been strong and fast, always known where her body was and what it could do if she asked it. She could lift, she could hit, she could pivot, she could glide. Her computer skills were very poor, but Jeff, getting up from the floor after she had hit him, told her they could soon teach her those, and offered her a job on the spot.

"Self-protection" had been a lifelong necessity for Amy, so the idea of protecting others seemed a natural fit.

Jeff then made her do a "Psychopath Test" of his own devising, and was delighted to see she scored eighty out of a hundred. Seventy-five was the cut-off point for Jeff: anything under that and you could be certain a new recruit would be "too emotional." Jeff himself had scored ninety-six, a number matched by only one other person, whose identity remained a secret but who was widely supposed to be Henk.

And now Jeff Nolan, a man provably lacking in gentle, emotional intelligence, "needs to talk." Anytime an ex-boyfriend had "needed to talk" Amy had gone for a long run, deleted his contact from her phone, and moved on. Lots of people "need to talk," but Amy is not one of them. And neither is Jeff Nolan.

Jeff must know what Amy knows. They haven't spoken about Bella Sanchez or Mark Gooch. The coincidence. But now they will surely have to? Andrew Fairbanks too? It's too much.

What will Jeff do? Will he give her some benefit of the doubt? Let her plead her case? She messages Jeff again.

I know what you're thinking. You have to trust me.

Amy looks out across the ocean to the mainland: the beautiful South Carolina shoreline, framed with oaks and cypresses, huge magnolia trees covered in moss, greens and whites and blues.

Amy needs to talk through everything that has happened with someone. To spell out the facts of the last few months. Would anyone understand?

Who can Amy trust right now, thousands of miles from home? She hears Rosie approach, flip-flops slapping on stone.

"Are we allowed to ask someone to come out to fix the sauna? I don't ask for much in this world, but two days without a sauna and I'll kill you and I'll kill Kevin and then I'll swim to the mainland."

"I'll do it myself," says Amy. "I'll watch a YouTube video. May I ask you about something?"

"You can ask me anything," says Rosie. "Ex-husbands, rehab, Burt Reynolds, I'm an open book."

"I might be in trouble," says Amy. "And I don't know if there's a way through it."

"There's always a way through trouble," says Rosie. "Often into more trouble, but at least it's different trouble. You fix my sauna, and I'll fix your problem."

Rosie pulls up a sun lounger and, as a mark of respect, sits on it, rather than lying down. She pours herself a large gin and tonic.

"May I have one too?" Amy asks. "D'you mind?"

"Finally!" says Rosie, unscrewing the cap once again. "I thought you never drank when you're on duty?"

"They don't test us for alcohol, only drugs," says Amy. "And I suspect I may no longer be on duty."

"Oh?" says Rosie.

"Oh," says Amy. "Let me tell you a story."

10

It's the same crowd in The Brass Monkey most lunchtimes and this Friday is no different. The widowers, the divorcées, and the lushes. Each has their own area of expertise. Steve himself (widower) is asked all the legal stuff; John Todd (lush), who used to work on the *Southampton Mercury*, gets asked the show business gossip; the mechanic Tony Taylor (long-term divorcé, long-term lush) takes care of all the car problems, occasionally branching out into microwave and coffee-machine repairs; and Dr. Jyoti Das (widow, alcohol tolerance building steadily) fields all and any medical questions, despite the fact she's a doctor of medieval history.

In the pub across the road, The Flagon, a similar, but by all accounts inferior, grouping can be found. Steve is very much the star man in The Brass Monkey, and occasionally there are entreaties from The Flagon as to whether he might be tempted across the street at some point. But Steve is loyal, Steve is steadfast, and, currently, Steve is having trouble with the clutch on his Vauxhall Corsa, something that Tony Taylor might be able to fix, so he is a Brass Monkey man through and through.

"That's what killed him, the shark?" asks Tony.

"Probably the bullet," says Steve. "The shark was attracted by the blood."

"You wouldn't want to be eaten by a shark," says John. "I was stung by a jellyfish once in Portugal, and it hurt like hell."

"You pee on it, don't you, Jyoti?" asks Tony. "A jellyfish sting?"

Dr. Jyoti Das, doctor of medieval history, nods. "Neutralizes the toxins."

"Who shot him?" asks John.

Steve shrugs. "I'll ask Amy about it. She'll know."

Amy will chat very happily about the killing. Too happily for Steve. Amy never talks about her childhood, but he picks up snatches here and there. It is clear that violence has been ever present in her life. She takes it in her stride in a way that makes Steve sad.

"How does Amy like Rosie D'Antonio?" John asks.

"Seems happy," says Steve, glad to think of something more positive. "Good fun, apparently."

"I'll bet," says Tony. "I'd love a crack at her, given the chance."

"I'll mention it to Amy," says Steve. "See if Rosie's in the market for a mechanic with kidney stones."

"Did you ever interview her, John?" asks Jyoti. "Rosie D'Antonio?"

"No," says John. "There was a bloke in Andover who wrote a book about horses once. I interviewed him. The author's life and whatnot. They kept me away from interviews, by and large."

"And this Andrew Fairbanks," says Jyoti. "Our shark friend. He was famous too? Have I got that right, Steve?"

"I'd never heard of him," says Steve. "But I've never heard of anyone these days." Steve thinks about those 18K followers again. Something doesn't sit right. Not his business, but he couldn't help that little old alarm going off in his head. And Letchworth Garden City? Come on now. If murder was still his business, that's where he'd start looking. But it's not, so he won't.

"Instagram," says Tony, and they all nod.

Their food is brought out and placed in front of them. Two shepherd's pies, a beer-battered fish and chips, and a lamb shank. Same as always. Tony collects the cutlery and napkins from the tin at the end of the bar and passes them round.

"Blue car in the car park last night, Steve," says John, tucking his napkin into his shirt like a cravat. "Appeared from nowhere."

"I'm across it," says Steve, starting to make inroads into the shepherd's pie.

"Greggs packet in the footwell too," says Tony. "Must have come from somewhere. Have I told you about my recycling bins?"

"No," says Steve, and signals for another pint.

"Someone's putting stuff in them," says Tony. "Like, I'll leave my glass bin out, and I wake up in the morning, and there're pizza boxes, all sorts in there. Anything you can do?"

Steve gives it some consideration. "Why don't I bring my Corsa round to yours this afternoon? The clutch's sticking. We can have a chat about the bins, while you take a look."

"Thanks, Steve," says Tony. "You're a mate. You can catch people on your doorbell these days, can't you? Could we try that?"

"That'd be perfect," says Steve. "I can take a look through the footage for you."

"What footage?" asks Tony.

"The footage from your doorbell," says Steve. "From the camera—you can download it."

"There's a camera on my doorbell?"

"What sort of doorbell do you have, Tony?"

"I don't know," says Tony. "I've had the same one since 1985. It came with the house."

"Okay," says Steve. "How did you think people were catching criminals with their doorbell? Just out of interest?"

"Fingerprints," says Tony.

Steve nods. Of the four of them, Tony is the one not on the quiz team.

"What was he doing there anyway?" says John.

"Who?" asks Steve. Sometimes this little lunchtime gang can lose focus.

"Fella on the boat," says John. "Shark boy."

"Advert," says Steve. "Flew over there to film something. Krusher Energy Drink."

"You'd solve it soon enough," says Jyoti.

"Not anymore," says Steve. "I don't solve murders."

Krusher Energy Drink, though. That's another lead, surely? How did they get involved? Why did they choose Andrew Fairbanks for this particular campaign?

They get back to their food.

"No doorbells on a boat either," says Tony.

"Wise words, Tony," says Steve. You wouldn't get this sort of quality at The Flagon.

11

The first one was a woman called Bella Sanchez," says Amy, sipping a gin and tonic through an elaborate straw, and shielding her eyes from the blazing South Carolina sun. "A client of Maximum Impact. I'd seen her on *Real Housewives of Cheshire*, then on *Cheshire Divorce Lawyers*, then on *Celebrities Go Dating*, and then back on *Real Housewives of Cheshire*."

"That's quite the arc," says Rosie. "I like the sound of her."

"She got called to a job in St. Lucia, an advert or something. You know, just a social media post—they get paid a fortune for this stuff."

"Did she have millions of followers?" asks Rosie. "Someone at my publishers does my Instagram for me. Probably for the best. I'd be canceled by lunchtime."

"No idea," says Amy. "Enough to do an ad, clearly."

"Good name for a book. *Canceled by Lunchtime*," says Rosie. "An assassin who works only in the morning? Something in that. In the eighties I advertised Dubonnet. Do they still make Dubonnet?"

"I don't know, I'm afraid," says Amy. "Do you want me to get to the murder or not?"

Rosie gestures to Amy that she has the floor. "Just adding some color, darling."

"She goes to a hotel in St. Lucia," says Amy. "She has a meeting with someone—"

"With whom?"

"Couldn't tell you—not my job to look into it," says Amy. "Penthouse suite. There's a final photo of her, lip-plumping gel held up to the light. That's what she was promoting. Then she's shot in the head. One bullet."

"Like Andrew Fairbanks," says Rosie.

"Very like him," agrees Amy. "Especially as she is then hung upside down from the balcony, for the world to see the following morning."

"Well," says Rosie. "Upside down. How dramatic. And a client of Maximum Impact?"

"A Platinum client, yes," says Amy.

"Why aren't I Platinum?" asks Rosie.

"Platinum is the lowest," says Amy. "It goes Platinum, Platinum Plus, Platinum XL, Platinum Gold, Platinum Diamond, and Platinum Platinum. You're Amber, because someone actually wants to kill you."

"What do you get for Platinum?"

"Consultancy, advice. Basic security checks as and when you might need them. But we wouldn't have been guarding her. Platinum clients don't get bodyguards."

"Andrew Fairbanks was Platinum too?"

Amy nods. "And then a month after Bella Sanchez was killed, a man called Mark Gooch, a financial influencer, another Platinum client of Maximum Impact, goes to Ireland."

"Uh oh," says Rosie.

"He's there to do an advert for a brand called Punk Wine. He's at a vineyard somewhere in County Cork."

"A vineyard in Ireland?"

"Climate change."

"Takes a final photo?" guesses Rosie.

"Takes a final photo," confirms Amy. "Sitting on the bough of a tree, top off, drinking from a can of wine. And his body is found about an hour later."

"Hanging from the tree?"

"Nailed to it," says Amy.

"Bit of variety," says Rosie. "But I get it. Three deaths, all linked, nice start to a story. But where do you come in? Hero? Villain?"

"Andrew Fairbanks was killed, let's say, fifty miles from here," says Amy.

"Or so," agrees Rosie. "And?"

"When Bella Sanchez was murdered in St. Lucia, I was in St. Lucia."

"Ah," says Rosie. "So perhaps you're not the hero?"

"I was maybe an hour away," says Amy. "I thought at the time, well, that's weird, but nothing more than that."

"What were you doing in St. Lucia?"

"Working with a musician, and—"

"Which musician?" asks Rosie.

"It doesn't matter," says Amy. "But I—"

"Come on," says Rosie. "Just say."

"I can't say, you know that," says Amy.

"Huh . . . you want my help, and yet here we are."

"Okay, it was Elton John," says Amy. "Now can we—"

"I've had some fun times with Elton," says Rosie. "Some fun times. He's calmed down a bit now, but haven't we all? Did you like him?"

"I did," says Amy.

"Did you like him more than you like me?"

"At this exact moment, yes," says Amy.

"Okay," says Rosie. "On with your story. So far you're on a killing spree."

"When Mark Gooch is found, just guess where I am?"

"Nearby?" says Rosie.

"Nearby," says Amy.

"With a hammer and some nails?" asks Rosie.

"In Dublin."

"With Bono?"

"No, with my husband. About an hour away by helicopter."

"I have a helicopter," says Rosie. "I think I do, I'm sure I bought one. I've definitely got a plane."

"So I was beginning to feel paranoid. Bella Sanchez, then Mark Gooch. Maybe just a coincidence, but it didn't feel right."

"And then I read you the Andrew Fairbanks story?"

"Three murders, three clients, and I'm in the neighborhood every time. Someone must be trying to connect me to these murders."

"You know I have to ask if you killed them?" says Rosie. "I'd get it. Capitalism isn't easy on any of us. You could just snap?"

"I didn't."

"Or perhaps someone was paying you?" Rosie suggests. "For insider information. You didn't pull the trigger, but there's still blood on your hands? Good money?"

"What does your instinct tell you, Rosie?"

"Oh, I know you didn't do it," says Rosie. "Not with those crazy ears. So is someone trying to frame you for three murders?"

Amy shakes her head. She doesn't know what's happening. Her phone pings. She looks at Rosie. "It's Jeff."

"The boss?"

Amy nods, and looks at the message.

Remember that job we did for François Loubet? He is behind this, and we are both in trouble. I need you back in London. We can discuss everything. Stay safe.

François Loubet, the money-smuggler. They'd been protecting a woman who worked for him. Henk had been furious that they were working for such a notorious crook. That was the start of the end for him and Jeff really.

"What's he saying?"

Amy is thinking. Fairbanks was found with a bag of money, that's for sure. But the others weren't. Another message comes through.

And do you know the name "Joe Blow"? Does that mean anything to you?

"Joe Blow"? Means nothing to Amy.

Nope. Should it?

"I mean, I'd be furious if I were him," says Rosie. "You just shot three people, hung two of them from ropes, and nailed the other one to a tree. I'd certainly be calling HR."

"He needs to talk to me," says Amy. "I have to get back to London."

Rosie gives a dubious purse of the lips.

"What?" Amy asks.

"Are you sure that's the best idea?" Rosie weighs up the question with her hands. "It's just that someone seems to be going to an awful lot of trouble to make it look like you killed three people. Someone who knows where you are at all times. And I'm guessing Jeff knows where you are at all times?"

"Jeff's on my side," says Amy. "But someone is setting me up, and I have zero idea of why."

Rosie shrugs. "I suppose the police, God bless them, didn't solve the other two murders? The lady and the man in the tree?"

"They didn't," says Amy.

"Then perhaps you should find out who actually did kill these three people? To rule yourself out? And, as you said, we're only about fifty miles from where Andrew Fairbanks was murdered. I mean, goodness, it's a hop and a skip, isn't it? It's sort of our duty to go take a look?"

Another message from Jeff.

And tell me if Henk tries to contact you. Do not trust him.

Jeff and Henk used to run Maximum Impact together. Henk had tried to poach her when he first left Maximum Impact Solutions, but Amy knocked him back, and she hasn't heard from him in months. Why would she hear from him now? And why shouldn't she trust him? There are more immediate considerations at this exact moment, however.

"Rosie," says Amy. "You are not leaving this island. Whatever is happening, there will be an explanation. I'll go back to London in the morning, Kevin will take care of you here, and it will be sorted out."

"Unless someone is out to get you," says Rosie. "And then you'll probably end up dead or in prison. Which I believe is very on-brand for Watford."

"Rosie, no one is out to get me. We've got three dead clients already. If I take you over to the mainland, you'll be an open target for Vasiliy Karpin. I'm not going to end up with four dead clients."

"*Four Dead Clients*," says Rosie. "Another good name for a book."

12

FROM THE DESK OF FRANÇOIS LOUBET
ChatGPT, rewrite in the style of a friendly English gentleman, please.

Mr. Kenna,

The time has come, old bean. Everything is in place, I trust?

Please advise when Amy Wheeler is dead.

Warmest regards,

François Loubet

"Old bean"? Sometimes ChatGPT can be a bit much!

Rob Kenna is my murder-broker, very good, you'd like him. I don't need him to tell me how Amy Wheeler is going to be killed; I simply trust that he is going to take care of it as a matter of urgency.

I almost feel sorry for her—she didn't ask for any of this, did she? She's simply the wrong person in the wrong place at the wrong time.

Just another layer of security for naughty François Loubet!

13

Gary Gough is nodding. "Uh huh, uh huh?"

"Only it was a lot of money," says Steve. "And the girl was terrified."

"Not sure I'm getting you," says Gary Gough.

"I just thought you might want to have a word with her," says Steve. "Ask her to lay off?"

"Not really my business," says Gary.

"Well, Lauren's your daughter," says Steve. "That's sort of your business."

"Kids," says Gary. "They've got lives of their own. If she wants to make a bit of money on the side, fair play to her. You can't watch them twenty-four hours a day. I'd rather she was beating up her classmates than on her bloody phone all day."

Steve used to have to deal with the Gary Goughs of this world day in, day out. Look around the New Forest long enough and there are still a few of them about. The ones successful enough never to have been caught. Clever enough never to have been too flashy, smart enough to have got out at the right time. With their high hedges and their ride-on mowers, going mad with money and gin. Gary will still have a trick or two up his sleeve, but Steve has no interest anymore. When you arrest a Gary Gough, another Gary Gough pops up in his place, then another, then another, then another. A sea of Gary Goughs, just waiting their turn. Sometimes one Gary Gough will shoot another Gary Gough, then a third Gary Gough will seek revenge. It's so bloody tiring, and so bloody boring.

But Steve can't stand a bully, so he thought he should at least pay a visit.

"How much?" says this particular Gary Gough.

"How much what?" asks Steve.

"How much for you to go away? How much did Lauren nick off the girl?"

"Three hundred," says Steve.

Gary laughs. "Christ, that's what you're here for, three hundred quid?" He opens his wallet and takes out a sheaf of fifties.

Steve waves the money away. "I gave her the three hundred; she doesn't need your money."

"You gave her the three hundred?"

"Someone from London overpaid me for finding a dog," says Steve, and Gary Gough nods in understanding. "I just thought you might have a word with Lauren? Ask her to leave this girl alone?"

"Pick on someone else?"

"Or maybe don't pick on anyone?" says Steve. And Gary laughs again.

"Law of the streets, old friend," he says. "Law of the streets."

"You don't live on the streets anymore," says Steve, getting up to leave. "You live in a mansion in a village with a delicatessen and a gastropub. Your daughter has a horse. She's not some tough kid fighting her way out of poverty like you were; she's a rich bully. So remember what you thought of rich bullies when you were growing up."

Steve takes his leave, walks around the side of Gary Gough's house, and gets into his Vauxhall Corsa. It is parked between a Range Rover and a Lexus. Steve had really been hoping to use Gary Gough's loo before he left, but he felt his parting shot was so good that he didn't want to draw focus from it.

Had Gary Gough been listening? Maybe, maybe not, but Steve had tried. He'll drive back the long route. It's Italian night at the pub this evening. They do a bolognese, and a bloke from Havant sings opera. He'll go home, have some quality time with Trouble, maybe collect his dry cleaning. Then a bit of TV and he'll head to Tony's, then the pub, remembering, of course, that he needs to collect the dog from Mollie Bright. Just ten minutes with Gary Gough had reminded him how much he hated his old world. Give him dogs and shops and ponies on notebooks. He messages Amy.

When's good to chat?

There is a delay in her reply.

Might need an hour or so?
You okay?

Another delay. Steve looks out of his window. The mighty forest growing about him, giving way to gorse-strewn heathland patrolled by armies of ponies.

Finally a reply.

All good here.

Amy is normally a little more chatty than this. Perhaps she is busy. Though how busy can you be on a private island? Steve asks her the question he's been dying to ask.

Glad to hear it. I want to talk to you about a man called Andrew Fairbanks. Heard of him? The shark influencer man?

He knows she'll respond with a bit more enthusiasm to this one. He passes a beautiful whitewashed pub. A man with his top off sits with a pint while his dog nuzzles the nose of a curious pony. Amy seems to be composing a reply for quite some while. And, when it arrives, it reads, simply:

Yes.

Less enthusiasm than he'd hoped for, but he's glad she's heard of the case. That'll be a fun chat.

Steve had looked up Krusher Energy Drink online. There didn't seem to be any adverts for it. A rudimentary website, where the "Buy Now" button didn't seem to work. And, strangest of all, the registered head office was at the same address as Vivid Viral Media. Must be owned by the same people. Makes sense, but a bit of Steve is tempted to go up to Letchworth Garden City. He's not sure why—it just feels like there's a stone in his shoe.

But. Not. His. Business.

When he gets home, he'll send Amy a heart emoji. Something in her tone has worried him. Probably nothing.

14

ubai, that gleaming temple of sunshine, money, and glorious possibility. Whether you're after a two hundred dollar steak or a rocket launcher, you will find it here, in a world of speed and heat and handshakes. Huge buildings reflect the sunlight, at once dazzling newcomers and hiding the insiders. The whole city is a giant turbine constantly eating and creating money. A merry-go-round that spins night and day. It has been the making of Rob Kenna.

To the outside world, Rob Kenna is a DJ, traveling from glamorous party to glamorous party. It's a hell of a lifestyle. Just take a look at his Instagram if you have any doubts about that. Look at Rob's villa on the Dubai Palm. Look at his Ferrari, wrapped in metallic gold. Must be a lot of money in DJing.

And there is a lot of money in it, that's for sure. Or there was, back in the day, at least. But even then there wasn't Ferrari money in it, Rob has always had side hustles on the go, and Dubai welcomes side hustles.

While DJing is not a bad business, murdering people for a living is a great business. Robust. Recession-proof.

The world economy can tank, fuel prices can rise, clubbers can stop listening to nineties trance music, and interest rates can go through the roof, but people will always want to murder other people. And Rob acts as the middleman. Tell him who you want killed and where, and he'll find someone for the job. No need to tell him why, any more than you'd need to tell a newsagent why you want to buy a paper.

Rob only started a couple of years back; he was into all sorts of other bits and bobs beforehand, but he's got some very nice contracts now. It all began with François Loubet, really. Loubet heard about him, used him, then used him again. Word got out that Loubet trusted him, and then the business started pouring in. Minimum charge a hundred grand, but that goes up steeply depending on the job, and no shortage of clients.

All Rob has to do is to pick up the phone to the right person and it's done. And Rob Kenna always knows the right person to ring.

And now a new job from Loubet, Amy Wheel—

"Hmm?" he says.

"Your shot, dickhead," says Big Mickey Moody.

"Miles away," says Rob. "Dreamland."

Mickey Moody, the big lunk, has never killed anyone, you can just tell. Some people don't have it in them, but that doesn't make them any less of a human being, does it? We're all built different. Big Mick hasn't killed anyone; Rob doesn't like sushi. Horses for courses. They both like golf and sunshine, though, and that's enough.

Rob steps up to the tee and pulls out his driver. He looks down the fairway, picturing his shot.

So François Loubet needs Amy Wheeler dead too? She's a professional, so it's not one for a gun-happy local cop. Fortunately the perfect man for the job is already there, and should be easily persuadable for the sort of money Rob can pay. Because Amy Wheeler is a pro, Rob's commission will be around two hundred grand. He'll offer the shooter fifty grand. Easy money for them both. He'll make the call.

Yep, he thinks, the Dubai sun dancing on his visor to the sound of birdsong and high-performance sports cars—it's not a bad old life, is it?

Rob Kenna then hooks his tee shot into the bushes. In fury he throws his driver over a ducking caddy and into the trees, while screaming an obscenity that frightens the birds.

"Unlucky, Rob," says Mickey Moody with a sympathetic smile. "Not always your day, is it?"

15

Amy is outside, on Rosie's afternoon-sun terrace. She hangs upside down from an exercise bar, and stares at her phone.

Steve wants to talk to her about Andrew Fairbanks? How can that be?

Something very strange is going on, and Amy is at the heart of it. Perhaps Rosie is right? Perhaps she should be cautious? Amy developed a keen sense of danger from a very young age.

But she also developed a keen sense of whom to trust. And she trusts Jeff.

The supply boat will be here in an hour or so. Amy plans to hitch a ride, and fly to London from Savannah later this afternoon.

She starts doing crunches, the power of her muscles defying the power of gravity.

Who is killing these influencers, and why? If it's all tied to François Loubet, is it a money-laundering scam? What if Bella Sanchez and Mark Gooch were carrying bags of cash too? How can she find out?

She starts working her body harder, adding a twist to the crunch.

Jeff will have answers, she's sure of that. She's sad to be leaving Rosie behind, but she will be in safe hands with Kevin. Amy just needs to get back to London, then she can—

"On the floor, hands on head. If you reach for your weapon, I will shoot."

Kevin. The man who had so recently brought her an oat-bran porridge with chia seeds now has his gun pointing directly at her head. Albeit upside down.

Amy maneuvers herself off the bar and gets onto her knees, her fingers laced behind her head. What's happening here?

"Where's Rosie?" Amy asks.

"I've told her to go to her panic room," says Kevin.

"You think I'm dangerous?" Amy asks. "That's been your observation, has it? Over the last few days?"

"Yep," says Kevin. He's no fool; Amy is dangerous.

Kevin circles behind her, gun still outstretched. Is she being abducted? By whom? Doesn't Kevin work for Jeff?

Amy weighs up the odds. Kevin is around six two, must weigh upward of 260 pounds. If she can unbalance him, it's an easy win for her. But Kevin is an ex–Navy SEAL. And Kevin knows that he is six two, and heavy, so Kevin also knows that if Amy can unbalance him it's an easy win for her. Kevin is therefore keeping his distance and letting the gun do the work. Amy hears handcuffs. The second Kevin reaches for her wrists, he will be doomed. Once she overpowers him, she can worry about what to do next.

But Kevin does not reach for her wrists. Instead he throws the handcuffs down onto the floor next to her.

"Put them on," he orders. "And I'll need to hear a click."

There is usually a way out of any situation, that is, if you really assess every angle. Would a leg sweep reach its target? No, Kevin is standing out of range. Might these handcuffs themselves be a weapon? An improvised nunchuck? She weighs them in her hand. Strong but light. No use. Negotiation, then.

"Did Jeff ask you to do this, Kevin? To take me in? Why the handcuffs?"

"Someone asked me," says Kevin. "You don't need to know who. And they said she'll beat you in a fight. And, if she can't beat you in a fight, she'll talk her way out of it instead. Handcuffs on now, or I fire."

"You don't need to handcuff me," says Amy. "I'm going back to London, I promise."

"You're not going to London, Amy," says Kevin. "Sorry. I've been given a job to do, and a lot of money to do it. So no fuss."

"Who gave you the job?" Amy asks. Where is Kevin going to take her? "Was it Jeff?"

"Handcuffs on now," repeats Kevin.

"You know that Jeff has—"

"If you say the word 'Jeff' one more time, I'll shoot," says Kevin. "That's a final warning. Now do me a big favor and click those handcuffs on."

Of course, sometimes the solution to a situation is that there is no solution. And in those instances you sit tight, shut up, and make sure you find a way of stopping yourself from getting killed. A very familiar feeling for her.

Amy reluctantly accepts that this is where she stands right now. She brings her hands slowly from behind her head.

"Even slower," commands Kevin.

She reaches down to her left to pick up the handcuffs.

"Behind your back," says Kevin.

"You think I can handcuff myself behind my back?"

"I do think that, yes," says Kevin. "If you fumble, I'll shoot you."

It is a breeze to handcuff oneself behind one's own back. Annoyingly easy. Amy places both wrists through the bracelets.

"And click," says Kevin. He still has a dab of flour behind his ear from making Rosie her pancakes this morning.

And click. That's it. Amy is handcuffed. She's on an island. She has a highly trained ex–Navy SEAL pointing a gun at her, and soon she will be either dead or on a one-way plane ride to God knows where. She also has a client shut up in a panic room.

The door opens.

"Well, I never," says Rosie D'Antonio, looking at the kneeling, handcuffed

Amy. "I have to say, my money was on Amy overpowering you. You clever thing, Kevin, all this, and you can also knock up a decent soufflé."

"I have to request that you return to the panic room, ma'am," says Kevin. He turns back to Amy. "Get on your feet."

"Yes, I decided I wouldn't go into the panic room until I knew Amy was okay," says Rosie. "You see the sort of person I am, Amy? Even after everything you've done?"

"I've done nothing," says Amy, getting up.

"I believed you at first," says Rosie. "But no smoke without fire. You can take the girl out of Watford, but can you ever take Watford out of the girl?"

Kevin nods. "I'm taking Amy into the panic room."

Kevin forces Amy forward, his gun in the small of her back. Amy is struggling to come up with a plan.

The door to the panic room is open. It is at least ten inches thick and framed with a vacuum seal.

He won't kill her, surely? Who on earth would want her dead? The room itself looks like a perfectly pleasant place to spend her next few hours. A big sofa, a TV, a drinks cabinet, another door leading to a bedroom. She'll be comfortable while she awaits her fate. Kevin forces her inside.

"At least tell me where you're taking me," says Amy.

"I'm not taking you anywhere, Amy," says Kevin. "I really am sorry, but it was a lot of money."

So this is it? In her line of work, she often thinks about where it's going to end. A military checkpoint in Syria? An opium den in San Salvador? That she made it through childhood was miracle enough, so she can't really complain. She thinks about Adam, and she thinks about Steve. Will they cry, she wonders.

Kevin digs his gun deeper into Amy's back and forces her onto the floor.

Of course they'll cry, Amy. They love you. They love you. You found love against all the odds.

The scene is playing out for Amy in the mirror above the bar. She looks

so beaten. Arms behind her back. Big Navy SEAL with a gun directly behind her. Who is doing this, who needs her dead? Why?

And then, and then.

Amy can see a golden trophy held by a small hand come crashing down
on Kevin's head. She spins as Kevin falls to the floor, and kicks his gun
across the panic room. Kevin is stunned but quickly back on his knees,
scrambling toward the gun. Amy drags herself to her feet and runs out of
the panic room, heading back into the house as Kevin aims and fires. She
falls in a heap on the hallway carpet just as Kevin's first bullet thuds into the
door of the panic room, which Rosie has swung shut. Closely followed by
the almost inaudible thuds of five more bullets ricocheting off that impreg-
nable closed door.

"Quick," shouts Amy. "Before he gets the door open."

"He can't open it without the code," says Rosie. "He's in there for the
long run."

As if to prove the point, very faint banging can now be heard from behind the door.

"That's good work, Rosie," says Amy.

"And without the upper-body strength I used to have," says Rosie, as
Amy gets to her feet. "I sensed you doubted me?"

"Well, I sensed you doubted *me*," says Amy.

"Let's promise neither of us will do that again," says Rosie. "I hit him
with an Oscar, you know, and not a scratch on it."

"When did you win an Oscar?"

"Best Cinematography 1974," says Rosie, showing Amy the Oscar. "Poker
game."

"I need to get off the island," says Amy.

"I'd say that I do too," says Rosie. "I just attacked a hitman with an Academy Award. We'd better get you out of those handcuffs."

"I get the feeling you've said that a few times in your life," says Amy. "I
can't take you with me, Rosie. It's too dangerous."

"You have no choice," says Rosie. "Come on, it'll be an adventure. Who else have you got on your side right now?"

Another text from Steve. A heart. Actually not bad timing, Steve.

"What's the plan?" Rosie asks.

"I could visit the sheriff who found the body?" says Amy. "You really should stay here until I can send help. Kevin can't get out."

"Someone is trying to have you killed," says Rosie.

"Yes, and Vasiliy Karpin is still trying to have *you* killed," says Amy.

"Listen," says Rosie, "sometimes a bit of attention is nice. But who's after you?"

"Fairbanks was found with a bag of money," says Amy.

"Almost a million dollars," says Rosie.

"And Jeff and I did a job a while ago for a man we really shouldn't have," says Amy. "A money-smuggler called François Loubet."

"Ah," says Rosie. "Nice guy? Single?"

"Never met him," says Amy. "All over encrypted messages, but, if he's after me, for whatever reason, I'm in real trouble. And Jeff's in real trouble too."

"And he knows where we are?" says Rosie.

"If it's him," says Amy.

"Sounds like you shouldn't leave me here on my own, then."

Amy doesn't have an answer to that.

"Good," says Rosie. "Now, why don't you load up on coffee and ammunition, while I go to pack my things?"

16

Jeff Nolan declines the Parmesan. "You know me and Parmesan, Bruno."

Bruno gives a slight bow to acknowledge the fact that he does indeed know Jeff and Parmesan, and Jeff returns to his files. The recent ones, of course, but also some much older. Jeff does not intend to lose his business. He knows that such things are sent to try us, and he is nothing if not a patient man.

Jeff always eats alone if he can help it. Sometimes there are clients to be entertained, or impressed, or mollified, and Susan Knox will book him into whichever restaurant is the hardest to get into that week. But usually he is at Bruno's. It feels like home.

Jeff started working in the City at seventeen, was making a bit of money by eighteen, and was making a lot of money by twenty-one. Bought a house in Sevenoaks when he was twenty-four, bought a bigger one two streets away at twenty-six, then, at twenty-eight, bought a town house in Mayfair for nine million. He can see it, across the street, through the windows of Bruno's.

Jeff likes to take care of details. That's what brought him into the close-protection business in the first place. He'd been doing a deal with a Saudi prince, and seen one of his security detail smoking and reading the paper. Jeff asked what the Saudi prince paid for his security, and whether he was happy with the job they did. The sum of money the prince mentioned, and the shrug he gave, told Jeff that this could be the business for him. He was thirty-five at this point and ready to retire, so it was perfect.

Jeff is rereading the reply he received from François Loubet after that first email. Before the killings started. Again, it might be evidence one of these days.

Mr. Nolan,

Thank you for your email, dated 14th of April.

I am sorry to hear of your clients' plight, I don't imagine jail is fun for anyone. However, it is the only proper punishment for smuggling money into a foreign country. We have laws for a reason.

As to your suggestion that I am somehow involved, well, I couldn't possibly comment! I will say, however, that I am a legitimate businessman with many interests worldwide, and my bookkeeping and tax records are, while private, exemplary.

I hope nothing unfortunate should befall your company, or any more of your clients, in the months ahead, but, if it does, might I suggest it is karma for the allegations you have made against me?

Meanwhile, you might do well to speak to your colleague "Joe Blow."

Proceed carefully, Mr. Nolan.

Warmest regards,

François Loubet

A clear and present threat from Loubet. No arguing with that. And the very first mention of "Joe Blow."

Bruno has returned to top up Jeff's glass. Jeff holds his hand flat to indi-
cate enough, and hears a noise from the street. A squeal of tires. Not the
sound of a car braking but the sound of a car suddenly speeding up.

And so it is that Jeff has already started sprinting before the black Jeep
crashes its way through the front windows of the restaurant. By the time the
two figures in balaclavas have leaped from the front seats brandishing pis-
tols, Jeff is already through the swinging double doors that lead to the
kitchen. And by the time the men follow him through the doors, firing
wildly, Jeff is gone.

Through the fire door, and into the backstreets of Mayfair.

17

Well, well, well, Rosie D'Antonio is thinking, this day is certainly looking up.

Rosie hadn't liked the death threats from Vasiliy Karpin, the chemicals billionaire, of course she hadn't, but these things come with the territory. If you have any sort of personality, someone will eventually want to kill you. And she shouldn't have done it, really: she should have hidden Vasiliy Karpin's identity. But she was bored, and when you're bored it's important to make things happen.

Which is also why she is now in a speedboat, water lapping around her Louboutins, helping a fugitive solve a murder. Not the most extraordinary Friday of her life but not a bad one.

Things used to happen to Rosie all the time. So many things. Parties, affairs, book launches, premieres, new deals, new lovers, tiffs, spats, beefs, kisses in swimming pools, photographers in bushes. Lawsuits, rehabs, husbands, cocaine on yachts, cocaine on rooftops, cocaine at the White House. Mustique, London, Capri, Aspen. Trouble and fun, fun and trouble. But people die or, worse, get married, people slow down, the photographers hide in other people's bushes now. They hide, Rosie guesses, in Taylor Swift's bushes. There is still romance, there's still booze, still the odd party here and there, people as old as she is clinking glasses and remembering who they all once were. And there's still the writing, which people seem to be enjoying again. Back on the bestseller lists. She was never in any danger of running out of money, but she had been in danger of running out of acclaim. Of running out of fame, the sparkling tonic she has long been able to add to the neat gin of her private life.

All in all, Rosie is quite happy to be on the boat. If you'd told her at forty that she'd still be doing this sort of thing many years later, she would have been very happy. And how nice to spend a bit of quality time with this charming young bruiser Amy, who is currently squatting, bailing water out of the leaky hull. Rosie only really has one rule in life: if you see a door, walk through it.

The mainland is just a thin, misty smudge, while the water in the speedboat is halfway up Rosie's calves. But Rosie chooses to remain confident. The boat, leaky though it might be, is so fast that, by the time it is ready to sink, they will have reached the mainland.

"Why don't you get a speedboat that doesn't leak?" Amy asks, above the noisy row between the engine and the ocean.

"Sentimental value," yells Rosie. "When I got my first-ever million-dollar royalty check—for *Tick-Tock, Death O'Clock*, I think—I bought a house, and that burned down. Then I bought a diamond ring, and my husband gave that to a Romanian gymnast. So I bought a racehorse and I bought this speedboat."

"What happened to the racehorse?"

"Don't ask. Mafia."

"It's taking on a lot of water," says Amy.

"That's life," says Rosie. "We take on a lot of water. The trick is to keep moving."

Rosie recognizes that keeping moving is Amy's only option for now. She is happy to join her. After all, someone is trying to kill them both. Not the same someone, she assumes, but you never know.

Visiting Justin Scroggie, the sheriff, was the best of their currently limited options. He had been at the crime scene, presumably searched it, maybe even had a theory or two. The presence of the famous Rosie D'Antonio, and the power of her credit card, might be enticing for a small-town sheriff. Fine by Rosie, nice to be needed.

"I think this is a losing battle," Amy says, still desperately bailing.

Rosie looks over to the land. "We'll be okay. Let's swim the last bit; the sharks never come this close to the shore. And can you carry my case on your back? I'm not as young as I once was."

18

It's your clutch cable," says Tony Taylor from underneath the hood of Steve's car. "Nice and simple."

Steve nods. "What do you need to do?"

"I need to replace your broken clutch cable with a new clutch cable," says Tony. "If that's not too technical for you?"

Tony unfolds himself and stands up straight. He wipes his hands on a rag that is slightly dirtier than his hands. "I'll have it done in twenty minutes, if you want to take a look at my bins?"

"Deal," says Steve. "I'm thinking of driving up to Letchworth Garden City, if you fancy a day out?"

"Letchworth Garden City?" says Tony. "What's there?"

"Just always fancied visiting," says Steve.

Tony nods. "How long are you planning to spend there?"

"Couple of hours," says Steve. "Three at the most."

Now Tony shakes his head. "Nope. Not going to work, Stevie. Think it through."

Steve cocks his head. He's happy to be dissuaded. Experience tells him you get so much more visiting someone in person, but he's not really investigating anything anyway. He could just send Vivid Viral an email?

"It's a good two and a half hours with those roadworks," says Tony, opening various workshop drawers. "A31, M27, come off at Junction 4 for the M3, M25 up to St. Albans, cross-country to the A1. Hell of a trip."

"Yeah," says Steve. "Five-hour round trip."

"Five-hour round trip. So even if you're only there for two hours you're going to hit rush hour one way or the other," says Tony, emerging with what Steve hopes and assumes is a clutch cable for a Vauxhall Corsa. "Rather you than me."

When Tony is right, he's right. Just send them an email. Or leave it altogether maybe? You don't have to play with every ball of string that comes your way. Time to take a look at those recycling bins.

They both turn at the sound of a knock on Tony's open garage door. A man is poking his head around. "Sorry to disturb you, gents. Which one of you is Steve Wheeler?"

"Who's asking?" says Steve.

The man, a tall, good-looking black guy, very nice coat, walks into the garage and extends his hand.

"Jeff. Jeff Nolan. I wonder if I might have a word?"

"Jeff Nolan, Amy's boss?" asks Steve, in a sudden panic. "Where is she?"

"Nothing to worry about, Steve," says Jeff, quickly. "Sorry, I shouldn't have surprised you like this, I should have thought. I just need a favor."

"You've come down from London?" asks Steve. "To see me?"

"I have," says Jeff. "Your address is in Amy's file. Your neighbor told me you'd be here."

"Where in London?" Tony asks.

"Mayfair," says Jeff.

Tony nods. "Did you go down through Brixton, M3 and across?"

"North Circular, M4," says Jeff.

"That's a long route," says Tony.

"I was concerned I was being followed by a hitman," says Jeff. "So it was a safer route."

Tony nods again. "Well, yeah, I mean."

"That a clutch cable for a Vauxhall Corsa?"

Tony looks at the clutch cable. "You know your clutch cables, my friend."

"I read a lot," says Jeff. "Always have. Shakespeare, encyclopedias, car manuals."

"If you like clutch cab—"

Steve steps in. "Does Amy know you're here?"

Jeff shakes his head. "I'll explain it all. Can you meet me in an hour? Somewhere private?" Jeff looks over at Tony. "No offense."

"I never take offense," says Tony. "Saved me a lot of time over the years."

"Sure," says Steve to Jeff. Amy likes Jeff, trusts him. So Steve does too. "That'll give me time to get my clutch cable fixed."

"And look at my bins," says Tony.

"And look at Tony's bins," agrees Steve. "You might find the pace of things down here a bit slow, Jeff."

"Suits me fine at the moment," says Jeff. "There's a campsite called Hollands Wood—do you know it?"

"Out by Brockenhurst, yeah, I know it," says Steve.

"Meet me there in an hour," says Jeff. "Pitch 46—it's tucked away out of sight."

"And Amy's okay?" says Steve.

"Amy's fine," says Jeff. "That's a promise. I'm just running out of people I can trust. So I'm turning to someone Amy trusts."

"Doesn't involve murders, does it?" says Steve.

"Hollands Wood in an hour?" says Jeff, without answering Steve's question. "I'll reveal all."

"B3055, then A337," says Tony, glad to be of some help.

19

N ice house," says Amy. Squatting in a bush for an hour is a good workout. Rosie is curled up, using a Louis Vuitton suitcase as a pillow.

"Too nice," says Rosie.

"You don't think cops should live in nice houses?" Amy asks.

"I don't think they can afford to live in houses this nice," says Rosie. "Not this nice. Criminals live on this street; cops live one street over."

"Perhaps he won the lottery?"

Rosie had been all for heading straight up to Scroggie's front door, giving it a rat-a-tat-tat and taking their chances. Amy understands that. By and large, people liked to talk to Rosie. If you found her at your front door, you'd invite her straight in. But Amy doesn't always trust law-enforcement officers, so it pays to be careful. They can get information from Scroggie without talking to the man. Get any information that might help, then try to head back to London and the safety of Jeff Nolan by any means possible.

The key is to stay as low profile as possible for the next few days. If Loubet paid Kevin to kill Amy, he will presumably still want Amy dead. And they are hardly inconspicuous, as she had pointed out to Rosie. Rosie accepted this; she was, for instance, wearing a tiara. "Always dress to impress—it doesn't matter where you are."

If Scroggie was investigating the Fairbanks death, Amy knew she might find something to her advantage in his house. Cops bring files home. The only alternative was breaking into police headquarters and, while Rosie was game, Amy told her she had tried that before ("in Venezuela") and advised against it.

In the time they'd been there, there had been no movement from the house. No noise, no lights, no deliveries. Amy looks at Rosie and nods.

"Okay, it's empty, let's go."

Amy runs in a low crouch, while Rosie saunters along behind her. They skirt around the side, and then the back of the Scroggie home.

"Do you know how to pick loc—" Rosie's question is interrupted by Amy taking a large rock and smashing one of Scroggie's back windows.

"Ah, I see you do."

Amy clears the remaining broken glass from the window frame and climbs inside. She then offers a hand to Rosie, who refuses it.

"I didn't get where I am without being flexible," Rosie says, squeezing herself onto Justin Scroggie's kitchen worktop. "What are we looking for?"

"Computer or phone," says Amy. "You check down here, and I'll check upstairs."

Amy takes the stairs three at a time. The house is very nice. Rosie had been right: too nice. Amy gets the feeling that whoever is paying Justin Scroggie, it isn't just the Lowesport Police Department. She notices that Scroggie has a top-of-the-range Peloton bike, currently being used as a drying rack. Amy has never understood why people cycle indoors. It's the same with boxing. Why punch bags when you can punch other people, and stop them from punching you back? People are so weird.

"Found it!" Rosie calls from downstairs, and Amy descends again. They are going to have to be quick. Who knows when Scroggie will be back? Amy isn't worried about escaping—she can escape from anywhere—but she doesn't want Scroggie to know she's been there. Doesn't want him to know that she's investigating the Fairbanks murder. Her plan is simple. Find something that might make some sense of what's happening, then escape unnoticed.

"Where was it?" Amy asks Rosie from the hallway.

"In here," says Rosie, from a den off the hallway. Amy heads through the door, to see Rosie proudly pointing at a computer.

"Good work," says Amy.

"Thanks," says Rosie, then cocks her thumb over her shoulder. "I spotted it straight after I saw his dead body."

Amy's eyes follow Rosie's thumb to the other side of the den, where the body of Sheriff Justin Scroggie is hanging by his bound hands from a ceiling joist. Amy looks back at Rosie.

"I'm a writer," says Rosie. "I notice things."

20

Jeff is speeding down back roads, away from the cameras. He has to get rid of his phone, though not before this one final call. He lets it ring and ring, but Amy is not answering. Jeff hopes this isn't bad news. Her voicemail cuts in. What information does he need her to have?

Amy, it's me.

Loubet's been using our clients to smuggle money. I called him out on it, and he threatened to kill me, and two gunmen just tried to kill me in Bruno's. So this will be our last communication for a while. I need to go completely off-grid.

I don't understand how you're involved in all this, but it looks like you are, so run.

We both need to keep our heads down and work out what's going on.

I'm going somewhere safe, and you should too.

He's working with someone we know. Someone connected to Maximum Impact. The name I mentioned, "Joe Blow." Don't trust anyone. Get rid of your phone.

I'm going to do what I can to find out what's going on. I suggest you do the same if you can.

This is a bad one, Ames, even for me. Take care and good luck.

Jeff ends the call, takes the SIM card from his phone, and snaps it in two. He then throws the SIM and the phone out of his window and drives on.

21

ChatGPT, rewrite in the style of a friendly English gentleman, please.

Another unwelcome email arrived a little after luncheon. What have I done to deserve this, I wonder? Have my sins found me out!!!

It was from Rob Kenna, my murder-broker. Now, if you don't have a murder-broker, you should get one, as it is most inconvenient to have to arrange these things yourself. Get yourself a good dentist, a good plumber, and a good murder-broker, and you won't go too far wrong in life.

> Mr. Loubet,
>
> Amy Wheeler has escaped, but situation under control. I have people tracking her on the ground in South Carolina. She won't get far. Will advise further.

Hmm. Situation under control? Well, I'll be the judge of that, won't I? Rob Kenna has not let me down before, but I await developments with some interest. Certainly if this were my dentist or plumber, I would be making a complaint.

You know, it's funny, I realize I don't even know what Amy Wheeler looks like. I know the name, of course, and that she is blonde, but other than that nothing. She must be wondering what on earth is going on, mustn't she?

Oh, and I know her blood type! Mustn't forget that!

22

I'm just saying, Amy," says Rosie, reasonably in her view. "Another dead body, and look who's nearby? You."

Amy ignores her. She learned to do that impressively early in their relationship. Rosie cannot resist someone who ignores her. Amy leans toward the computer screen.

"Locked."

"Then perhaps it might be a good time to leave?" suggests Rosie, looking back at the hanging corpse of Justin Scroggie. "Unless you're a computer hacker too?"

Amy keeps looking at the screen. "Cut him down for me. Keep your gloves on."

Rosie looks at the corpse again. "I've had to free a few men from ceilings in my time, but they've almost all been alive. Where are we taking him?"

"I just need him for a moment," says Amy.

Rosie stands on a small cabinet and spots a ceremonial sword mounted on Scroggie's wall. She cuts through the rope and Scroggie's body falls to the floor. Amy steps over to the corpse.

"Help me drag him."

"You've gone from *I can't possibly let you off the island, Rosie* to *Help me drag a corpse, Rosie* ever so quickly you know?"

"Get him onto this office chair," says Amy, and the two women manage to manhandle Scroggie into place. Dead people are always so much heavier than you think they're going to be. "Do you have a makeup wipe?"

"I have clarifying wipes," says Rosie. "But extremely expensive ones."

"So long as they're good with blood, I'll take one," says Amy.

Rosie reaches into her bag, pulls one out, and hands it to Amy.

Amy feels it. "It's so soft. Where do you even buy these?"

"Tibet," says Rosie. "I'll order you some."

Amy grasps the index finger of Scroggie's right hand and wipes it clean of blood. She then places the index finger onto the keyboard's touch sensor.

"Oh, that's clever," says Rosie. "Fingerprint recognition. Can I use that in a book? *The Corpse Hacker.*"

"Not clever enough, though," says Amy, looking at the resolutely locked computer screen. "He doesn't use it."

"Mine uses iris recognition," says Rosie. "Because of my high-maintenance nails."

Amy and Rosie look at Scroggie's face. His eyelids are puffy, deep purple, and clamped closed. They look at each other.

"I've done worse," says Rosie, and maneuvers the swollen eyelids of Scroggie's dead left eye open, with a great deal of difficulty.

"You're a trouper," says Amy. "I'll give you that."

Amy swivels the office chair just a jot so that Scroggie is "looking" directly into the camera and, with a happy ping, the computer springs into life.

"Teamwork makes the dream work," says Rosie.

23

H ollands Wood Campsite is on the right, just after you've driven through Brockenhurst. If you see the Balmer Lawn Hotel, you're almost there.

Steve is trying very hard to stay calm. Whatever Jeff needs to talk to him about, it'll be fine. Amy is okay; he's been assured of that.

The site is huge, each pitch shielded by trees, and dappled in golden sunlight. Steve sees families sitting outside tents and caravans, eating salads from fold-up tables. Kids playing football with new friends, couples on bikes, and ponies poking their heads through tent flaps. The speed limit around the site is 5 mph, and the Corsa has rarely been happier. Unlike Steve. What could Jeff Nolan possibly need from him?

Deeper into the campsite, the pitches get further and further apart, and, Steve guesses, become more expensive; a few are unoccupied, even in August. Birdsong is everywhere, the odd radio playing quietly. Steve sees a couple sitting together under a caravan awning, both white-haired and tanned. She's doing the crossword. One of his hands is holding a book, the other touching her arm.

It's the sort of scene that Steve had always imagined for him and Debbie, but that will never happen now. But Steve has learned you must never resent other people for their happiness. Everyone is taking the best shot they've got, and some shots are just luckier than yours. Anytime you feel your unhappiness turning into bitterness, you have to check yourself. You can live with unhappiness, but bitterness will kill you.

He drives past Pitch 38, so it can't be far now. The forest is all around him. It'll be something simple, Steve is sure. Won't it? Why has Jeff insisted on privacy? Who is he hiding their meeting from? Steve has messaged Amy, but she hasn't picked it up yet.

Steve reaches Pitch 46, and immediately knows that Jeff is in trouble.

Jeff's car, a black BMW, is parked on the grass. The driver's door and front passenger door are both wide-open.

Steve parks the Corsa and approaches the BMW. The driver's side window has been smashed, and in the driver's seat he sees a pool of blood, still wet. The blood continues, streaked across the passenger seat. Steve walks around to the other side of the car. The streak of blood continues across the grass and into some gorse bushes. Steve navigates his way through the gorse and comes out on another pitch. More blood, which stops in the middle of the pitch. And what starts in the middle of the pitch are tire tracks.

Steve takes out his Dictaphone. "I couldn't swear by it, but I'd say they're the tire tracks of a Volvo XC90."

So what is this? A kidnapping or a murder? And is Jeff Nolan the victim or the perpetrator?

Steve would be happy to leave it. Delighted to leave it, in fact. Turn the whole thing over to the police and forget about it. But Jeff Nolan had come down to see him about something. Something that was troubling him, and something he needed help with.

And the only thing the two men have in common is Amy.

Is she in trouble? Surely she would have told him?

24

In the hazy heat of a South Carolina noon, another bullet cracks through the air.

"We need to steal a car," says Amy to Rosie. "A fast one."

"We're currently being shot at," says Rosie. "Perhaps focus on that?"

"They're not shooting at us," says Amy. "They're shooting near us. And a professional wouldn't be shooting at all, so stop being so melodramatic. They'll get bored in seven minutes or so."

"I'll settle in, then," says Rosie. "I could just hire us a car, by the way? Unless that's not cool enough for you?"

"Can't use your credit card," says Amy. "From now on. Nothing traceable."

She has just listened to Jeff's message. Professional, and to the point, even though he seems to have no idea why she is being targeted. He made it clear that she and Rosie must go entirely under the radar. Also, they can't return to London: Jeff has gone, and he's told her to not trust anyone else. She and Rosie are going to have to keep moving. Amy is a little shaken, but Jeff will be okay; he's a professional. She understands, though, that they're now on their own.

"No credit cards?" Rosie says. "Kill me now, Amy."

Another burst of gunfire. A little further away? There is a woodland just behind Scroggie's house, a perfect hiding place. Which is why Amy and Rosie are hidden, instead, in a neighbor's garden, underneath a pool cover.

Only their heads are above water. On the side of the pool are the documents they printed out in Scroggie's house, and Rosie's handbag. Rosie's Louis Vuitton case is currently under a trampoline.

The gunman had run straight into the woodland. As Amy had known he would. Gunmen, by and large, are idiots.

Sheriff Scroggie's home and computer had been a treasure trove. His personal email accounts had been full of boasts to pals about coming into some money ("More than usual, ya pal Scroggie just hit the big time"), and being asked to do an important job for some important guys ("Asked for me personal like. Heard I got jobs done, I guess").

So Scroggie wasn't going to lead them to the killer of Andrew Fairbanks. Scroggie *was* the killer.

Three other things stood out.

Firstly, his corpse: that was hard to ignore. Murdered, certainly. By Loubet? Looking at the handiwork, Amy was certain it had been done by someone incredibly committed to murdering people, so it could well be.

Secondly, a grocery bag containing a hundred thousand dollars that Rosie found in an upstairs cupboard. Scroggie must have stolen it from the bag that was found on the boat. It would explain why the bag had contained $900K. Either way, it was an idiotic move on Scroggie's part. The hundred grand is currently under a lawn chair in the backyard where they're hiding. It will come in handy now Amy has to stay off-grid.

And then, thirdly, and most pressingly at the current moment, somebody opened fire on them the instant they climbed out of Scroggie's house.

"Who do you suppose is shooting at us?" asks Rosie. "Assassins?"

"Assassin," says Amy. "There's only one of them. Not a very good one either—all this shooting is just giving away their location. Sounds like a Glock 22, so I'm guessing police. If they've got Scroggie on the payroll, they could have all sorts of cops on the lookout for me."

"You know a lot about guns," says Rosie.

Another gunshot, further in the distance again, the gunman trying to scare them out of hiding.

"I've just realized we're in the shallow end and I can put my feet on the bottom," says Rosie. "Do you get shot at a lot?"

"Yes," says Amy.

"First time for me," says Rosie. "No, wait, second. Even so, I told you we'd have fun if we left the island. You didn't believe me."

"Who do you trust most in the world?" says Amy.

"Who do I trust?" says Rosie. "Goodness. At a push, maybe Cher?"

"We're going to need help," says Amy. "We can't go back to London. Where can we stay, within a four- or five-hour drive?"

"My friend Barb will put us up," says Rosie. "You just worry about stealing a car. Does this mean you're not going to leave me behind?"

"You don't leave my side," says Amy. Jeff was also supposed to be dealing with the Vasiliy Karpin problem. Jeff being out of commission means Karpin will remain a threat to Rosie. Another complication for Amy.

The gunshots are becoming faint now. Give it three minutes, then go. Steal a car, visit whoever Barb is, and regroup. Try to work out what the hell is going on. Why is François Loubet after her? Why has Jeff warned her about Henk, his former best friend? And how is it all linked to Andrew Fairbanks, Bella Sanchez, and Mark Gooch? It's too much for Amy to take in.

"Who do *you* trust, by the way?" Rosie asks. "We might need more help than my friend Barb. She's eighty."

And that was the biggest question of all. Who did Amy trust in this world? Who can she turn to now?

She trusts her husband, Adam, implicitly. Early in their relationship she'd had a lie-detector machine in her carry-on suitcase, and he'd agreed to be hooked up to it and answer any question she had. Which is how she knows that Adam loves her, that he will never cheat on her, and that he secretly loves "My Heart Will Go On" by Celine Dion.

But Adam is in Macau, and Adam curls up into a ball at the first sign of trouble. That's why they work so well together.

Jeff Nolan. She trusts Jeff Nolan with her life. Has literally trusted him with her life many times. But he has now found himself caught up in all this trouble himself.

Rosie? Does she trust Rosie? Amy supposes so, as she watches her now, neck deep in water, reapplying her lipstick by the light of her phone.

But she needs immediate help, and there's only one other person in the world that she truly trusts. And he would actually be useful in the current situation. Someone who has solved a murder or two in his time.

Steve.

But Steve is not going to like it. Amy turns to Rosie.

"Can I ask you a question?"

"If it's the question I get asked most often," says Rosie, "then the answer is Jack Nicholson."

"Did you say you have a private plane?"

Rosie laughs. "Of course I've got a private plane. I've got eighties money."

Okay, then. Time to go steal a car and send for the cavalry.

Nope, Steve is not going to like this one bit.

25

As Steve is contemplating the BMW full of blood and bullet holes, his phone rings. It's Amy.

"Jesus Christ, at last," he says. "Are you okay?"

"I'm always okay. What are you doing this evening?" Amy asks. Straight out.

"It's Italian night at The Brass Monkey. Where are you? I've got very bad news."

"That makes two of us," says Amy.

"I think Jeff Nolan might be dead," says Steve.

"What?" says Amy. "Where are you?"

"Or he's been kidnapped," says Steve. "Or he's killed someone. But I think he's dead. Are you in a car?"

"Yes," says Amy. "Steve, you're not making sense. How do you know this?"

"He came to see me," says Steve.

"Jeff came to see you? Why?" says Amy. Steve hears an older woman's voice in the background, asking, "What's happening? Is he coming?"

"I thought *you* might know," says Steve. "He came to see me. Then he told me to meet him at Hollands Wood—it's a campsite—which I did, and his car is all shot up, blood everywhere."

"Jesus," says Amy. "He told me he was in danger. There's no body, though?"

"Just blood," says Steve. "How are you in a car when you're on a small private island?"

"We've left the island," says Amy. "If there's no body, he's not dead. I guarantee it."

Steve hears the woman give a "Yeehaw" and realizes that it must be Rosie D'Antonio. Steve hopes Amy knows what she's doing. If Jeff is in danger, is Amy?

"Did Jeff say anything?" Amy asks. "Did he look scared?"

"I'd say he looked mildly concerned," says Steve. "Nothing more than that."

"Jeff looking mildly concerned is like me screaming in terror," says Amy.

"You've never screamed in terror," says Steve.

"Exactly," says Amy. "Christ, what a mess."

In the background Rosie D'Antonio says, "If you don't tell me what he's saying, I'm going to grab the wheel and steer the car into a bridge."

"What's this about, Amy?"

"I'll explain everything when you get here," says Amy.

"Get where? America?" says Steve. "I'm staying here. I've just witnessed the aftermath of a murder."

"Do the police know you witnessed it?"

"No, I'm about to ring in an anonymous tip," says Steve. "And then drive away as fast as I can. Tony Taylor just fitted me a new clutch cable. You didn't need to know that last bit."

"Then you're free to come help your daughter-in-law," says Amy. "You said you've been reading about Andrew Fairbanks? How come?"

"Is that what all this is about?" says Steve. "Fairbanks? I was just reading about it because you were nearby. You're not involved?"

"I need you to fly over," says Amy.

So she really *does* mean America. I mean, in all honesty, no thanks. That heat, and the TV shows are all different. And no doubt there are insects, and maybe even alligators. Do they have alligators in South Carolina? Steve hadn't known they had sharks in South Carolina until he'd read about Andrew Fairbanks.

"I need to stay in England," says Steve. "If this is about Andrew Fairbanks, I can be much more useful here. I've got a lead. Have you ever been to Letch—"

"It's bigger than Andrew Fairbanks," says Amy. "Three people have been murdered."

Steve hears Rosie D'Antonio say, "Four people."

"Four people have been murdered," says Amy. "And I'm on my own."

Steve hears Rosie D'Antonio snort.

"Are you okay, though?" asks Steve. "Are you safe?"

"No," says Amy. "I'm not safe. Somebody just tried to kill me, and someone will try again. I need someone I can trust. And I'm afraid that's you, so buckle up."

"Someone tried to kill you?" says Steve.

"Yes," says Amy. "An ex–Navy SEAL. And I think a local cop's just been shooting at me too."

This is all Steve needs. Jeez. There must be a way of helping from home, surely? No need to go to America. Letchworth Garden City is where the answer is. He can feel it.

"I appreciate the sentiment," says Steve. "But America is not my speed at all. Not at all. A much smarter move is to ask one of your mates. The bodyguards? I'll do all I can here. I've got the internet."

Steve looks over at the BMW again. He really needs to get out of here. "And I've got no one to look after Trouble."

"Margaret can look after him." Amy sounds irritated. *She's* irritated? No one's asking her to fly to America, are they? *She's* in a car with a famous author. He's at a dreadful crime scene. When was the last time she was at a dreadful crime scene?

"Look, I can't promise you," says Steve, "but I could look into flights on the computer? See if I can get a cheap deal next week? Maybe you'll have solved it by then?"

"There'll be a plane waiting for you at Farnborough," says Amy. "Rosie's private jet."

"Give over," says Steve. "Farnborough. Is there parking?"

"A car will come to your house. It'll drive you to the plane."

"Wait a minute," says Steve.

"I need you, Steve," says Amy. "Get the plane."

"I'll have to mull it ov—"

"What would Debbie tell you to do?"

Steve knows exactly what Debbie would tell him to do. She's telling him right now. He feels sick.

But then he realizes there's another feeling too. One that he can't quite put his finger on. Surely not excitement? At being wanted? At being needed? At *danger*? No, he must just be in shock.

"Are there alligators?"

Steve hears Amy put this question to Rosie, who replies, "God, yes, huge ones."

If Steve does go to America, he's going to have to rearrange that shelf delivery. That'll be another half an hour on hold to the call center. And there will be no bolognese.

And, worst of all, four murders. Or, given what he has just seen, maybe five?

"Steve, I need someone I can trust," says Amy. She is quieter now. She knows that she has him. "There are murders to be solved, and I can't do it by myself. It's you and me."

"But we don't solve murders," says Steve.

He can hear Amy smiling down the phone. "Then we're going to have to start."

PART TWO

From South Carolina to Dubai

*(via St. Lucia and County Cork,
and a brief return to the New Forest)*

26

ChatGPT, rewrite in the style of a friendly English gentleman, please.

Another email from Rob Kenna, my trusty murder-broker. I almost forgot to put my ChatGPT on, by the way! What a shock you would have had, hearing the real me!

Amy Wheeler still at large. Apologies. Being dealt with.

Well, I really have got myself into something of a pickle here, haven't I?

Let me tell you a little about myself, so I can explain all! If you're reading this, it's either because I'm dead or I'm in prison. There is also the slight chance that these little notes might be intercepted by the authorities one day, so I will continue to cloak myself. But that's unlikely, because I take care. And that's also why I very much doubt that I will ever end up in prison. And that's because I always take out insurance.

Money-smuggling is the biggest business of them all—that's the first thing you need to understand. Every single illegal activity in the world is made up of two sides. The buyers and the sellers. The sellers offer all sorts of different things: drugs, guns, people, counterfeit clothing, secrets, rare-bird eggs, military-weapons systems. But the buyers, by and large, offer just one thing—money.

And so it goes, that in the sum of the parts of all the illegal activities anywhere in the world, trillions of dollars' worth of good old-fashioned cash money is just sloshing about, looking for a safe harbor.

And, for the most part, that money is nothing but trouble. Have you ever tried paying a million pounds into your local bank branch? Try it. See where that gets you. In the old days they turned a blind eye. A pile of fifties stained with blood? Let me count that for you, sir.

But now? Sometimes it's honestly not worth the bother. Anti-money-laundering laws are a real disincentive to entrepreneurs. Just last week a friend told me she had sighed when being handed a bag containing ten million dollars, dismayed by the thought of the effort and time and expense it would take to clean it all up.

And that's why people employ me. If you need your money laundered, fed through fake companies, washed through casinos or money exchanges, I am a veritable one-stop shop!

So that's me! Now, about this current scheme, which has begun to backfire like a cheap motor car!

A lot of the job is electronic these days—transfers upon transfers upon transfers, a long, laborious process that means it might be months before you have some actual cash in your hands.

Which is why one of the fun parts of the job is when circumstance forces one to physically move money around the world. A client in São Paolo needs a million dollars in cash by Tuesday. An Australian mining magnate needs untraceable currency to pay a bribe at a weekend barbecue. Sometimes people just need cash, and they need it quickly.

This is where couriers come in. Just as mules smuggle drugs, so couriers smuggle money. Every day, sums large and small pass through the scanners and security checks of airports and docks around the world. Much of it controlled by my good self—the man known as François Loubet, though, by the time this is being read, you will of course be familiar with my real name!

Now, at any given time, I have an awful lot of smuggling schemes on the go. I diversify. I refuse to put all my eggs in one egg-receptacle.

So when did this "influencer" scheme begin? Two years ago, something like that?

I had been using the services of a company called Maximum Impact Solutions. Just a bit of light security work for one of my people in London. They were perfectly fine, efficient, didn't ask too many questions, and they didn't balk when they were paid in Rwandan francs through a bank in Indonesia.

Then a week or so later I received an email from someone called "Joe Blow," who was clearly connected with Maximum Impact. "Joe Blow" had rather a neat proposal to supply me with couriers.

Influencers.

I hadn't even really known what the word meant when Joe Blow emailed me out of the blue and suggested it to me. I'd heard of it, of course, but hadn't paid it any heed. But, it turns out, they are the perfect couriers.

You see, if you want to smuggle large sums of money around the world— and I do very much want to do that—here is the question you must ask yourself.

Who has a jet-set lifestyle? Who might travel halfway around the world for only a day or two? With bulky luggage? Without it looking too suspicious?

Famous people would be the answer. Hiding in plain sight, taking selfies on the plane, always with the perfect reason to be flying to America, or St. Lucia, or the Cayman Islands.

But what's the problem with most of the famous people who lead these jet-set lifestyles?

You're ahead of me, I'm certain. They're already rich.

So this is where these influencers come in. The influencers with limited numbers of followers. They can fly around the world raising no suspicion. But they have no money. And therefore they can be bought.

Simply set up a few dummy companies, I have many of them already. Joe Blow and I use a company called Vivid Viral Media for this scheme. Then book your influencers on a few fake assignments abroad, advertising the products of other front companies you already own, and, unbeknownst to them, give them a big bag of money to smuggle through customs every time.

Well, almost every time. Sometimes your poor couriers, usually with no idea what they're carrying, get caught. And that's the origin of this current brouhaha!

Joe Blow is clearly high up at Maximum Impact, with access to this email address certainly. I don't give it out willy-nilly!

At first I simply assumed that Joe Blow was Jeff Nolan. He seemed like a good guy who would happily put his clients at risk for an immense payday. However, I fear I was mistaken, because, after two of our couriers had been caught by customs officials, Jeff Nolan himself sent me a very rude email. Accusing me of all sorts. Quite the nerve.

So I decided to move on. As I say, I have plenty of these schemes; as soon as one gives me gip, I move along posthaste.

But, before I did, I sent Jeff Nolan a message in return. And by "message," I mean I had one of the couriers killed, very publicly. No point pussy-footing around, is there? It was simply a gentle warning to back away, a shot across Jeff Nolan's bows, and I thought that would be the end of it.

But no. There was a further email from Jeff Nolan. He had taken offense at the murder, for goodness' sake, and wasn't backing down. He wished to expose me. You know that sort of nonsense. All ego.

My response was the only reasonable one in the circumstances. To have another courier killed. Inconvenient for me, but one must always respond to threats, mustn't one? I can't abide a bully.

But still Nolan wouldn't back down.

The third murder was a few days ago. South Carolina, I believe. I'm not fully across the details. This time I even told Rob Kenna to leave the money with the body. A million dollars. That was me saying, very simply, to Jeff Nolan, "This isn't about the blasted money, old thing, this is about the blasted principle, so we must let bygones be bygones and live in harmony."

Nothing from him since, so perhaps this has done the trick, and I can get on with the rest of my business in peace?

Back to the email from Rob Kenna, though. Amy Wheeler on the run.

Where does Amy Wheeler come in? And why do I want her dead? I did tell you that I always take out insurance, and, on this occasion, Amy Wheeler is my unwitting insurance policy. I will explain more when she's dead. I don't want to get too cocky!

I know that Amy Wheeler is far from a fool, you see, and, though I trust Rob Kenna to get the job done, it won't do any harm to send him a note of encouragement.

Mr. Kenna,

I understand completely; these things happen. While I still have great faith in you, be assured that if Amy Wheeler is not dead within a week, you will be.

Warmest regards,
François Loubet

Hopefully that should focus his mind. Chop-chop, Robert!

27

S ushi, sir?" The attendant is wearing an all-black uniform.

There had been a driver, wearing a hat, if you can believe that, waiting for Steve back at the cottage. Steve had invited him in for a cup of tea, but the driver, Ken, had refused.

Steve had then taken a call from his old colleague Linda, now at Hampshire Police. Of course she can tip him the wink when they get the blood results back from the Hollands Wood scene. Why did Steve want to know? Oh, no reason, no reason. Linda then asked if Steve fancied a drink, and Steve pretended he had plans. It always makes him feel awkward, that sort of thing, women asking him round to supper, or out for drinks. Feeling sorry for the widower. Steve berated himself for a while for pretending he had plans, before realizing that, for once, he actually did have plans.

He is flying to America to stop somebody from killing Amy.

Steve had then knocked for Margaret, told her the situation—"Just a couple of days, surprise party, don't forget Trouble needs eye drops"—and packed a bag. Steve couldn't find any details of how much luggage you could take on a private plane, so had packed just a small rucksack in case. He took a cup of tea out to Ken, because the poor man had been waiting for nearly forty-five minutes. He told Ken he'd need to stop at a cashpoint, as he had no money to pay him, but Ken said it was all already paid for. His printer was out of ink, so over he went to Margaret's again to use hers, and printed out the documents Amy had sent him. A topless man, smiling on a yacht, and then a mutilated torso, and pages and pages of notes about a woman called Bella Sanchez and a man called Mark Gooch. He would read them on the plane. He packed a toothbrush and a phone charger, a book of word search puzzles, three pairs of underwear, a shirt, just in case they had to go anywhere nice, a packet of chocolate digestives, in case there was nothing to eat on the plane, a Van Halen T-shirt, a Def Leppard T-shirt, and a smart denim jacket with holes at the elbows.

When Steve got into the front of Ken's car, Ken said that most people sat in the back, but Steve said that sitting in the backs of cars was only for children or prisoners, so he stayed where he was, and they had a good chat all the way to Farnborough. Steve said he wasn't sure which terminal he was going to, but Ken said not to worry, and when they got to the airport, he drove the car all the way up to the plane steps, where Steve was met by a passport officer with a stamp, and Brad with a glass of champagne. He said his farewells to Ken, and they swapped numbers because Ken plays bass in a Kiss tribute band who sometimes gig at a pub up in Lyndhurst, and he'd wondered if Steve would ever fancy coming along.

Up the steps and on board, Steve looked around for other passengers, but there were none. The pilot, Saskia, asked if he would like to sit in the cockpit for take off, and Steve said that he would like that very much indeed. She even let him press a button. Which was the first good thing to happen today, apart from finally getting his clutch cable fixed.

Eventually, when they'd reached cruising altitude, Steve said to Saskia, "I'll let you get on," and, as he left the cockpit, he saw her stretch out and pick up a book. When Steve returns to his seat—a sofa, of all things—Brad offers him sushi on a silver tray.

Steve takes a look. "Do you have anything else?" he asks. "A sausage roll? Some crisps?"

"I think we have some Parmesan croutons?" says Brad. "I'll ask the chef."

"Or a Scotch egg?" says Steve. "Whatever you've got. I was supposed to be having bolognese tonight, so if there's any bolognese?"

"Of course," says Brad. "And can I get you a drink? We have eighteen types of vodka."

"Do you have beer?" asks Steve.

"We have twelve types of beer," says Brad.

"Do you have an ale? Something with a bit of oomph?"

"I couldn't say," says Brad. "Why don't I bring out all twelve, and we'll have a tasting?"

Steve agrees that this sounds like a fine idea. From his window he sees the lights of the English coast. Soon they will be out above open sea. The last time Steve went abroad was a week in Turkey with Debbie on a flight that had neither sushi nor eighteen types of vodka. He ended up with an upset stomach and had to stay in the hotel room. And the only English thing on the TV was an international news channel that repeated everything on a half-hour loop. He learned an awful lot about the disputed elections in Burkina Faso on that trip.

Steve takes out his papers, in an effort to distract himself from going abroad.

Andrew Fairbanks. Killed on a yacht, tied to a rope, and thrown overboard, bobbing along on the Atlantic Ocean until the alarm was raised.

The trip had been booked through a trendy media agency with offices in decidedly untrendy Letchworth Garden City. Steve knows all about that. He hasn't sent them an email yet; he's not quite sure what question he wants to ask. He also doesn't want to alert them to his suspicions.

Steve reads on. Fairbanks is met at the airport, the same airport Steve is now flying to, by a driver, no name provided, and driven to Lowesport, where he was to meet a yacht, and a photographer. Again, no names provided. Steve takes out his Dictaphone.

"Who met him? CCTV at the airport."

On to François Loubet, a new name for Steve. Amy has sketched out a few details for him. Finding him seems to be her priority. And Amy also mentions a Joe Blow, perhaps an insider at Maximum Impact Solutions. Both these names had come from Jeff Nolan. Steve takes out his Dictaphone.

"Who is François Loubet? Who is Joe Blow?"

Brad arrives with twelve shot glasses, each filled with liquids of varying shades of amber.

"Shall we?" asks Brad.

"Will you join me?" Steve asks.

"Not allowed to drink with passengers, I'm afraid."

"Says who?"

"I think it's international law," says Brad. "But the pilot too. She needs me sober. In case of emergency."

Steve raises his finger, asking Brad to give him a moment, and walks to the cockpit. As he opens the door, Saskia looks up from her book. It is Rosie D'Antonio's latest, *Dead Men & Diamonds*.

"Can Brad have a drink with me?" he asks. "It's a long flight."

"Sure," says Saskia. "There's a wrap of coke in the Business Suite too. Fill your boots."

"You're okay," says Steve. "But thank you."

Shutting the door, Steve takes out his Dictaphone again. "Debs, I'm on a private jet. There's a gold toilet, and cocaine, but no crisps. Anyway, no doubt we'll crash, but, if not, let's chat later. Love you, babe."

Steve returns to his sofa. Brad raises an inquiring eyebrow.

"Saskia says go for it."

Brad smiles, and raises the first glass. "We start with a cheeky little lager from Japan."

28

Bonnie Gregor's influencer dream had started small.

And yet here she is, just a year later, on a train to Letchworth Garden City.

Bonnie had posted a photograph of her newly painted pink toilet door on Instagram. At the time she had six followers: her mum, her sister, two of the girls from work, Gail and Reba, Reba's husband, Mike, and a pornographic bot from South Korea.

Bonnie scrolls through her Instagram now—14K followers, thank you very much—trying to choose some highlights to show to Felicity Woollaston at Vivid Viral Media. Felicity doesn't know she's coming, but sometimes you have to make things happen. Big things happen to other people, so why not to her too? The kids are with her mum for the day.

Bonnie has no sense of Felicity's age, but she's guessing mid-twenties hipster. Fourteen K followers in just a year. Imagine where she could go next? Reba and Mike have since divorced, but the porn bot is still there. That's loyalty.

She had included #LooWithAView in her photograph caption. She had taken the photo while sitting on the loo, and you could just see the tips of her knees in the bottom of the shot. It got four likes, Mike and the porn bot being the only dissenters. Early signs there that Mike was not to be relied upon.

It soon trailed off into that vast forgotten ocean of Instagram posts that fortunate future historians will spend whole careers interpreting.

A few weeks later the paint started peeling a little; she'd bought the wrong sort, it was only a bit of fun. So she scraped it off. She briefly experimented with hanging a picture of Harry Styles on the door, but it seemed disrespectful to him, and what if, unlikely Bonnie knew, he ever came round? His car broke down on her street, say, and he needed the toilet?

The train is now pulling into Letchworth Garden City. Bonnie is a little nervous, but nothing ventured, nothing gained. It was Reba really who planted the idea. "Fourteen K followers? That makes you an influencer."

She had Reba to thank for the whole thing. It was Reba who had posted Bonnie's photo on Facebook in the "Bathroom Inspiration" group, where it had been seen by a woman who had turned out to be Fearne Cotton's mum; so then Fearne Cotton had seen it and had posted it on her own Instagram with the hashtags #ILoveMyLooToo, #LoveThisIdea, #GoBonnie in her caption.

The followers started flooding in, but, after they liked the toilet-door post, there was nothing else for them to see, other than a photograph of Bonnie's lunch that day, a tuna bake. They soon started flooding away again.

So, as a stopgap, Bonnie had painted "ILoveMyKitchen" on one of her kitchen cabinets. Pink again—she had a bit of the paint left. That photo seemed to please the hordes. "Love this idea," "So fresh," "Makes you think about kitchens. Like, what are they? Thanks for the inspo." And so Bonnie then painted on her living-room wall, her bedroom wall, and the spare bedroom wall, realizing after she had finished that she had run out of rooms.

The walk from Letchworth Garden City Station to the high street is surprisingly pleasant. Bonnie sits on a bench and takes out her phone. She unpeels one of her stickers ("£4.99 for a roll of 60," direct from her website), which reads "I LOVE MY _____." She writes the word "bench" with a pink glitter pen ("£6.99 for 6," direct from her website) and sticks it onto the bench. She then takes a photo of herself on the bench, next to the sticker, and pulls a mildly bemused face as if to say, "Wait, I love a bench. I might be a little crazy," applies a few filters, adds #LovinLetchworth and #BenchesNeedLoveToo, and posts it.

As she sets off to meet Felicity, she feels her phone buzz with notifications as people like the post. That gives her some confidence. She knows it's silly, really, but she also knows that she spreads a tiny bit of happiness in a world that needs all the happiness it can find. Who knows what advice Felicity Woollaston might have for her? The stickers and the pens and the paint sets and the stencils are all well and good, but she barely covers her costs. She certainly couldn't give up her job. Maybe Felicity can change all that? Elevate her to the next level. Bonnie has plenty of ideas, but she knows that Felicity is the expert.

And, above all, Bonnie knows you have to dream your dream, and see where it takes you.

29

Amy is still driving.

"Will I like him?" asks Rosie. "Your father-in-law? Is he rugged?"

"Do you like the type of man who eats all his meals in his local pub?" asks Amy. "And looks like a roadie for Iron Maiden?"

"Well, you're hot, which means that you probably married a hot guy. And hot guys usually have hot dads. So I like my chances."

"No touching," says Amy. "I mean it."

"The heart wants what it wants, Amy," says Rosie. "I'm often powerless."

Has Amy done the right thing, involving Steve? It's a good question. She goes through her six-point checklist. Jeff had drummed it into her during her training.

Point One: Assess the situation. The situation is that it seems that François Loubet is trying to murder her. That's Jeff's understanding of the situation. And she is almost certainly being implicated in three murders she hasn't committed with no idea why.

Point Two: Assess your strengths. Her strengths are ten years in the field, a bag containing a hundred grand in cash, safe harbor with an eighty-year-old woman named Barbara, and a window of two or three days in which to investigate the murders. Also, implicate her in these killings all you like, but there's no way anyone could ever tie a single one to her. She might have been nearby, but there is no direct evidence anywhere.

Three: Assess your weaknesses. Her weaknesses are a complete lack of experience in murder investigation; Loubet wanting her dead; and Jeff Nolan possibly having been murdered. Add to these an indeterminately aged woman in a rhinestone jumpsuit who might be shot by a Russian billionaire at any moment. Or who might try to seduce her father-in-law.

Four: Can you build on your strengths? Yes. Calling Steve was doing precisely that: he's a man she can trust, and a man who can investigate. Albeit, a man who phoned her from an airport runway in Hampshire to ask how much it might cost to use his mobile phone in America and, when she had no immediate answer, switched his phone off and hasn't been contactable since.

Five: Can you control your weaknesses? No such luck. Rosie is smoking a cigarette with mischief in her eyes.

And Point Six: Act decisively, which she is doing. Amy is not a dweller on things. She tends to concentrate on what is right in front of her at any given time. Someone is killing clients, and perhaps that same someone is framing her for it. Again, if she can't kick it or hit it, it's not particularly in Amy's area of specialty. But right now Amy's best protection is to investigate, and to try to solve, the murders of Andrew Fairbanks, Bella Sanchez, and Mark Gooch.

She needs to sit down with Steve and talk it all through. Well, she'll talk it through; he'll nod and listen; and then he'll suggest what they might do. Perhaps she should have cleared all this with Adam? Before inviting his dad to join a slightly perilous murder investigation 4,000 miles from home? She texts him with voice activation.

**Ads, might ask your dad for a bit of advice. Work stuff.
Okay by you?**

That should cover it. The key with Adam is to make him feel part of whatever's going on. He's just flown from Macau to Singapore, to broker a lucrative deal between two companies that don't seem to own anything or make anything, but that are, nevertheless, worth billions each. Adam tries to explain sometimes, but, really, so long as he's enjoying himself, Amy is happy. The disembodied voice of Siri reads his reply.

> **That'll be nice for him, Ames, he likes to feel involved.**
> **Love you to the moon and back xxx**

Amy smiles. She loves Adam to the moon and back too, and decides she should tell him.

> **Same.**

She is a romantic fool sometimes.

Another ping. Steve has finally turned his phone back on. Siri gets to work again.

> **Have landed. No crisps on flight, but we made the most of**
> **what we had. Might be a while getting through customs.**

Amy knows customs won't be a problem. Checks are cursory at the Emory Executive Airfield. Too many clients with too much to hide. Steve will be waved through. Unless he attempts to joke with the border official, which she wouldn't put past him. But, all things being well, he should be with them soon. She voice-messages back.

> **Get the car to take you to the Eternal Glade Wellness**
> **Retreat Resort near Greenville. Ask for Barbara Elliot.**

Another message from Steve.

> **Do you know where the toilet is at the airport? I didn't go**
> **on the plane because it was so small and I was worried**
> **Brad might hear.**

Amy shakes her head at this message, and then glances over at Rosie, who is somehow simultaneously singing, smoking a cigarette, and flipping the bird at a truck driver as they speed past him.

Amy has four murders to solve, with just Rosie D'Antonio and her father-in-law, Steve, to help her.

She gives a little smile, finding that she actually rather likes those odds.

Her old friend adrenaline has returned.

30

Rob Kenna, murder-broker, knows exactly who to call. He always knows exactly who to call. That's the job.

The key here, despite Loubet's email, is not to panic. The ex–Navy SEAL, Kevin, has messed up. And there was a local cop who had done a nice job of killing the sheriff, but a very bad job of shooting a fleeing Amy Wheeler. He needs someone new. He presses the "call" button on his Zoom. It's not actually "Zoom": it's a heavily encrypted video-conferencing app he bought from a Russian at the Emirates Squash Club. It's called "Shhhh!"

Rob is calling home. London. Very specifically, East London, where he grew up, a place where he knows he'll find someone he can trust. And there, speak of the devil, is Eddie Flood himself, looming into frame and looking for the camera.

He's still fit, is Eddie. Hair nicely cropped, gone to fat a bit, but not as much as the other lads they'd grown up with. Eddie was always a little smarter than the rest.

"Eddie, you're looking well," says Rob.

"You too, brother, been too long," says Eddie.

Rob looks behind Eddie. "Nice dartboard. I'd kill for a game."

Eddie looks surprised. "You not got one?"

"They don't do darts out here," says Rob. "They do polo, but it's not the same, is it?"

"Polo?" says Eddie. "No, it's not the same as darts."

"How do you fancy a trip to America, Eddie?" Rob asks. To business now, no more time to waste.

"America? Not much," says Eddie. "We not having a gossip first?"

"No time," says Rob. "How you doing for money?"

"Badly," says Eddie. "You?"

"Good, thanks," says Rob. "How about thirty grand to kill someone for me? Half now, half when it's done."

Eddie considers this. "Does it have to be in America?"

"'Fraid so, old son."

Eddie puffs out his cheeks. "Why me?"

"I trust you," he says. "The woman I need you to kill is a piece of work. I need someone good. You still do the odd job?"

"Now and then," says Eddie.

"Course you do," says Rob. This is all part of the business. Rob hires the right person for the job, Rob gets paid, and Rob doesn't get killed by François Loubet. The circle of life.

"I don't know, though," says Eddie now, shaking his massive head. "America? A woman?"

"Yeah, but thirty grand, Eddie. And I need the best."

"Yeah," agrees Eddie. "I suppose so."

Rob holds up a photo to the camera. Two women. Taken a couple of hours ago. "You kill the young one. Amy Wheeler."

"What if I have to kill the older one?" asks Eddie.

"Don't," he says. "She's famous, and we don't need the attention. She's Rosie D'Antonio."

Rob sees Eddie look away from the camera, trying to hide something in his eyes. "Rosie D'Antonio?"

"The writer, yeah," says Rob. "You all right there? Look like you've seen a ghost?"

"Right as rain," says Eddie, seemingly fully recovered from whatever that was. "When do I go?"

"Now," he says. "For reasons we don't have the time to talk about, I need this done quickly. City Airport as soon as you can. Use my plane."

"You got a plane now?"

"Two. One in Dubai, one in London."

Eddie nods and looks around at the golden decor behind Rob. "Two planes and no dartboards. Times change, eh?"

"They do, Eddie old son. They do."

Eddie will get the job done, Rob knows that. No flash, no ego. Not like that dumb Navy SEAL, Kevin. Just in, bang, bang, out. Then Rob can stop worrying about François Loubet.

And that's why old friends are so important.

31

Steve Wheeler stands at the top of the steps leading down from the private jet. He has drunk probably the equivalent of six pints, and the onboard chef had fashioned him a rudimentary "steak bake" from veal, Wagyu beef, and panko breadcrumbs. The moment the hatch opens, the humid South Carolina air hits him like the breath of an angry beast. He probably shouldn't be wearing a denim jacket and a sweatshirt. But that's what he always wears, and America will have to change before Steve does.

The sky is the blue of a dream. He is no longer in England, and that thought makes him want to turn back immediately. He is sure they will fly him home again if he asks politely. On the horizon he sees a freeway, speeding cars glinting and metallic in a way familiar from films but alien to Hampshire. Also the freeway signs are the wrong color. And why does he have the word "freeway" in his head? It's a "motorway," Steve, don't get sucked in.

The adverts on the side of the small private terminal building seem so tantalizingly similar to adverts he might see at home. And yet the teeth are whiter, the hair shinier, and the slogans more sure of themselves. Steve runs a hand through his hair, touches his teeth with his tongue, and feels considerably less confident than he has been in a long time. What will they make of him here?

Brad, the flight attendant, stands behind him, swaying slightly, in the manner of a man unused to drinking a great deal of beer at altitude.

"You might want to put on your sunglasses," Brad suggests.

"I don't have sunglasses," says Steve. "I'm not a male model."

"A hat, then," says Brad. "A hat at least."

"I don't have a hat," says Steve. "Who has hats at their beck and call? Perhaps we should just turn round and head back? Can we do that?"

"Sure," says Brad. "Depends if you came here to do anything important."

That's annoying. He did come here to do something important. He came here to help Amy. Though Lord alone knows how. The very idea that Amy might need any sort of help seems ridiculous to Steve.

Amy was made of steel from the day they met, and for the last five years she has been the helper.

They don't really talk *about* anything, Steve and Amy, in their daily chats. Steve is not a lonely man, no, not that, think of his friends in the village, there's always someone there, someone to have a pint with. So she isn't there to stop him feeling lonely.

So what is it that Amy does? When they chat about nothing?

They certainly don't talk about grief. There are other people to talk to about that if he ever felt the need. Margaret from next door lost her father not so long ago. Tony Taylor from the pub, his wife left him, and there are online forums if things get bad.

The police offer a grief-counseling service to former officers, but he'd be laughed out of town if he took them up on that sort of thing. Resilience is an underrated quality in Steve's mind, and so grief counseling was never for him.

He often explains this to Amy on their calls. Talks through why he doesn't need grief counseling, why he can handle it himself. Why grief is private. Amy is very good about it, to be fair, never presses the point. They just have a good old chat about their days instead, maybe talk about Debbie for a bit, and sometimes Amy will tell a funny story she has remembered about her. Yep, plenty of people bang on about grief counseling, but Amy isn't one of them. She respects his opinion, Steve reckons, knows he doesn't need it. So they'll laugh and cry about all sorts of things, the two of them, but no one ever mentions grief.

He descends the steps. Welcome to America.

There will be another car to meet him, he knows that—Amy has arranged it all—but the car will have to wait, because Steve needs a little snoop around the airport first. This was where Andrew Fairbanks arrived, wasn't it? Where he was picked up by some mystery man? Steve feels like there is something here that he could usefully look into. Some actual investigating. This way, he arrives with a present.

Brad is removing Steve's luggage from the hold of the jet. His camping rucksack, the bottom held together by duct tape. Everything in this place—the plane, the staff, the terminal, the grass, the lights, everything—is gleaming and sparkling and at the top of its game. Everything, that is, except for Steve's rucksack, and for Steve himself. Ragged and baggy but does the job.

Steve refuses to let Brad carry the rucksack to the terminal. Can you imagine? Brad, ever the professional, looks a little put out, though he also looks like a man for whom beer and Parmesan croutons don't mix.

"What's in the building?" Steve asks. "Passport control, all that?"

"Your passport will be checked in the Arrivals Suite," says Brad. "Then Border Protection. They never check bags, though."

Steve is relieved—he doesn't need a bored man with a gun questioning why he's only packed three pairs of underpants. "Many staff?"

"I'm afraid I don't have that information," says Brad. "But it's a small airport."

"So everyone will know everything," says Steve.

Brad doesn't understand the question but nods regardless.

Sliding doors open in front of them, and the air-conditioning instantly transforms Steve's pools of uncomfortable hot sweat into pools of uncomfortable cold sweat. He feels like he is growing stalactites. He follows the sign that says ARRIVALS SUITE. US CUSTOMS AND BORDER PROTECTION WELCOMES YOU. A hefty man in a blue uniform and aviator shades holds out his massive hand for Steve's passport. The name on his gold badge says CARLOS MOSS.

"Purpose of travel, sir," says Carlos Moss, as Steve rummages around in his rucksack.

"Family visit," says Steve, eyeing the man's gun. After twenty-five years on the force, there are very few fellow officers he would have trusted with a gun. It looks good on Carlos Moss, though.

"I'm in the job too," says Steve. "Twenty-five years in the police. Private investigator now."

"I'm Customs and Border Protection, sir," says Carlos, unimpressed. "That's a different job."

"For sure," says Steve, seeing his awkward frame reflected in the sun-glasses. "For sure. But, you know, hunting down the bad guys, right? That's what we do."

"And bad women," says the man. "Don't profile, please. What family are you visiting, sir?"

"Daughter-in-law," says Steve. "I'd love, man to man here, to take a look around. See your systems. The CCTV, you know. I'd get a kick out of that, as a professional."

Carlos looks down at Steve, and lowers his aviator shades for the first time.

"Sir, are you on drugs?"

"No," says Steve. Okay, plan B, then. Steve nods at the man's gun.

"You ever shoot that?"

"Sir?"

"Your gun?" says Steve, finally finding his passport and handing it over. "Can't imagine you get a lot of trouble here?"

"Sir," says the man, flicking through Steve's passport and looking at him again, "I hope you don't think we're having a conversation?"

"No," says Steve. "No, apologies. Just, this would be an easy airport to smuggle a gun into. Everything a bit lax. No real cops."

That should do it, surely? He just needs to get inside the security hub.

"This your bag?" Carlos Moss motions to Steve's rucksack.

"The bag I just carried all the way from the plane and pulled my passport out of?" says Steve. "Yes, it's my bag, Sherlock."

Bit much?

"Is that humor, sir? I hope not."

"Long flight," says Steve. "Also, I'm English. Also, stupid question, Carlos."

Carlos lowers his aviator shades once more. "Sir, you've made me lower my sunglasses two times now. That's plenty enough. You want me to search this bag? You want to see the parts of this airport that ain't so pretty?"

That's exactly what Steve wants. At any regular US airport he would have been in a back room after his first remark. But they have obviously been told not to cause a fuss here. No wonder rich people got away with so much. So he might need one more push.

"If I'd packed a gun, you wouldn't find it, however hard you searched."

"Sir?"

"You'd never find it," says Steve. "It's the American mindset. Too obvious."

Steve already thought that Carlos Moss was tall, but he now uncoils himself further. Carlos finally takes off his shades. "Sir, I'm going to have to ask you to accompany me for a full search."

Bingo, thinks Steve, job done. He then wonders exactly what his plan is now. Whatever it is, he hopes he'll figure it out before the man pulls on a latex glove.

Carlos leads Steve to exactly the spot he had hoped for: the bit of the airport that the tourists never see, unless that tourist has a suitcase full of cocaine or some such. Carlos swings Steve's bag onto a metal table and starts undoing the flimsy clasps.

"Sir, what exactly is your business in the United States?" Carlos has begun delving into Steve's luggage. "You pack light, sir. How long are you staying?"

"Not long, hopefully," says Steve. "Not that this isn't a lovely place to be. But there's the quiz on Wednesday, and Margaret's very good with Trouble, but he misses me."

"Trouble?"

"My cat," says Steve.

"You're a cat guy," says Carlos, nodding. He spends a moment or two looking Steve up and down. "What sort of a cat?"

"Rescued stray," says Steve.

"Good," says Carlos, pulling a Van Halen T-shirt out of Steve's bag. "You a Halen fan?"

"Greatest band of all time," says Steve.

"You got that right, sir," says Carlos.

"Call me Steve," says Steve.

Carlos shakes his head. "No, sir. So why you here?"

"Have you heard of a man called Andrew Fairbanks?" asks Steve.

"Can't say as I have." Carlos now pulls a Def Leppard T-shirt from Steve's rucksack, and nods approvingly. "Two T-shirts for the whole trip?"

"Should do it, don't you think?" says Steve. "And you have washing machines over here. Andrew Fairbanks is the guy who died on the yacht."

"Tied him to a rope and the sharks got him?"

"That's the fella," says Steve. Carlos is repacking his rucksack. Much neater than Steve had done. "Can I show you a photo of him?"

Carlos tightens the drawstring at the top of Steve's bag. "Sir—"

"Steve."

"Sir, you are subject to a search by Customs and Border Protection. I'm within my rights to demand silence from you, but, seeing as you love cats, and you understand where Van Halen sits in the scheme of things, I've given you a little leeway. But you're in no position to be showing me photos, except the one on your passport, where you look a lot more respectable than the guy standing in front of me."

Steve gives his passport photo a peek. "My wife made me dress up. Have a haircut."

"Your wife traveling with you?"

"She's dead," says Steve. "She died."

"Sorry to hear that," says Carlos. "I know what that feels like. So you're here to visit your daughter-in-law?"

"Amy," says Steve. "You'd love her."

"I'm sure," says Carlos. "The two of you got plans?"

"If I say 'investigating a murder,' will you send me back to England?"

"You armed?" asks Carlos.

"No," says Steve.

"I'd recommend it," says Carlos. "What murder? Andrew Fairbanks?"

"Are you interested in that?" Steve asks.

"I'm interested in a lot of things," says Carlos. "Orchids."

"He used this airport you know?" says Steve.

"Did he now?" Carlos replies.

"Tuesday," says Steve. "Were you here?"

"Day off. I was at an airship show," says Carlos. "I like blimps."

Steve *loves* airships. But maybe that's for another time. Focus now. "A driver picked up Fairbanks at the airport, but no one knows who. Has anyone been asking?"

"Not as far as I know," says Carlos. "Just you."

"Local police?"

"Not a soul," says Carlos.

"Would be fun to look at your CCTV, wouldn't it?" says Steve. "See what we can see? Perhaps whoever picked him up killed him?"

"I have another flight landing in twenty minutes, sir."

"Steve."

"Take it to the cops, Steve," says Carlos.

"You're not curious?" Steve asks.

"I'll be curious about whether you're smuggling drugs in your back passage if you don't let this go," says Carlos.

"I'll tell you what I'll do," says Steve. He pulls his Ponies of the New Forest notebook from his bag. "I'm going to write down the name of the greatest ever Van Halen song in this notebook. You do the same in your notebook. And if we both choose the same track, you let me take a look at the CCTV, which you're dying to look at anyway?"

Steve starts to write, and then hands his pen to Carlos. Carlos hesitates, but Steve knows that most people find it impossible to resist the opportunity to voice their opinion on this sort of thing. He also knows that Carlos is going to choose "Unchained"; he can read him. Carlos sighs, pulls his small notebook from his shirt pocket, and starts writing. Got him. Carlos finishes writing and hands back the pen.

Steve opens his notebook, places it on the table, and spins it to face Carlos. There, in capital letters, is "UNCHAINED."

Carlos nods, and places his notebook on the table too. He spins it, and then he opens it. It reads "When It's Love."

Steve looks at the name, then at Carlos.

"Come on, man."

"I like the gentler stuff," says Carlos. "Sorry, Steve. Now, if you don't mind, I've got some more billionaires to pretend to frisk."

The door to the security office swings open, and a young woman pokes her head into the room.

"The Cessna from London's delayed by an hour—why don't you take your break, Carlos?"

"Sure, ma'am," says Carlos.

"Y'all done here?" she asks, looking at Steve and his bag.

"Pretty much," says Carlos. "Few more questions and I'll have this gentleman on his way."

The woman disappears again.

"Okay, Steve," says Carlos. "I'll give you twenty minutes with the CCTV, but you have to fill me in on everything."

In every investigation there is a first step, a little toehold to start you on the climb ahead.

François Loubet, Joe Blow, Letchworth Garden City. It's all in there somewhere.

32

In the boardroom of Maximum Impact Solutions, Susan Knox, Jeff's right-hand woman and head of HR, is looking through Jeff's file on François Loubet. Bloomberg News is on the conference room TV. They are bemoaning the stubborn problem of high interest rates.

There must be a clue in here somewhere.

Susan has no idea if Jeff is alive or dead. If anyone else's car had been found riddled with bullet holes and soaked in their own blood, you could be fairly sure they were a goner. But Jeff?

She tries his numbers constantly. Jeff has so many phones, but at the moment she is getting zero response from any of them.

Susan Knox has also accessed a few of Jeff's bank accounts; he has many different accounts for many different purposes, from a high-yield tax-free investment account in the Cayman Islands to the NatWest account his granddad started for him with five pounds nearly forty years ago. That account's got more than five pounds in it now. Susan looks at the balance: something just over two million. But, more importantly, she looks at "recent transactions." Nothing, except for his regular payments, gas, broadband, five thousand a month to Save the Children. The most recent transaction is for fuel at a petrol station in South London several days ago. In account after account she finds the same pattern. Balances in the millions; recent transactions, none. The two accounts she is most familiar with are empty, but they have been for a while, so no clues there either.

So if Jeff *is* alive, he isn't using his phones, and he isn't spending his money. Though he will have phones and money hidden away somewhere, surely?

With Jeff absent—missing, presumed neither alive nor dead but pending—who can she turn to? Most of the work at Maximum Impact Solutions is done by freelancers, out in the field, and the office is deathly quiet this late. Her old boss, Henk? Jeff's best friend for so many years. Surely he would help out if Jeff has been killed?

She continues reading Loubet's emails to Jeff: they become increasingly threatening, yet they're all written in that strangely jolly tone of his. Who is this man? There must be something that gives him away? A turn of phrase, *anything?*

Throughout the file are little scribbled question marks. Clearly Jeff has tried to do what she is trying to do right now: work out the identity of François Loubet. There is also a row of question marks next to the reference to "Joe Blow."

The last two pages of the file are François Loubet's "Client Identity Form." It is laughably brief: Loubet's name, the name of an Indonesian bank, and blank boxes. She has been through the whole file. The man is a ghost.

There is nothing here she can use to identify Loubet, and nothing that will help to identify Joe Blow.

What to do next?

She can't talk to Jeff.

Susan looks at the boardroom mirror that hides Henk's secret den. She's not a hundred percent sure she should trust Henk van Veen either. But does she have a better option? Amy Wheeler?

As Bloomberg News continues to chatter behind her, Susan decides that Amy has to be worth a shot. Somebody else needs to read these files, before anybody else dies.

33

I want you to think about your fears."

Amy rolls her eyes. Rosie whispers to her.

"If you don't take this seriously, I'm going to hand you in to the police. Or the people trying to kill you."

They are sitting, cross-legged, in a small clearing, in a woodland at the Eternal Glade Wellness Retreat. In front of them Barb is banging a small gong and, from time to time, humming. Night-lights twinkle on the deck.

"Think about what your fears represent," says Barb. "How your fears might help you. How your fears might control you. Greet them, sit with them, break bread with those fears."

Amy wonders when Steve might arrive. Soon, she hopes. There is plenty of work to do. They need to go through the printouts from Sheriff Scroggie's computer. She has been reading them but is yet to find the smoking gun. There is no doubt that Scroggie killed Andrew Fairbanks on the boat. But is there anything in Scroggie's papers that could lead them directly to François Loubet?

"Rosie," says Barb, "can you feel the vibrations of the gong?"

"Do you know, I think I can, Barb," says Rosie. Amy knows it is important for Rosie to enter into the spirit of the thing. Barb is putting them up at the retreat after all.

"Don't call me Barb," says Barb, banging the gong once again.

"Sorry, Barb," says Rosie. "What was it again?"

"Gray Panther," says Barb.

"Okay," says Rosie. "Why not Silver Panther? Wouldn't that be cooler?"

Barb looks at Rosie, the wisdom and serenity departing her face for a brief moment. "I didn't think of it. No matter. I want you both—"

"You could change it now?" Amy suggests. She's worried that she's been a bit quiet, and that Barb might be offended. "We can just call you Silver Panther?"

"I'm afraid you must be known by whichever spirit calls you," says Barb. "And, besides, it's on all my business cards, so too late."

Amy hasn't yet got to the bottom of how Rosie and Barb know each other. Barb is in her eighties, and looks it, in a comfortable, well-earned way. Surely Rosie isn't eighty too? Amy sneaks a peek. I mean, *possibly?* With a lot of work? Was Barb also an author at some point? A rival turned friend? Perhaps an editor?

"I want you to name your fears, Rosie," Barb continues. "Give them wings and let them fly among us."

Amy sees Rosie close her eyes.

"I fear mental and physical decline," says Rosie. "I fear the loss of friends, and loves."

Barb bangs the gong after each fear.

"I fear being misunderstood," says Rosie. "Being seen as an inconsequential person, a joke. I fear being forgotten. I fear being remembered for hair and lipstick and leopard print, and sunglasses, and not for what I worked for, and what I am proud of."

The gong continues. Amy wonders if this is what therapy is like?

"I fear connection," says Rosie, "and I fear a lack of connection. I fear that perhaps I am not real. That I have been imagined as so many things by so many people that my soul is now in them, and no longer in myself."

It occurs to Amy that Barb will be asking her the same question in a matter of moments, so she'd better start thinking. What does she fear? Amy feels like she got all her fears out of the way in childhood. If the worst possible things have happened to you already, what can the world do to you?

Rosie is still releasing her many fears into the world.

"I fear that people see the mask and not the face," continues Rosie. "I fear that I will forget the little girl I once was, many years ago."

How many years ago, though? thinks Amy.

"I fear being small," says Rosie. "Being vulnerable, being powerless. I refuse to fear death, but I do fear life."

Rosie keeps her eyes closed for a few more moments, then breathes in slowly and opens them. Amy sees tears that are refusing to fall.

"Thank you, Rosie," says Barb. "For your honesty, for your bravery, and for your wisdom."

Barb turns to Amy, as Amy had known she would.

"Amy," says Barb, with a light gong bang, "you are welcome here, and you are valued here."

"Thank you, Gray Panther," says Amy. Very much not for her, any of this, but needs must.

"Amy, I want you to name your fears," says Barb. "Give them wings and let them fly among us."

Amy closes her eyes, as Rosie had done.

"I fear . . ." starts Amy, wanting to be as truthful as she possibly can.

She dives as deeply as she is able into the blackness of her mind. Into the void she knows is always there, but that she carefully steps around. It's funny, she and Steve never talk about her childhood. He knows she doesn't need to, and he knows the importance of resilience. They just chat about nothing instead. He tells her how much he loves her, and how special she is, how they are a family, but they never have to talk about her childhood.

Down and down Amy goes, searching for a fear. Searching for the thing that scares her the most. She finds it.

"I fear," Amy says, and stops. She takes her time, as she has never acknowledged this before. "Spiders."

Amy waits a few seconds, breathes out, and opens her eyes. "Thank you, it felt good to admit that. It's the way they move, I think."

Barb looks at her for a moment and then, in Amy's opinion a little sarcastically, bangs the gong.

There is a rustling in the trees ahead of them, and Amy pulls her gun. She nods at Rosie to get behind her.

"I'm not going to take orders from someone who's afraid of spiders," says Rosie.

"And, strictly speaking, it's no guns here," says Barb.

A figure emerges from the trees. A figure wearing a Van Halen T-shirt and carrying a small rucksack. Amy rushes toward him and hugs him, careful to point the gun away from his neck as she does.

"You made it!"

"Car was waiting at the airport," says Steve.

Rosie D'Antonio has somehow crept up on him without making a single sound. She extends a hand.

"Well, you must be Steve," she says.

He takes her hand. "Pleasure to meet you, Rosie."

"The pleasure is mine, I assure you," says Rosie, holding on to Steve's hand for longer than Amy is comfortable with. "That's quite a grip you have."

"Put him down, Rosie," says Amy.

Rosie lets go of Steve's hand but maintains eye contact.

"I don't suppose you ride a motorbike, Steve?"

"A motorbike?" says Steve. "No."

"Oh, you should," says Rosie. "It would suit you."

"She's scared of life, apparently," Amy says to Steve. "Wouldn't know it, would you? Do you need rest or are you ready to work? I've got a million files for you."

"I'm ready," says Steve. "And I come bearing gifts."

He takes a sheet of paper from his rucksack and shows it to Amy and Rosie.

"CCTV from the airport," says Steve. "Shows Andrew Fairbanks being picked up."

In the image Andrew Fairbanks is greeted, then led away, by a slim woman with long red hair tied in a ponytail. Fairbanks carries one of his suitcases, and the woman, despite being half his size, carries the other. A leather holdall.

"How did you get this?" Rosie asks.

"Airships and Van Halen," says Steve.

"I've ridden both in my time," says Rosie.

"I think that might be our cue to do some work," says Amy.

"You get anything from Scroggie?" Steve asks. "The sheriff?"

"His corpse was hanging from the ceiling," says Amy.

"Ah . . ."

Barb approaches the group.

"Steve," says Amy. "This is Barb. She's hiding us away from prying eyes."

"You have," says Barb to Steve, "if you don't mind my saying, the eyes of a kind soul."

"She says that to everyone," says Rosie. "Knock it off, Barb."

"That's very kind of you, Barbara," says Steve, as Barb kisses him on both cheeks.

"It's not Barbara," says Barb.

"I see," says Steve. "So where does 'Barb' come from?"

"It's a nickname," says Rosie. "For thirty years she controlled the barbiturates trade across the entire East Coast."

So *that's* how Rosie and Barb know each other, thinks Amy. Mystery solved.

And, speaking of mysteries, time to get to work. Amy has been backed into corners her whole life. And she learned a long time ago that the only way out of a corner is to fight.

"Someone is trying to kill me," says Amy. "And someone from Maximum Impact is helping them. So let's shoot some people until we find out who."

Steve nods. "Or gather some clues, sure."

"And then shooting," says Amy.

"We'll see," says Steve. "We'll see."

It really is nice to have him here.

34

ddie Flood exits the plane, steps into the South Carolina humidity, and immediately puts on his sunglasses. He texts Rob Kenna.

Landed.

What is he doing here? Hired to kill a woman for thirty thousand pounds.

That's not all, of course, but he can't tell Rob Kenna everything he's here to do.

Rob would kill him if he knew the whole truth.

In his suitcase there are clothes to make him look like a tourist, clothes to make him look like a business traveler, and there are combat fatigues for the job at hand.

He also has his laptop. As always. He'd been researching bullets on the flight. Entry wounds, exit wounds. The time flew by.

Entering the small terminal building, Eddie sees two customs officers. One is a white guy with a small mustache and a thin mouth; the other a large black guy who stands like a man who can handle himself in a fight. Eddie chooses the black guy. Looks much more his type. As he approaches, he sees the name tag: CARLOS MOSS.

"Passport, please, sir," says Carlos.

"Beautiful day, Carlos," says Eddie.

"I don't believe we know each other, sir," says Carlos. "Passport, please."

Eddie takes his passport from his jacket and hands it to Carlos.

"Purpose of visit?" Carlos asks.

"Pleasure," says Eddie.

Carlos lowers his aviator shades and looks Eddie in the eye. No worries for Eddie: he has many faults but being easily intimidated is not one of them.

"What kind of pleasure, sir?"

Eddie likes where this is going. He needs information and Carlos seems to be the kind of guy who could help him.

"I heard this is where Rosie D'Antonio lives," says Eddie. "The author. I'm a big fan."

"That so?" says Carlos.

"She's the best," says Eddie.

"Favorite book, Edward?"

"Too many good ones to choose between," says Eddie. "Call me Eddie—everybody does."

"Everybody but me," says Carlos, and takes a look at Eddie's suitcase. "You pack this suitcase yourself, sir?"

Eddie glances at the other border officer, stamping passports without looking, and smiling at passengers.

"Uh, yes," says Eddie. He's very glad he's not carrying a gun; he'll be picking that up at a gas station on something called Route 47, from a man named Duke. "What's the pay like here, Carlos?"

"Excuse me?" says Carlos.

"The pay," repeats Eddie. He has access to a few expenses. "You get treated well?"

"Do you have a reason for asking?"

"Just making conversation," says Eddie.

"Then I'd advise you to make it with somebody else," says Carlos.

"Sorry," says Eddie. "Long flight. And I'm English. Bad combination."

"Sir, I meet a lot of people who've been on flights," says Carlos.

"Must do," says Eddie. "Must do. I bet she's got a plane somewhere here, hasn't she?"

"Sir?"

"Rosie D'Antonio? Bet she's got a hell of a plane? I know you can't tell me that sort of thing, but, you know? Maybe you can?"

There are a few moments of silence as the two men look at each other.

"Sir, I'm going to ask you to come with me for a moment," says Carlos, and he takes Eddie's elbow.

"Course, course," says Eddie. "Is something wrong?"

"Just a random check," says Carlos. "Bring your baggage. I'll have you on your way in no time."

Bingo. A quiet back room somewhere. Eddie can bung this Carlos geezer a few hundred dollars.

"Lead the way, Carlos old son," says Eddie. "So, Rosie D'Antonio? Back and forth all the time, is she?"

"That feels a lot like business, sir," says Carlos. "And none of your business at that."

Carlos opens the door to what looks very much to Eddie like an interrogation room. And Eddie knows what an interrogation room looks like. The key now is to make a connection with Carlos Moss, and then seal the deal.

"What kind of music do you like?" Eddie asks. As good a start as any.

"Sir, this is a United States Port of Entry," says Carlos. "Not a dating app."

"Big hip-hop fan myself," says Eddie. This is a lie, but he is taking a punt. He's a pretty good reader of people. His favorite band is actually Van Halen, but that's not going to fly here.

"I need you to sit here for a moment," says Carlos and, once Eddie has sat down, he walks out of the door and closes it behind him.

And, Eddie notes, he locks it from the outside. Another sensation he is familiar with.

Eddie can authorize a payment of up to a thousand dollars for information. He'll start with an offer of three hundred, and work his way up if need be. He'll settle in for now, and wait for Carlos to do whatever he needs to do.

He takes out his laptop again. No point wasting time; he's got business to take care of.

35

Steve has woken up in a tree house. A tree mansion, really, built into the boughs of a South Carolina elm, one of a series connected by walkways through the forest canopy. The tree house has a porch with views for many miles. Steve is now reading the documents from Scroggie's computer spread out on a low bamboo table in front of him.

Barb is setting them up for the day ahead.

"I could get you a rosehip-tea infusion, or a jasmine and honeysuckle, or a clean juice, or an anti-oxidizing water," says Barb. "Rosie is having a cactus smoothie, and your lovely daughter-in-law is having water with agave syrup."

"I don't suppose I could have a beer?" Steve asks. It would be lunchtime back home.

"No alcohol," says Barb. "I don't think we need it, do we?"

"I mean, it's a point of view," says Steve.

In the blazing heat, Steve is now wearing his Def Leppard T-shirt, and a pair of blue satin gym shorts Barb has brought him from the lost and found. He has refused, however, to wear flip-flops—there are lines he will not cross—and so is still wearing combat boots.

"No alcohol, no dairy, no meat," says Barb. "Clean air, clean living."

"And yet you were a major-league drug dealer for many years, Barb?"

"God don't care about yesterday," says Barb. "God cares about tomorrow. I'll make you a rosehip infusion, and I'll put a bit of kale in it. But only because you're so handsome."

Steve sees Rosie and Amy crossing the walkway toward him. Time for business.

Barb gives him a wink and heads off to get his drink.

Amy and Rosie climb onto the porch and, after hugs and greetings, and a number of comments about Steve's shorts, attention is turned to murder.

"Fairbanks, Sanchez, Gooch," says Amy. "All influencers, all flown out to aspirational locations for photo shoots, all shot pretty much the moment they arrive, and all left out on display for the world to see."

"And all three killed within an hour or so of where you happened to be?" Steve says to Amy.

"And all three clients of Maximum Impact," says Rosie.

"Two key questions, then," says Steve. "Why were they killed? And why were you in the vicinity every time?"

"I like the way you say 'vicinity,'" says Rosie.

"Have you found anything in Scroggie's computer records?" asks Amy.

"One major thing," says Steve. "I don't know what we read into this, but it worried me. When Scroggie is sent his instructions for the murder, he is also sent a blood sample."

"A blood sample?" says Amy.

Steve nods. "And he is asked to leave it at the scene of the killing."

"To incriminate someone," says Rosie.

"Presumably," says Steve.

"Whose blood sample?" Amy asks. "Don't say mine, Jesus, don't say mine."

Steve holds up his hands. "No idea. But is there any way someone could get hold of your blood?"

"Your mandatory drug tests?" suggests Rosie.

"Every three months," says Amy, nodding. "They take a sample at Maximum Impact."

"And could Loubet get hold of that?" Steve asks.

"I hope to God he couldn't," says Amy.

36

Max Highfield, the World's Seventh Sexiest Male, not that the Academy seems to care about that, sits in a huge Winnebago, dressed as a Roman centurion. He is reading lines from a thick yellow script opposite a film director. She is wearing headphones around her neck, and is also holding a script.

"I shall not praise Caesar this day. This victory does not honor him, for there is no honor in sight upon this field. The bloodshed stains his hands, and the bones of children we see scattered around us will bury him. We remember, soldiers, we remember this day as we march on Rome, as we march toward destiny. Death to Caesar!"

Max puts the script down. "I think I'll just say 'Death to Caesar!' and do the rest with my eyes."

The director nods, and draws some lines through her script.

There is a knock on the Winnebago door.

"Come," says Max.

A runner enters with a bouquet of flowers. "Just delivered for you."

Max looks at the flowers, and returns to his centurion voice. "They please me."

The runner nods, uncertainly. "Can I get you a coffee?"

"A coffee, by my oath?" says Max. "And think you, does a Roman centurion drink coffee, messenger?"

"I don't know," says the runner. "We've got Coke Zero?"

"I think Roman centurions drank coffee, Max," says the director. "It's been around for thousands of years."

"Mmm," grunts Max. "Then I shall have a coffee upon your return."

The runner nods. "How do you take it?"

"Soy milk latte," says Max. "And hasten!"

The runner nods and puts the flowers on a table. As the runner leaves, Max picks up the card that came with the flowers and opens it. It reads:

YOU'RE DEAD

37

Jeff could get hold of your blood, though?" Rosie says, quietly.

"It wouldn't be Jeff," says Amy. "He's the one who warned me about Loubet and about Joe Blow."

"Though he did know where you were, when all three of them were murdered," says Steve. "And he knew where you were when Kevin came calling. Who else at Maximum Impact might be involved?"

"Henk van Veen," says Amy. "Left the company three months ago, been stealing clients ever since."

"So maybe killing clients as well?" suggests Rosie. "Scare people away from Maximum Impact?"

"Where is Henk?" Steve asks.

"Back in England, as far as I know," says Amy. "But he wouldn't know my movements."

"But he could have taken your blood," says Steve. "Months ago?"

"And Susan Knox," says Amy. "She's Jeff's right-hand woman. She'd know where I was, and she'd know where my blood was."

"I think we have to keep moving," says Rosie. "If Amy's blood is at that scene, then—"

"Could the police match it to you, though, Amy?" Steve asks. "Is your DNA in any database?"

"Well, I've never been arrested," says Amy. "Another thing Maximum Impact insists on. But I don't want to take any chances. If that's my blood at the scene, I want to get as far away from South Carolina as I can."

"Come on, let's go to St. Lucia," suggests Rosie. "Keep investigating."

"I don't know," says Steve, glancing into his tree house. "I've just unpacked, and I'm settled in, and I don't—"

"How long did unpacking take?" Amy asks.

"It doesn't matter how long it took," says Steve. "If I unpack, I settle. You know that, Amy. I've only just got here."

"I think I'd like to go down there," says Amy. "I have to keep moving, so I might as well go somewhere I can be useful. See what we can find out about Bella Sanchez. Was she carrying money too? Was she shot by a local cop for hire?"

"Did they find blood at the scene?" says Rosie.

Amy nods. "At least then I can feel like I'm doing something."

"She's right, Stevie," says Rosie.

"It's just Steve," says Steve.

"You suit Stevie," says Rosie.

"What I suit is staying in Hampshire," says Steve.

"But you love Amy, so here we are," says Rosie. "Relax into it. Do you smoke marijuana?"

"Take a guess," says Amy.

"Where I should really be is Letchworth Garden City," says Steve, finding one of his files. "Andrew Fairbanks was hired by the Vivid Viral Agency, address Letchworth Garden City. Not the natural home for a hip media company."

"I like that you say hip," says Rosie. "Takes me back."

"He was advertising Krusher Energy Drink," continues Steve. "A company also registered at that same address in Letchworth Garden City."

"Companies have offices everywhere," says Amy. "Rosie's right: we have to go to St. Lucia. I'll pack for you."

Steve's phone rings. The display says CARLOS AIRSHIP.

"Excuse me a second." He takes the call. "Carlos?"

"You told me to tell you if anyone was asking after Ms. D'Antonio?"

"Uh huh?" Steve looks over at Rosie and whispers, "Just a friend I met at the airport."

"I got a guy in a cell right now asking questions about her . . ."

"What sort of guy?"

"English. Named Eddie Flood. Looks like a boxer who gets beaten up a lot. He has the address of a gas station in his bag, and it's the kind of gas station where you can buy more than just gas. I can keep him here for maybe two more hours before I get fired."

"Carlos, you're a hero," says Steve. "You're wrong about Van Halen, but you're a hero."

"Back atcha, brother," says Carlos. "Talk soon."

Rosie and Amy are both looking at him.

"Okay," says Steve to Rosie and Amy. "A development. It looks like a new guy is on his way here to kill Amy."

"St. Lucia, then," says Amy.

"If he's followed us here, he can follow us to St. Lucia," says Steve.

"Your hot dad is right," says Rosie. "They'll be tracking my plane."

Barb arrives with the drinks. As she places the tray on the table, she looks at the photos Rosie took of Justin Scroggie's dead body. She raises an eyebrow to Rosie, and Rosie raises a finger to her lips. Barb does the same in return.

Steve is thinking. Rosie and Amy are right; he knows it. They should go to St. Lucia. That's how you investigate stuff. Perhaps he can get somebody else to take a look at Letchworth Garden City? But how to shake Eddie off their tail? Carlos can't hold him back forever.

But there is a way, though. He messages Carlos.

Might have a little job for you.

"I have a plan," he announces to Amy and Rosie.

"If it involves Letchworth Garden City, we've heard it," says Amy.

Steve shakes his head and takes a sip of his rosehip-and-kale tea. What is it now? Saturday? Hopefully they can wrap this all up before the quiz night next Wednesday.

"Where's your pilot?" Steve asks Rosie.

"Hilton Head," says Rosie. "She does a few tourist trips for the locals while she waits for me to call."

"Can you get her to the airport?"

"Sure," says Rosie. "She might take a while to sober up. Where's she flying? St. Lucia or Letchworth?"

"Neither," says Steve.

38

Carlos could not be more apologetic. Eddie has to hand it to the guy. "Bureaucracy, man," says Carlos. "I'm sorry. When the computer beeps, it beeps."

"I get it," says Eddie, folding away his laptop. How long has he been locked in here? "Same the world over."

"Tell you the truth," says Carlos, "computer wanted to keep you in for longer. You ever been arrested?"

"Couple of times," says Eddie. "Couple of times."

His passport was supposed to have been wiped clean, though. Rob Kenna had assured him.

"That'll be it," says Carlos. "Knew it as soon as I saw you. Game recognizes game. I had to pull a little magic trick to ease your way through the system."

Eddie knew it. All the talk of hip-hop and money had done the trick. This could have ended very badly for Eddie. He was lucky he'd chosen to stand in Carlos's queue. Well, a bit of luck, a bit of judgment.

He stands and stretches, and follows Carlos out of the interrogation room.

"I appreciate that, Carlos," says Eddie. "Can I call you Carlos?"

"You sure can, brother," says Carlos. "And maybe I can make it up to you? This little delay?"

"You've done enough," says Eddie, as Carlos opens the door leading back to the immigration hall.

"It's just you were asking about Rosie D'Antonio? The writer?"

"Uh huh?" says Eddie. This is suddenly getting very interesting. Perhaps the delay will have been worth it?

"Her plane is getting ready to fly."

"You're sure?"

Carlos motions out of the terminal windows to the runway. A Gulfstream is taxiing. On the tail is the code TC-816. Rosie D'Antonio's plane.

"And she's on it?"

"I can't . . ." starts Carlos. "Listen, I'd love to help, you know that. But—"

"I mean, we could help each other?" suggests Eddie.

Carlos looks both ways, checking to see if he is being watched, then ducks behind a computer terminal. "I gotta be mad."

Outside the window, Rosie's jet is picking up speed.

"Okay," says Carlos, coming back around from the computer. "Strictly brother to brother. She's on board. With another woman."

"Heading where?"

"Hawaii," says Carlos. "That's all I've got."

Eddie thinks.

"Are there other planes I can hire? If I wanted to go to Hawaii too?"

"You really like Rosie D'Antonio, huh?" says Carlos.

"It's a hobby, sure," says Eddie.

"I'll walk you to the charter desk," says Carlos. "I'm sure we can get you in the air within an hour."

What on earth would Eddie have done without Carlos? He's not even going to waste his time offering him three hundred. Just slip him the full thousand for a job well done.

Eddie is heading to Hawaii. And Rosie and Amy will have no idea he's on their tail.

Rob is going to be very pleased with him indeed.

39

Felicity Woollaston rarely has visitors, but she has made Bonnie Gregor as welcome as she can. Fortunately Bonnie drinks herbal tea, so Felicity hasn't had to pop out to buy milk this time.

"I'm sorry to just turn up," says Bonnie. "I feel silly now."

"Not at all," says Felicity. Bonnie was the lady whose email she had read. Two kids? Something to do with houses?

"It's just, my friends all told me, you have to shoot your shot sometimes. So I thought, be brave, Bonnie."

Bonnie seems very nervous. Felicity can't remember the last time someone was nervous in her company.

"A good maxim for life," agrees Felicity. "I wonder what I might be able to do for you?"

"I just," starts Bonnie. "I just, well, I'm not sure. I thought you could tell me?"

"What I could do for you?"

"I just typed in 'influencer agencies,'" says Bonnie. "And you were the closest, and my mum can only look after the kids for a few hours, so I thought I'd come and see you, and ask you about everything."

"Mmm," says Felicity. "And if you were to narrow down 'everything'?"

"It's not my world," says Bonnie. "Well, I suppose it is in a way, and I'd like it to be. It's probably ridiculous, though."

"The world of influencers?" asks Felicity, looking for a foothold in the conversation.

"It's just, I have 14K followers now, on Instagram, and I know that might not be enough for Vivid Viral, but maybe it is, I don't know?"

Felicity senses she has been asked a question. She really should know a lot more about Vivid Viral.

"Fourteen K?" says Felicity, mulling it over. Fourteen thousand—is that a lot? "Quality is often just as important as quantity, isn't it? How is your tea?"

"It's perfect, thank you," says Bonnie. "Calming. Could I ask you a few questions? If you get bored, just send me away, I know you must be busy."

Felicity clicks her mouse, closing down the Sudoku she has been playing on her computer. "Ask me anything."

Bonnie takes out a notebook. "Sorry, I wrote them down, I knew I'd be nervous. What is the best way to grow and monetize my social media following?"

"Gosh," says Felicity. "How long is a piece of string, I suppose?"

Bonnie nods, and writes this down. "Yes. And in numbers what might that mean?"

"Well," says Felicity, "it can mean whatever you'd like it to mean. What would your expectations be?"

"I don't need to be a millionaire or anything," says Bonnie. "Just, I suppose, one day, maybe give up my job? Do this full-time?"

"Influencing?"

"Sorry, you think that's, no, of course, but I don't need much," says Bonnie.

Felicity is desperately trying to remember details from Bonnie's email.

"Perhaps," says Felicity, "perhaps I could see some examples of your . . . of what you do?"

"Of course," says Bonnie. "Of course, I don't really know how these things work, sorry, I've never been in this sort of meeting before."

You and me both, thinks Felicity. But she is enjoying the company, and she realizes she feels rather protective toward Bonnie. Perhaps she can put a good word in for her with her new bosses. Whoever they might be.

"It's all on Insta," says Bonnie. "@bonnieinspo."

It is clear from Bonnie's body language that she is expecting Felicity to somehow use this information. On the computer perhaps? She clicks the mouse a few times and pretends to tut. "Bloody thing," Felicity says. "IT department said they'd fixed it. Perhaps you could show me on your phone?"

Felicity makes her way around from behind her desk and pulls up a chair to sit next to Bonnie. How lovely to have someone in the office. Would Bonnie think it peculiar if she were to ask her out to lunch? They could go to the Pizza Express? When was the last time Felicity went there? Bonnie shows her a stream of photographs, slogans painted on walls and doors in striking pink. Lots of "love" and "hope" and "cherish." Felicity isn't entirely sure what she is supposed to be looking at, but she welcomes the love and the hope.

"Wonderful," says Felicity. "Wonderful."

Bonnie smiles, as Felicity makes her way back to her desk. "You really think?"

"Very vibrant," says Felicity. "Positive and refreshing."

"Is there . . ." Bonnie begins. "Do you think there might be brands who would want to work with me?"

"Goodness me," says Felicity. "Isn't that the question? I don't see why not, Bonnie."

"Wow," says Bonnie. "What sort of brands?"

"Paint," says Felicity. "Paint brands? Decorating?"

"Yes," says Bonnie. "Yes, exactly. Interior design."

"Interior design," agrees Felicity. Now she is starting to feel guilty. It's the happiness in Bonnie's eyes. She should just come clean, send Bonnie somewhere else. To someone who knows what they are doing. To someone who is not a fossil. Felicity is useless. Useless.

"What sort of brands do you work with?"

Felicity doesn't work with any brands. She works with UKTV Gold and sometimes the *Letchworth Courier*. Poor Bonnie. Felicity looks over to the pallets of products stacked up against her office wall. She points them out to Bonnie. "I mean . . ."

Bonnie swivels, and takes in the random wall of products.

"Oh my God, Krusher Energy Drink!"

"Yes," says Felicity. The purple drink she has learned never to stare at directly.

"Does that mean . . ." Bonnie teases.

Felicity raises one eyebrow, hoping Bonnie will provide her with more information as to what that might or might not mean.

"Does that mean Andrew Fairbanks?"

"It's precisely what that means," says Felicity, wondering who on earth Andrew Fairbanks might be.

Bonnie is shaking her head in disbelief, so Andrew Fairbanks must be a big deal. "You must be very busy at the moment, I'm so sorry."

"Not at all," says Felicity, waving away the concern. "Not at all. Part of the job."

"Andrew Fairbanks," says Bonnie. "Wait till I tell my mum."

Felicity suddenly feels a ridiculous but visceral desire to be Bonnie's mother. Or grandmother. For someone to come home to her and tell her their news.

"So do you think you can help?" Bonnie asks. "You can say no, I promise."

Surely the big bosses at Vivid Viral owe Felicity a few favors, for whatever it is that she does for them? Surely she can send an email and recommend Bonnie? She's new, she's hungry, she'll do anything, try anything? Felicity feels sure that they'll listen to her. And that she can help out this lovely, funny, nervous woman, who has traveled to Letchworth Garden City because her friends have told her to shoot her shot.

"I'll tell you what," Felicity says, "why don't we chat about it over a pizza?"

40

In the parking lot of Emory Executive Airfield, Rosie, Amy, and Steve see Eddie Flood's plane fly up into the clear blue sky.

"He'll have fun in Hawaii," says Steve.

"Not as much fun as Barb and her daughter are going to have," says Rosie.

They even have his name now, and a scan of his passport photo from Carlos Moss. Eddie Flood, the man who has been sent to kill Amy, is currently on a ten-hour flight to a holiday paradise in pursuit of an eighty-year-old health retreat owner and her grateful daughter.

Steve takes his small rucksack from the back seat as Rosie's Vuitton suitcase is lifted carefully from the boot by Carlos Moss.

"St. Lucia here we come," says Rosie. "I'm just going to google what's legal and illegal there."

"Thank you, Carlos," says Amy, as they walk toward the terminal building.

"My pleasure, ma'am," says Carlos. "They've just refueled a Falcon for you. It's a nice one."

Ahead of them is Steve, still in T-shirt, gym shorts, and combat boots, his back covered in sweat patches. Rosie is trying to take his arm, but he is resisting.

"He sure loves you, huh?" says Carlos.

"I find it quite hard to accept love," says Amy.

"I hear you," says Carlos. "You should work on that, though."

Amy nods. A porter with a trolley has arrived to take the cases. Carlos approaches Steve for a hug.

"I don't hug, I'm afraid," says Steve.

"Well, I do," says Carlos and hugs him.

"I'm sorry I'm so sweaty," says Steve.

"It's South Carolina," says Carlos. "Sweating's what we do. You have a good flight, folks, and don't get killed. Steve and I have got airships to see."

He bows to Rosie. "Miss D'Antonio."

"Thank you, Carlos," says Rosie.

Carlos returns to work, and Rosie, Steve, and Amy head toward the tarmac.

"You should put Carlos in one of your books," says Amy. "As a thank-you."

"I know Carlos very well," says Rosie. "He's already been in one of my books. You ever read *While You Were Dead?*"

"No point in pretending I haven't anymore," says Amy. "So who's Carlos in that? The security guard at the end?"

"The ex-Marine the writer sleeps with in the private airport terminal," says Rosie.

"Of course he is," says Amy. "Of course he is."

Rosie points the porter in the direction of their chartered plane.

41

ax Highfield is meeting Henk van Veen in the library of The Wilberforce, a London private members' club, just off Pall Mall. From the reception desk he can see oak and leather and hear whispered conversations between men and women in suits and ties. This is where Henk likes to meet.

Max has actually been here before. They sometimes hire it out for film shoots. He once shot a Nazi in the gents' toilet.

"I'm sorry, sir, no trainers," says a porter in a bowler hat.

"Excuse me?" Max replies. Perhaps the porter has not recognized him. Max takes off his beanie and runs his big hand through his thick hair with intent.

"No trainers," the porter repeats, seemingly oblivious even to the hair.

"You may not have recognized me," says Max. This, he has learned, is politer than "Don't you know who I am?"

"I certainly recognize you, Mr. Highfield," says the porter. "From the films and such. It is a great pleasure to have you here at The Wilberforce, but I'm afraid that trainers are not allowed. Even on your esteemed feet."

Max chooses to reason with the man. "But these trainers cost over seven hundred pounds."

The porter simply raises a single eyebrow and asks, "What, each?"

Max is allowed everywhere. Wearing anything. This is the man who went to a royal wedding barefoot and in a sarong. An Alexander McQueen sarong, certainly, but a sarong all the same. This is some insane nonsense right here. Keep your cool, though, Max: don't forget, the little people buy tickets.

"I'm meeting Henk van Veen," says Max. Henk's name will carry some weight here, Max is sure of it.

"Certainly, sir," says the porter. "I believe Mr. Van Veen is waiting for you in the library. Wearing shoes."

"Can I borrow some shoes?" Max asks.

"Certainly, Mr. Highfield. What size would you like?"

Max Highfield's feet are a size six. "Ten, please."

The porter disappears into a closet and returns with a pair of size ten brown brogues.

"Brown?" says Max. "But I'm wearing black."

"They're the only size tens I have, I'm afraid, sir," says the porter. "I have a black in a nine if you think you could squeeze into them?"

"Even tens are tight," says Max. "I'll take the brown. But I need absolute assurance I won't be photographed while I'm in the building."

"Sir, this is The Wilberforce," says the porter. "Within these walls you have more chance of being oil-painted than photographed."

Max nods, takes himself over to an antique banquette, and slips on his new shoes. He is proud of how he handled himself there. Old Max would have lost his temper, screamed the place down, but therapy is working nicely for him.

"I very much enjoyed *Rampage 7*, sir," says the porter. He's actually not that bad a guy. Just doing his job.

"Thanks, man," says Max. "I read a lot of Chekhov and Ibsen before filming. I think it showed."

"It shone through," confirms the porter.

Max feels his toes finish their journey roughly halfway down the shoe. He doesn't feel great coming to see Henk, but Jeff Nolan is no longer returning his calls. So you go to the next best option, right? It's pretty much the same service. Henk knows that Max will bring him other clients too, so there's a deal to be done there.

And another message arrived on the heels of the first. A note slipped under the dressing-room door. *You will die, Highfield.*

As to where Jeff Nolan is, that's a question for other people to work out. Max has only one rule in life. Keep moving forward and never look back. Or is that two rules? His therapist asked him to think long and hard about whether this was a good tactic. Is it healthy for you, and those around you, the people you work with, the people you love, to only look forward?

Max had taken the therapist's advice. He had a long, hard think about it, before coming to the conclusion that, yes, it *was* healthy for him, and for those around him. He really does love therapy. It's even tax-deductible.

He'd explained to his therapist, Melanie—a woman, sure, but older, so it sort of works—that after making *Rampage 7* you have to make *Rampage 8*, right? You don't go back and make *Rampage 6* again, do you? You move forward. She has countered that perhaps you didn't have to make any *Rampage* movies at all, and that's when he realized that, while she might be wise in all sorts of areas, she had no idea at all about box-office numbers. He asked if she even read the trades and she asked what the trades were, so that was that. Therapists can't do everything. She's very good on why his dad was never able to truly love him, but very bad on why he is so ambitious.

And then, as it turns out, *Rampage 8* is actually going to be a prequel, so you can go forward and backward at the same time. Where does that leave her theory?

"Sir?" says the porter.

"Hmm?" says Max.

"Forgive me, sir, you've been whispering something to yourself for the last minute or so, but I wondered if I should interrupt and take you up to the library?"

"Yes, yes," says Max, standing. He stands and hands the porter his trainers. Neon blue and pastel pink, charcoal in the sole.

"Can you assure me that no one will steal my trainers while I'm here?"

The porter takes a look at the trainers. "I think I can assure you of that, sir, yes."

The porter places the trainers behind his desk and leads Max up a small flight of wide, carpeted steps.

Max follows, feet slip-slapping like a police frogman on a steep canal bank.

42

Rosie and Steve are sitting on a cream leather sofa in the Falcon, looking like an extremely ill-matched mum and dad, while Amy sulkily looks at her phone in a velvet armchair opposite them. Amy and Steve are both wearing their seat belts because the pilot had warned them of turbulence. Rosie "doesn't believe in turbulence."

Steve and Rosie are singing along to a song about country roads that she has never heard. If someone really is going to kill her, please let it be now.

They will find out what they can about Bella Sanchez. If they can tie her killing to money-smuggling too, everything will point to Loubet. But if it is Loubet, what next? Where is he? Who is he, for God's sake?

Her phone pings. An unknown number.

I wish to speak with you.

Jeff? It doesn't sound like Jeff? But a lot of people are putting all of their communications through AI filters these days, so who knows? She replies.

Jeff?

Opposite her, Mum and Dad are now singing about a showgirl called Lola. How do they know the words to these things?

No, it is Henk. Henk van Veen, in case you know more than one Henk, which is possible. Where are you? I can help you. You want help?

Henk? The man who has profited the most from these murders? What on earth can she reply?

Where's Jeff, Henk?

She shouldn't have kept this phone. But she needs to keep the number, for when Jeff finally breaks cover and needs to contact her.

I heard Jeff died. Did you hear that? I don't know. I don't think Jeff can die.

Steve raises his chin an inch in her direction. "You messaging your friends?"

"I'm trying to find out who wants to kill me," says Amy.

"It probably is one of your friends," says Rosie from the sofa.

Are you trying to kill me, Henk? You've made a bad job of it so far.

What's the play here?

I am not trying to kill you, Amy. If I was trying to kill you, you would be dead! LOL (Laughing Out Loud)!

"Who is it?" Steve asks, obviously seeing her look.

"Henk van Veen," says Amy.

"Jeff Nolan's old business partner?" says Steve.

Amy nods. "And best mate. Very Dutch. Jeff warned me about him before he went missing."

"You shouldn't use your phone on a flight," says Steve.

"Sure," says Amy. "God forbid I should put us in danger."

Amy decides to reply to Henk. See if she can draw him out.

> **You know where I am, Henk. You just hired the wrong guy
> to follow me. And I've got a hundred thousand dollars,
> which I'm guessing belonged to you in the first place?**

Amy looks at Steve. If Henk really is trying to kill her, he might well suc-
ceed. And if he does kill her, who's to say that Steve won't get caught in the
cross fire too? She shouldn't have brought him out here.

A new song starts playing, "Take On Me." Finally one she's heard.

And now she really looks at Steve. There is something in his eyes she
hasn't seen for a long time. He turns down the spliff that Rosie hands to
him, but with a smile on his face that looks real. He and Rosie are singing
along. Rosie is up and dancing, and Amy gets the feeling that Steve would
get up and join her if the seat belt lights weren't still on. There is another
ping on her phone.

> **Is someone trying to kill you? I am very sorry to hear that.
> I am about to meet an old client of yours and it made me
> think of you. I am always looking for good people to join
> me at Henk Industries. Can we talk?**

Can we talk? That again? No, Henk, we cannot talk. Amy slides the
SIM card from her phone, takes some nail scissors from her bag, and cuts it
into small pieces. Jeff will find a way of reaching her. She instantly feels
freer. Just her, Steve, and Rosie against the world now.

Amy is half expecting Steve to tell her she's not allowed to take scissors on a plane, but she sees that he is too busy preparing his falsetto for the chorus of "Take On Me."

The chorus begins, and the three of them belt it out together, as the shape of St. Lucia comes into view in the Caribbean Sea far below.

43

A few years ago Max Highfield would have felt out of place in this room. But now Max doesn't feel out of place anywhere. He's earned the right to go where he chooses, when he chooses. Even if sometimes he's not allowed to wear his trainers. Max can't help worrying that the porter just put his trainers behind a reception desk, rather than putting them in a locker or, better still, a safe.

The library has floor-to-ceiling shelves, floor-to-ceiling windows, a temple to dark oak and green leather and books. There are writing desks along a side wall, circular tables covered in new books and thick magazines. The light is provided by three huge chandeliers and a succession of brass reading lamps. It's so big that Max thinks he could strip the whole lot out and have room for a swimming pool, gym, and sauna complex if this were his own house. And he could call his complex "The Library" to show that he is a reader.

Henk is hidden away behind the medical periodicals, filling the corner of a large, green leather sofa, a book open in his hand.

The only other person in the library is a woman in her eighties, reading a book on the philosophy of grief. She clocked him as he came in, though—he can always tell.

Max takes a deep armchair opposite Henk. Henk puts down his book and nods toward it.

"Spinoza," says Henk. "Have you read him?"

"Spinoza?" says Max. "No. Good?"

"Not bad," says Henk. "Not bad. And, in my view, without Spinoza, we have no Kant, we have no Goethe."

"No," agrees Max.

"Do we even have George Eliot, I wonder?" Henk asks. "Do we have *Middlemarch* without this Dutch genius?"

Henk chuckles, and so Max does too, then says, "Thanks for seeing me."

"I was expecting you," says Henk. "Lot of problems at your current agency. Can't be so easy for you to stay loyal?"

"I stay loyal to Max Highfield," says Max.

"That is a moral paradox," says Henk.

"Thanks," says Max. "Someone said Jeff's dead? Like, in real life?"

"Jeff?" says Henk, as if remembering a forgotten childhood friend. "He is no longer my concern, Max. Sometimes people who live by the sword also die by the sword."

Max looks quizzical. "Are you talking about that film I did? *Die by the Sword?*"

"No," says Henk. "It's an idiom."

"Agree to disagree," says Max. "I don't suppose you'd be interested in looking after my close-protection needs?"

"In looking after you?" says Henk. "I think that sounds wise. I think even our friend Spinoza might approve, don't you?"

"I mean, if I joined you," says Max, "I have certain needs. Expectations."

"Full security cover," says Henk, "twenty-four seven, and you take your pick of my people. And I give you two million a year to act as an ambassador."

Max picks up a book from the oak table beside his armchair. It is called *Fourteenth-Century Iran: The Howl of Uncertainty.* He puts it down.

"Is there something else, Max?" Henk asks.

Max takes a card from his jacket and gives it to Henk.

"*You're dead*. My, my. Any idea who this might be from?"

"None," says Max. "I'm universally loved. They even said that in *Grazia*."

"I shall look into it for you," says Henk. "It seems that Maximum Impact are not taking care of you as they should."

Max picks up his book again, before remembering that it is called *Fourteenth-Century Iran: The Howl of Uncertainty*. He puts it down once again.

"Have a lot of Jeff's clients come to you?" says Max.

"The seagulls follow the trawler," says Henk.

Max nods. "And did you really tell Jeff I didn't hold my gun properly?"

"Excuse me, Max?"

"In *Rampage 7*?"

"I don't know what *Rampage 7* is."

Now Max laughs. "Nice one, Henk."

"Thank you, Max," says Henk.

Max stands and slaps Henk on the back. "You get a contract knocked up, and I'll sign it."

"Pleasure seeing you, Max," says Henk, returning to his book. "I will ensure that nobody kills you."

As Max leaves, he sees that the old woman reading the book about grief is silently sobbing. Max studies her for a while, pretending to be reading a magazine about yachts. Max has never quite been able to cry on camera. If he ever sees crying in a script, he makes sure they change it to "a roar of anger," which he can do very well.

He approaches the woman, places a hand on her shoulder, and gives his kindest smile.

"Would you like an autograph?"

The woman looks up, tears still streaming down her face. "I'm afraid I don't know who you are, dear. I would advise you to take your hand off my shoulder, though."

Max nods, slowly. He gets it. Grief does the funniest things to people.

44

Amy has been in mortal danger in many countries over the last few years, but St. Lucia has to be one of the most beautiful.

"Only country in the world named after a woman," Rosie tells her.

"What about Georgia?" says Amy.

"Georgia is named after St. George," says Steve, and he and Rosie roll their eyes at each other. Amy could live without that little alliance developing.

They are climbing higher and higher on the coast road. Endless blue falling away to one side of them, and endless, mountainous green rising up on the other. Colorful villages cling to bends in the road, with wooden porches looking out over the Caribbean.

Amy is enjoying the view but she is also aware that Steve has been determinedly looking down at his phone for the entire ride.

"It's a beautiful view, Steve," says Amy.

"I'm okay," says Steve, still looking at his phone. "Are we going much higher, Ferdy?"

Ferdy, the taxi driver, turns around almost 180 degrees. "Another two kilometers up, then three kilometers down. You want me to speed up?"

"Yes, please," say Amy and Rosie.

"No, thanks," says Steve, eyes still glued to the phone on his lap.

Amy looks down at his phone. "What are you reading?"

"Nothing," says Steve.

Amy takes a closer look. He does actually mean "nothing." The phone is off.

"Why is your phone off?"

"I read something in the paper about roaming charges when you go abroad. Someone went to Tenerife and had a five-grand bill. So I'm keeping it off."

"If it's off," says Rosie, from the front passenger seat, "why are you looking at it?"

"We're just . . ." says Steve, tilting his head toward the window without raising it. "We're just quite high up. And I don't see any barriers."

Ferdy turns 180 degrees again. "You're safe with me. Never had a fatal accident."

"Turn your phone back on," says Amy. "It won't cost you anything unless you download something without Wi-Fi."

"Will they have Wi-Fi at the hotel?" Steve asks.

"One of Condé Nast's Ten Most Luxurious Hotels in the World?" says Rosie. "Yes, they might have Wi-Fi."

Steve switches his phone back on, and it slowly springs to life with message alerts.

"Are any of those from Hampshire Police?" asks Amy.

"They're mainly Margaret from next door, sending me pictures of Trouble."

"Trouble?" says Rosie, reacting to the word like a meerkat.

"Steve's cat," says Amy.

"A cat called Trouble," says Rosie. "I like the sound of her."

"Him," says Steve.

"Well, you can't have everything," says Rosie. "Ferdy, why does everybody here wave at you?"

"They all know me," says Ferdy. "I'm a politician; they see me on the news sometimes."

"And Companies House have sent me all the information I requested on Vivid Viral."

"And?" asks Amy.

"It seems to be a new name for an older company. Felicity Woollaston Associates," says Steve. "A theatrical agency, TV and what have you."

"Can I ask why you're driving a taxi?" Rosie asks Ferdy. "If you're a politician."

"Because I always lose," says Ferdy, swerving at the last moment to avoid a concrete truck. "Every time I lose."

Ferdy beeps his horn at a group of young children waving at him from a bright yellow veranda.

"They still seem to like you, though," says Rosie.

"That's because I lose," says Ferdy. "If I'd won, they'd hate me. That's politics."

"Felicity Woollaston is the sole director of the company," says Steve. "Born eighteenth of March 1951."

"Is that before or after you, Rosie?" Amy asks.

"I'm talking to Ferdy, dear," Rosie replies.

"What's a woman in her seventies doing single-handedly running a digital media agency?"

Amy shrugs. Perhaps Steve does have a point, though. Why Vivid Viral? Amy will be annoyed if this whole investigation ends up being solved by Companies House rather than by a gunfight.

"Will you look into her a bit more?"

Steve nods. "As soon as I've got Wi-Fi."

"Just a little way to Emerald Bay now," says Ferdy from the front.

Amy sees Steve breathe a slight sigh of relief.

"Though I should warn you," says Ferdy, "the last stretch is terrifying."

Amy sees Steve's knuckles whiten around his phone. God bless that man.

"Do you take everyone to Emerald Bay?" Rosie asks Ferdy. "You're the official driver?"

"Most people," says Ferdy. "Sure, most people. Some people take a heli-copter because the drive is so dangerous. Or you can take the boat. Much safer. Zero deaths."

"I don't suppose you took this woman? Bella Sanchez?" Rosie asks, showing Ferdy a picture of Bella Sanchez. Ferdy takes the briefest of glances.

"I remember her," says Ferdy.

"You drove her?" asks Amy from the back.

"No. But I remember her," says Ferdy. "She got picked up by a private car. Never saw it before."

"Did you see the driver?" Amy asks.

"Only when they crashed," says Ferdy.

"They crashed?" says Rosie.

"Everybody crashes," says Ferdy.

"Except you," says Amy, squeezing Steve's hand.

"Oh, I crash plenty," says Ferdy. "Don't you worry about that. That final kilometer is crazy: they won't pave it, because they want the resort to be pri-vate. If it was easy to get to, everyone would drive down and use the beach. All the beaches here are public."

"So you saw the driver?"

"Saw her," says Ferdy. "Tried to drag the car out too. Went about two meters down the rocks, got stopped by a tree. I stopped to give them a hand."

"Could you describe her?"

"White lady," says Ferdy. "Long, red hair, baseball cap."

Sounds a lot like the woman who picked up Andrew Fairbanks. So proof, at least, that the deaths are connected. Amy is glad of the certainty.

"Did you happen to see Miss Sanchez's luggage at all?" asks Rosie.

"Sure," says Ferdy. "Clambered down the rocks to get it for her. Three big cases."

"You can't carry three cases," says Amy.

"I carried two," says Ferdy. "The driver insisted on carrying the other one."

"What sort of bag was that?" Rosie asks.

"Big leather holdall," says Ferdy. "Brown. Expensive-looking."

"Anything like this bag?" Amy asks. She shows Ferdy a photograph of the bag found with Andrew Fairbanks on the yacht. The bag containing the money.

"Identical," says Ferdy. "Same bag."

For the first time Steve dares to look up. "Same driver, same bag."

Amy nods. That's more like it. Forget Companies House. A real-life killer, and a real-life bag of money.

"I told you it was worth coming to St. Lucia," says Rosie.

"You guys movie people?" Ferdy asks. "Sounds like you're working on a script? We get a lot of movie people here. Stallone was here. He couldn't believe I was more famous than him."

"Just tourists," says Steve.

"Private tourists," says Amy. "So if anyone ever describes us to you, you never met us."

"I never speak about anyone I drive," says Ferdy. "You have total privacy."

"Though you did just tell us about Stallone," says Rosie.

"Yeah," says Ferdy. "But, with respect to the three of you, that's Stallone, isn't it?"

"And if anyone tries to ask you about Bella Sanchez," says Steve, "will you let me know? I'll leave my number with you."

"You got it, boss," says Ferdy. "Yeah, she got real lucky, that Bella Sanchez. Couple of feet either side of that tree and she could have died that day. Lucky, lucky lady."

"Up to a point," says Rosie.

"Okay," says Ferdy. "Final kilometer. Buckle up, it's a bumpy ride."

Rosie claps her hands with delight.

Amy sees Steve once again staring, determinedly, at his phone. She squeezes his arm. "You just keep pretending to read your emails. I won't let anything happen to you."

Steve continues staring. "I'm not pretending to read. Email from Hampshire Police."

"About Jeff?" Amy asks. Still no contact from him.

"The blood in the car," says Steve. "It was Jeff's. They checked it against his file at work. And there was an awful lot of it in that car."

"This sounds exciting," says Ferdy from the front.

Steve is reading on. "They're saying he must be dead."

"Lot of people die in cars," says Ferdy, turning round to Steve and nodding.

"Jeff's not dead," says Amy. Though with a little less conviction than she has managed before. If he's not dead, where is he? Why isn't he helping her? And if he is dead, who killed him? Henk? They were best friends, the two of them, before all this.

A silence descends. The car is shaking and rattling on the dirt road like a washing machine on spin cycle.

"This is the most action I've had in weeks," says Rosie. "Where would a woman buy drugs around here, Ferdy?"

"Some boys in Soufrière, down by the jetty; they'll get you anything you need," says Ferdy.

"No," says Rosie. "Real drugs. Kilos, that sort of thing. If I had a bag full of cash, where would I be taking it?"

"Nelson Nunez," says Ferdy. "Lives up at Bluff Point, about five miles up the coast. But if you visit without an appointment, he'll kill you. And if you do have an appointment, he'll probably kill you too, but at least you'll know when."

"Is he a friend of yours?" asks Rosie.

"I know him enough," says Ferdy. "You want to meet him?"

"Very much," says Amy from the back. Bella Sanchez brought money into the country. That money wasn't found. Nelson Nunez sounds like a good place to start looking for it.

"If someone was murdered on St. Lucia," says Rosie, "is Nelson the sort of man who might know who did it?"

"Nelson?" says Ferdy. "Sure, if he didn't do it himself. When's this movie coming out? You need a driver?"

"Driver?" says Rosie. "I see you more as an actor, Ferdy."

"I'll talk to him," says Ferdy, nodding in agreement. "Tell him a big-name writer wants to talk to him."

Amy has yet to encounter a door that wasn't open to Rosie D'Antonio.

"How do you know Nelson Nunez, Ferdy?" Amy asks.

"He's the one who always beats me in the elections."

45

teve has never been anywhere like it.

There is a swimming pool actually inside his room, brilliant sapphire blue, marbled with dancing veins of sunlight in gold and silver. Tiny birds are cheeping and chirruping on the wide, high terrace, and three bottles of beer sit sweating with frost in an ice bucket. In the far distance twin volcanoes jut out into the sea, two perfect triangles dipping their toes into the Caribbean.

They hadn't crashed, and this suite is Steve's reward. He takes out the Dictaphone and looks down to the bay, where colorful dive boats criss cross the waves.

"Hey, dollface, I'm sitting on a balcony, next to a private pool in the biggest hotel room I've ever seen. It's bigger than our house. Well, until we put the conservatory on, then it's probably about the same. I'm even wearing shorts, so get your laughing out of the way. I've still got shoes and socks on, though.

"You wanted to go to the Caribbean; you sent me links and all sorts. It was always the wrong time of year, though. You know I did my research. I couldn't find a single month that wasn't either too rainy or too hot or too expensive. And I read about the hurricanes too, because that would be just my luck. And you said, 'One day' and I agreed 'One day, for sure,' didn't I? But that day never came, eh? Sorry, Debs. Sorry for not living when I had the chance."

Steve opens one of the ice-cold beers and calms himself down.

"Rosie knows the bloke who owns this, so we're all in suites. She's in the Presidential Suite. They threw out the prime minister of Japan to put her in there. We're all off to see a man called Nelson Nunez tomorrow. A drug dealer. I'm assuming drug dealers are roughly the same in St. Lucia as they are in London. I'll let you know. Unless I'm cut down in a hail of gunfire, in which case I'll see you, won't I? I'll be walking through the door, full of bullets, great big smile on my face. Give you a big cuddle."

Steve switches off the Dictaphone and breathes deeply before switching it back on. He feels shaky and tearful. He'd been warned about jet lag.

"There're restaurants here that do all sorts: they've got barbecue on the beach, they've got Italian—I missed bolognese night at The Brass Monkey, as you know—they've got fresh sea fish in a little shack. We should have come out, shouldn't we? We should've. God, I'm sorry, I'm hopeless. I could have sat by the pool while you went scuba diving or talked to people. I don't know why I didn't just do it. We should have taken our chances with the weather. It's nice out here now. Hot but with a breeze off the sea. When you get here, luxury resorts aren't actually as bad as you think."

What does Steve need to ask Debbie about the case?

"So Bella Sanchez had a bag full of money too, and got picked up by the same driver as Fairbanks, which means it's all connected. So we're looking for this François Loubet. And trying to work out who was involved at Maximum Impact."

Steve pauses for a moment, listening to what Debbie has to say about it all.

"I know, doll, I know, I'm tired of saying it to Rosie and Amy, but you're right. The Vivid Viral Agency thing is the bit that really makes no sense. I'm starting to think I might not be back in England anytime soon, so I need to find another way to take a look at them. Also there's this guy Henk, who started his own close-protection business three months ago, which is convenient timing."

A bell rings at the door of the suite, and Steve puts down his machine and answers the door. A young St. Lucian man in a jade uniform has a large black bag folded over his arm. He gives it to Steve.

"From Miss D'Antonio in the Presidential Suite, sir. A suit to wear for this evening's dinner."

"A suit?" says Steve. "I don't need a suit to eat barbecue."

"Sir," says the young man, "tonight you are dining at our sushi restaurant with the owner of Emerald Bay."

Oh, man. *Sushi?*

"Miss D'Antonio also said you can wear it to meet the drug dealer tomorrow. I didn't wish to pass this message on, sir, but she gave me a substantial tip."

Steve thanks the young man and takes the suit inside. He throws it on the bed before thinking that, actually, he should probably hang it up. He picks up the Dictaphone again.

"Bloody sushi, in a bloody suit. First I miss the bolognese, now this. I wonder if Tony Taylor would drive up to Letchworth for me? Have a poke around? That's a thought, isn't it?"

Steve looks out over the Caribbean Sea, and feels the breeze on his face. He extends an arm to one side, and imagines for a moment that Debbie is there with him, safe in his embrace. But she is not in his embrace, and she was not safe. And a better man than Steve would have come here long ago. What chances he had.

If there's trouble tomorrow, if bullets fly his way, if one should hit him, would that be such a bad thing?

There is another knock at the door. Steve finishes his message. "Love you, baby, I'm so sorry you couldn't come here with me."

He opens the door to Rosie D'Antonio.

"Hello, Stevie," says Rosie. "Have you been crying?"

"No," says Steve, honestly, before registering the heat behind his eyes and realizing that he has. "Why did you buy me a suit?"

Rosie smiles. "One of my favorite things in the world is handsome men who are very badly dressed. There's so much you can do with them."

"I don't wear suits," says Steve.

"You have very certain rules, Stevie," says Rosie.

"I know what I like, and what I don't like," says Steve.

"That is very evident, Stevie," says Rosie. "You like your routine?"

"Yes."

"You like your home?"

"Yes."

"You like to feel safe, and you like to feel prepared?"

"Yes."

"I see," says Rosie. "And how is all that working out for you?"

"It's working out well," says Steve, but the question has hit home. His world has become so small. What must Amy think of him? What must Debbie have thought?

"Good," says Rosie. "Now, take my arm, and let's walk along the beach and talk about murder. And then you can tell me all about your beautiful wife, and how much you miss her. Would you like that?"

Steve nods. He would.

"I would too," says Rosie.

46

Amy is running along a sandy beach, her feet splashing in the water every time a wave comes in. Her wraparound sunglasses and her headphones cocoon her. She speeds up, sprinting now, the effort beginning to show on her face. As she passes a bright yellow rowing boat pulled up onto the beach, Amy collapses to the ground, as if she has reached an imaginary finishing line.

Taking huge gulps of air, she looks back toward the beautiful resort that towers over Emerald Bay, and then looks around the desirable stretch of beach she now finds herself on. She takes out a cheap phone and punches in a number.

Susan Knox is at her desk, trading software open in front of her. A mobile phone buzzes somewhere, but she can't immediately locate it. It is certainly not the one on her desk. She searches for a moment before realizing the buzzing is coming from the bottom drawer of her desk. At speed she reaches her arm underneath her desk and knocks on a panel; a key drops to the floor. The mobile is still ringing as she grabs the key and uses it to unlock the bottom drawer. The ringing gets louder as she pulls out a phone and answers.

"Jeff???"

"It's Amy."

"Jesus, Amy," says Susan. "You're still alive?"

"Out of breath but alive," says Amy. "So nothing from Jeff?"

"Nothing," says Susan. "You?"

"I'm uncontactable," says Amy. "Henk was trying to track me down. I didn't like it."

"What do you need, Amy? Did you find anything in the files I sent you?"

"This is going to sound ridiculous," says Amy. "But the blood tests we do?"

"The drug tests?"

"Where are they kept?"

Susan stops for a moment. She looks over her shoulder.

"So Jeff told you what happened?" Susan says.

There is no reply from Amy.

"Amy, the room was locked, and the freezer was locked; we have no idea how it happened, and I promise it won't happen again."

"Remind me again," says Amy. "It was only my blood that went missing?"

"Only yours," says Susan. "Full disclosure, Amy. I thought maybe you'd stolen it yourself, you know, because you were worried about what it would show? So I didn't look into it as much as I should have. And Jeff didn't disagree."

"Well, I didn't take it," says Amy. "But somebody did. Who would have access?"

"Ten or twelve people at most," says Susan. "Our medical people, some of the senior staff. Anyone else would have to have found a way to break in."

"You'd have access?" Amy asks.

"Me, absolutely," says Susan.

"And Jeff?"

"Jeff, yes," says Susan.

There is another pause. "Remind me how long ago this was? I don't think Jeff was clear?"

"End of April," says Susan. "Something like that. I'm really terribly sorry, Amy. It shouldn't have happened, and I shouldn't have suspected it was you."

"And Henk was still at the company then," says Amy. "He would have had access too?"

"He would," confirms Susan.

"And could any clients have had access?" Amy asks.

"I mean, we show people around from time to time," says Susan. "To show off our facilities. But I don't see how that could happen."

"If anyone, anyone, speaks to you—the police, Henk, anyone—you haven't heard from me."

"Of course, of course," says Susan. "Amy, what's happening? Where on earth is Jeff? Are you safe?"

"I don't think anyone is safe, Susan," says Amy.

47

Rob Kenna, his ball in a bunker, is not best pleased.

Eddie has flown to Hawaii and Amy Wheeler, according to sources, is alive and well in St. Lucia. Well, of course she is; he should have anticipated that. It seems she's following the path of the murders. Investigating them, presumably.

She won't find anything there, Rob's fairly sure of that. The Bella Sanchez murder was just another local cop earning a payday, with no idea who from. Same if Amy decides to go to Ireland.

But she'll be dead before she gets the chance.

The key thing is to surround yourself. Layer upon layer of people. And you'd have to unreel an awful lot of layers before you got to Rob Kenna. Still, you have to protect each and every layer if you can.

François Loubet is the same. This is the fourth job Rob has had from him, and he's still never met the man, wouldn't recognize him if he passed him in the street. Layer upon layer upon layer.

Eddie's getting the first plane over from Hawaii, which is expensive, but money's no object with Loubet. So now Rob has to find Eddie a gun in St. Lucia.

He'll talk to the guy who helped him out before. Nelson Nunez.

The nice thing about Dubai, one of the many nice things, is that a man like Rob can get everything he needs.

You need a gun in St. Lucia? You just chat to the Chilean arms dealer with the villa up the street from yours, he talks to a Venezuelan drugs middleman he knows from the tennis club, and, before you know it, introductions are made, encrypted emails are sent, and Nelson Nunez is hiding a semi-automatic pistol under an unusually shaped rock on a St. Lucian back road. Dubai really is that sort of community. Everyone helps everyone.

Rob doesn't want to let Loubet down, though. That could be very dangerous.

"You look like you've got the worries of the world on your shoulders," says Big Mick.

"Work," says Rob.

Big Mick laughs. "I remember work. Overrated."

Mick, a proper old geezer, sold his scrap-metal yard and retired out here ten years ago. Not much of a conversationalist but lives next to the course, and always free for a game of golf. The men play a couple of times a week.

He hacks his ball out of the bunker, and levers himself back onto terra firma.

Rob and Mick walk down toward the green, Big Mick's ball a good twenty yards or so to the left of Rob's.

As he waits for Big Mick to reach his ball, Rob sends a message to Nelson Nunez. Rob writes:

Friend visiting, needs gun. Same place, same terms. 24 hours?

Big Mick has reached his ball, and signals for Rob to hit his next shot. It lands in a bit of trouble about five yards over the green. Rob likes landing in trouble; it forces you to use your brain, to adapt. Up ahead, Big Mick hits his next to within eight feet of the hole.

Nelson replies:

I have the perfect thing. Advise if further help needed.

Rob realizes that Nelson might actually be of further use. Much as he loves Eddie, his old pal might need some help finding where Amy Wheeler is. And if Rob knows islands, it won't have escaped St. Lucia that Rosie D'Antonio has come visiting.

> **If you hear where Rosie D'Antonio is, let me know. The**
> **person she's traveling with is the target.**

Nelson replies:

> **I might be able to take care of it myself? For a fee?**

That's a thought. Eddie might take a while to arrive, and Nelson Nunez knows his work.

> **Sure, if opportunity presents itself. Two hundred. But**
> **don't harm Rosie D'Antonio. Too much publicity if she dies.**

Nelson replies with a thumbs-up. Rob is reassured. It's a small island, and he has Eddie Flood and Nelson Nunez to help him. If one of them doesn't kill Amy Wheeler, the other one surely will.

Big Mick and Rob reach the green. Big Mick steps onto the beautifully manicured surface, a nice gentle putt in front of him, while Rob just keeps on walking toward the deep trouble.

48

"May I make you a cup of tea, Mr. Taylor?"

"Only if you're having one?" says Tony Taylor. "I don't want to impose."

"Couldn't harm, could it? After your journey?"

The journey had been a pleasant surprise, if Tony Taylor is honest. The A31 turned out to be clear as a bell—couldn't believe his luck there. M27, no major problems. The traffic backed up around Junction 2 of the M3—but when doesn't it? The usual fun and games on the M25, but then clear from Junction 9 all the way to Letchworth Garden City. So, all in all, Tony couldn't complain. Should have taken two hours and twenty-three minutes, actually took two hours and fifteen minutes.

Tony had been tempted to say no to the whole plan, but Steve was a good mate, and so, against his better judgment, he decided that, just this one time, he would risk the traffic.

"Couldn't harm at all," says Tony. "Nice cuppa."

He gave back the time he'd saved, however, because parking was prohibitive in the center of Letchworth Garden City ("£2.40 an hour?" he'd said to the attendant. "Who do you think I am? Rockefeller?") and so he had parked on a residential street eight minutes away from Felicity Woollaston's office. So it was swings and roundabouts.

"A nice cuppa," agrees Felicity. She must be, what, seventy-odd, good nick, great hair. "I'm guessing you'd like PG Tips?"

"Then you're guessing right," says Tony. "Give that woman a goldfish!"

Felicity laughs as she fills the kettle. Apropos of absolutely nothing, Tony thinks she has a delightful laugh.

"Thanks for seeing me at short notice," says Tony. "I'm not really in show business, so I've no idea how it all works."

"What are you in, Mr. Taylor?" Felicity asks as she uncouples a pair of tea bags.

"Cars," says Tony. "And call me Tony. Only the taxman calls me Mr. Taylor!"

Felicity laughs again. "Taxman indeed. Are you sure you're not in comedy? You're a hoot."

Tony knows he is a funny guy, but people often tell him that he's not. It is refreshing to see his banter making an impact. And on a professional.

Steve had called him yesterday, outlined what he needed. Just a bit of info, Tony, tell a few white lies. "Like a spy?" Tony had asked, and Steve had said, "Well, no, not really, just a friendly chat, see what you can see," and Tony had said, "That sounds a lot like a spy to me," and Steve had said, "Look, mate, would it make you happier if I said you were a spy?" and Tony had said, "Me? No? No skin off my nose, I'm just saying, call it what it is," and Steve had said, "Okay, you're a spy," and Tony had sucked his teeth and given it some thought and said, "Okay, I'll do it, for you, mate. I'll spy." Then they'd talked about the weather in St. Lucia for a bit, too hot, but Tony could have told him that, and how Amy was, she's very well, and what Rosie D'Antonio was like. "Very much her own woman," apparently.

"So what brings you to Letchworth Garden City, Tony?" Felicity asks.

"My nephew," says Tony. "He's an influencer, you see."

"I see," says Felicity, filling their mugs. "In what area?"

"Southampton," says Tony.

"No, what's his area? His specialty? Who does he influence?"

Tony knew he should have thought his story through more on the journey up. But spies have to think quick.

"Spies," says Tony. The word was in his head, and now it is on the table.

"Spies?" says Felicity. "Goodness me. How does one influence spies?"

"Instagram," says Tony. He had done *some* thinking.

"And what does he do on Instagram?"

Tony hadn't expected the third degree. He takes a sip of his tea. It is much too hot, but it gives him vital thinking time. "Gadgets. Secret bugs and . . . spy guns."

"Is that tea not too hot?" asks Felicity.

"No, it's perfect," says Tony. "So what does a viral media company do?"

"Gracious," says Felicity. "I mean, what *don't* we do?"

"Yeah," says Tony. "It's like people ask what I do all day. Clutches, brake pedals, dings, used to do MOTs but lost my license."

"Exactly," says Felicity. "Clutches, brake pedals. Et cetera."

"Et cetera," agrees Tony. "But if my nephew—"

"What's your nephew's name, Tony?"

Again, he could have prepped this. "He's called Tony."

"Tony like you," says Felicity. "I approve, keep it in the family. And what would he like to do?"

"He read about influencers doing adverts," says Tony. This bit he's remembered. "How does that all work?"

"How does it work?" muses Felicity. "How does it work? That's the million-dollar question."

"Literally I hope!" says Tony, and there's that laugh again. "But, seriously, as the expert, how does it work?"

"Well," says Felicity, "as the expert, lots of ways, really."

She's being quite secretive. Avoiding the questions. Tony will report this back.

"But, what, like," says Tony. "So a company has got like a drink, or a hi-fi, or a Walkman, and they come to you, and you give them an influencer?"

"Pretty much," says Felicity. "You've hit the nail on the head there, Tony."

"And what would he get paid?" says Tony.

"I mean, hmm," says Felicity. "Six of one, half a dozen of the other? You know?"

Tony nods; he does know. Something he won't share with Steve is how much he likes what he sees. How easy it seems to be to talk to Felicity Woollaston. Spies mustn't fall in love, though. It's the first rule.

"Do you have any of his work I could look at?" Felicity asks. Are her eyes blue or gray?

"Whose work, sorry?" says Tony. Remain focused, fella. Look sharp.

"Tony's work," says Felicity. "Tony's spy work?"

"Didn't bring any with me, I'm afraid," says Tony.

"But we can look online?" says Felicity.

"If you have it," says Tony.

Felicity laughs again. Tony didn't even know he was being funny this time. Felicity just seems to bring it out in him.

"You have a very nice smile, Tony," says Felicity. "It would really work on camera. That's a professional opinion."

"Thank you," says Tony. "Thank you. You have a very nice dress."

"Thank you."

"And face."

Felicity smiles again. Wow. Tony wants to invite her to the pub. Have a bit of lunch, talk about something else. But he knows he can't. He hasn't got a single piece of information out of her that he can pass on to Steve. The only information he has gleaned so far is that there is a picture of a man on her desk, but she is not wearing a wedding ring. No, he has to stay here and ask more questions about her agency. Be professional, Tony—what would James Bond do?

"I was wondering if you'd like to go to the pub?" says Tony. "Get a spot of lunch?"

He sees Felicity freeze for a moment. Of course, of *course*, he's been an idiot. Tony realizes she was just laughing to be polite, she said he had a nice smile to be polite, she's got a lovely guy waiting for her at home with a big dog and all his hair.

"Sorry," says Tony. "Of course not, you must be very busy. Stupid of me to ask."

Felicity thinks for a moment more, then leans forward.

"Tony, can I tell you a secret?"

"You're not hungry?" guesses Tony.

"Well, that wouldn't be a secret, silly," says Felicity. "Tony, I feel like I can trust you?"

"You can," agrees Tony. "Everybody can."

Felicity looks around her, trying to form her thoughts into words. "I'm not busy, you see. I'm never busy. I don't really *do* anything."

"Okay," says Tony.

"I just . . . I don't really know what I do anymore, or what my company does. And I've been thinking lately that it would be very nice to talk to someone about it."

"I see," says Tony.

"And then in you walk," says Felicity. "With your lovely smile and your big hands."

She doesn't do anything? Doesn't actually know what her business is? Tony is dimly aware that Steve will want to know this. But for the moment he's too busy looking at his own hands.

"Shall we?" says Felicity, standing. "There's a posh pub, or there's The Crown, where you can get a shepherd's pie?"

"Shepherd's pie for me," says Tony. "Unless you—"

"Shepherd's pie is perfect," says Felicity. "Absolutely perfect."

Tony Taylor smiles. It is a reminder that, sometimes in life, you really should risk the traffic.

49

Rosie is driving them to see Nelson Nunez at Bluff Point. As expected, her name did the trick. Nelson had announced he would be "delighted" to see them at nine a.m., so here they are, bright and early on a Sunday of all days, on their way to a drug dealer's home. She turns off the coast road, and onto a rough track. The house is nearby, she knows that, but it is nowhere to be seen. Drug dealers, like celebrities, will pay a great deal of money for privacy. And often for the same reasons.

"So someone steals your blood, presumably Joe Blow, sends it to Loubet, and there you are," says Steve. "You're physically present at every scene?"

"They've got me," says Amy.

"But no one's going to believe you killed them," says Rosie. "Why would you?"

"They won't need to believe it," says Steve. "If there's solid proof, there's solid proof. So we need some proof of our own that somebody else did it."

Rosie looks at Steve in the rearview mirror. This guy can really fill out a suit. He is sweating fairly profusely, but these things can't be rushed. She takes the next bend much too fast, because where's the fun in doing anything else, and finally sees high iron gates set into a stone wall. On the gates are three signs. One says GUARD DOGS ON PATROL, the second says TRESPASSERS WILL BE SHOT, and the third says ST. LUCIA WELCOMES CAREFUL DRIVERS.

Rosie winds down her window and presses the intercom button on a security post. There is a quick back-and-forth, and the gates swing open. As she continues down the driveway, a Land Rover emerges from bushes to her right and settles in behind her. Mounted in the flatbed of the Land Rover is a machine gun, currently manned by a young man in a Coldplay T-shirt.

"Welcoming committee," says Rosie. "That's nice."

"I'd hate to see what happens when he's not delighted to see someone," says Steve.

"They'll frisk me for my gun," says Amy. "Rosie, you take it."

"You think they won't frisk me?" says Rosie.

"I wouldn't," says Steve.

"Never say never, Stevie," says Rosie, leaning her arm around her seat to take Amy's gun. The house comes into view now: pretty enough, white wood and painted green shutters.

"Smaller than you'd think," says Amy. "For a big-time drug dealer."

Rosie pulls up on a tarmac strip at the front of the house, the main doors swing open, and a man who can only be Nelson Nunez steps out onto a wide porch carrying a tray of glasses and a pitcher of orange liquid that, to Rosie's trained eye, looks lethally alcoholic. The drive home will be even more fun.

Rosie, Amy, and Steve exit the car. Rosie has hidden the gun where she has hidden many things over the years. Not easy in a jumpsuit. It is a testament to the trust she has in Amy that she didn't even double-check if the safety was definitely on. As Steve walks around the car to join Rosie and Amy, she sees Nelson's face change.

"There are three of you?" says Nelson.

They look at each other, as if to confirm this.

"My friends," says Rosie. "Amy and Steve."

They take their drinks.

"Okay," says Nelson, clearly thinking something through. "Then we have a problem."

The Land Rover pulls up behind Rosie's hire car, and the young man in the Coldplay T-shirt jumps down. Nelson looks at him, and then looks at his guests.

"Well," he says. "Come in. I'm sure we can sort this out between us."

As Rosie walks up the two steps to the porch, she sees Nelson give a slight nod to the boy from the Land Rover, and receive a slight nod in return. She is glad, not for the first time in her life, to have a gun.

50

FROM THE DESK OF FRANÇOIS LOUBET

ChatGPT, rewrite in the style of a friendly English gentleman, please.

I'm still here! Don't you worry about that. Patience beginning to wear thin, but these things are sent to try us.

Further correspondence has arrived from my pal Joe Blow.

> Monsieur Loubet,
>
> You do not have to kill Amy Wheeler. She is no danger to you. This has all gone too far.
>
> Joe Blow

Sometimes you simply have to laugh, don't you? What else is there to do when confronted with this buffoonery? Of course I have to kill Amy Wheeler. Goodness, it's like explaining things to a child sometimes. I declare it to be so!

You see, Amy Wheeler was the bodyguard who worked for me in London, the capital city of England. She was very diligent, by all accounts. When I decided to order my, let's not be coy here, *killing spree*, I needed insurance. I hired Rob Kenna: that's one layer of insurance; he has no idea who I am. I then also needed to choose a handy scapegoat, because I always do. And Amy Wheeler was perfect. She worked for Maximum Impact, she was a trained killer, and I could always find out where she was. Bad luck for her but good luck for me. Just the way I like it.

Granted, these are not the sort of murders that get looked into too closely, mainly because they were all carried out by local police officers, but, if someone did decide to investigate properly, they would soon find an easy culprit in Amy Wheeler. I was able to source her blood, and it has been placed at each scene. If I wish to draw their attention to it, the police won't look any further than that. She has no motive, of course, but, with her blood at all three scenes, and her proximity to each, no jury is going to worry too much about that. Even her friends and family might think twice about her guilt. Could she have? Would she have?

Insurance, you see.

However, there is one person in the world who knows for a fact that Amy Wheeler didn't kill the three influencers. One person who would never buy that particular story.

And that person is Amy Wheeler.

So what's the harm in taking care of her? Putting a bullet in that little noggin of hers, and moving right along? Nothing to see here.

You see, alive, Amy Wheeler is a nice little insurance policy. But insurance doesn't always pay out, does it?

The moment she dies, I shall alert the authorities that they might like to cross-check the blood samples at the three scenes, and, what do you know, they can compare it with the recently spilled, still-warm blood of her fresh corpse!

Dead, she is the end of the story altogether. So you see why I am anxious to get that sorted out once and for all?

My understanding is that she is still yet to die, but it is all in hand! Jolly good, I should hope so too. Rob Kenna knows her death is a priority, and knows the penalty if he fails.

And, now that I really think about it, after Amy Wheeler dies, I should probably find out who Joe Blow is, and have them killed too.

These are all loose ends for another day, however, as my mind is already on other things. All ties must be cut with Maximum Impact, that's very clear, but I do plan to keep using influencers to smuggle my money. There seem to be an awful lot of them about.

Vivid Viral Media, the company Joe Blow and I have been using for this scheme, is fully under my control, so I have decided to keep using it, and find my influencers there.

There's always another fool around another corner!

51

You're not really supposed to have your phone on school premises. They tell the kids not to bring them in, so it does look bad when the adults do. Some of the teachers pay no attention to this rule. They glue themselves to their phones, every break time in the staff room, quickly hiding them, and tutting, if a child knocks on the door.

Bonnie would love to be brave enough to do the same, but, as a teaching assistant, she feels she doesn't have the status to be able to pull it off. But, equally, when you are checking for likes and waiting for news, you *do* have to look at your phone *sometimes*.

And this is why Bonnie is in a cubicle in the girls' toilet outside Unicorn Class when she gets the news she's been praying for.

The email is not from Felicity, which is what she would have expected, but instead from a "Bookings Committee." Would Bonnie be free to fly to São Paulo, in Brazil, on Thursday, to film a three-minute promotional video for an organic paint brand? Non-negotiable fee of £20,000. Please confirm.

Bonnie rereads the email. Then re-rereads it. Perhaps she is getting it wrong somehow? Brazil? Twenty thousand pounds?

This can't be right.

Twenty thousand pounds will change her life.

She checks *again*. It must say £2,000 surely? Even that is beyond her dreams. But it doesn't say £2,000, it says £20,000.

As quietly as she is able, Bonnie starts to cry. She's thinking of the friends who encouraged her. Who told her to dream her dream. How close she came to ignoring them, to thinking that things like this don't happen to people like her. Even on the morning she visited Felicity Woollaston, she'd nearly turned back, thought better of it, doubted herself.

"Impostor syndrome," her best friend had called it. The feeling that you're not good enough, that you don't know enough, that you're not worthy enough. But Bonnie had swallowed her fear, and got on the train.

And now here she was. Heading to Brazil, with an unimaginable amount of money coming her way. Mum will look after the kids, she's sure of that. And as for her job here, well, she loves the children, even likes a few of the teachers, but they will all understand when she hands in her notice. Some of them will even be happy for her.

Organic paint? Bonnie hadn't realized that paint wasn't already organic. She should have been aware, she supposes. She will do some reading up. "Hi, I'm Bonnie Gregor, I'm just in Brazil, enjoying the sunshine, I try to get out here two or three times a year if I can, just to top up my tan . . ."

Note to self: book spray tan.

". . . and I'm hopping on Instagram to let you know about an insane new product I think you're going to love. A lot of people don't realize that paint isn't organic, and, I guess, to me, organic is so important. That's why I was excited to come across . . ."

Note to self: find out the name of the paint.

". . . XXX Paint. No chemicals, no e-numbers, no artificial colorings, just paint as it should be, natural, fragrance-free, whol—"

There is a knock at the door, and a young child says, "I really need the toilet."

"One minute," says Bonnie.

"Okay," says the young child, doubtfully. Bonnie feels bad, but these kids do wee themselves an awful lot, and this is a special occasion for her.

What will she wear? They'll probably tell her, won't they? And she can treat herself to a new top or two now, can't she? Her sister-in-law Clarissa went to Barbados last year and didn't stop going on about it for months. Bonnie can't wait to see the look on her face.

But, no, that's mean.

She texts her mum.

Thank you for believing in me. I love you, Mama.

Bonnie reads the email one final time. She dreamed her dream, and it has come true.

She replies to the email.

Dear Bookings Committee,

Thank you, I would like to confirm. Where will I need to get a plane from, and should I book somewhere to stay? What is the name of the paint? Sorry for so many questions.

Yours sincerely,
Bonnie Gregor

She presses "send," and knows that, thanks to Vivid Viral Media Agency, her life is about to change forever.

52

It all happened quickly, as ambushes are wont to do.

The moment they had stepped into Bluff Point, the young man in the Coldplay T-shirt stepped up behind them, with his gun raised, and Nelson Nunez did the same from the front. You'd never get this sort of thing from someone in a Van Halen T-shirt, thought Steve, before being ordered to lie face down on the ground.

Steve and Amy are now lashed to kitchen chairs. Rosie is also strapped to a chair but has avoided being frisked by saying, "Please, feel free, I think you'll find exactly what you're looking for in my knickers."

Nelson genuinely looks upset. Not especially angry, and not especially evil, for a man who has a machine gun mounted on a Land Rover—just upset. Steve has seen the look sometimes in armed robbers who thought it was unfair that they had been caught. But Nelson holds all the cards, so what is upsetting him?

"I was told you were on the island," says Nelson to Rosie.

"By Ferdy?" says Amy.

"By someone else," says Nelson. "He asked me to tell him if I found you."

"You found me," says Rosie. "I don't suppose it was a disgruntled Russian chemicals billionaire?"

"It wasn't," says Nelson. "At least I don't think so."

"So it's not Vasiliy Karpin," says Rosie, then looks at Amy. "I had honestly forgotten he was threatening to kill me. Seems a long time ago now."

"What's the problem here, chief?" Steve asks. Time for him to prove his worth. "Man to man, let the women go."

"The seventies called, Stevie," says Rosie. "It wants its attitudes back."

"Sorry," says Steve. Even as he was saying it, he knew it would get him in trouble.

"It was sort of sweet, though," says Rosie. "And I appreciate it's a mine-field for your generation."

It really is, thinks Steve.

"Okay," says Nelson. "Here is my problem. I have been offered a lot of money to kill one of you."

"Okay," says Steve.

"But," continues Nelson, "I don't know which one of you I'm supposed to kill."

There is a silence that suggests Nelson is looking for a reply.

"Sorry, you want our help?" says Amy.

"Here is the information I have," says Nelson. "'Rosie D'Antonio is coming to the island, and you must not, under any circumstances, kill her.'"

"Yessss!" says Rosie.

"Right," says Steve, and looks at Amy. Steve can see Rosie sawing at the cable ties binding her hands with her nails. Five hundred dollars, she said her last manicure had cost. Time to see if it was money well spent.

"But he said that Mrs. D'Antonio—"

"Miss D'Antonio," says Rosie, still sawing.

"That Miss D'Antonio would be with somebody, and that he would like that person killed."

"Okay," says Amy.

"And now two of you are here," says Nelson. "So you see my problem, I think? Who do I kill?"

Again, it seems as if Nelson is looking for an answer.

"Both of them would be the obvious answer," says Rosie. "Wouldn't you think?"

Steve gives her a questioning glance. Amy doesn't react.

"I think you are right," says Nelson. "I'll only get paid once, but it can't do any harm, can it?"

"Problem solved," says Rosie.

Steve assumes that Rosie is going somewhere with this, but he doesn't yet know her quite well enough to be absolutely certain.

"Ah but . . ." says Rosie.

Phew, thinks Steve.

". . . what would you do with me afterward? You see, you've been expressly forbidden from killing me, and yet I will know that you killed my friends, and I will, of course, hunt you down and have you tortured and then murdered. I am fabulously wealthy and I thrive on revenge."

"Listen," says Nelson, but then seems to be unable to follow this up.

"Who is asking you to kill one of us?" Steve asks.

"I just get messages," says Nelson, nodding toward his phone. "From a guy in Dubai."

"He told you he lived in Dubai?" Amy asks.

"Anyone who lives in Dubai tells you they live in Dubai," says Nelson.

"I don't suppose his name is François Loubet?" Amy asks.

Nelson doesn't react, but Steve can see that he knows the name. He also sees that Nelson is sending a message.

"What happens if you don't kill any of us?" Amy asks.

"If I don't kill any of you?" says Nelson, and then takes a moment to think. "Nothing happens to me."

"It's just you don't seem like an assassin?" says Amy. "And I know a lot of assassins."

"I'm *not* an assassin," says Nelson, his tone very reasonable. "I'm just, you know, a regular criminal and politician."

"Well, then," says Rosie.

"Seemed like easy money, given you were coming here anyway. All I'm really supposed to do is hide a gun for someone else who's coming to kill you. One of you."

"Problem solved, buddy," says Steve. "Untie us, and we'll be on our way."

Nelson nods for a while, thinking this through. "Okay. So I let you go, and we're cool? This never happened?"

"We're cool," says Amy. "Never happened."

Nelson nods again, happy with that deal, and then his phone buzzes. He looks down, reads, and then smiles.

"On second thought, forgive me. I know who to kill now. Blonde woman, early thirties. That was very good timing for me. And very bad timing for"—he looks at his phone again—"Amy Wheeler."

"But you're still not an assassin, Nelson," says Steve. He needs to keep this conversation going for as long as possible.

"I know," says Nelson. "But come on. All that money for one little bullet."

Steve sees that Rosie is so nearly through the cable ties. But she's not going to make it. He thinks back to his conversation with Ferdy earlier when he gave the driver his tip.

Rosie plays for time too. "You'll still have the two of us to worry about."

Nelson bobs his head for a moment, weighing this up.

"I saw you driving up here," he says. "Very fast, on very dangerous roads. I think we can wait for sundown and see if you don't drive your car over a cliff. Terrible accident, no trouble for me. No trouble, only money."

"Nelson," says Amy. "You recognized the name François Loubet?"

Nelson shakes his head at Amy. He then nods to his young bodyguard. The boy points his gun at Amy, closes one eye, and squints along the barrel. The time has come.

Steve's nails, often bitten, never softened or filed, never bathed in ewe's milk or coated in Ecuadorean honey, have done the job that a $500 manicure could never manage. He breaks free of his ties, thrusts his hands inside Rosie's jumpsuit, pulls out the gun, and fires.

He has never fired a gun before, but after the deafening gunshot the young man in the Coldplay T-shirt is moaning in pain on the ground, a bullet hole through his shoulder. Steve, now in a crouching stance, gun raised, looks at Rosie and Amy. Amy has a look of shock, whereas Rosie's look is—what—surprise and lust? She breaks free of her ties.

Nelson makes a run for the door. Steve stays in his crouch, shoots, and hits Nelson in the leg. He goes down too.

"Have you ever shot anyone before?" Rosie asks Steve, while snapping through Amy's cable ties.

"No," says Steve. "But the Coldplay T-shirt made it easier."

Rosie nods down at her jumpsuit. "You know that means we're married now?"

Steve stands over Nelson and offers his hand. Nelson is in a great deal of pain, as is his bodyguard.

"Let's get you both to a hospital, shall we?" says Steve.

"Plenty of time for that," says Amy. "He's got a good four hours before he bleeds out. So maybe a few questions first."

Steve drags Nelson to his feet and helps him over to a sofa. Amy slings the young bodyguard over her shoulder and dumps him next to Nelson.

"Tell us about Bella Sanchez," says Amy.

Nelson looks blank.

"The girl who got murdered at Emerald Bay?" says Amy. "With a bag full of money."

"I don't know anything," says Nelson. "I know a girl got murdered, that's it."

Amy motions for Steve to hand over his gun. Steve shakes his head. Amy gives him a withering look. Steve rolls his eyes and hands it over. Amy takes the gun and holds it against the whimpering Nelson's left temple.

"I don't believe you," says Amy. "Tell me everything you know or I pull the trigger right now."

"Steady on, Ames," says Steve, then turns to Rosie. "This is why we always let her win board games at Christmas."

Amy hasn't taken her eyes off Nelson. "Somebody is trying to kill me."

"Me too," says Nelson.

Rosie laughs, then mouths a silent "sorry" to the furious-looking Amy.

"Forget these two," says Amy to Nelson. "I'm the one you have to worry about here. If I shoot you, it won't be in the leg. Who's your guy in Dubai?"

"I don't know," says Nelson, and tilts his head toward his injured body-guard. "Can we get him to a hospital?"

Steve can see the bodyguard slipping into unconsciousness.

"Amy," says Rosie, "I trust you know what you're doing? There are few things in life I haven't tried at least once, but I don't want to add killing someone to the list."

"You've never killed anyone?" Steve asks. "I'm actually surprised."

"A Danish pop star once had a heart attack in my hotel hot tub," says Rosie. "But that was different."

Amy looks at her watch and says, "He's fine."

"He's my nephew," says Nelson. "My sister will kill me."

"Not if I kill you first," says Amy. "Who killed Bella?"

"A local cop," says Nelson. "Bought a speedboat right after."

"Anything else?"

"They found blood at the scene," says Nelson. "But it didn't match no one."

"There we go," says Steve.

Amy nods. "Okay. I need you to send your friend a message."

"Anything," says Nelson.

"Tell him that Rosie D'Antonio and Amy Wheeler are flying to Alaska."

"Okay, sure, okay," says Nelson. "Alaska."

"No," says Steve. "Eddie's not going to fall for the same trick twice. Tell him they're still holed up at Emerald Bay. A little truth will keep Eddie on St. Lucia longer than a big lie."

Amy nods. "Okay. And do it while I'm watching."

Amy watches Nelson key in the message. Steve is still thinking of Nelson's reaction to the name "François Loubet."

Satisfied the message has been sent, Amy picks up the unconscious nephew once again and carries him over her shoulder.

Steve helps Nelson to his feet, and Nelson drapes an arm around his shoulder.

"I don't think Nelson is going to report us to the police," says Amy. "Let's get Coldplay to a hospital, pick up our passports, and head to the airport before Eddie Flood shows up to waste his time at Emerald Bay."

"Who do you think is messaging you, Nelson?" Steve asks. "If you had to guess? It's François Loubet, isn't it?"

Nelson gives a small laugh.

"You don't think so?"

"I'll tell you one more thing," says Nelson.

"Go on," says Steve.

"François Loubet."

"You know him?" Steve asks.

"I got a message from him once," says Nelson.

"And?" says Amy.

"And whoever he is," says Nelson, "he's not a French guy called François. That message was from an English guy, for sure."

Steve, his arm around a drug dealer he has just shot, has an idea.

53

Eddie Flood gets ready to disembark from the Piper. St. Lucia looks beautiful, but then Hawaii had looked beautiful too, and look how that turned out. Eddie ended up having a drink with Barb in one of the airport bars, no hard feelings. She gave him some amphetamines to help him get over his jet lag, and to prepare him for the flight to St. Lucia.

Eddie yawns with real intent. In his head, Hawaii and St. Lucia were fairly near each other. A two-hour flight maybe? Hopefully even shorter.

He certainly hadn't expected a thirteen-hour flight. Hawaii was a quick ferry ride from California, right? It's America, after all. Looking at the map on his phone, he could sort of see it now, though.

Of course, the thirteen-hour plane journey had had its upsides and its downsides. Downside: he is arriving in St. Lucia nearly twenty hours after Amy Wheeler and Rosie D'Antonio. Upside, he has had plenty of time to work. He's been looking into bribes, police corruption, that sort of thing. The sort of money it takes to get the police to work for you.

He closes his laptop and packs it away. Private jets are pretty good for concentration.

Eddie recognizes, though, that the downside of the unnecessary journey was worse. If he doesn't kill Amy Wheeler this time, then, old friend or not, Rob Kenna might decide he is surplus to requirements. And that would be bad timing, given Eddie's plans.

The door of the plane folds down in front of him, transforming itself into steps. At the bottom of the steps a taxi awaits. Eddie needs to pick up the gun, then find Amy Wheeler. Again, if she's still traveling with Rosie D'Antonio, that shouldn't be a problem. Eddie very much hopes that she is.

As he reaches the bottom of the steps, the driver offers his hand. Eddie shakes it.

"Eddie," says Eddie.

"Ferdy," says Ferdy. "Welcome to St. Lucia."

Eddie's phone buzzes. Rob Kenna is the only one who knows the number.

Found her. Emerald Bay Resort. If you lose her, I'll bet any money she'll head to Dublin next.

Dublin? Quite the tour Amy Wheeler is taking.

"Where can I take you?" Ferdy asks.

"Emerald Bay Resort," says Eddie. "You know it?"

"Sure," says Ferdy, laughing. "Been there once or twice!"

"Great," says Eddie. "You take a lot of people there?"

"Lot of people," confirms Ferdy. "Lot of people. Stallone once."

Eddie nods. "Rosie D'Antonio?"

"Rosie D'Antonio?" Eddie sees that Ferdy is now studying him in the rearview mirror.

"The writer," says Eddie. "My favorite. I read somewhere that she comes here."

"Sure," says Ferdy. "She was staying there, but I drove her back here an hour ago. She's flying to Fiji."

"Fiji?" says Eddie.

"It's an island," says Ferdy. "She's researching a book."

So Rob says that Rosie is at Emerald Bay, and suddenly a random driver says she has gone to Fiji. Why does Eddie feel like he's been given the runaround again?

"You know what," says Eddie, "is there a bar at the terminal? I need a bit of thinking time."

"Sure, boss," says Ferdy. "Whatever you need."

Having just sat through a thirteen-hour journey, Eddie is not in the mood to mess around. He opens up the FlightStats app on his phone and checks the three most recent private jet departures from the airport. Fiji is nowhere to be seen.

So why is this man who recently drove Rosie D'Antonio, and presumably Amy Wheeler, lying to him?

One of the most recent flights was to Charlottesville, one was to Bogotá, and the third?

Well, the third, which took off just forty-five minutes ago, was to Dublin.

Nice try, Amy Wheeler, nice try. This time Eddie has got them. Game on.

54

Rob Kenna knew his luck would change.

Someone had been trying to fool them, but Eddie saw through it, and he is now on a flight to Dublin. This one is costing Rob another fortune, but it will pay him back handsomely.

You see, *this* is why Rob had gone to Eddie. It's going to take a proper professional to kill Amy Wheeler. This woman knows what she's doing. If you need some average Joe off the street killed, you can hire another average Joe to do it. Like that South Carolina cop who stole some of Loubet's money. They would have had to kill him anyway, but he made it a lot worse for himself, that one.

But a special target, like Amy Wheeler, calls for a special killer. And Nelson had been right: they had stayed at Emerald Bay. It didn't lead to anything, but Rob will send Nelson a thank-you fee anyway; it pays to keep in with good people. The murder business is a relationships business.

Relationships like Eddie Flood. Eddie grew up on the same streets as Rob: East London when they started out, then Soho when the stakes got a little higher. Eddie was the best. He had no flash, no ego, took no joy in his work, just worked for the paycheck, and made sure he earned every penny of it.

He really could have gone places, Eddie, but he didn't have Rob's ambitions. As Rob built his empire, the two men drifted apart. No reason why

Eddie shouldn't be right here on this golf course, nice villa on the Arabian Gulf. He had the brains, the skills, but he didn't want it enough. Rob wonders what Eddie does want. What other people want?

Rob watches as Big Mick smashes his ball off the tee. His swing is crude but effective. There's another man who lacks ambition. Who's happy with his lot. Must have made a million or two, surely, and then just thought, that's it, that'll do me. Rob can't understand it. Enough is never enough.

"You know what I do for a living, Mick?"

"I heard you were a DJ," says Big Mick. "Apart from that, I don't want to know."

"You never fancied being a billionaire?" Rob asks.

"What for?" says Mick. "You'd never be able to spend it all."

"But you could look at it," says Rob. "And other people could look at it."

Rob bets that François Loubet is a billionaire. Must be.

"Also, it'd wipe the smile off my dad's face."

"There it is," says Mick. "Proving something to your dad. You never will."

They have reached the green. Rob lines up his putt. It's nice talking to Big Mickey Moody. Rob's putt rolls two feet past the hole.

Mickey Moody is lining up his own putt. "I never knew my dad, you see. My two grannies brought me up, and they'd be proud of me whatever I earned."

"Taught you right from wrong, did they?" says Rob.

"Taught me to work hard," says Mickey, as his putt curls into the hole. "Strong women."

"Yeah, " says Rob. "Nice putt. Maybe I should quit while I'm ahead?"

"Do what makes you happy, that's my advice," says Mick.

What makes you happy? Huh, that's a good question. Rob holes his putt, and the two men walk to the next tee. Rob's phone buzzes again. It's Nelson Nunez.

Am coming to Dubai. Can we meet?

Nelson Nunez is coming to Dubai?

Purpose of visit?

Rob sees the three dots dancing.

Diamond Conference, gems are one of my many sidelines.
I have a proposition for you. You'll like it.

Rob Kenna senses money. The feeling rises in his chest. Of course, that's what makes him happy. And that's okay.

People like his dad, people like Eddie, people like Big Mickey Moody would never understand it. That drive. That was okay; there were others who got it. People like François Loubet and Nelson Nunez. And they were the people who kept him in business.

55

So what did they know now? The same woman picked up both Andrew Fairbanks and Bella Sanchez from the airport, both were carrying identical bags, and both influencers were murdered, then left on display.

In Ireland, they will try to discover if the same is true of Mark Gooch.

As for who François Loubet might be, they hadn't found the answer in St. Lucia. But they know that a man in Dubai has been tasked with killing Amy by any means possible. As for Nelson's François Loubet theory, knowing he isn't French hasn't exactly narrowed things down.

Steve has also received a message from Ferdy, telling him that Eddie Flood is on his way to Fiji. So that is one less thing to worry about for now. Poor Eddie, you had to feel for the guy.

On the flatscreen TV is Tony Taylor, with the rest of The Brass Monkey crowd, Dr. Jyoti Das, and John Todd. Jyoti is the only one who seems to know how to use Zoom properly.

"Guys," says Steve. "I'm so sorry I might miss the quiz this week. I hate to let you down."

"You're solving a murder, mate," says John. "Don't even think about it."

"So will Tony take my place?" Steve asks.

"So you've got some information, Tony?" says Amy, keen to hurry things along. "About Vivid Viral? Something that could help us?"

"Tony on the quiz team?" laughs Jyoti. "Come on. We love him, but come on."

"She's right," says Tony. "I'm not a thinker."

"Do you work with your hands, Tony?" Rosie asks, taking a long drag on her cigarette.

"What's the information, Tony?" Amy asks. "Something that helps the case?"

"So who will you get on the team this week?" says Steve. "Not Mildred from the Cottages?"

"Bloke called Martin, just met him," says John. "He's a loss adjuster from Lymington. Boring but knows his capital cities."

"Knows everything," says Jyoti.

"So, Tony—" starts Amy, one more time.

"I don't like the sound of him," says Steve.

"Needs must," says Jyoti. "He is very good."

"You've been up to Letchworth, Tony," says Amy. "We're on a tight sched—"

"He knows it's not permanent, right?" says Steve. "This loss-adjuster? He knows I'm back next week?"

Rosie looks at him. "Oh, we're wrapping all this up by then, are we, Stevie?"

"We'd better," says Steve.

"Martin knows it's temporary," says Jyoti.

Amy decides she might just let this play out. She guesses they will get to Letchworth, and Tony's information, when they're good and ready.

"*Martin*," says Steve, shaking his head. "Riding in on his white charger."

"He gets it," agrees John. "He knows it's a lucky break, but he understands it can't last."

"Make sure he does," says Steve.

"So," says Amy. Are they finished?

"This is the most macho I've ever seen you, Steve," says Rosie. "And I've seen you shoot a drug dealer."

"You shot a drug dealer?" says Tony.

"Only in the leg," says Steve.

"Still," says Jyoti.

"Yes, still," agrees John.

"So, Tony, you've been to Letchworth," says Amy. "I wonder if you have information that could lead to me not being killed?"

"Of course, of course, sorry, Amy," says Tony, finally focusing. "Felicity says she's making a lot of money, but she can't understand where it's coming from."

"Do you wear oily overalls in your job, Tony?" asks Rosie.

"Not now, Rosie," says Amy. "How much is she making?"

"Felicity says—" starts Tony.

"Felicity says," repeats John, and gets a punch on the upper arm for his troubles.

"She says," Tony continues, "she's making about forty grand a month. Has done for the last two years."

"What would she normally make?" asks Steve. He has got a bit of color from their St. Lucia stay. Albeit the color red. Should have upped the SPF.

"Five or six," says Tony. "In a good month. She was ready to jack it in."

Amy and Steve are both writing this down. "And she doesn't have to do anything?"

"Forward a few emails," says Tony. "Lots of post arrives for lots of different companies, but someone picks that up. She met with a new influencer the other day, but that's not usual."

Amy has a good guess as to what's going on here. "So it's a front? Someone is using her?"

"She's very bright," says Tony.

"But Andrew Fairbanks was on her books?" Amy asks. "And Bella Sanchez, and Mark Gooch?"

"Steve sent me the names," says Tony, "and she hadn't heard of any of them. Went through her emails and everything."

Rosie levers herself up from the sofa. "Can I get anyone a tequila?"

"We're working, Rosie," says Steve.

"Yes, please," says Amy. She is more relaxed now she knows Eddie Flood is about to be 10,000 miles away. Rosie goes off to raid the drinks cabinet.

"I can't believe that's really Rosie D'Antonio," says John.

"Believe it, Johnny," Rosie shouts as she pours tequila into shot glasses.

"So someone is paying Felicity a lot of money to use her company," says Steve. "Clients are being booked by the company, but she knows nothing about them. And she hasn't spoken to anyone about this?"

"I don't think she's had anyone to speak to," says Tony.

"Until now," says Jyoti.

"But she must know it's dodgy?" says Amy.

"I think she's been kidding herself," says Tony. "She's a very moral woman."

"Sorry to hear that, Tony," says Rosie, sitting back down again with three shot glasses of tequila. She and Amy knock theirs back; Steve pushes his to one side.

"Okay," says Amy. "We need Felicity to send us everything she has: accounts, emails, everything. Whoever's using her company as a front has killed three people, and is trying to kill me."

"I'll ask her," says Tony. "Who do you think it is? She won't be in danger? If she sends you her records?"

"Tony," says Steve, "the people she's working for have sent three people to their deaths. So you have to think maybe she's in danger, either way."

"They could kill her?" Tony asks.

"Seems to me like they could kill everyone," says Rosie, returning to the sofa with three more shots.

"Except you," says Amy, "because you're a celebrity."

"What if this story ends with everybody dead except me?" says Rosie, downing her shot. "Hell of a final scene. I love it."

"You'll keep Felicity safe?" Tony asks.

"We'll keep everyone safe," says Steve. "Is there anything else she can tell us?"

"What did Felicity say about the one in prison?" John asks Tony.

"Which one?" replies Tony.

"The one in the prison in Dubai?" says John. "The influencer stopped at customs? Weren't you telling us about it earlier?"

"I don't think Felicity told me that," says Tony.

"What girl?" Amy asks.

"Can't remember the name," says Jyoti. "Kylie? She got ten years. Dubai, smuggling something."

Amy sees Steve on his phone. He's gone from being a man who was scared to turn his phone on in mid air a week ago to a man now using a burner phone with Wi-Fi at 25,000 feet.

"Courtney Lewis?" he asks. "Ten years, Al-Awir Prison, Dubai?"

"That's the one," says John. "All connected."

"Courtney, Kylie," says Jyoti. "I see what I was thinking."

"And she's connected?" Amy asks.

"Felicity seems to think so," says John.

"Okay, we're on it," says Amy.

Rosie is pouring more shots. Amy hears Tony say, "I don't remember telling you that," but it gets a little lost in people saying their goodbyes.

"So perhaps we should go to see this Courtney woman in prison?"

"We can't get to Dubai anytime soon," says Steve. "We're going to need a few days in Ireland. Then I thought maybe I'd head back to Axley for a day or tw—"

"We don't need to go to Dubai," says Amy.

"Why?" asks Steve.

"I'm just going to send a text to the newest member of our team," says Amy, downing her shot.

56

Adam Wheeler has had a successful day. Meeting after meeting, listening, writing things down, thinking things through. He's sold a stake in a Singaporean cinema chain, and bought a stake in a South Korean AI software start-up, and he had a nice sandwich for lunch.

He's flying to Dubai on Tuesday, where there's a diamond conference; it's a good place to chat to a few of his clients. By and large people enjoy chatting with Adam, because he listens more than he talks, and he usually makes them money.

Amy was supposed to be joining him in Dubai, but her contract with Rosie D'Antonio has been extended. It's a shame. He misses Amy, but he understands her work, and she understands his. They both have things to prove, and they need time and freedom in which to do it.

She's with his dad, apparently. Adam wonders why. There will be a reason, but the last few days have been too busy for him to spend time thinking what that reason might be.

Some of his colleagues, the brokers, the senior analysts, the traders, are going out tonight. A meal, casino, the men picking up women, the women picking up men, or whichever way around works for them. It's a free-for-all. That's his world. Put in the hours, reap the profits, buy watches and cars and houses, sleep with anyone and anything that moves. Cocaine, ketamine, whisky, money, money, money.

Adam is going to get room service and watch a film on his laptop instead. He's downloaded *Rampage 5*. He might have a gin and tonic from the minibar, although it's £12. One of his colleagues, Wanda, bought a Rolex last time they were all in Singapore—£25,000. For a watch. Back in London she wore it on an evening out, and a teenage boy on a moped with a gun took it off her. Adam is no apologist for teenage criminals, but if you're going to wear £25,000 on your wrist, then, in Adam's view, two crimes have been committed.

Adam loads up *Rampage 5* on his laptop. He had thought the *Rampage* movies were Jason Statham, but now he sees that it's Max Highfield. Not as good as Statham, in Adam's opinion, but probably the next best thing if Statham is unavailable. The Jean-Claude Van Damme to Statham's Schwarzenegger. Adam remembers Max Highfield starting out. He was a minor character in a soap opera, had an affair with someone, or burned down a launderette or something, so perhaps that stops him from taking Max Highfield seriously as a Hollywood A-lister.

Not that someone like Max Highfield would ever care what someone like Adam thinks.

Wanda is married to a guy Adam knows from his banking days. She's also having an affair with a Finnish hedge-fund manager. Adam doesn't like to judge, although, honestly, he can't help but think that sort of life must be exhausting. He doesn't get casinos or infidelity. Why earn money, just to lose it, and why look for love, just to betray it? Adam has been very smart with his money. Amy doesn't know exactly how much he has put away over the last few years, nor, Adam knows, does she particularly care, but he is looking forward to telling her one day.

Adam has also been very smart with his love. When he and Amy met, neither was in the right place for a long-term relationship, each traveling the world, Amy punching people, and Adam looking for value in zinc derivatives. By rights, the whole thing should never have got off the ground. But both knew what they had found in each other. They discussed things openly and honestly. Amy had no interest in settling in one place, in nesting, raising a family, getting a mortgage, painting a living room, and being a wife. But, she stressed, she wanted to stay with Adam forever. Adam, for his part, agreed. For now, any sort of traditional marriage would be a disaster, but, equally, the thought of spending the rest of his life without Amy was unthinkable.

So what to do?

On Adam's laptop screen Max Highfield is driving a sports car underneath a moving airplane. Highfield's wife, as far as Adam can follow, has been kidnapped, and is on the plane. He is shooting at the fuselage, which seems foolhardy to Adam if his wife *is* on the plane. The plane then takes flight and Max Highfield lets out a roar of anger. Not bad.

Years ago, when Adam was more junior, he was on a desk that dealt almost exclusively in "options." If you think a particular stock is going to rise in the future, you simply make a bet, a "call option," allowing you to buy that stock at a predetermined price at a future date.

He had explained this to Amy, in the context of their relationship. They could both take out a "call option" on each other, if they felt their love was likely to grow, but they didn't currently have the emotional bandwidth to commit to each other. Amy had said that this was quite unromantic, but she was also of the view that romance was overrated, and so was happy to hear more.

Adam further explained that taking out a "call option" on their relationship was an incredibly efficient way of leveraging their emotional investment, while also representing their faith in a directional bet as to which way their love might go.

At this point Amy had said that this was actually too much information, and Adam had agreed. They had kissed, and Adam had asked if Amy would like to meet his mum and dad.

But, from that day, they both understood the contract. They loved each other, they would have a life together, but they would do it when they were good and ready. They married; Amy had held him at his mum's funeral; Amy formed a bond with Adam's dad, which was great news, because Adam had never quite been able to do it; and they traveled the world, counting down the days until they were ready to cash in on their love. So theirs was a fairy tale that might not have started with a "Once upon a time," but they are both confident it will end with a "Happily ever after."

Back on his screen, Max Highfield has just thrown a hand grenade out of a helicopter. Perhaps Adam will ask Amy whether she's ever done anything similar? He had been looking forward to seeing her in Dubai. They are both self-reliant, that's for sure, but there are evenings when he aches for her.

Come on, Adam, it's every evening.

Now Max is killing the helicopter pilot, so one assumes that he is a qualified pilot also.

Adam's phone buzzes. A message from Amy. His heart pulses at the sight of her name. So silly, really.

Will you be in Dubai on Tuesday?

Adam pauses the film. Max is kicking a hole in the windscreen of the helicopter, for no reason that Adam can fathom. He replies:

Land at 9ish, Dubai time.

Perhaps she is coming after all? Job finished? Another message.

Do you mind going to Al-Awir Prison?

So she's not finished. Prison in Dubai? Well, that's a good question. I mean, he wouldn't choose to go there, but Amy wouldn't be asking without good reason, would she?

Yes, I'd love to. Do you fancy a chat? I'm between meetings.

Can't right now. Drinking tequila with your dad.

Dad doesn't drink tequila?

> He does now. You need to talk to a Courtney Lewis. She's there on smuggling charges. Let her talk, and take notes, they're expecting you. Are you going to be in meetings all evening? We could chat later?

Adam looks at his laptop. There is literally nothing to be gained by kicking a hole in the windscreen of that helicopter. He would love to speak to Amy, but he doesn't want to seem needy. He can sense she's busy.

I'm going to be stacked back-to-back this evening. Ames, can I ask you a question?

> If the question is "Do I love you," the answer is "Yes."

Well, likewise. But I really wanted to ask if you've ever thrown a hand grenade out of a helicopter?

> Also yes. Take care, my prince. Should I give your love to your dad?

Say hi, yeah.

So now he has to go to a Dubai prison. But he's doing it for Amy.

In Adam's business that's called breaking even. He googles the prison, while Max Highfield rides a snowmobile over a waterfall.

57

S teve has never liked flying, even back in the days when he wasn't so frightened of everything.

He thinks about the facts of the situation. He is traveling at 600 mph, high in the heavens, in a metal tube whose upkeep and safety are in the hands of a series of human beings, some of whom, statistically, must be going through a divorce or a battle with addictions, or perhaps missing sleep because of a new baby or an old worry.

Given that Steve knows all these things, he is surprised at how calm this plane feels, almost serene, as it cuts a smooth path through the dark night toward Dublin. He is surprised about the calm he feels too. Rosie is asleep on a sofa. Steve places a blanket over her. Rosie asleep has a vulnerability that you never see in Rosie awake. Or she never lets you see.

Everyone is vulnerable. For some people, for Steve, it comes out as fear, avoiding situations where the vulnerability is exposed. For others, for an awful lot of people these days, vulnerability comes out as anger, pushing away anything that feels like it might pierce their shell. Steve watches people on TV sometimes, shouting the odds about this, that, or the other, railing against the truth of reality, and he always sees the pain first. They have lost someone, or they never had someone, and so now they have lost themselves.

Rosie hides her vulnerability with her brilliance; the brightness of her light is all that you can see. But, lying on the sofa, in the same sleep as the rest of us, Steve sees her.

My God, it is peaceful up here. That might be the tequila talking, but Steve can't help but feel it. He is far from home for the first time in a long time. The safety of his routine has been left behind in an empty house. It must be echoing off the walls by now. Up at eight, feed Trouble, watch the news with Trouble curled on his lap as if he hasn't just been sleeping all night. Weetabix for breakfast, sometimes with berries if he's remembered to buy them. Walk to the shops, buy the paper and maybe something for tea. Say "Good morning" to the people whose routines coincide with his. Home, quick crossword, Sudoku, let Trouble out when he meows with the plaintive sorrow of a thousand dying suns, then let him back in again immediately. Lunch at the pub, good friends, variable conversation.

How safe that all makes him feel, but how small his world has become without his noticing. Up here, with the world stretched below him, looking at the names on the flight map of the world, he sees it now. He spins the globe on the screen. Will he ever visit Dar es Salaam? Jeddah? There's Dubai.

Looking at Rosie again, Steve wonders now what he must look like asleep? How small he must look, how fragile. Sometimes when Steve wakes, Trouble is curled up on his chest. Steve has always thought that Trouble was looking for Steve's protection, but what if Trouble is protecting him? What if Trouble sees the young child Steve still is—that we all still are when we sleep—and understands that he needs protecting?

Amy is working on her laptop, her face lit by the glow of the screen, looking at the files that Susan Knox has sent over. How does Amy hide? Steve wonders. Where does she go?

Steve touches her arm, and Amy looks up. Everything is silent except the cocooning drone of the engines keeping them alive.

"Are you scared?" Steve asks. He has wanted to ask her this many times, but he was frightened of the answer.

Amy smiles at him. "Yes. Are you?"

"Of course," says Steve. "I'm always scared."

"Me too," says Amy. "I'm just very good at running away from it."

"I know," says Steve. "Or punching it, or shooting it. You know . . . if you ever wanted . . . we could talk about you growing up? All of that?"

"I know we could," says Amy. "And you know we could talk about how sad you feel?"

"I know we could," says Steve. "You found anything else in those files?"

"Nope," says Amy. "No François Loubet, no Joe Blow. You?"

"Nope," says Steve. He's lying. There is a very interesting name hidden in the files. A name Steve recognizes. Though he has a lot of work to do before he can say anything. He also has another worry.

"Seeing as Courtney Lewis, our friend imprisoned in Dubai, was another Vivid Viral booking, we should probably think a bit more about Felicity Woollaston."

"Tony Taylor's new girlfriend?" Amy arches an eyebrow. "She's just being used."

"Maybe," says Steve. "I hope so, for Tony's sake."

"Adam's seeing Courtney Lewis when he gets to Dubai; she'll have some answers," says Amy. "Quick tour of the vineyard, see what we can see, talk to whoever will talk to us, then get Ads on Zoom and put our heads together."

"I'm glad you asked Adam to help," says Steve.

"He's very good, you know," says Amy.

"At what?" says Steve.

"At everything," says Amy. "He's an amazing man."

"That's nice to hear," says Steve. "I still see the boy."

"That's because you're both idiots, and you don't spend any time together," says Amy. "Believe it or not, you'd get on."

"You don't spend much time with him either," says Steve. "I worry about that sometimes."

"We don't need to spend time together for now," says Amy.

"That doesn't make sense, Amy," says Steve.

"It would make sense if you understood leveraged futures options," says Amy. "We have forever."

"No one has forever," says Steve.

"God, no, sorry," says Amy, putting her hand on Steve's arm. "Let's both spend more time with your son."

"Why don't you get some sleep?" Steve suggests. "I'm going to do a bit more thinking about Jeff. This case goes off in very different directions, depending on whether he's alive or dead."

Amy shuts her laptop. She looks over at her father-in-law. "Thank you, Steve."

"Always a pleasure," says Steve. "What for?"

"For asking if I was scared," says Amy. "No one ever asks, but sometimes I am. I don't want to die."

Steve gives his daughter-in-law a hug. This beautiful, brave woman scared of dying, and this silly, cowardly man afraid of living.

As Amy closes her eyes, Steve opens his file again. Has he discovered the identity of Joe Blow? He'll soon find out.

58

I am very happy with this poached egg," says Henk van Veen. "Very happy indeed."

"I'm pleased to hear it," says the young man, Ashley, who has just served him.

"Poached eggs are hard to get exactly right," says Henk. "Firstly you have to select the correct egg. Free range is an absolute must. I weep to think about battery chickens, do you?"

"I do," says Ashley.

"They are unhappy," says Henk, "they are unfulfilled, and no amount of salt can hide it. I will not put salt on a poached egg unless it is absolutely necessary. Today, I am glad to note, it is not necessary."

"Terrific," says Ashley.

"Secondly, the color," says Henk. "I'm sorry, am I keeping you, Ashley?"

"Not at all," says Ashley. "I am enjoying talking about eggs with you, Mr. Van Veen."

"So, the color," Henk continues. "The British often favor a yolk that is altogether too yellow. A good yolk should be orange, in my view. In fact, not just in my view but in the correct, natural order of things."

"Yes," agrees Ashley.

"It can also be too orange, of course," says Henk. "The perfect color is somewhere between the beauty of an English sunrise and the color of the Dutch national football kit. Again, today's egg is perfect."

"Can I get you more coffee, perhaps?" asks Ashley.

Henk holds up a finger to Ashley, indicating that they will get on to coffee, but, for now, he has more to say about eggs. "Consistency? Once the white—firm but yielding—is breached, the yolk must be unstoppable but also determined to take its time. Say the yolk of an egg, Ashley, is the lava from a volcano, and the toast is Pompeii. For me, Pompeii must eventually be destroyed, but the townsfolk should have time to vacate with their belongings before they perish. They can't dawdle too long, but, if everybody operates in good order, then there should be no casualties."

"We went to Pompeii on a school trip," says Ashley.

"The toast is also paramount," says Henk. "I mean, of course it is. The English have started insisting on sourdough, and this will not do for me. Quite why it will do for anyone is beyond the limit of my powers. Spinoza once said, 'I have made a ceaseless effort not to bewail human actions, but to understand them.' I say this, Ashley, Spinoza, faultless in so many other ways, had clearly not come across sourdough toast. Seeded granary, lightly toasted and still warm, is the trick, and today that trick has been pulled off with aplomb. And, thank you, I will now have a coffee."

"Certainly," says Ashley. "How do you take it?"

"Oh, just as it comes," says Henk. "I'm not fussy."

Ashley leaves to get Henk his coffee.

Henk is aware that what makes today's egg perfection all the more extraordinary is that this feat has been managed aboard a plane. Napkin tucked into his shirt, final piece of toast mopping up final smear of yolk, he will have to pay his compliments to the chef.

Amy Wheeler's phone is no longer active, which is to be expected from a professional, so Henk has had to take matters into his own hands. She had been in South Carolina, that he knew for certain. MailOnline has a photograph of Rosie D'Antonio at the airport in St. Lucia, so that must have been their next port of call. It stands to reason, doesn't it, that they are following the path of the murders? Andrew Fairbanks in South Carolina, Bella Sanchez in St. Lucia, so next stop will be Mark Gooch, a few miles outside Cork in Ireland. So that is exactly where Henk is headed.

All things being equal, Henk might even arrive there before them. Could be there to greet Amy and her merry band. That would be the ideal for him.

Henk dabs at his mouth with the napkin, rises, and stretches. He walks toward the galley to thank the chef, and perhaps discuss technique. Maybe even get a card? Henk's personal chef is very good, but what if he were to die? Or find another job? You must always have contingencies, and anyone who can cook the perfect poached egg at 25,000 feet is going to be of interest.

The steward, Ashley, perfectly good at his job, gives him a pleasant smile.

"Mr. Van Veen, we've already begun our descent into Cork. It might be more comfortable for you to take your seat and fasten your belt."

Henk shakes his head. "I like to stand in the aisle when the plane is landing. It is a thrill for me. A small thrill but a thrill all the same. You must take thrills where you can get them, Ashley."

"I certainly try," says Ashley. "But I am legally obliged to ask you to return to your seat."

"I know you are," says Henk. "That's one of the reasons it's a thrill. To surf the landing. You will join me, perhaps. There is such a minuscule risk of death."

Ashley takes a look over his shoulder toward the cockpit. "Okay," he says.

Henk smiles. Today will be a good day. The perfect egg, a spot of plane-surfing, a gun wrapped in so much sawdust it will clear all cursory airport checks, and, above all, a minuscule risk of death.

For him, at least.

59

The Arrivals Hall at Dublin Airport is quiet.

"You take a taxi into town," says Amy. "I have to see a man about a gun."

She doesn't have to see a man about a gun. She's actually picking one up from a quiet suburban house to the west of Dublin on Tuesday morning. But her business at the airport is not finished, and she doesn't want to worry Steve and Rosie.

Amy senses danger, and she learned long ago to trust her senses.

It is around twelve a.m. on Monday, though with time differences it could be the middle of the day. That sort of thing never really worries Amy. Rosie has booked them all into a hotel in the middle of Dublin, and on Tuesday she has arranged for a helicopter to fly them to the vineyard near Cork. Apparently the private hangar at Cork was full on Monday.

"A night out for you and me later, then, Stevie," says Rosie. "I have a few contacts in Dublin."

"Not for me," says Steve. "I'm going to stay in my room."

"No, you're not," says Rosie.

"You've never been to Dublin before," says Amy. "Why not see a bit of it, before we head to Cork tomorrow?"

"I'm sure Dublin is lovely," says Steve. "But I have a few films to watch."

"You're coming drinking tonight," says Rosie. "If I have to drag you by the hair."

"I haven't watched any TV for days," says Steve. "Surely no one would begrudge me?"

Rosie rolls her eyes.

"He's been through a lot," says Amy. "Perhaps we let him win this one?"

Amy sees them both into a taxi. Hopefully by the next time she sees them everything will be settled. She looks at her watch, then at the multistory car park opposite the cab rank.

"You're coming out drinking when you're finished, though," says Rosie out of the cab window.

"You have my guarantee," says Amy. "Night night, Steve. Love you."

The taxi drives off. Amy will definitely join Rosie for that drink, if she survives the next thirty minutes.

60

When was the last time Tony Taylor had a date? Hard to remember—1987, something like that? The Thatcher era, certainly.

But, despite his rustiness, it had gone well. Felicity talked about television, famous actors, presenters you'd have heard of; Tony talked about the parking problems in Axley, and the Ford Sierra Cosworth he's currently fine-tuning. They both asked questions, they both drank wine, and neither could keep the silly grins from their faces.

He had taken Felicity to a restaurant called The Pig, in Brockenhurst, not far from Axley. It was wonderful, as it should be at those prices. It is very important to show a bit of class on a first date—Tony certainly remembers that much—but he hopes that Felicity doesn't come to expect this sort of thing regularly. He is a modest man of modest means.

They took a walk around the gardens after dinner, and they kissed under a sycamore tree.

Felicity is going to stay in Steve's empty house this evening; Steve has okayed it. Tomorrow morning, Tony is taking her on a tour of the New Forest. Lymington, Beaulieu, the forest walk at Boldre, the old shipyard at Buckler's Hard, all the sights. Get some fudge maybe.

Tony was very glad when she agreed to a nightcap back in Axley, at The Brass Monkey. Much more his speed.

Tony has just nipped back from the gents' and stops for a moment to watch Felicity in animated conversation with John and Jyoti. He wonders what they're talking about. Hopefully not him—John and Jyoti are both liabilities in that regard.

He wishes Steve was here too, but Amy needs him, and a man's got to do what a man's got to do. If you can say that sort of thing these days. Steve says the fella who came to his garage the other day was murdered down at Hollands Wood. Not something Tony has mentioned to Felicity, because not everyone liked talking about murder, did they? Especially on a first date.

He walks over to the table they are sharing and takes his seat, next to his pint.

"Blood everywhere," says John.

"Shot him, then dragged his body away," Jyoti adds.

"Did Steve see the body?" Felicity asks.

"We don't need to hear about all this," says Tony.

Felicity smiles at Tony. "I can't believe you talked about a Ford Sierra instead of this."

"It's a Sierra Cosworth," says John. "To be fair to Tony."

"I just didn't want you to think that the New Forest is all murders," says Tony. "There are ponies, all sorts."

"I can handle ponies *and* murders," says Felicity.

"She's a keeper," says Jyoti.

"Tell us more about this woman in prison, Tony," says John.

"Tell you about what?" says Felicity, sipping her pint.

"Your client," says Jyoti. "In prison in Dubai?"

"I don't think I've got any clients in prison in Dubai," says Felicity. "Unless Alan Baxter has started drinking again."

"Tony told us about her," says John. "At the lock-in the other night. We were all talking about Steve's murders."

"Yeah, I don't think I did," says Tony. "I wasn't even at the lock-in."

"Then who told us?" says Jyoti.

John shrugs and downs his pint. "Well, *someone* did. Who's for another round?"

Jyoti raises her empty glass in assent. Tony sneaks a look at Felicity. He motions toward the door with his eyes, and she gives a small nod. First the kiss under the sycamore tree, and now the small nod. What a night.

"I'm going to walk Felicity home," says Tony.

"I'll bet you are," says John, then extends his hand. "Felicity, a great pleasure. You've got a good one here."

"Thank you," says Felicity. "And thank you for the graphic descriptions of the murder."

"Not at all," says John. "You wouldn't get that at The Flagon."

Jyoti stands too and embraces Felicity. "I hope we see a lot more of you in Axley."

"I hope so too," says Felicity.

As Felicity turns, letting Tony help her into her jacket, Jyoti puts her hand on her heart and nods at Tony. Tony smiles in return. When was the last good thing that happened to him?

He follows Felicity out into the summer evening air, and they link arms and walk up the hill toward Steve's house. Tony carries her overnight bag.

"It's very beautiful here," says Felicity. "I might come back again, you know."

"I think my friends liked you," says Tony.

"I liked them too," says Felicity. "What was that about Dubai?"

"Honestly?" says Tony. "They drink a fair bit, those two. A couple of weeks ago John said he saw Camilla Parker Bowles in the Brockenhurst Co-op."

Felicity smiles.

"This is us," says Tony, as they reach Steve's cottage.

"Oh, it's lovely," says Felicity. "And so much more private than the sycamore tree. Will you join me for a coffee, Tony?"

"I don't really drink cof—" Tony starts, before catching Felicity's look. "Of course. I'll get you settled in, show you where the fuse box is."

As he puts Steve's spare key in the lock, Tony could swear he sees a flash of light from an upstairs window. As if a curtain has been drawn back and quickly replaced.

Is someone in the house? Impossible. But he opens the door with care, just in case.

As Felicity slips off her jacket, Tony jumps at a sudden noise. Then sees a familiar black cat pad down the stairs with something to say for himself.

Of course there was no one in the house.

It was just Trouble.

61

Amy needs to stay awake just a while longer. Fortunately she has thinking to do. Thinking about Henk van Veen, thinking about Jeff, thinking about Joe Blow and François Loubet. What *has* she got herself caught up in here?

She thinks about being killed. Thinks about Steve being killed. Thinks about Adam being on the other side of the world.

When did she become so sentimental? It's ridiculous.

One thing she can control is being good at her job. Trusting her instincts and taking pains.

Whoever is trying to kill her is no fool. They've got away with killing four people already, with almost no leads left behind. They hired Kevin to kill her, and he wasn't bad. He wasn't good enough, but not many are. You can prepare for pretty much anything in this game, but nobody expects to be bludgeoned by a shoulder-padded novelist with a cinematography Oscar. That was bad luck.

It follows therefore that Eddie Flood is no fool either. Whether Henk hired him, or Loubet hired him, or Henk *is* Loubet, Eddie will be a professional. A professional who just fell for a sucker's trick and flew to Hawaii. Will they really catch Eddie out with the same trick twice? Amy doubts it.

It's lovely to believe that Eddie is, even now, enjoying a gin and tonic on his way to Fiji, but Amy is placing a different bet. Amy is placing a bet that

Eddie is on the plane with the call sign F716A that left St. Lucia just three hours after her own.

And that's why she has broken into this very comfortable Mercedes in the long-stay car park of Dublin Airport, with a perfect view of the taxi queue. Below her is a floral display spelling out WELCOME TO DUBLIN. She plans to give Eddie a welcome of her own. Follow him, question him, and, if it comes to it, kill him. If that happens tonight, it will have to be with her bare hands.

It is very possible, though, that Eddie won't even know who has hired him. Kevin hadn't seemed to.

If Eddie is on that plane, no doubt he'll rest up in Dublin for the day, before heading to Cork in the morning. The row of taxis is getting very little business at this time of night, the drivers all standing around a single car and discussing the events of their days.

Flight F716A touched down about fifteen minutes ago. Amy gives Eddie twenty-five minutes or so to taxi toward the terminal and to clear customs.

Amy has tried to find who chartered flight F716A, with very little luck. The world of private jets can be opaque at times.

The airport is quieting down, and the electronic doors on the front of the terminal are shut more than they're open. Every time they burp someone out Amy is on full alert.

It's all very well thinking about Henk, and about François Loubet, but Amy can't stop a niggling little voice from saying Jeff Nolan's name too. Jeff knew where all three victims would be, Jeff knew they were all unprotected, and, to cap it all, Jeff must have signed off on Kevin working with her and Rosie. Could Jeff be a killer? Yes. Would Jeff try to kill her? Again, all you can do is to trust your instincts, and her instincts say no.

Her instincts certainly say that Jeff is not dead, but perhaps that is her being sentimental again. It's a curse.

Amy's phone buzzes: a message from Rosie at the hotel. It's a photograph. They're in the residents' bar, Rosie looking mischievous, raising a glass of Guinness to the camera, her arm round Steve, who is doing the same.

It's not a long drive from the airport to the hotel—ten minutes or so—but Rosie had clearly worked her magic in that time. Steve looks happy. Rosie always looks happy.

The sliding doors open once again, and three students with rucksacks emerge. Eddie is taking his sweet time. What if customs have stopped him? He wouldn't be stupid enough to carry a gun, surely? There are ways of smuggling . . .

A sudden noise, and the back windscreen of the Mercedes shatters. Amy throws herself down. Someone is firing from directly behind the car. Firing and getting closer. She risks a look into the rearview mirror. It's Eddie Flood.

He's not just good, he's very good. But she's still alive.

Eddie has a gun, and Amy has nothing. She has a car, sure, but no way of starting it. Amy lies flat across the front two seats. If Eddie wants to check she's alive, he's not going to be able to do it from any of the back windows; he'll have to go to the driver's side door.

Right on cue, Eddie appears at the window and levels his gun. Amy hooks one foot under the door release, and then kicks out with the other leg, sending the door swinging open and Eddie flying across the concrete. Amy springs up, opens the passenger side door, and, as Eddie regains his balance, she dives over the parapet of the car park, landing on the WELCOME TO DUBLIN floral display. Eddie fires one more shot from above, before, sensibly in Amy's view, realizing this is all too public. The few onlookers were already screaming and pointing. The taxi drivers suddenly have something new to talk about.

Amy runs across the airport access road and jumps into the first taxi on the rank.

"Temple Bar Hotel," she says to the driver, while keeping her head out of sight.

"That's a nice hotel, right enough," says the driver. "That's you being shot at, is it?"

"Afraid so," says Amy.

"Welcome to Dublin," says the taxi driver, putting her foot hard to the floor and screeching away. As they take a bend at speed, one final shot smashes the back window.

The driver looks at where her window used to be, and at Amy brushing glass from her jacket.

"I'll not ask if it's business or pleasure."

62

I t's such an honor," says Mark, the makeup artist. "But it's very hard to make you look any more fabulous."

"Thank you," says Rosie. "And I've had almost no sleep."

"You are so drama," says Mark. "So drama. I love it."

"Whenever drama is in short supply, you must create your own," says Rosie. "When I'm not writing stories, I try to live them."

"Oh, you are *extra*," says Mark. "You are extra extra, you know what I mean?"

Rosie does know what he means. She is "drama," and she is "extra." She has always been able to create chaos out of nothing, to spin the people around her like plates. Rosie can turn a calm sea into a maelstrom with a single word here, or a single glance there. It can be tiring, but it keeps reality from the door.

"You're like Lizzo," says Mark. "We've had her on. She brought her own makeup people, though."

Chaos is a jungle in which it's easy to hide, and Rosie has, therefore, enjoyed the last day or so very much. And she is aware there is more fun to come.

Rosie had taken Steve for a drink straightaway. Steve had objected at first, but Rosie had once persuaded a Buddhist monk to do LSD in an infinity pool, so Steve was no match for her. "Just one pint," he had said.

Several hours later, they were still in the residents' bar when Amy had appeared, with a slight limp and a story to tell.

A floor manager pokes her head around the door of the makeup room. "On air in five?"

"She hardly needs a thing," says Mark. "I told her, you're like Lizzo."

Amy had told them that Eddie was in Dublin after all, the sly old fox, armed to the teeth and determined to finish the job that Kevin had started. Amy didn't give them the whole story, however much Rosie pleaded, but she had broken glass and magnolia petals in her pocket, so something interesting had gone on. Rosie ordered more drinks for them all.

"What's the big announcement, then?" Mark asks, adding some final hair spray.

"Secret, I'm afraid," says Rosie.

"What's said in the makeup room, stays in the makeup room," says Mark. "It's like Vegas."

But what to do about Eddie. He was in Ireland, he was armed, and he would surely be following them to Cork. So, Amy is currently buying a gun for €4,000, while Rosie waits to go on Ireland's leading breakfast television show. You have to play to your own strengths.

One drink turned into another and then, as so often in life, into another, at which point Rosie's current plan to foil Eddie Flood came into focus. At six p.m., as the bar started to fill with revelers just beginning their evening, Rosie sent a message to a man called Michael O'Doherty, the producer of *An Irish Breakfast*, promising a scoop, and they all promptly went to bed.

Michael, whose main guest of that morning was due to be a pet psychic, jumped at the chance, and at 6:45 a.m. a car came to the hotel to take Rosie to the studios of RTÉ. They stopped en route at a newsagent with a photocopier, stopped once again for Steve to be sick, dropped Amy off on a nondescript suburban street corner with her pockets filled with cash, and arrived at the studio with time to spare.

Steve is currently lying down in a darkened dressing room. Some people just can't handle twelve pints of Guinness. Rosie and Amy were fresh as daisies.

On the TV high on the wall of the makeup room, Rosie hears one of the hosts, Kellie, say, "And, coming up, one of our favorite guests is back. Rosie D'Antonio will be joining us on the sofa with a big announcement. And she needs *your* help."

Her co host, Ryan, casually handsome, like so many Irish men, moves on. "More on the shots fired at Dublin Airport early Monday morning. There are no confirmed casualties. Niall Clark has this report."

The floor manager reappears. "Okay, that's us. After this VT, can I get you into the studio?"

Rosie takes one last look at the screen, where a group of animated taxi drivers are being interviewed. She is led through a heavy metal door, into the air-lock space they always have in TV studios to let you know that you are leaving the world of reality and entering the world of television. The floor manager opens a second metal door, and Rosie finds herself in the *Irish Breakfast* studio. Niall Clark is finishing his report as the two hosts ignore the VT, heads down in their scripts.

On the screen a female taxi driver is saying, "I never saw anything," though Rosie notes that she has plastic sheeting taped across the space where her rear passenger window should be.

Kellie and Ryan look up as Rosie is seated next to them. They look thrilled to see her, as well they might, knowing they've been saved an interview with a man staring into the eyes of a dog and saying, "I feel like he's *lost* someone recently."

They whisper their happy "hellos" as the countdown for the end of the VT begins in the studio. Rosie checks herself on the studio monitor. Say what you like about her, she can hold her drink.

"Niall Clark reporting there," says Kellie. "Quite the mystery at Dublin Airport."

"And speaking of mystery," says Ryan. "She's sold over fifty million books—"

"Over sixty million," says Rosie.

"Over sixty million books," says Ryan. "Apologies. She's got through five husbands—am I right there?"

"The third one wasn't strictly legal," says Rosie. "So four and a half. But still looking for more, Ryan."

"And we always love having her on *An Irish Breakfast*. It's Rosie D'Antonio. Welcome to Ireland, Rosie."

"Thank you, Ryan," says Rosie. "You smell amazing, by the way."

Ryan gives a bashful gesture of dismissal.

"Now," says Kellie, "how are you enjoying Ireland?"

"Well," says Rosie. "I had twelve pints of Guinness yesterday."

"A woman after our own hearts," says Ryan. "And have you murder on your mind while you're here?"

"Honestly, yes, I do," says Rosie.

"But you have an announcement to make, I think?" says Kellie. "You're looking for some help?"

"I am," says Rosie. "And thank you for letting me use your viewers—"

"What, both of them?" says Ryan, with the laugh of a man who knows he has Ireland's biggest breakfast show. Rosie laughs too, because he really is very handsome.

"I was recently swimming on a lake in South Carolina, you see," starts Rosie, always at ease with stories. "A lovely warm day, I was wearing virtually nothing, can you imagine, Ryan?"

Ryan pretends to fan himself.

"And I got into trouble," says Rosie.

Kellie leans forward in concern. Ryan nods, sternly, in concern.

"There was a strong current," says Rosie. "And I'm not as young as I once was."

According to Wikipedia, she is actually five years younger than she was seven years ago. Rosie likes to think of herself as "age-fluid."

"Now, I've killed a lot of people over the years," says Rosie. "In my books. But I began to think, 'This is it for me.' You know?"

"How terrifying," says Kellie.

"But, then, as I started to go under, I felt two strong arms pull me up."

"Oh, it's like something from a book," says Kellie. "Like something you'd read."

"A man swam me to shallower waters," says Rosie, "and I thanked him for saving my life, and he just said, 'No problem, no problem.' I asked him what I could do for him—could I reward him? Did he live nearby, could I send him something?"

"I mean, you've sold over sixty million books," says Ryan.

"But he asked for nothing," says Rosie. "He just said, 'I'm here as a tourist.' He got out of the lake, took a round of applause, and disappeared."

"A hero," says Kellie. "An absolute hero. God bless his soul."

"I see," says Ryan. "Now where do we come in?"

"Well," says Rosie. "I told you he said, 'No problem, no problem.' But what I didn't tell you was that he said it in an Irish accent."

Kellie gasps. She is a great audience.

"I'd say specifically a Cork accent," says Rosie. "And so I'm here to find him, and to thank him for saving my life."

"Wonderful," says Ryan. "Can you describe him?"

"I can do better than that," says Rosie. "One of the onlookers took his photo, and I have it."

Kellie is being told something in her ear. "I think we can see it now."

On the screens in the studio, and on the screens of a million breakfasting Irish folk, appears the face of Eddie Flood. Steve had found it on a Facebook group for fans of Lambrettas.

"If you recognize him," says Rosie, "if you see him anywhere, particularly if you're in Cork, somewhere round there, there's an email address where you can contact my people. If you can tell me exactly where he is, there's a reward of twenty thousand euros."

"Twenty thousand euros if our viewers can spot him?"

Eddie's face fills the screen again. An email address appears underneath. Amy set it up last night.

"You have to email the moment you see him, and tell me exactly where he is. Maybe have your photo taken with him. I so want to thank him. Hug him for me too, all of you."

"What a wonderful story," says Ryan. "And what a wonderful opportunity for the people of Cork. Twenty thousand euros up for grabs if you can tell Rosie where this hero is."

"That goes for the police too," says Rosie. "Whoever spots him gets the money. I want everyone in Ireland keeping an eye out for this man, and telling me exactly where he is."

"Thank you, Rosie D'Antonio," says Ryan. "And hurry back. Now, a mystery in a sleepy Cork village. A local police officer tells pals he's won the lottery, and is found dead just days later. With th—"

Rosie is led off set. Steve has made his way out of the darkened dressing room and onto the studio floor.

"Did I do good?" Rosie asks.

"I'm afraid I had my head in a bucket," says Steve.

Rosie slaps him on the back. "Come on, soldier, we've got a helicopter to catch."

63

Eddie Flood knows the game is up. Time to ring Rob. He's already emailed over the footage of Rosie on *An Irish Breakfast*.

"Boss," says Eddie, as Rob picks up.

"Never seen anything like it," says Rob. "How's your morning been?"

"Busy," says Eddie. He hadn't had a clue what was going on. He was mobbed in the foyer, chased into his cab, followed to the airfield by three kids on motorbikes, photographed by his cabbie, by the airfield porter, by the helicopter pilot, and met by a crowd of around forty to fifty people at the small landing field outside Cork, all of whom had been alerted to his movements and keen to make a bit of money. "Popular show."

"How did she know you were there?"

"Took a shot at Amy Wheeler yesterday morning," says Eddie. "And didn't hit her."

"Christ, Eddie," says Rob. "You're supposed to be good at this. You used to be."

"Yeah," sighs Eddie. "She was in a Mercedes, tinted back window, so I didn't get a clear shot. And I didn't think she was going to jump out of a multistory car park."

"You're off the job," says Rob. "You understand?"

"Course," says Eddie. "Let you down. Let myself down."

"And your photo is everywhere," says Rob.

"Yeah," agrees Eddie. "Not good, not good. Understood."

"Keep the fifteen grand, Eddie," says Rob. "But that's the best I can do. And it's only because you're a mate."

"Thanks, boss," says Eddie. He was going to keep the fifteen grand anyway, whatever Rob had said. He has something he needs to spend it on.

"Now I've got to find somebody else to kill her," says Rob. Eddie is barely listening. He's thinking ahead. This latest development might actually be useful to him. "When a Navy SEAL and an East Ham hardman have already failed."

"Feel for you," says Eddie. "Why not try a Scandinavian? They don't muck about."

"If she doesn't die, I'm dead," says Rob. "Got to go, it's my putt."

Eddie clicks his phone off and wonders again who Rob is working for. It would be very useful to work it out, for obvious reasons. To be the one to fit that jigsaw together. That's information he could use to his advantage. But he's got his own ghost to worry about.

What to do right now is the big question. Rob is off his case—that's good. He's got fifteen grand to help him along—that's good too. How long does he need? Another week maybe? And until then, though, he needs to keep close to Amy Wheeler, because her next move will be his next move.

The back windscreen of the Mercedes hadn't been tinted. Eddie had had a clear head shot. He could have killed Amy Wheeler in a heartbeat. He'd had a clear shot at the taxi too. He shot and missed for two very good reasons.

Firstly, he needs Amy Wheeler to stay alive and, secondly, he needs to be noticed.

Staring at his own picture on the Sky News app on his laptop, captioned with "Who is this mystery hero?" Eddie would say it was mission accomplished.

He won't be able to get anywhere near them for now, but that's okay—gives him time to finish everything, make it perfect.

64

Henk has never drunk Irish wine before, but he is a firm believer in fitting in. Fitting in is the very best way to hide.

Left to his own devices, Henk would drink only milk, but, for reasons he cannot begin to understand, that seems to unnerve people.

With a little time to kill, he has tagged along with a tour group, currently being guided around Rockgrove Vineyard. It is terrifically interesting. As they walk between low rows of green vines, Henk spies the tree where Mark Gooch was found dead. He points at it and addresses the group.

"Ah, the tree where Mark Gooch was found dead."

This is met with the muted horror he has come to expect from other people. Civilians.

"You know," says Henk. "The influencer. They nailed him to it. Perhaps the holes are still there?"

Henk recognizes that sometimes he is simply *too* Dutch, but he never sees the need to leave a truth unsaid. The tour guide is hurriedly changing the subject.

"And the Bacchus grape, originally imported from Germany, is fast becoming a staple of Irish wine production."

The rest of the group are now keeping a discreet distance from Henk. They'd be keeping even more of a distance if they'd known he had a gun tucked into his waistband. Henk checks the updates on his phone. Amy Wheeler should be here in the next half hour or so. What will they do once they arrive? He supposes they will talk to the people he has already spoken to. The manager, the staff who were working there on the day Mark Gooch died. What will they discover? They will discover that Mark Gooch arrived in a taxi driven by a woman with long, red hair. They will discover that he was carrying a large leather holdall that was later nowhere to be seen, and they will discover that he was found by a local off-duty police officer, who happened to be wandering around the vineyard as dusk turned to night. They will discover what they already know. But then, when they sit down to lunch, they will discover something else. They will discover Henk van Veen with a gun, and with a piece of information that will unlock their puzzle once and for all. That Jeff Nolan is behind everything.

It is very good, thinks Henk, to be in the fresh air, with justice on one's mind. He wanders over to the tree. The holes have been filled in with wood glue, then painted over. You would have to look very closely to know that anything had happened at all.

Henk thinks this is most interesting, so shouts over to the rest of the tour party, "They have filled all the holes with wood glue! Really tremendous job!"

65

Steve had suggested that they should leave him behind in Dublin, but here he is, banking steeply in a small helicopter, buffeted by winds and with a keg of Guinness refusing to leave his belly. The pilot had told him, "If you're going to be sick, make sure we're over fields," and he has been vomit-bombing the beautiful green patchwork of Ireland with regularity since they took to the air.

Amy's phone rings. She looks at the name on the screen and answers. She speaks over the noise of the rotors.

"Adam. Yes. Yes, I know. I'm in a helicopter . . . No, a helicopter . . . Ireland . . . Ireland. The country . . . Bono. The Corrs . . . *The Corrs* . . . Yes, he's with me, he's throwing up . . . Guinness . . . Guinness . . . Well, now he does drink it. What did you get from Courtney? . . . Yep . . . Yep . . . Uh huh . . . yeah . . . you sure? . . . What are you having for dinner? . . . For dinner? . . . Yeah . . . yep . . . Not much . . . someone tried to shoot me . . . shoot me . . . *shoot me* . . . yeah, yeah, he missed . . . he missed . . . shall we talk when I'm not in a helicopter? . . . I miss you . . . miss you . . . No, I miss you, Adam . . . I mi— . . . Doesn't matter, talk later."

"That's literally the most romantic I've ever heard you," shouts Rosie.

"Whenever I get shot at, I miss him," Amy shouts back. "Steve, you must be out of vomit by now."

Steve nods, and tries to sit up straight. "This poor country. So Adam saw Courtney Lewis?"

"He went to see her," shouts Amy. "But he didn't see her."

"He shouldn't have taken no for an answer," says Rosie.

"He didn't," says Amy. "She's dead."

"She's what?" Steve asks.

Amy shouts into his ear, "She's dead. They found her in her cell the day before."

The pilot turns to them. "Beginning descent. No more vomiting."

Steve gives him a weak thumbs-up.

"How did she die?" Rosie asks.

"They wouldn't tell him," says Amy.

"Did they know Adam was going to see her?" asks Steve.

"Of course," says Amy. "Believe it or not, you have to make an appointment to visit someone in a Dubai prison."

"So," says Steve, "we find out about Courtney Lewis from Felicity Woollaston, and the next moment she's dead?"

The vineyard is rising up to meet them, green on green, an impossible beauty.

"You need to ring Tony Taylor," says Amy. "Get more details. We need to know exactly what Felicity Woollaston knows."

"And who she's told," says Rosie.

The helicopter reaches solid ground. Steve closes his eyes in silent thanks.

"Hope you enjoyed your first helicopter trip?" the pilot asks him.

"Please apologize to the Irish countryside from me. Are people sick all the time in helicopters?"

"Happens a lot," says the pilot. "But you're my new record holder."

Steve looks over at Rosie. "You're not hungover? Not queasy?"

Rosie shakes her head. "I've kept myself topped up since 1978."

They exit the helicopter, Steve ducking below the slowing blades, Amy and Rosie walking tall, confident of the five-foot gap between their heads and the rotors.

"Ring Tony," Amy tells Steve.

Steve does as he is told, and Tony Taylor answers on the third ring.

"Steven Wheeler," says Tony. "Late of this parish. How might I help you?"

"You sound chipper," says Steve.

"Walking through the forest with Felicity," says Tony.

"We've got bad news for her," says Steve. "Her client, Courtney Lewis. She's dead."

"One second," says Tony.

Tony puts his finger over the microphone, so Steve only hears a muffled chat. Tony and Felicity, eh? Seems to be going well. The line clears again.

"She's never heard of her," says Tony.

"Courtney Lewis?"

"Never heard of her," says Tony.

"But you told us about her," says Steve. "So how did you hear about her? It's literally impossible that anyone else in Axley would know the connection."

"You're the detective, mate," says Tony. "Felicity says hi, by the way. She was eating an ice cream, and she got some on her nose. Honestly, it's the cutest thing you've ever seen."

Steve hears Felicity giggle. Actually giggle. My God, love is a wonderful, but also sickening, thing.

"Listen," says Steve. "Say hi back from me, and enjoy yourself."

"Aye, aye, captain," says Tony. "Over and out."

Steve hears Felicity giggle again. Bit much now. He puts his phone back in his pocket. Amy and Rosie are waiting for his news.

"The information didn't come from Tony; he swears to it. And Felicity says she's never heard of Courtney Lewis."

"So?" Rosie's question hangs in the air.

"So, listen," says Steve. "Perhaps someone else in Axley just happened to have that information? Just happened to be in the pub and mention it?"

"Or?" says Amy, knowing Steve well enough to not finish the sentence.

"Or Felicity Woollaston is lying to Tony."

"And lying to us," says Amy.

Is Felicity Woollaston lying to them? How much does Tony really know about her?

"Well, while you work your way through that, let's interview someone about a man nailed to a tree," says Rosie, walking toward the winery. She looks back at them, over her shoulder. "And I wouldn't say no to a drink."

66

Max Highfield is so furious, he can barely enjoy the Emirates First Class Lounge. Where is his bodyguard? They had a deal. Max takes his business to Henk; Henk hires the best bodyguard he has for him. So why is he sitting here alone? Why did he just have to get his own salad? Why is the bodyguard meeting him in Dubai and not here?

A nervous-looking teenager approaches him. "Are you Max Highfield?"

Well, well, well, here we go. This is what happens. *Are you Max Highfield?* Take a wild guess, kid. Who else looks like this? Who else is wearing a custom-made Gucci knitted tank top in First Class? Max raises his sunglasses to confirm that it is indeed him. And then motions to his salad to let the teenager know it is rude to approach someone when they're eating. Good to learn that lesson young.

"*Titans of War* is my favorite film," says the teenager, not picking up on Max's salad cue. "It's so good."

"They underused me in that," says Max. Could this kid have picked a more annoying film? Why doesn't anyone mention *The Rose of Sarasota?* "I was like, I don't just do action, you know?"

The teenager nods uncertainly. "Yeah, I liked it when you kicked that man off that spaceship."

How does a teenager get into the Emirates First Class Lounge anyway? If Max was actually paying for his ticket, he'd be even more angry. The Diamond Conference people are paying. Max is hosting, and two writers called Shaun and Christine have written a few jokes for him. "It's the only ceremony with more carats than the British Vegetarian Awards." That one is a pun about "carats," as in diamonds, sounding the same as "carrots," as in vegetables. They had explained it, and guaranteed it would work.

The teenager is still staring at him. Max puts his sunglasses back on, and starts to eat his salad.

"Could I get a photograph?" asks the teenager.

This is why Max will never forgive Henk. He's on his own here. Henk should have someone with him 24/7, except when Max doesn't want someone with him. But here he is, defenseless.

"Sure," says Max. The youngster takes out his phone. He's trembling, which is something at least, a mark of respect. The boy gives a shy smile, and Max gives a tough-guy scowl. He is lucky in that people prefer it when he scowls. He knows some actors who have to smile when they meet members of the public, and it kills them.

"Thank you," says the kid. He's not a bad kid, but this is not something Max should be dealing with alone. Max nods to him and goes back to his kale. The kid runs back excitedly to his parents. The dad gives Max a thumbs-up. Another invasion of privacy. Can't a man just kick back in his lime-green tank top and get a bit of peace?

Max rings Henk.

One of the lounge staff approaches. "Sorry, sir, no calls in the lounge."

"I know," says Max. "But I'm Max Highfield."

The woman has no answer to this.

Henk isn't answering. You wouldn't get this from Jeff Nolan. Jeff would see his name and pick up. Middle of the night, whenever. Perhaps it's not going to work out with Henk after all? But Max has burned all his bridges by now.

Max will see how the Dubai bodyguard goes. He's taking a keener interest these days. Previously Max had had bodyguards only because everyone else had them, and he didn't want to feel less important than, say, Ben

Affleck. But now, since the messages have started, the death threats, he feels he might actually need one.

The last one read:

I know what you did. And you won't get away with it. RIP.

What has he got himself mixed up in?

Not that he would admit this to Henk, or to Jeff, or to his therapist. But somebody has his number, in more ways than one.

In *The Rose of Sarasota* Max plays a soldier back from Vietnam, or possibly Korea, but Max can't see what an American soldier would have been doing in Korea, so probably Vietnam. He has an illness; in the script it was cancer, but Max didn't think that was glamorous enough, so in the end they left it vague. He remembers the key was it had to be an illness that wouldn't cause him to lose weight, because he was filming *Hercules versus Poseidon* straight afterward. So he had this illness, and he was in a hospice, coughing, etc., telling old women he loved them, and he really thought, this is it, this is the Oscar, but no. The movie industry buried it—politics again—and it wasn't even on Netflix last time Max looked (which was yesterday; he will check again this evening). The only country where it did good numbers was China, and that, Max later discovered, was because they edited in lots of clips of Max from a Second World War film he'd shot, and pretended they were flashbacks.

You do have to take the rough with the smooth, but Max had been very angry that *The Rose of Sarasota* hadn't been a hit. Very angry and, just sometimes, when he woke in the middle of the night, very sad too.

Max doesn't think about death all that much. Death to him is dummy guns and blood-spatter packs, and stuntmen falling onto crash mats. But he thought about death when he was filming *The Rose of Sarasota*.

And, in the brutal, lonely luxury of the Emirates First Class Lounge, he is thinking about death once again.

67

I had to come and see you," says Henk. "Because you wouldn't return my calls."

Henk had been waiting for them in the private dining room of the Rockgrove Vineyard. Amy should have known. They had just shaken Eddie off their tail, and now this.

"I wish to inform you that I have a gun," says Henk.

"You're not going to shoot me here, Henk," says Amy. "So stop showing off."

"Why would you want to kill Amy?" asks Rosie, sitting down. "I'm Rosie D'Antonio."

"It is my great pleasure, Ms. D'Antonio," says Henk. "I know many people enjoy your books, and surely they can't all be wrong?"

"I might put that on my next front cover," says Rosie.

"Steve Wheeler," says Steve, shaking Henk's hand. "Father-in-law."

"Ah, the mystery man," says Henk. "I hope I haven't frightened you, Mr. Wheeler? You look pale?"

Steve waves this away and sits down.

"You're here to kill me, Henk?" says Amy.

"Goodness, no," says Henk, laughing at the very thought.

Amy isn't laughing. "Then why do you have a gun?"

"To protect myself from you, and to deliver you to the relevant authorities," says Henk. "I thought that would be obvious?"

"You think Amy has something to do with the murders?" Steve asks.

Henk nods. "Mmm hmm. I trust you visited the tree, as I did?"

Steve looks out of the window toward the tree. "They've done a lovely job with that wood glue."

"Is that the first time you've seen that tree, Amy?" Henk asks.

Amy looks at him and nods.

"Haven't nailed anyone to it?" asks Henk. "In recent memory?"

"No," says Amy. "Same question to you."

"No, dear me, no," says Henk. "Why would you think I was involved? You must know quite the opposite to be true?"

Amy thinks about Jeff's warning: don't trust Henk.

"I know you split with Jeff, and then Jeff's clients started dying."

"And we know you've been very keen to track Amy down," says Steve.

"Well, of course," says Henk. "I'm trying to solve the murders and Amy is my chief suspect."

"I'm your chief suspect?"

"You're my only suspect, I would say." Henk smiles. "That's why I have a gun. Jeff was working with François Loubet. You all know that, surely? He took him on as a client, Jeff was able to have direct contact with him, and Jeff was able to know the whereabouts of all clients at all times."

Amy shakes her head. Jeff can't be Joe Blow. "Come on, the two of you were best friends."

"That's why I left Maximum Impact Solutions," says Henk. "When our clients started to get arrested. It wasn't difficult to fathom what was happening. And the information Loubet needed for his scheme could only have come from myself or Jeff. And it didn't come from me."

"Other people had access to those files," says Steve. "Susan Knox?"

Henk shakes his head and pulls an envelope from a briefcase set down by his chair.

"You have proof it's Jeff in that little envelope of yours?" Rosie asks.

"Firstly, it is not a little envelope, it is an A4," says Henk.

"Apologies," says Rosie, raising her glass to him.

"And, secondly, yes," says Henk. "I have proof in this normal-sized envelope. The master client files from Maximum Impact. They show that the following five people—Jackson Lynch, Courtney Lewis, Mark Gooch, Bella Sanchez, and Andrew Fairbanks—were all recruited to the company personally by Jeff Nolan."

"All of them?" asks Amy.

"All of them," confirms Henk. "And every single other client who has been on an assignment for Vivid Viral Media—there are thirty-five in all—was recruited by Jeff."

"Oh, that looks bad," says Rosie.

It does look bad. But Steve is thinking about something else. About who else would have known about Courtney Lewis being in that Dubai prison cell.

"So Jeff was running an international money-smuggling operation with François Loubet?" says Amy, combatively. "That's your big theory?"

"Yes," says Henk. "Jeff was working with François Loubet, the world's most successful money-smuggler. I will stake my entire reputation on that. And you were his soldier. I don't know why you both had to kill those people—you will have had your reasons—but I believe that you did."

There is silence around the table. Broken by Steve.

"I'm just thinking about the pub quiz," says Steve. "Tomorrow night at The Brass Monkey. The four of us are going."

Rosie laughs.

"No one is to kill anyone for the next twenty-four hours," says Steve. "That's all I ask, and Henk, I need to take a look at those files, please."

"Don't bother shredding them," says Henk. "I have copies."

"Time to go home," says Steve. "There's someone I need you all to meet."

68

ChatGPT, rewrite in the style of a friendly English gentleman, please.

I had a tremendous laugh, I must say, at Rob Kenna's latest tale. His hitman outwitted by Rosie D'Antonio, the famous writer and also attractive woman. Just because business is serious doesn't mean you can't enjoy it from time to time—that is another lesson for you.

We all like a good chuckle, so I suspect Rob was hoping I might be understanding, but I am not.

In truth, he has lost my confidence. Enough is enough. I have decided that, though it ill behooves me to so do, I must now also involve the police. I shall ensure they are aware of Amy Wheeler's blood being found at all three scenes. What a careless ninny she has been!

If Amy Wheeler doesn't die within the next forty-eight hours, she will most certainly be arrested!

Dead would be best, but one mustn't get too greedy.

In better news, I have a shipment leaving London for São Paulo in two days' time. And I don't need Joe Blow this time. It has been booked directly through Vivid Viral.

Praise be to the heavens, commerce stops for no man!

69

Bonnie Gregor is doing some packing. Her mum is overseeing the operation, and her kids, Mimi and Maxie, are doing their best to help.

Bonnie knows what to pack. She has watched an awful lot of influencers online in the last few days. She used to do this for fun, but now she is doing it for research.

She packs a selection of bikinis.

"They won't expect that of you, surely?" says her mum, Lois. "Who advertises paint in a bikini?"

"Influencers do, Mum," says Bonnie, with the sigh of someone who knows more than a parent. She has lost a bit of weight in the past few days, but she still wouldn't describe herself as "beach body ready."

"Flencers do," parrots Mimi, currently attempting a cartwheel on the bed.

Bonnie has already packed indoor clothes and outdoor clothes. She has packed jumpers for the evening, a nice dress from M&S for smart, and she has packed shoes for every occasion.

"You won't get any more in there," says Lois. "The zip'll go."

Mimi crashes to the floor. Maxie puts her arms around her sister.

"I'm going to have to," says Bonnie. "I haven't even started on my bits and bobs yet."

They won't be photographing her in her underwear, she's fairly certain of that, but you have to be the full package.

"Take another case," says Lois. "We've got an old one of your dad's in the loft. I'll fetch it down."

"Can I help?" asks Maxie.

"Can't take another case," says Bonnie, trying to choose between two identical black blouses, before packing them both. She wonders if anyone else sweats when they are packing.

"Go over your lines again," Lois says. Her mum is as excited as she is. Bonnie knows her mum has always been proud of her, and she knows that not all mums are proud of their daughters. But, even so. Bonnie is so happy to see her mum so happy. Bonnie gets it. If one of her children suddenly got the job of their dreams, her heart would burst. As she watches Mimi and Maxie play dress-up with one of her bras, she wonders what it is they might end up doing.

"They haven't given me my lines yet," says Bonnie to Lois, wondering if she needs eight pairs of shoes, and deciding that she does. "I think I have to make them up."

"Well, you're very good at that," says Lois. "I couldn't do it. I wouldn't know what to say. You've always been a talker, though—that yellow top won't go with anything—always chattering away, I don't know where you get it from, on my life I don't—I like that blouse, make sure the iron's not too hot in the hotel, use it on a towel, test it out. Maxie, that doesn't go up your nose, darling. They'll have an iron in the hotel, won't they? It'll be that sort of hotel, won't it? Iron, en suite, minibar, the works. What's the name? I'll look it up."

"They haven't told me my hotel yet," says Bonnie. "Maxie, not up Mimi's nose either. They're meeting me off the plane and driving me."

Bonnie wishes they would tell her the name of the hotel. She'd like to look at everything before she goes. Look at the rooms, see if there's a restaurant, see if there's room service. She can just imagine that, having breakfast delivered. Maxie and Mimi brought her breakfast in bed on Mother's Day: a packet of custard creams and a flower Maxie had kept in her pocket. So, yes, it would be nice to have the name of the hotel, but perhaps influencers are a bit cooler about that sort of thing.

"I've got all sorts planned with the kids," says Lois. "We're going to visit Graham—"

"Yes, Graham!" shouts Maxie.

"Graham!" repeats Mimi.

"You know, Graham from the club, he's got an allotment and he says the kids can do some digging. I've bought them some stickers too. There's a mark on the back of those jeans. We'll have a whale of a time."

"We see a whale!" squeals Maxie.

Bonnie is now resorting to sitting on the clothes in her case.

"And you don't need to ring every day," says Lois. "If you're busy. I know you'll be rushing around doing your influencing."

"We can all go on holiday when I get back," says Bonnie. She's never been able to say anything like that before. She's heard people say it on TV, and now it's her turn. "Me, you, the kids. Wherever you fancy. France, Florida."

"The moon," suggests Maxie.

Bonnie really has a lot to thank that Felicity Woollaston for. She clearly believed in her. Bonnie had thought of sending Felicity an email, thanking her. But she doesn't want to seem uncool. Felicity does these deals all the time, and Bonnie is keen to fit in, to take all this in her stride. She will send Felicity a thank-you afterward. Maybe take her to lunch when she's back from the trip? Is that uncool too?

"I don't need a holiday," says Lois. "You enjoy the money, you've earned it. Spoil the kids. You're really not getting anything more in that case. I'm fetching the old one."

"I can't take another case," says Bonnie.

The kids zoom out of the room in search of a whale.

"You can take two cases," says Lois.

"I'm already taking another case," says Bonnie.

"What other case?"

"It's part of the job," says Bonnie. "You've watched 'unboxing' videos?"

Lois shakes her head.

"Opening something on camera, like a new product, a surprise, and then you can record your reactions. So it's real."

"And you're going to do that with paint?"

"Organic paint, Mum," says Bonnie. "They've got a new product. They want me to take it with me, and then open it on camera. They're sending it to me today."

"No way you won't take a peek first," says Lois. "You know what you're like at Christmas."

"It's got a lock," says Bonnie. "I get the combination on camera, and then open it up."

"And people watch that?" Lois asks.

"It's very popular," says Bonnie. She's just watched a makeup influencer from Austria open a box of concealer up an Alp.

Lois goes into the pose and voice of a customs officer. "Excuse me, madam, did you pack this bag yourself?"

Bonnie and Lois laugh together. Her mum hasn't had the easiest time of it lately—who has?—and it's lovely to see her dancing eyes. Honestly, this whole thing is a dream. Who knew that things like this could happen to people like her?

Whether it's uncool or not, Bonnie decides she will take Felicity out for lunch the moment she gets back.

70

Killing someone in a prison is very easy. Even in a Dubai prison. The place is full of murderers who will do anything for money. And that's before you even get to the prisoners.

But why had Rob been hired to kill Courtney Lewis in the first place? A girl from Essex, caught with a bag of money. Loubet's money, no doubt. So is Loubet panicking? And, if Loubet is panicking, should Rob be panicking? Rob thinks again about the layers he has built around himself. The layers of expendable people who protect him.

It occurs to him now, probably later than it should, that he is one of Loubet's expendable layers.

Perhaps they need to meet, finally? How would Rob go about that?

The more immediate question, of course, is who might Loubet be worried about? Who is getting too close for comfort?

It must be Amy Wheeler, no? She's bang in the middle of it. What if she's figured it all out? Rosie D'Antonio is smart too—she writes books, doesn't she? And the old guy Amy is with? The father-in-law, Eddie reckons. Ex-cop, for what that's worth. What if they've put their heads together? What if they're headed to Dubai and that's why Loubet wanted Courtney Lewis killed?

With Eddie out of the picture, and things getting closer to home, Rob thinks it might be time to break the habit of a lifetime and kill Amy Wheeler himself. No one else seems capable.

Mickey Moody comes back with two pints. "You look stressed."

Maybe Mickey could do it? Or help at least? Keep an eye out for Amy Wheeler arriving in Dubai?

Rob picks up his pint. "Work."

Mickey laughs. "Why do you all work? I don't get it."

"I like it, Mickey," says Rob.

"You like the stress?"

"I like to be busy," says Rob. "You fancy a job, by the way?"

"A job?" Mickey Moody laughs. "Listen, you know I never ask what any of you boys do for a living. But I know I don't want to be a part of it. No offense. I just enjoy the golf."

"It'd only be sitting at the airport for a day or two," says Rob. "Keeping an eye out for someone."

Mickey shakes his head. "Not for all the money in the world."

"Thirty grand," says Rob. "A hundred if you're interested in something more serious?"

Mickey looks at him. "There's a different way of living, you know?"

Rob smiles into his pint. A different way of living? Too late for all that. "Sorry, Mickey, I shouldn't have asked."

"That's okay, son," says Mickey. "Nice to know someone doesn't think I'm useless."

"You're a useless putter," says Rob, and Mickey clinks his glass against Rob's.

There is something admirable about people like Mickey, Rob supposes. Rob's got a few old friends who never got tempted. Who kept their souls safe and raised families and lived in small houses in small towns. Then there're others, like Eddie, who've skirted around the business, poking their heads up every time they needed a payday. But Rob is in it for life. Death is his life. Death is what he is good at.

So no panicking. There might be three people on his trail, but he has an advantage.

Ordinarily, tracking someone like Amy Wheeler would be an enormous headache, with favors called in all over the place—police officers bribed, all at some cost. But Amy has chosen to travel with one of the most famous women in the world, and that makes Rob's job an awful lot easier. He has alerts set up on all the big social media sites. If anyone posts an excited selfie with Rosie D'Antonio anywhere in the world, he will hear about it.

Perhaps it will be Dubai; perhaps it will be somewhere else. It doesn't really matter, because the moment he sees a selfie Rob will go into action himself. Needs must, and murder's not so difficult. Wear gloves, and don't drive the getaway car too fast.

Perhaps he should kill the father-in-law too? Better safe than sorry.

So, no, Rob won't lose any sleep over Amy Wheeler just yet.

Will he lose sleep over François Loubet? Perhaps a little, but Rob has never needed a lot of sleep. He's like Maggie Thatcher in that regard.

And, besides, when you're in the business of death, it comes with the territory.

71

This time Steve doesn't duck when he gets out of the helicopter. You don't need to show Steve anything twice.

Had it only been five days since he'd last been at this house? Confronting Gary Gough about his daughter's behavior. He sees Gary Gough approach the helicopter. Steve extends his hand.

"Sorry, Gary, needed somewhere quiet to land, and didn't know who else to ask."

"No problem," says Gary. "Not everyone with a helipad doesn't mind breaking the law."

"Everyone with a helipad is a crook," says Rosie, also shaking Gary's hand. "I'm Rosie."

"Welcome to the New Forest," says Gary. "I'm a legitimate businessman."

"Amy," says Amy, sizing up Gary. "I hear you used to smuggle cocaine on submarines?"

Gary shrugs, and turns to Steve. "What's this all about? Looks super-dodgy. Any way I can get involved?"

"I am Henk," says Henk, bringing up the rear. "I am Dutch."

"I can believe that," says Gary, shaking Henk's hand.

"Someone was trying to kill Rosie," says Steve. "And now someone's trying to kill Amy."

Gary gives a "fair enough" expression. "You know, when I see an ex-cop, a celebrity, a bodyguard, and a Dutch guy, I smell money."

"Well, I smell danger," says Henk. "So if they find me dead, tell the police that these three did it."

"I haven't said anything except 'No comment' to a police officer in over thirty years," says Gary.

"Yes, of course," says Henk. "In which case, just avenge my death."

Gary leads them toward the house. On a large patio, in the far distance, Steve sees Lauren Gough, the schoolgirl extortionist, playing with a friend. They are laughing at videos on the friend's phone. To his great surprise Steve sees that the friend is Mollie Bright. The girls haven't spotted this unusual new gang. Helicopters must be a familiar sight here. Steve looks at Gary, and motions toward the girls in surprise.

"You were right," says Gary. "Your little lecture. When I grew up I had to fight. No one gave me anything. I had to scrap for it."

"Oh, boohoo," says Amy.

"But Lauren's got everything, and she still fights," says Gary. "Which made her a bully. We've been chatting. She wants to be a vet, but she never told me."

"High suicide rate, vets," says Rosie.

"I made her apologize to Mollie," says Gary. "They hugged, and they haven't been off YouTube since."

Steve nods. They are now walking around the side of the house, and Steve sees the large gravel turning circle at the front of the house.

"Where are you headed?" Gary asks. "You all right for a lift?"

"Tony Taylor's coming to pick us up," says Steve. "He's just retuned a school minibus."

"I'm not getting in a minibus," says Rosie. "No disrespect to anyone."

"I've got a Range Rover," says Gary, pointing to his Range Rover.

"Thank you kindly," says Rosie, and walks to the Range Rover. "Did you really used to smuggle cocaine in submarines?"

"No," says Gary. "Submersibles."

Gary opens one of the back doors of his car for Rosie, but she stays still, until he shuts it and opens the driver's door instead. Tony Taylor's minibus approaches.

Rosie gets into the driver's seat of the Range Rover. "So I shall see you all in Axley this evening?"

Steve nods. "The Brass Monkey, seven thirty. First question at eight."

Tony's minibus pulls up, with the unnecessary flourish of a wheelspin. There is a woman in her early seventies in the passenger seat. She exits the minibus, as Tony walks around from the driver's side. She is positively glowing.

"You must be Felicity," says Steve. "A pleasure to meet you."

"And you," says Felicity. "Thank you for letting me use your home. I've tidied your cupboards for you."

"Much obliged," says Steve. "By and large I never open them."

"And, by the way," says Felicity, "I love Trouble."

Steve smiles. "Talking of trouble . . ."

Tony gives Steve a big hug, then gives Amy a big hug, and then stops in front of Henk, who has his arm outstretched.

"I am Henk."

"And I'm Tony Taylor. And I believe you're sleeping on my sofa this evening. I've washed the cushion covers."

"*I've* washed the cushion covers," says Felicity.

"I didn't even know you could," says Tony, turning back to Steve. "What's the big plan?"

"All will be revealed at the pub quiz," says Steve, feeling truly relaxed for the first time in a week. "But, first, I have a cat to see."

As Steve opens the minibus door, he sees Lauren Gough leap down the steps from the front door of Gary Gough's house. She makes a beeline for the Range Rover.

"You're Rosie D'Antonio," Lauren says to Rosie.

"Accept no substitute," says Rosie.

"You're famous," says Lauren.

"I try," agrees Rosie.

Lauren looks down for a moment, nervous. She looks at her dad, then back at Rosie.

"Can I get a selfie?"

Rosie smiles. Ever the pro.

72

Eddie had a decision to make. Amy, Rosie, and Steve had flown to England; a little bribe at the airfield was enough to tell him that. They'd landed somewhere in the New Forest. Eddie had looked up the New Forest on the map. Lot of trees—the clue was in the name.

So Eddie has headed over too, just to keep an eye on everything.

And no need to tell Rob Kenna this time. Amy Wheeler was someone else's problem now, so Eddie could concentrate on the job at hand.

He's still got most of Rob's fifteen grand, so he booked himself into a hotel called The Pig. It's the perfect place to hole up for a couple of days, and to do what needs to be done. It's quiet, great food, lovely staff, private. You can see deer out of your window in the morning.

Is Eddie ready? He's still not sure. It has to be exactly right before he makes his move. He's only going to get one shot. But he still needs the answer to this final tricky question: can you shoot somebody through a pane of glass in a high building? Would it deflect the bullet? If you *can*, he is all set.

Eddie heads down to the hotel dining room. It is a relief, after Ireland, not to be mobbed. Perhaps this will be the final stop on the impromptu world tour he finds himself on. That would be nice. He could handle staying here until the deed is done. There's even an herb garden.

As Eddie reaches the third step from the bottom of the staircase, he has a view into the restaurant. It's classy but also cozy—that's a nice combination. He's already read the menu, of course he has, he's only human, and is looking forward to the fish and chips. The fish has been caught locally, and the potatoes grown locally. As for the batter, that's anyone's guess.

There is sunlight pouring into the room, and, before Eddie reaches the bottom step, he sees it glint off a ruby-and-emerald brooch of a crouching tiger. There, at a window table, is Rosie D'Antonio, talking to an older guy. The guy is wearing a waxed Barbour jacket and purple cords. You saw that a lot with people who've had to wear suits all their lives. No idea how to dress without one.

Eddie backs up the stairs one by one, making no sound. An elderly couple walks past him on the stairs, and he gives them a gentle wave.

So Rosie D'Antonio is in the hotel? Perhaps she's staying here? That would make things even easier.

Time for Eddie to get room service, and finalize his plan.

73

I'm sorry," says Derek Charters. "I didn't realize we were dressing up."

Rosie laughs. "This isn't me dressing up. And you suit purple cords. I'm sorry to get straight down to business, but did you take a look at everything Steve sent you?"

"Steve, is it?" says Derek. "New man of yours, I suppose?"

"No," says Rosie. "Not for want of trying, though. This New Forest trout is delicious by the way. When did England learn to do food?"

"Nineties," says Derek. "I took a look, and Vivid Viral Media seems to be up-front."

"Up-front?" Rosie is surprised by this.

"They're an agency," says Derek. "Long established, changed course recently, but that's business, isn't it? It seems that this Felicity Woollaston spotted a gap in the market. Social media influencers. Huge sums of money flying around. There's a hundred and fifty thousand pounds, for example, to a man called Mark Gooch, two hundred thousand to a man named Jackson Lynch. It's big business."

"But not dodgy?" asks Rosie. "As far as you can tell?"

"It's a real company," says Derek Charters, "with a real history. But there is a question I would be asking if I thought this company was being used to launder money."

"What might that question be?" Rosie asks.

"Why did they choose this particular company?" Derek says. "Why did the cuckoo choose this particular nest? It won't have been at random; that's far too dangerous."

"So somebody must already have had a connection with Felicity Woollaston?" says Rosie.

"I'd say so," says Derek. "That's business. Did I ever tell you about the time I bought an Estonian bank?"

"Let's say yes, so I don't have to hear about it," says Rosie. "How's Carol, by the way?"

"Oh, she's right as rain," says Derek. "Living in Jamaica with a ski instructor."

"In Jamaica with a ski instructor?"

Derek shrugs.

"Carol's stories were always better than yours," says Rosie.

"Why the interest in Vivid Viral?" asks Derek. "Anything I can make some money out of?"

"Ever the investment banker, Derek," says Rosie. "Murders. They're trying to kill a good friend of mine."

"Murders are your specialty," says Derek. "No one is trying to kill you, though, I hope?"

"Well, funnily enough, someone was," says Rosie. "A Russian billionaire. I don't suppose you're a hitman?"

"With my arthritis?" says Derek.

Rosie laughs. It's funny, across a lifetime, the people you pick up. It's often the most unexpected ones who stick around. There are friendships forged in fire, which end up disappearing like smoke, and other casual, nodding friendships, which will stay with you for the rest of your life.

From the corner of her eye, Rosie catches a movement. It's on the staircase in the hallway and looks an awful lot like a tracksuit bottom moving slowly up the stairs.

Eddie Flood? How has he managed to follow them again? Here's a guy who doesn't give up.

She will have to tell Amy immediately, of course, but a further, troubling, thought occurs to Rosie.

Of all the places to stay, why is Eddie here?

What if Vasiliy Karpin hasn't given up on her? Jeff Nolan was supposed to be brokering a deal with him, but Jeff Nolan is very missing, presumed very dead.

Has Rosie taken her eye off the ball? What if Eddie had been hired to kill *her* all along? Shooting at Amy was just to get her out of the way?

"Can I top you up?" asks Derek, tipping the wine bottle toward her.

Rosie puts her hand over the top of her glass. "I'm going to stick to water, I think."

"Rosie D'Antonio and water," says Derek. "Goes together like ski instructors and Jamaica."

Rosie musters a smile. On the staircase, Eddie has disappeared. But she knows he will be here for a reason.

She needs to focus a little.

Because, while Rosie is busy protecting Amy, is anybody busy protecting her?

74

Amy and Steve are waiting outside The Brass Monkey.

Amy has to admit it has a certain charm. The white portico and thick oak door are garlanded with red and yellow flowers. Amy doesn't know what kind of flowers they are. All flowers are roughly the same, aren't they, apart from the colors? The summer air is slowing everything and everyone. Ponies chew on hanging baskets with a leisurely concentration, while human beings vape and gossip all around them. There is a burst of amber light and laughter each time the door opens.

"Happy to be back?" Amy asks.

Steve nods.

"Ever going to leave again?"

"Shouldn't have thought so," says Steve.

"Do we really have to do the quiz?" asks Amy.

"You'll see," says Steve. "What's the point of vaping? Do you know?"

"No idea," says Amy. "What flowers are these?"

"No idea," says Steve.

"I've missed these chats," says Amy, and Steve laughs. It's true, though. Amy likes to hear about New Forest roadworks and missing postmen. She likes to hear about the normality of life, though she has no interest in living it.

Rosie is the first teammate to appear, carrying an overnight bag. Amy looks at her quizzically.

"Something wrong with The Pig?" she asks.

"It's almost perfect," says Rosie, putting down her bag by the picnic bench. "Food great, terrific barman, soft beds, the views, honestly, all you could ask for. If I have one gripe, it's that there's a hitman there."

Rosie sits.

"Not Eddie?" Amy asks.

"Persistent little bugger," says Rosie. "Staying on that subject, I wonder if we know whether Vasiliy Karpin is still trying to kill me? You seem to have forgotten him in all the excitement."

"Uh—" starts Amy.

"Sorry to be all 'me, me, me,'" says Rosie.

"Jeff was handling it," says Amy.

"Jeff was handling it," repeats Rosie. "That's good, that's put my mind at rest. Dead Jeff will protect me. The guy in the BMW full of bullet holes has got my back."

"*BMW Full of Bullet Holes* is a good name for a b—"

"Not now, Stevie," says Rosie.

"Whether Eddie is here to kill you, or me, we should probably go inside," says Amy. Rosie is right, though. Amy *should* be thinking about Vasiliy Karpin. He's still out there somewhere, and still, presumably, gunning for her client. "Client"? Funny to think how quickly Rosie turned from being her "client" to being something quite different. A friend? It's not *quite* that. When Amy has more time on her hands, she will work out just what sort of relationship she and this woman old enough to be her grandmother have developed.

"You ever have a drive-by shooting in Axley?" Rosie asks Steve.

"Someone crashed a moped into a bollard once," says Steve. "But that's the worst we've had. Are you ready to quiz?"

"No, of course not," says Rosie. "Before I go in, I need to know exactly who's there, exactly what's going to happen, and exactly how early I can leave."

"My normal quiz team will be there," says Steve. "John and Jyoti. They don't know we're coming, so my replacement, Martin, the loss-adjuster from Lymington, will be there, and apart from that it's just us."

There is an approaching voice. "What a time I have had of it this afternoon. Is there a sight more beguiling, I wonder, than an English churchyard? 'The paths of glory lead but to the grave.' That is your Thomas Gray, I believe. You will correct me if I'm wrong, but I do believe it is Gray?"

"And Henk," says Steve. "Hello, Henk. You fancy a pint?"

"When in Rome," says Henk. He looks at the flowers climbing across the entrance to the pub. "Ah, crocosmia, beautiful. You know they are South African originally?"

"Okay, Henk can be on our team too," says Steve. "We all set?"

"Steve, I implore you to tell us what is going on," says Henk. "I implore you."

"Through this door," says Steve, and leads his motley team into the pub.

Amy has been in The Brass Monkey a few times before—Christmas, Debbie's birthday one year. Tonight it is rammed, the quiz being the weekly highlight of the Axley social calendar. Every table is filled with men in short-sleeved shirts and women in floral blouses, doing the pre-hunch of teams agreeing on names. At a table in the far corner, Amy sees Jyoti half stand and raise her arm to grab their attention. John is setting down three drinks on their table and the loss-adjuster, Martin, sits with his back to them.

Steve snakes his way through the tables toward his friends. Just before Steve reaches the table, Amy finally understands why they are there. If she were the sort of person to gasp, she would gasp.

Martin turns, a handsome black guy in a cloth cap. His salt-and-pepper beard not hiding for one moment that Martin from Lymington is, as alive as you like, Jeff Nolan.

"You look well, Jeff," says Steve. "Considering."

Jeff gives an impressed smile. "You found me?"

Steve smiles back. "Who else would have dropped the information about Courtney Lewis into a Brass Monkey lock-in?"

"Couldn't think of any other way to get in touch," says Jeff.

"Who's Jeff?" asks Jyoti. "Hello, Steve!"

If Jeff is surprised to see Steve, he hides it with great skill. He stands and hugs Amy.

"So you're not dead," says Amy.

"Why would he be dead?" says John. "He's a loss-adjuster."

"From Lymington," adds Jyoti.

"Kept five pints of my blood in the fridge," says Jeff. "Fired a few shots in the Beamer and tipped it over the front seat."

"That's what I said you would do," says Amy.

Rosie offers her cheek to him and says, "Ah, the elusive Jeff. The elusive, surprisingly handsome Jeff. I'm Rosie."

"That's Rosie D'Antonio," says John to Jyoti. "At the quiz!"

"Amy doing a good job looking after you?" Jeff asks.

"Terrible," says Rosie. "But we're having a lot of fun."

"What's going on, Jeff?" says Amy. What is he doing here, in Axley? How did Steve know he would be here? And is Henk right about him? And, the most important question of all: are they really going to have to do an entire pub quiz before she finds out?

"It suited me to be dead for a few days," says Jeff. "François Loubet was trying to kill me."

"How do you know it was Loubet?" Steve asks.

"I've got the emails to prove it," says Jeff.

"Where have you been staying?" Steve asks.

"Well," says Jeff. "Full disclosure. I've been in the spare room at yours."

"Huh," says Steve.

"Apart from the last couple of nights. A man and a woman showed up, so I made a sharp exit. I've been sleeping in a ditch."

"You look good on it," says Rosie.

"It was a comfortable ditch," says Jeff.

This is it, is it? They're just going to make small talk? "Why are you here?" Amy asks in frustration. "In Axley?"

"Mainly because Loubet was trying to kill me," says Jeff. "But also I love a quiz. I just thought, where better to hide out while you solved the case?"

"And Loubet is trying to kill me too?" Amy asks.

"With a bit of help from Joe Blow," says Jeff.

"And who's Joe Blow?" Amy asks.

Jeff nods over to the bar. "Henk, of course."

They all look over toward Henk, currently trying to carry four pints at once.

"Who's Henk?" says Jyoti.

"But Henk says you're working with Loubet?" says Rosie.

"Other way round," says Jeff. "You'll see."

"We still need a team name," says John.

Henk is focusing his eyes on the carpet as he weaves through the crowd. And then, flicking his eyes toward his destination, he sees Jeff.

The voice of a young woman now pipes through the speakers. "*Okay, Brass Monkey, pens in hand and brains in gear, please. Question one. On which soap opera did actor Max Highfield begin his career?*"

Henk reaches the group. Steve motions for them all to sit down at an empty table next to his usual team. "We quiz, then we discuss who is trying to kill whom—agreed?"

"No," says Henk. "We need to sort this out right now. Steve, you have tricked me. Jeff, we must talk immediately."

Steve jabs his finger at Henk's chest. "Henk, I've put my priorities on hold for a number of days now. I've been tied up, I've been threatened with a gun, I've been in a helicopter with a hangover, and I've eaten kale. Now, sit down, shut up, and, for the next ninety minutes, or more if there's a tiebreak, *let me quiz*."

The quizmaster repeats the question. "*That's Max Highfield—I definitely would—on which soap opera did he start his career?*"

Henk nods at Steve, and, as they both sit, he says, "*EastEnders.*"

"You're sure?" says Steve.

"Definite," says Henk. "And I know Max Highfield, so maybe we can get a point for that?"

"It's *Coronation Street,*" says Jeff. "Guaranteed. And I also know Max Highfield. So."

"*EastEnders,*" says Henk.

"*Coronation Street,*" says Jeff.

Henk looks at Jeff. Jeff looks at Henk.

"Well, you can't both be right," says Steve.

Neither man will back down and break their stare.

"Oh, for God's sake," says Amy, taking the pen and answer sheet from Jeff. "It's *Hollyoaks.*"

"*Okay. Question two . . .*"

onnie Gregor is stretched out in her childhood bed, staring at the ceiling. The ceiling is a painting of the night sky, dark blue and covered in stick-on gold stars. Her dad painted it for her when she was six or seven, and when she was a little girl she would sometimes stare at it all night. It seemed so immense, so full of a twinkling promise. A world her dad had made for her, and so close she could almost touch it.

Then, after her dad died, she would stare at it all night and wonder where he might be? If he was up there, and if he was all alone? As she grew taller, sometimes she would stand on her bed, on tiptoes, and reach up to touch it.

Lying here now, Bonnie realizes that if you look at the stars, the sky seems full. But if you look at the darkness, the sky seems empty.

Tonight Bonnie is looking at the stars. She's flying tomorrow, the four p.m. from Heathrow. It says on the website to get to the airport at least three hours before departure, so that's one p.m. It says on Google that the journey to Heathrow will be just over an hour, but you never know with daytime traffic, so she has allowed two hours, which means leaving at eleven a.m., and then, just for added peace of mind, she has given herself an extra hour and has decided to leave at ten a.m. That should do it.

Her next-door neighbor's husband has agreed to drive her to Heathrow for petrol money because he loves planes.

She looks up at the golden stars; she has mapped them in her brain, forty-one of them, only three peeling, even after all this time. She goes through her lines once again. Quietly. The kids are sleeping next door in her mum's room. They are very excited to be staying at Grandma's for the week, though not half as excited as their grandma is.

She's written a few things she thinks might work.

"What is paint? Paint is color. And what is color? Color can be anything you want. Color can make you happy, it can brighten your day and slap a smile on your face. A bright orange—bosh!—a bright yellow—bosh! bosh! . . ."

She is experimenting with "bosh," because she doesn't really have a catchphrase, and it would be useful to have one. Something to say when you can't think of anything else, something to fill in the gaps. She's not sure if she's cracked it yet, though. "Splosh!" Is that better?

"So if paint is color, and color is happiness, a tin of paint is a tin of happiness!"

That's the bit she's most confident about. She's been through the whole thing with her mum over and over. She will try "Splosh!" out on her in the morning.

The bag arrived today, not a case, as she had expected, but a brown leather holdall.

She has learned the names of all the colors in the range. "Lipstick Red," "Hello Yellow," "Pretty Pink," "Lady Lime," "Hi-Ho Silver," "Baby Blue," and "Agent Orange."

She knows all about vegan paint, breathable paint, and non-toxic nursery paint. She knows all about zero VOC paints. Volatile Organic Compounds, compounds with "a high vapor pressure at ordinary room temperatures," and is confident that she can talk about them while sitting by a pool drinking a mai tai.

She hasn't told her mum yet, but the first half of the money came through this morning. She checked her balance at the cashpoint in Morrisons, and there it was.

The other thing she hasn't told her mum, though she's certain it's fine, is the way she is being paid. It is something to do with Vivid Viral Media's tax systems; they explained it, but Bonnie's probably not the right person to understand, so she doubts her mum would be. Either way, Vivid Viral, instead of just paying her the twenty thousand, actually pays her two hundred thousand, and then they arrange a transfer of the extra one hundred and eighty thousand to another company. It's not a scam, because Bonnie keeps the twenty thousand. It's fascinating, really, to see the way things are done. One day this will all be second nature to her, and she'll be able to sit her mum down and go through it all.

On Bonnie's bedside table are two "Good Luck" cards. One from her mum that says "Chase the Dream" and one from the kids, of a 3D unicorn saying, "I love you."

Bonnie checks her alarm once again. If she's leaving at 10:00, or perhaps 9:30 if she's ready, she'll make sure she's up by 6:00, just in case there's a last-minute crisis. She can make breakfast for the kids and her mum. She lies back again.

"Forest Paints. Breathe. Believe. Achieve."

This time tomorrow she'll be on the plane. Up in the night sky, up among the stars. She can talk to her dad while she's up there. Tell him all about her new adventure.

Bonnie can feel her eyes beginning to shut. She is sleeping easier these days. Less to worry about, knowing she can make Maxie and Mimi happy and safe. That's the secret to happiness, isn't it? She looks up at the ceiling again and thinks about her dad with the paint roller, waiting for it all to dry, and working out exactly where to put all the stars. The perfect pattern to make his daughter happy. That's all you can do for your kids, isn't it? Try to arrange the stars.

Bonnie pushes herself up and stands on her bed. She doesn't need tiptoes anymore, as she reaches up and touches the ceiling.

Bonnie looks down and checks the corner of the room. Her bags are safe and sound. There's her case, with the wonky wheels, packed with every possible combination of outfit. And there's the big leather holdall, secured with a safety lock.

She has lifted it of course—there were no rules against that—and it was heavy. But then paint is heavy, isn't it? What could it be? A new color launch? "Princess Purple"? Perhaps body paint? Or tile paint? That would actually be useful.

The possibilities are endless. Bonnie shuts her eyes. She can't wait to open the bag and find out.

76

Even with an illegal number of team members they finished second in the quiz. By one point.

Jeff and Henk pretty much canceled each other out, and the only question Rosie got right all evening was about Diane Keaton. She told Steve that they'd "shared an orthodontist," and then winked at him.

Steve is still hurting, but he supposes there are more important matters at hand this evening, and, when he turned his phone back on, Steve received the message he'd been waiting for. Now he has *two* pieces of information for everyone. It's so nice to be home.

The whole gang has decamped to Steve's living room. Felicity and Tony have also joined the crew. Steve notes they have not let go of each other's hand at any point. Good for Tony—there really is someone for everyone. He is still keeping a close eye on Felicity.

Losing by one point, though. So close.

Jyoti and John had wanted to join this little chat, but were finally dissuaded when Amy told them that an awful lot of people were being murdered, and Rosie agreed to give John an autograph.

Jeff Nolan is in Steve's favorite armchair, and an audience now sits around him. Trouble settles on Jeff's lap. Curls himself around Jeff's laptop.

"Seems I have a fan," says Jeff, very happy with himself.

"That's because of the laptop," says Steve, annoyed at Trouble's lack of loyalty. "He can't resist them."

"So this is from two days ago," says Jeff. "Encrypted, as always." He reads from the screen.

Dear Mr. Nolan,

They say you are dead, but people say an awful lot of things, don't they? I'm afraid I don't believe them. They say you cannot pull the wool over the eyes of someone who wishes to pull the wool over your own eyes!

Your lesson has been learned, I hope? You wanted to interfere in my business, so I had to interfere in yours. But with those three strikes, I am out, and you will hear nothing more from me so long as I hear nothing more from you.

I wish you no malice, but I must protect my own interests, in the same way I understand you must protect yours. So I shall look elsewhere for my helpers, and leave Maximum Impact in peace.

Should you decide to interfere in my business again, I shall return to interfere in yours. But, for now, this is farewell.

Again, I was sorry to hear about the attempt on your life. You must have made an enemy somewhere!

I suspect that if you are more careful in future you will be quite safe.

I regret that the same cannot be said of Amy Wheeler. I hear there is a mountain of evidence piling up against her? Poor Amy.

Please pass on my fondest wishes to Joe Blow.

With warmest regards,
François

Jeff closes his laptop. "You see why I think this is Henk? Overwritten. Obvious."

"Excuse me," says Henk, on a kitchen chair, "if I don't take a lecture on what is obvious from a man who couldn't name England's leading goalscorer in the Sport round."

"You're going to have to let that go," says Steve. Steve can't help but blame himself too. He'd known it was Kane, not Rooney. With that extra point they'd have been in a tiebreak.

"Henk, it could only be one of us," says Jeff. "Our client list is confidential. No one else could have known that Bella Sanchez, Mark Gooch, and Andrew Fairbanks were all clients of Maximum Impact."

"I agree," says Henk. "Which is how I know it is you."

"I'll go and make some tea," says Felicity, getting off the sofa. "Sorry, Steve, I don't mean to take over your house!"

"I don't think there is any tea," says Steve.

"Well, there wasn't, but I bought some," says Felicity, and disappears into the kitchen.

Henk shoos Trouble away, which only makes Trouble more determined to be stroked by him.

"For example," says Henk, "I couldn't have been involved in booking your Navy SEAL, Kevin, in South Carolina, unlike Jeff."

"I liked him," says Rosie. "Did he ever get out?"

"I had someone let him out yesterday," says Jeff. "I think five days in your panic room had been quite enough."

"So that's who's been using my Netflix account," says Rosie. "I wondered who was watching all the Guy Ritchie films and that Formula 1 documentary."

"He died of a bullet to the head within eight hours of our letting him out," says Jeff. "So that's what we're dealing with. And he had no idea who'd hired him to kill Amy."

"Oh, I have the answer to that," says Steve, pulling a mobile phone from his pocket. "A man named Rob Kenna, based in Dubai, which is where it seems all roads lead."

"How did you find that out?" Amy asks.

"I took Nelson's SIM card from his phone while he was bleeding on me," says Steve. "Rob Kenna and I have been having quite the chat. I've told him I need to see him about a couple of troublesome rivals, and he's invited me for a round of golf."

"So you think Rob Kenna hired Eddie too?" asks Amy.

"No idea," says Steve. "But he hired Kevin to kill you, and he hired Nelson to kill you, so you'd have to guess so. Who else would have hired him?"

"There's no possibility, I suppose, Jeff," says Rosie, "that Eddie has been sent to kill *me*? By Vasiliy Karpin? He just shot at Amy to get her out of the way?"

Jeff weighs this up. "Let me try to get in touch with Vasiliy."

"I mean, if you would," says Rosie. "I don't mean to be a fusspot, but somebody might be trying to kill me, and I think I'm still paying you."

"And we think that Rob Kenna is working for Loubet?" Amy asks.

"Correct," says Jeff. "And Loubet is working with Henk."

"And Loubet is working with Jeff," says Henk. "It has to be one of us."

"Oh, this is a bit of fun," says Rosie.

If Steve is completely honest with himself, he threw away another point when he'd insisted that Lily Savage had taken over from Terry Wogan as the host of *Blankety Blank*. That will be keeping him awake tonight. Forgetting that it was Les Dawson in between. But for now he must concentrate—back to the business at hand. Time to let Jeff Nolan and Henk van Veen know what he's found out.

"Neither of you is working with Loubet," says Steve.

Even Trouble turns to look at him.

"Because anybody with any real skill in investigation would have spotted something else in your files."

"Susan Knox?" says Henk.

"Who?" says Tony.

"Their head of HR," says Amy. "Has access to everything."

"Not Susan Knox," says Steve. "Someone far more interesting."

Steve takes Henk's envelope from a coffee table.

"You see, Jeff certainly signed off on all these clients. Thirty-five times. But something else happened thirty-five times, according to the files that Susan Knox sent us."

"What?" asks Rosie.

"On all thirty-five occasions, an introduction fee of ten thousand pounds is paid to Max Highfield."

The room is silent in amazement.

"Max Highfield recruited every single one of them," says Steve.

Jeff laughs.

"No way," says Jeff. "Max Highfield is working for François Loubet? I don't buy it."

"Hell of a coincidence, then," says Steve. "He introduced each and every one of these influencers to the company. A payment of ten grand to him for each one. Anyone here believe in coincidences?"

Jeff shakes his head. "Max doesn't have the brains, Steve. And I mean he really doesn't have the brains."

"And how would Max have got Loubet's email address?" says Henk. "It's in one file, a classified one."

"And we're still not addressing the most important point," says Rosie. "Why did they choose Felicity's company? It can't just be random. Why do your business through a small TV agent in Hertfordshire? That's the weak link, that's where we can unravel all this."

"She's a medium-sized TV agent," says Tony. "Not small."

"I agree with Rosie," says Henk. "Sorry, Steve, I'm sure you used to be a perfectly adequate detective, but I think Max Highfield actually is just a co-incidence."

Felicity walks back in with a pot of tea and some mugs on a tray.

"Max Highfield?" she says. "Oh, I could tell you some stories about him."

"Stories?" Amy asks. All eyes are now turned to Felicity Woollaston.

She smiles. "Only nice ones. I was his very first agent. Got him the *Holly-oaks* job."

"Max Highfield was your client?" says Steve.

"Always knew he'd go far," says Felicity, beaming proudly.

77

The bright lights of Dubai shine through a panoramic window. Rob Kenna has three guns laid out on his bed in order of size.

He picks up the first one, a small handgun, and poses with it.

"Amy Wheeler, I presume?"

Blam! Blam! He blows across the barrel. Next he picks up a compact machine pistol.

"You defeated the rest, Amy Wheeler, but you just met the best."

He sprays imaginary bullets around the room, then throws it back down on the bed. He picks up the final weapon, a sawn-off shotgun.

"Welcome to Dubai, Amy. It'll blow you away."

Kablammo!

Rob throws the gun back onto the bed. He's almost looking forward to it.

"You need a job done properly, sometimes you gotta do it yourself."

78

M ax wouldn't," says Felicity. "He couldn't possibly. He was the sweetest boy. I went to his final show at drama school, and he couldn't act, but he had something."

"Height?" suggests Jeff Nolan.

There is a knock at the door. Everyone looks at each other, then at Steve. One by one, Amy, Jeff, and Henk stand, pull guns, and point them toward the hallway of the house. Amy then pulls a second gun from her thigh, and throws it to Steve.

"Blimey," says Tony.

Steve walks out into the hallway. Two heads are silhouetted behind the glass in his front door. Steve turns back to the living room. Amy is in a crouch, gun in hand. Henk is secreted behind an IKEA multimedia unit, gun up to his eye, and Jeff is standing, bold as brass in the middle of the room, gun arm extended. Rosie is draped on the sofa, enjoying the show. Jeff nods to Steve.

Steve slips his gun into his waistband, and calls out, "Yes?"

"Hampshire Police, sir," comes a voice from the other side of the door. "We're looking for an Amy Wheeler. We believe she's in your property."

Amy once told Steve that the first time she enters any building she looks for every possible escape route. Steve used to do it himself, but, as he's got older, the first thing he looks for is where the loo might be.

"Sir?" says the same voice.

"She's not here, I'm afraid," says Steve. The "mountain of evidence" that Loubet had mentioned. Has he given up trying to kill her and is now planning to get her locked up instead? "Gone back to London."

"If we could just double-check, sir," says the voice. "Put our minds at rest?"

That should have given her enough time, Steve thinks. He opens the door a crack, and is gratified to see it really is two Hampshire Police officers.

"Come in," says Steve. "Come in."

As Steve leads the officers into the living room, Henk and Jeff are playing chess, each with a cup of tea, Tony and Rosie are watching *Married at First Sight: Australia* on the TV, and Felicity is walking around the room with a plate of biscuits. Amy is nowhere to be seen. You had to hand it to the lot of them—that was quick.

Steve wonders where all the guns are, and feels his own poking into his lower back.

"We have a warrant for Mrs. Wheeler's arrest," says the older detective. "If you know where she is, you'd do well to tell us."

Everyone looks at each other.

"What's she done now?" says Rosie.

"Murder, madam," says the older detective, "I'm afraid."

"That's our Amy," says Rosie.

"She left for London," says Jeff. "Hours ago."

"And you are, sir?"

"Me?" says Jeff. "None of your business."

"We might choose to make it our business," says the younger detective without bravado or fear.

Jeff looks at her. "I don't suppose you'd like a job?"

"I was just thinking the same," says Henk. "She carries herself very well."

"If she gets in touch," says the older detective, giving Steve his card, "you give me a call?"

"Of course," says Steve. "You're investigating a murder."

"So you're Steve Wheeler?" the detective says. "Heard a lot about you."

"Rest assured," says Steve, "I'm always happy to help out the Hampshire Police."

The detective sizes up the room of people in front of him. "Look, I don't know who you all are, or what you're all doing, but we're trying to investigate three murders here."

"Gosh," says Rosie. "Imagine."

The younger detective looks at her. "Are you Rosie D'Antonio?"

Rosie waves this observation away.

The older detective looks at them one by one. "I'm going to ask all of you not to leave the country."

At any other time, thinks Steve, that would be music to his ears.

79

lot of people are finding it hard to sleep tonight. All for their own reasons.

STEVE Wheeler is finding it hard to sleep, because Trouble is insisting on sleeping on his chest. Steve feels that is fair, given that he has been away for so long. Trouble doesn't ask much from him.

So Max Highfield is Joe Blow.

He'd made the connection as soon as he'd read the files. Cross-referenced with the information Henk had given him. Max Highfield of all people. Steve had stopped watching the *Rampage* movies after *Rampage 3*. No way someone fires a bullet on the Space Shuttle.

Add in his connection to Felicity Woollaston and he has to be involved in this. And he's currently in Dubai, home of Rob Kenna. Isn't that convenient?

Actually, it's not convenient, because it means Steve has to take yet another flight first thing in the morning. At least he got to do the quiz, though.

Rosie's coming with him; Jeff is staying where he is. Loubet thinks Jeff might be dead, and Jeff wants to keep it that way for now. He's going to go back to the office and see what else he can find.

Steve gently strokes the sleeping cat's head as he thinks about what is to come. He feels his eyes begin to close. Perhaps this will be the first night he doesn't need to walk through the streets of Axley? To sit on the bench and talk to Debbie?

But won't Debbie miss him? Sitting there all alone?

ROSIE D'Antonio is wide awake, because she is waiting for the lightest of taps on her bedroom door from Jeff Nolan. She is in Steve's spare room, and Jeff is downstairs on the sofa, despite her fairly unambiguous invitation. She will give him another five minutes before taking a handful of melatonin on top of a bellyful of whisky.

She feels safe at least. Steve is in the room next door, Jeff on the downstairs sofa, and Henk across the village in Tony Taylor's house. That's some fairly hefty security.

She hopes Jeff will knock. They usually do in her experience. And she hasn't slept with anyone in over two weeks. She has ruled Steve out now. She sees his vulnerabilities and, while ordinarily she would be happy to take advantage of them, she feels it would be inappropriate. Her therapist often accuses her of having no boundaries, so it shows what he knows.

There was Kevin the bodyguard; he was a contender. Something could have happened there, couldn't it? If he hadn't tried to kill Amy? Even then you never know.

Carlos Moss at the airport, of course. Been there, done that, but would recommend to others. The drug dealer on St. Lucia, Nelson. He had a certain something until Steve shot him in the leg. Again, even then . . .

The TV host in Ireland? She would have loved a crack at him, but there was a helicopter waiting. Often the way, in her experience. Even Eddie Flood has a certain rugged charm, though she is increasingly coming to suspect that he has been hired by a Russian chemicals billionaire to kill her. What a way to go, though.

All that frustration, all of those missed opportunities, and still she hasn't turned her headlights on Steve. That's real progress. She looks forward to reporting back to her therapist on this with well-earned pride. *See, Jonathan? I do have boundaries.*

In fact, now she thinks about it, Jonathan was the last person she slept with.

JEFF Nolan can't sleep. The two nights in a ditch, idyllic and "back to basics" though it was in some ways, have not been kind to his back, and Steve's sofa is finishing the job. He misses the lovely spare-room bed, but he was never going to take that from Rosie. He is half tempted to tiptoe upstairs, knock on Steve's door, and ask if they could share for the night. But Steve's only experience of him so far involves him faking his own death and then breaking into his house, so it might still be a little early in their relationship to be roommates.

At least this sleeplessness is giving him time to think. He will head back to London in the morning. Steve had composed a simple email to send to Loubet's encrypted email address.

Dear Mr. Loubet,

We know you are in Dubai, and we know about Max Highfield and Rob Kenna. We are coming to find you.

There's really no point in sending it, but Steve was very keen. "Let's flush everyone out" had been the logic.

Jeff is a little jealous that Trouble is upstairs with Steve. He thought they had a bond.

HENK van Veen is wide awake, walking down the high street. Tony Taylor's sofa had been surprisingly comfortable, and he was settling very nicely when the sounds of vigorous lovemaking reached him from the floor above, and he thought it might be a good time to take the air. Upon returning an hour later, he found that the noises were, if anything, louder still, so he headed straight back out again.

Max Highfield, though? Really? And does he trust Jeff now? Well, no.

Henk finds a bench by the pond and sits down. There is a plaque on the bench dedicated to a woman named Debbie. Nice to be remembered. Nice to be loved. Henk doesn't see his family so much. One day he would like to again, but how does one go about healing wounds?

Perhaps he can heal his wounds with Jeff too? They were a good team.

BONNIE Gregor can't sleep. She's just had a thought. About what her mum said the other day.

That moment when they ask, "Did you pack these bags yourself?" What happens if you say no? She's never heard anyone say that, so she doesn't know.

On reflection, it's probably best to say that she did, isn't it?

Yes. That's probably what people do. Go back to sleep, Bonnie.

EDDIE Flood can't sleep. He has become a prisoner to the alarm setting on his iPhone.

Once Eddie set a seven a.m. alarm for seven p.m. by mistake and, as a result, was late for a prison-van hijack. Tonight he has set the alarm on his phone for five a.m., and he keeps rolling over and rechecking that he's set it properly. Then he checks that the alarm will work even though the volume is off. He dozes briefly and, half asleep, tells himself that his alarm has gone off, but when he checks he sees it has only just gone midnight. What if he does fall asleep, dream that his alarm has gone off, and then, in his sleep, *actually* turn it off?

Whether he does eventually fall asleep, or whether "alarm-related sleep anxiety" keeps him up all night, he will rise at 5:00. Wherever Rosie D'Antonio goes tomorrow, Eddie will go.

He decides to read up on undetectable poisons to send himself to sleep.

It's four a.m. in Dubai and Max Highfield has no intention of sleeping anytime soon. He was delighted to find that the VIP room at Ekwinox Night Club had its own even smaller VIP room, and that is where he is now, snorting cocaine with a boxer, a diamond dealer, and a billionaire. He is sure he has read somewhere that you're not supposed to take cocaine in Dubai, but they say you're not supposed to take cocaine in London either, and it's virtually compulsory there.

And, besides, if it was illegal, would a billionaire arms dealer and a boxer be doing it?

Henk has given him a bodyguard. She is only five foot two, but she has already shown him how to mine for Bitcoin.

Billionaires and celebrities. Max is glad that he is one, and looks forward to being the other.

Amy Wheeler is fast asleep in the guest wing of Gary Gough's country home, about as safe from police officers as it is possible to be. There are busy times ahead. She will do her job, and she knows that Steve and Rosie will do theirs too.

PART THREE

From Dubai
to a small bench
by a quiet pond

80

He can't stay as François Loubet for much longer, that's clear now. It was a good run, but there's too much heat. Time for a change of identity. What will it be this time? Colombian? Turkish? Change everything, numbers, emails, the lot.

Merci beaucoup, though, François, you've had police the world over looking for you, and you never even existed.

Things change, things stay the same.

The man who was François Loubet smiles, pours himself a whisky, and opens his emails for the final time.

81

On the flight from St. Lucia to Dublin, when Steve first started to suspect Max Highfield, he'd read an interview in which Max had named *The Rose of Sarasota* as his finest film. It had taken Steve a while to track it down, as none of the usual streamers seem to have shared Max's opinion.

Having just watched the first eight minutes of *The Rose of Sarasota*, Steve understands why. He only made it as far as eight minutes in, because it was at that point that Max Highfield had revealed that his character, an army explosives expert, had the nickname "Joe Blow."

A nice thing to add to the pile of evidence, as he and Rosie fly out to Dubai. Steve sits back in his seat, but it's not as comfortable as some of the other private jets they've taken.

Steve remembers that he used to buy Trouble his cat food from the local shop in Axley. You got it in pouches, twenty or so in a box. There was a duck flavor, a salmon flavor, perhaps a beef one, something like that. Trouble never stopped to ask; he just loved food that he hadn't had to catch or scavenge for himself.

Then one day Margaret next door made a roast chicken for her family and brought Steve the leftovers. Steve fed some of the roast chicken to Trouble, just as a treat, and, as anyone with a cat could have told him, from that day forward Trouble refused to eat cat food.

If you try him with it, he'll tip his head and look at you in utter incomprehension. We both know I only eat roast chicken, mate, come on.

And that, Steve realizes, is how *he* is now about private jets. This private jet—it's a Learjet—is slightly smaller than the ones he has become used to in the last week and he is feeling a little cramped. He's also just found out that there is no private chef, and he had really been looking forward to a bacon sandwich.

So, just as cat food has been ruined for Trouble, so air travel has now forever been ruined for Steve.

Which is actually fine by him, because as soon as they trap Max Highfield and talk to Rob Kenna, and as soon as they work out who François Loubet is, Steve intends never to fly anywhere ever again.

He sits opposite Rosie, knees almost touching, because of the slightly reduced legroom.

"So we know for sure that Max Highfield is Joe Blow," says Steve. "All of the influencers we know about were recruited to Maximum Impact through his recommendations, the connection with Felicity Woollaston, and now the name."

"Bang to rights," agrees Rosie. "Thanks to you. Is this private jet a bit too small, do you think?"

Steve shakes his head in shock. "Rosie, I'm not the sort of person who goes around thinking that private jets are too small."

"Oh my God," says Rosie. "You *do* think it's too small. You'll be complaining there's no chef next."

Steve waves this away but, not for the first time, feels utterly naked in front of Rosie's gaze. "We just need to be able to outwit Max Highfield."

"How are we going to get to him, though?" Rosie asks. "According to the *Tatler*, Max Highfield is the world's fourteenth biggest film star."

"You could get a meeting with him?" Steve suggests. "As the world's second biggest author?"

Steve had caught Rosie putting her books in front of Lee Child's at the WHSmith in the airport.

"Maybe," says Rosie. "Usually when a celebrity meets another celebrity they only ever talk about Tom Cruise, or how much tax they paid last year. But perhaps I could pitch him an idea?"

Steve nods, and Rosie takes out her phone. Steve looks out of the window. Where are they flying over? Bulgaria perhaps? If you fly over somewhere, can you say you've been there? That would be handy. Think of the places he'll have been then?

"Are you still worried that Eddie Flood is trying to kill you?"

Rosie shrugs but unconvincingly. "Certainly, if he turns up in Dubai, we'll know it's trouble. Or if Vasiliy Karpin puts in an appearance."

"Well," says Steve, "I honestly hope no one kills you."

"That means a lot, Stevie, thank you," says Rosie. "That's the closest you've ever come to flirting with me."

"Did you enjoy the quiz?" Steve asks.

"The quiz?" says Rosie. "God no."

"Only, I saw you laughing quite a lot," says Steve.

"I'm on painkiller medication."

Steve smiles. "There's always a place on the team for you."

"I don't do pub quizzes, Stevie," says Rosie. "I live on a private island."

"By yourself," says Steve.

"Yes, that's what makes it private," says Rosie.

"You don't get lonely?"

"Says the man whose best friend is a cat."

They both laugh. Steve looks down at the map on the flight computer. They are now over Armenia. That's another country ticked off the list. Armenia? Yep, been there. Very hilly.

"I'm not lonely," says Rosie. "That's not the word. There are just fewer people around nowadays. Fewer friends."

"People die," says Steve.

"And a lot more people die when you get to my age," says Rosie.

"Remind me what age that is again?" asks Steve.

"Thirty years younger than my first husband," says Rosie. "And thirty years older than my next husband."

"There are still plenty of people out there," says Steve. "Plenty of friends. If you want them."

"But they'll die too," says Rosie. "Won't they? Everybody dies."

"That's the spirit," says Steve.

"Urghh, ignore me," says Rosie. "A bit of me thinks if Vasiliy Karpin did kill me, would that be such a bad thing?"

"I said the same to Debbie the other day," says Steve. "About me dying, not you dying."

"Would Debbie have liked me?" Rosie asks.

"She'd have loved you," says Steve. "And you'd have loved her. She was more fun than me."

"I do want to catch Loubet," says Rosie. "But I'll be sad when this is all over. What do you think Amy and Jeff will get up to?"

"Go through all the records back in London," says Steve. "See when Max started to get involved. Find any clues to Loubet's identity."

"And we trust Jeff?" Rosie asks.

"Why wouldn't we?" says Steve. "Unless you think he's been sending the Loubet emails to himself?"

Rosie goes back to her phone. Steve tries to get comfortable. Tony Taylor used to send emails to himself, as part of an elaborate tax fraud. Too elaborate for Tony, anyway, that's why he's not allowed to do MOTs anymore. Steve looks over at Rosie again. Are they friends now? Will they stay in touch after all this? Always assuming they're both still alive? Steve has a thought.

"This might be crazy," says Steve, "but are we certain that Max Highfield isn't François Loubet himself?"

"I'm not sure he has the brains," says Rosie. "I saw an interview with him in *Vanity Fair* in which he hadn't heard of Ukraine."

"Perhaps he's street smart," says Steve.

"He also thought Princess Diana was fictional," says Rosie.

"Who is François Loubet?" says Steve. "It's driving me crazy."

"You worked out that Max Highfield is Joe Blow," says Rosie. "You worked out that Rob Kenna is working for Loubet. And now one of them will lead us to François Loubet."

Steve nods. Rosie's right. Just keep following the clues. "By the way, did you notice the loo roll in the toilet isn't double-ply?"

"I never go to the toilet, Stevie," says Rosie, looking up from her phone. "You know that."

As he sprays a lavender, chamomile, and musk mist onto his goose-down pillow, Steve realizes he's going to miss all this too.

82

The journey to Heathrow Airport hadn't taken as long as you'd think, and Bonnie is relieved that she's arrived in plenty of time for her plane. Her next-door neighbor's husband was kind enough to carry her leather holdall ("What you got in here? Gold bars?") all the way to the check-in queue, Bonnie struggling behind with her big case on its wonky wheels.

The line is long—lucky Bonnie got here early, you just never knew. She'll be happy to get the case and the bag off her hands. And then there's security to get through too—who knows how long that might take? She looks at the clock on the wall: plenty of time, Bonnie, plenty of time.

As the queue inches forward in front of her, Bonnie uses her foot to push the leather holdall forward. It doesn't feel like tins of paint. Perhaps that's the point? No more tins? Paint in a bag? Could be, couldn't it?

Maxie and Mimi were excited to see her off this morning. They waved from the front door, and she promised to bring them presents. Her mum was crying, so Bonnie promised to bring her back a big bar of Toblerone, but her mum said, "Just bring yourself back safely."

Bonnie nudges the bag forward once again. Heavy, but with a bit of give. Why in the world is she doing this? Is she an idiot for taking a bag on a plane when she has no idea what's in it? Could be a bomb, couldn't it?

That's like something her mum would have said, but her mum doesn't understand Instagram.

There are only two check-in desks open. Perhaps she should email Felicity while she waits? Just to put her mind at rest? She composes an email on her phone.

Felicity, hi!

On my way to sunny São Paulo. At the airport in plenty of time.

Super quick one. They've given me a bag with a lock on it, and I don't know what's in it.

It's for a surprise unboxing video (bit 2022 right???). Just checking this is normal?

Sorry to be a pain, first time and everything!

Thanks again, I owe you so much.

Bonnie

Her finger hovers above the "send" button as she rereads it. Imagines Felicity, in her office, reading it. She moves her finger away. No. Felicity will think she's a drama queen. Come on, Bonnie, you're a grown-up. She imagines Felicity forwarding the email on to her colleagues with a few cry-laugh emojis. What if Forest Paints get to hear about it? The influencer who thought their paint samples were a bomb?

"Next, please," says a smiling woman at one of the check-in desks. Bonnie sends the email to "Drafts" and gives her leather holdall a series of shuffling kicks toward the desk.

She hands over her passport.

"Where are you flying to today, m'love?" asks the check-in clerk.

"São Paulo," says Bonnie.

"Ooh, lovely," says the clerk, checking her passport. "Little holiday?"

"Business, actually," says Bonnie, feeling ten feet tall.

The clerk looks at Bonnie's case and holdall. "And just the two bags to check in?"

Bonnie nods.

"Stick them on the scales for me, my darling," says the clerk. "What's your booking number?"

Bonnie lugs the holdall onto the rubber conveyor belt next to the check-in desk and hands over her booking confirmation.

"And you packed the bags yourself, Bonnie?"

The moment she hears the question, Bonnie knows she should have sent the email. Just to be certain. She'll be worried there's a bomb in the hold for the whole flight. Good luck enjoying a Jennifer Aniston film now. But if it was a bomb, she'd have been able to feel it, surely? It felt softer than that? What if it's drugs? But why would it be? She had sat face-to-face with Felicity. They even went to Pizza Express, for goodness' sake.

"Yes," says Bonnie. Felicity is not going to send Bonnie to São Paulo with a holdall full of drugs. You're an influencer now, Bonnie, so act like an influencer, not a child.

As Bonnie is about to put the case with the wonky wheels onto the belt, the clerk scans her confirmation QR code.

"Ah, m'darling," she says. "You're on the four p.m. flight?"

Bonnie nods.

The clerk looks at her watch. "Only it's nine thirty in the morning."

"I didn't want to miss the flight," says Bonnie. In the end they had left at 8:30, because she was packed and ready, and what harm could it do to get there a bit early?

"Your check-in doesn't open till one," says the clerk. "There's a Costa and a Boots if you get bored. Do you want to pop your bag back down for me?"

Bonnie heaves the first bag back off the belt. Better to be early than late, though, isn't it?

"I'll sit in Costa for a bit, thank you," says Bonnie.

"Probably cost you as much as the flight," laughs the clerk.

"I know," says Bonnie, now swinging the heavy holdall back down to the floor. "Who has that kind of money?"

83

Amy is curled up in the boot of Gary Gough's Land Rover.

He has kindly agreed to drive her all the way to London. As it happens, he needs to be there for a lunch with an amphetamine dealer from Liverpool anyway, so he promises it is no inconvenience.

There are police officers all over Axley and the surrounding villages looking for her. That's why she's in the boot. An officer had even knocked at Gary Gough's door last night, and Gary had pointed to the name of his house, carved into a beautiful New Forest log. Amy hadn't noticed before that Gary Gough's house is called No Comment.

She could probably have got out of the boot by now, as they speed up the M3, but it is comfortable and comforting. Gary had sent her a text message from the front seat asking if she was okay, and she had texted back a "thumbs-up" and a "Zzz," so he'd left her in peace.

She feels bad sending Steve and Rosie on their own to Dubai, but she has no choice but to lie low. Whatever "evidence" has appeared at the scenes of the three crimes will, no doubt, be very bad for her. Her only hope is that they can discover who François Loubet is, and stop him.

She also feels nervous that Steve and Rosie are in Dubai together. Who knows what the two of them will do without what she considers to be her calming presence?

Gary is going to drop her in the underground car park of Maximum

Impact, where she will spend the night. Tomorrow, she and Jeff are going to go through the François Loubet files with a magnifying glass to help the cause. Neither of them is great with files, but that's their only option for now.

In the boot Amy finds a metal case, and inside the case there are two handguns. She texts Gary and asks if she can take one. He replies with a thumbs-up and a gun emoji.

She always feels safer with two guns.

There's another thing she's worrying about.

Steve is staying with Adam at the villa. You could tell they were both sort of mortified when they realized it would be just the two of them there. Rosie was about to offer Steve a room in her hotel, but Amy hushed her.

It will do Steve and Adam some good, spending time with each other. Father and son. It's healthy. But Amy can't help wondering what they'll be talking about. They both talk about Debbie with Amy, but never with each other.

As Amy feels the car slow from the speed of the motorway to the crawl of London, she hopes they are talking about Debbie now.

84

Flew over on Tuesday, yeah," says Adam.

Steve nods. "Got the plane, yeah?"

"Got the plane," confirms Adam.

"Best thing," says Steve. "Be a long time in a boat."

"Long time," agrees Adam.

When was the last time Steve and his son had chatted without somebody else in the room? Even at Christmas, if Amy pops into the kitchen to make a cuppa, Adam will say, "Let me help you." And if he doesn't say, "Let me help you," Steve will say it instead. Anything but being stuck together.

"You know where the loo is?" Adam asks. "If you need it?"

"Hallway," says Steve. "Clocked it on the way in."

Adam nods, and sips his tea again.

What did they used to talk about? Dinosaurs, when Adam was very young, but conversation has been limited since then. Two awkward men on either side of a canyon of silence.

Steve tries something.

"How's the flush?" he says. "Good water pressure?"

"Dad," says Adam, "we could talk about the murders, you know?"

"Well, uh, okay," says Steve. "I didn't know if you'd be interested?"

"I'm interested," says Adam. "I don't go to prisons in Dubai to visit dead women very often."

"They're trying to kill Amy," says Steve.

"I mean, that's another reason why I'm interested," says Adam. "Do you know who?"

"A man called Rob Kenna, hired by a man called François Loubet."

"And they're in Dubai?"

"Kenna is for sure," says Steve. "That's why I popped into the golf club on the way here. Kenna was sitting at the bar wearing sunglasses indoors. He's a DJ."

"A DJ's trying to kill Amy? She must hate that. Did you speak to him?"

"No need to make a fuss in public," says Steve. "I'll get him. He was playing golf with an old Cockney bloke who looked like a talker."

Adam nods. "And where's François Loubet?"

"'Where's Loubet?' isn't the question," says Steve. "The question is 'Who's Loubet?'"

"Okay," says Adam. "Who's Loubet?"

"That's what I'm trying to find out," says Steve.

The two men sit in silence for a while longer. Every time Steve thinks of something to say, he gets embarrassed. What does Adam want to hear? They occasionally give each other a little smile and nod. Adam is having the same struggle, Steve can tell. Perhaps, one day, he should talk to Adam about Deb—

"I might hit the hay," says Adam. "Long day."

"Good idea," says Steve. Great idea. Problem solved. "I'm going to see if there's anything on the telly."

"Yeah," says Adam.

Adam stands and salutes "Good night." This is to avoid a hug both of them would be too embarrassed to have.

"Night, skipper," says Adam. "There're towels in the airing cupboard."

Maybe they *should* talk about Debbie? But how? How do you raise that sort of thing? It's just too much. Adam reaches the door.

"Stegosaurus," says Steve, taking himself by surprise.

Adam turns around. "Stegosaurus?"

"That was your favorite, wasn't it?" Steve says. "Stegosaurus. And you liked a triceratops too."

Adam nods. "Didn't mind a triceratops. To be fair."

"Triceratops," repeats Steve.

"Diplodocus," says Adam.

The two grown men look at each other, both waiting for the other to say something more. Steve finally cracks.

"Can I ask you another question?"

"Of course, Dad," says Adam. "Anything."

"What are you supposed to wear in a sauna?"

The pause suggests that this wasn't a question Adam was expecting.

"In a sauna? Nothing," says Adam. "Just a towel."

"I feared as much," says Steve.

He nods at his son, five feet from him but so far away.

"Airing cupboard, yeah?"

"Airing cupboard," says Adam. "Night, Dad."

85

In the end, Bonnie Gregor spent just over three hours in Costa Coffee. She was about to leave after ninety minutes, because she thought the nice Albanian girl behind the counter was judging her for spending so long over a single cup of coffee, but then the shifts changed, and she was replaced by a girl with glasses who read a book when she wasn't serving. Bonnie also bought a lemon-and-poppy-seed muffin, because she is aware that Costa Coffee is a business, and business is tough these days.

She sent the email to Felicity, because manners are important, and also because it is better safe than sorry, isn't it?

Check-in for her flight has finally opened, and she has returned to kick-nudging her leather holdall through the queue. Waiting had given her plenty of time to think. Working for brands like Forest Paints is all well and good, but it's her own brand she really wants to work on. So perhaps she can put some of this twenty thousand toward some new equipment, new stock, stronger ideas? She knows she makes people smile, and the more people smiling in the world, the better. Would Felicity help her? As soon as she is back from São Paulo, Bonnie will go back to Letchworth and they can start working on next steps.

Bonnie reaches the front of the queue. The same woman is still working on the check-in desk. She flashes the same smile.

"Don't tell me," she says. "São Paulo, business, just bankrupted yourself in Costa?"

Bonnie laughs along with her, and hands over her passport and boarding pass.

"And the two bags?" the woman says. "Just pop the case up here for me, m'darling."

Bonnie heaves the case with the wonky wheel up onto the belt.

"And you packed this yourself?"

Bonnie nods. She actually did pack this one herself. Well, with her mum's help. The woman ties a sticky label around the handle.

"And the other one, m'dear."

Bonnie lifts up the leather holdall.

"And you packed this one yourself too?"

"Mmm hmm," says Bonnie. "Mmm hmm."

Just as a label is being tied to the handle of the holdall, there is a commotion behind her in the queue. The woman looks over Bonnie's shoulder and points at someone.

"There's a queue, sir."

Bonnie turns to see who is causing the problem. A man in his late fifties is barging his way to the front, to the fury of the other passengers.

"Sir . . ."

The man, a little out of breath, heads straight for Bonnie and snatches the leather holdall from the belt.

"That's my b—" begins Bonnie, before seeing another figure pushing to the front of the queue. Felicity Woollaston. "Felicity?"

Felicity puts her hands on her knees as she catches her breath. "So sorry, Bonnie, my mistake. Booked you on the wrong flight." She nods toward Tony. "This is Tony."

"Hello, Bonnie," says Tony, now taking her case off the luggage belt too and placing it next to the holdall.

"Is everything okay, m'darling?" asks the check-in clerk.

"Yes, all fine," says Bonnie. "This is my agent. What's happening?"

"Just a mix-up," says Felicity. "Nothing to worry about."

Tony picks up the cases and leads Bonnie and Felicity away from the desks. "You got my email?"

"In the nick of time," says Felicity. "We nearly didn't make it."

"Roadworks on the M3 slip road," says Tony. "As per."

"Let's get you a Costa, and have a little chat, shall we?" says Felicity. "My treat."

86

As so often, the sun shines brightly on a brand-new Dubai day. Everything is possible here.

Rosie is enjoying the view from the breakfast terrace. Henk has arranged for them to have a meeting with Max Highfield before the Diamond Conference a little later this morning. She has a plan to get him to talk, or at least to find out if he's lying. Rosie will be pretending that she wants Max to star in the film of one of her books. Steve is going to play a big-shot movie producer, and Rosie is already looking forward to dressing him up.

Does Max even know who François Loubet is, though? Amy will not be safe until he's found. All of this journey will have been wasted. But she knows Steve will find—

Suddenly a very large figure blots out the sun.

"Miss D'Antonio, I wonder if I might join you?"

Rosie looks up at the obstruction, a bear of a man in a tank top and Speedos. He must be very rich indeed to be wearing those in this hotel. Russian accent. She knows precisely who he is, and today there is no Amy to protect her. While they were chasing the ghost of François Loubet, the flesh and blood of Vasiliy Karpin has been chasing her.

What unfortunate timing. If she'd known she was going to die this morning, she would have ordered the pancakes.

Okay, how to play this.

"I'm afraid that I have a rule," says Rosie. "I won't have breakfast with anyone who wants to kill me."

"Lucky I don't have the same rule," says the man. "I would never eat. My name is Vasiliy Karpin."

Rosie hadn't needed telling. "You'd better sit, Mr. Karpin. I'm assuming you can't kill me right here, but perhaps you'll prove me wrong."

Vasiliy Karpin lowers himself onto the chair. You had to admire chairs sometimes, those thin legs, but look at the weight they could carry.

"So, Mr. Karpin," Rosie begins, "are you looking for an apology or a corpse?"

"Oh, neither, neither," says Vasiliy. "I am looking for myself to apologize. Even though I believe you described my face as that of 'a bulldog chewing a nettle'?"

"Not at all," says Rosie. "I think that was a mistranslation. It was 'a bull-frog chewing a nettle.'"

Vasiliy laughs, like an elephant seal in great distress. "My wife's sister, you don't know her, she says you are right. That is what I look like!"

Vasiliy reaches into a cloth swimming bag, and Rosie tenses. He brings out a book and a pen. It is *Dead Men & Diamonds*.

"Do you think you could sign it for her?"

Rosie raises an inquiring eyebrow.

"For my sister-in-law," says Vasiliy. "She will kill me if I don't get it signed."

"Of course," says Rosie, taking the book. "What's her name?"

"Yevdokiya-Ivanovna," says Vasiliy.

Rosie nods. "And how do I spell that?"

"Just the normal way," says Vasiliy. "We were at a barbecue, in Sochi, and I was angry about something, I don't know what, and I saw she had your book and I say, 'Oh, that's the lady I am going to kill!' and Yevdokiya-Ivanovna says, 'She is my favorite writer, she is beautiful; if you kill her, I will kill you back,' and if you know my sister-in-law, you know she means it, so I said I won't kill her."

"When was this?" Rosie asks.

"A few weeks ago," says Vasiliy. "Something like that."

Rosie signs the book and hands it back. "And you didn't tell anyone you'd called off the hit?"

Vasiliy shrugs. "I call for so many hits, I call off so many hits. It would be a full-time job."

"So I've had a bodyguard for no reason?"

"No such thing as no reason," says Vasiliy. "Everything has a reason."

He has a point there. But it does leave one loose end hanging.

"So you haven't hired a man called Eddie Flood to kill me?"

"Never heard of him," says Vasiliy.

Rosie nods. "Sorry I used your name in my book. I shouldn't have, really."

"I got a signed book out of it," says Vasiliy. "And if you ever need me to kill anyone?"

Vasiliy stands, with some effort, and shakes Rosie's hand.

"That's terrifically kind of you," says Rosie, having to avert her eyes from the departing Russian's Speedos.

On the way up to her suite last night Rosie had seen a familiar sight. Eddie Flood hiding badly.

But if Eddie Flood *isn't* here to kill her, and he isn't here to kill Amy, what *is* he here for?

87

Eddie Flood stretches and looks at his watch. He's had a good nine hours' kip. That'll serve him well. You have to sleep well.

He's decided. Today's the day.

The odds are against him, he knows that. But he's been in that position many times before.

Is he nervous? Sure. But is he ready? Yes.

He packs his bag and pats it for good luck.

He'll follow Rosie this morning, then, as soon as she's by herself in her room, that's his cue to strike.

He walks over to his window and draws back the curtains. His view is of aluminum air-conditioning ducts, snaking up a crumbling stone wall. Rob Kenna's fifteen grand was never going to last forever.

And that's why today's the day.

88

Max Highfield is lying naked, save for some white briefs, on a sheepskin rug, with diamonds sprinkled on his bare chest.

A photographer moves around him, exhorting him to "Look mean, Max," "Look sexy, Max," "Think deep thoughts, okay, okay, even deeper thoughts if you can."

Rosie is sitting on a yoga ball, smoking a joint.

"What would my character be called?" Max looks into the distance, as if at the explosion of a distant planet he once called home.

"Do you want to hear the idea first?" Rosie asks.

Max's bodyguard, a woman in her twenties called Abby, who has been sitting at a laptop up to now, stands.

"Okay, that's time."

"Just two or three more," says the photographer, still snapping away.

Abby takes the camera in her fist and places it gently on the floor. "I said that's time. Tux on now, Mr. Highfield."

She hands Max Highfield a tuxedo, and he turns to Rosie.

"Name first," says Max. "Let me get the vibe of the thing."

"He's called Blake Scott," says Rosie.

"I like it," says Max, grunting. "Blake Scott. What does he look like?"

"Like you," says Rosie. "Exactly like you."

Max pulls a dress shirt over his head. "Maybe he could have a mustache?"

"Could do," agrees Rosie. She has dealt with, dated, and divorced many actors in her time. "I wouldn't have thought of that."

"That's what you get with Max Highfield," says Max Highfield. He motions for Abby to pass him a bow tie. "So Henk says you're a writer?"

"Me?" says Rosie. "Yes."

"I write too," says Max, now reaching his hand out to Abby for a thick, green smoothie.

"Have you sold sixty million books?" Rosie asks.

"Nah," says Max. "Books are too twentieth century. I write poems mainly. Stream-of-consciousness stuff. Not even poems, really, a whole different art form. I don't think you'd be able to describe them."

"Oh, I bet I could have a good go," says Rosie.

"So I'm Blake Scott," says Max. "And I've got a mustache. What else? It's pretty thin so far, writer."

Max nods over to Steve.

"And who's he?"

"Steve," says Steve. "I'm the producer."

Max nods. "You sweat a lot, my friend."

"It's very hot," says Steve. "And I'm wearing a suit."

"I don't sweat," says Max.

"No?" says Rosie.

"A lot of good people don't," says Max. "Okay, I don't like this idea."

"You haven't heard it yet," says Rosie.

"I'm not feeling it, though," says Max.

This is one of the many reasons why, whenever Rosie sells one of her books to Hollywood, she doesn't like to get involved. Bank the check, turn up at the premiere, chat with Graham Norton, job done.

"Also, I don't just do action," says Max. "I did Shakespeare at school. But go on, I've got a couple of minutes till I'm onstage."

"It's a story about money-smuggling, Max," Rosie begins.

"Like . . . smuggling money?" replies Max.

"Yes, like that," confirms Rosie. "It's the story of a syndicate that pays influencers to smuggle bags of money around the world."

Not a flicker from Max, so far. "And that's illegal?"

"Yes," says Steve. "It is."

"This bloody government," says Max. "Okay, so is Blake Scott an influencer?"

"No," says Steve. "He's the one in control of the syndicate."

"So he's a bad guy?" says Max, finally pulling on some trousers. "I don't really play bad guys."

"He's nuanced," says Rosie.

"I don't do nuance either," says Max. "Nuance is too woke."

"I've hacked into The Hampstead Dog Hotel," Abby announces, bringing her laptop over to Max.

Max eagerly takes the laptop and starts cooing. Rosie raises an eyebrow at Abby.

"Mr. Highfield's dogs are at a residential facility in North London," says Abby. "I've just hacked into their outdoor security cameras so he can see his dogs."

"Is *that* legal?" Steve asks.

"Any cameras facing public spaces are legal to view," says Abby. "Very difficult to access but legal to view."

Max is tearing up. "They look so happy. Thanks, Abby."

Abby takes the laptop back.

"Would you like to hear more of the story?" Rosie asks.

"Sure," says Max. "Maybe Blake Scott has two dogs?"

"I'll note that down," says Rosie.

"Only the influencers—the ones smuggling all the money—start getting shot," says Steve. "One by one."

"This actually happened to a friend of mine," says Max.

"Yes?" says Rosie.

"Yeah, Jeff Nolan. Good guy."

"This exact story?" Rosie asks. If Max is involved in all this, he is covering it very well.

"Same thing," says Max. "Influencers getting shot. I don't think they were money-smugglers, though. That's a nice twist."

"You like the idea?" Rosie asks.

"Sure," says Max. "Where would we film?"

"We'd start in South Carolina," says Steve. "Then St. Lucia, then Ireland."

"And we'd finish the whole thing in Dubai," says Rosie.

"Sounds nice," says Max, expertly looping his bow tie. Again, no sign that any of this is ringing alarm bells for him.

Max slips into a pair of dress shoes. "Send it to my agent. Tell him I said yes. But I need my character to be a good guy. Make someone else the baddie, and I kill him."

"There's another character who would be perfect as the bad guy," says Rosie.

"Great," says Max, heading toward the stage.

"François Loubet?"

Max thinks. "I've heard that name before. French?"

"One supposes so," says Rosie.

"Great," says Max. "I'll ask Timothée Chalamet. He's a mate. I come first in the billing, though."

Max disappears onto the stage and they hear applause. Abby follows to the side of the stage with her laptop.

"You're good," says Rosie to Abby. "I'll tell Henk."

"Thank you, ma'am," says Abby, and is gone. They hear Max start his speech.

"Now what's beautiful, ultra-hard, and incredibly expensive? No, not me. Diamonds. The last time I was around this many carats, I was in Sainsbury's."

Rosie turns to Steve.

"Not a flicker," says Rosie. "The whole way through the pitch."

"Because Sainsbury's is an English supermarket, you see, and they sell carrots."

"But if Max isn't Joe Blow," says Steve, "who is? Because either he's not involved at all, or he's a very good actor."

Rosie looks at Steve. "And I think we both know the answer to that."

89

D awn rises in the City of London. On the eightieth floor of a building that nobody can mention for reasons of security, Amy, Jeff Nolan, and Susan Knox, Jeff's head of HR, sit at a boardroom table, files of paper spread out between them. The first rays of sun pick up dust in the air.

"Every single one of them," says Amy.

"Thirty-five clients," confirms Susan Knox. "All of whom have worked for Vivid Viral, and all of whom were introduced to Maximum Impact by Max Highfield. There are payments of ten grand directly into his account for each of them."

Amy leafs through the new file. "This goes back just over two years. Name after name, introduced by Highfield, including Courtney Lewis, where the whole plan began to unravel."

"Are there details of any of the jobs they did?" Jeff asks. "Where they might have traveled and when?"

"Low-value clients," says Susan. "No one in this file could have afforded to have us accompany them on a trip. That's why they were chosen."

"Not a single clue?" Amy asks.

"The file is just names, numbers, and addresses," says Susan. "Everything else must have gone through Vivid Viral, I suppose."

"Then none of this brings us any closer to Loubet," says Amy.

Jeff is studying something intently. "Max would have needed help."

"Jesus," says Amy. "Who would be stupid enough to help Max Highfield?"

Jeff looks at Susan, and then at Amy. The sunlight now pierces the window blinds, throwing black stripes onto his face. "I think you know who, Amy."

What's happening here? Amy feels like she is walking into a trap.

"The first name on this list," says Jeff, "was introduced to me by Max Highfield three days after he came back from a trip to San Francisco."

"Come on—" Amy starts. Now she sees.

"Where his close-protection officer," says Jeff, "was Amy Wheeler."

"Amy?" says Susan.

"And on the day that the second name on the list was introduced, who was Amy working for?" Jeff pauses for an effect that is not needed, because they all know the answer. "François Loubet."

"No," says Amy.

"We both know exactly what's happened here, Amy," says Jeff.

90

Steve has never been in a sauna before, and he is fairly sure he never will be again. But he's investigating, and investigating always involves some sort of sacrifice.

What he needs right now is a friendly introduction to Rob Kenna, and he has found just the man for the job.

He sits on a bench diagonally opposite the big Cockney he'd seen playing golf with Rob yesterday. Could be an ex-cop, this fella, open, dependable face, bald, red head pouring with sweat.

"Like a sauna in here, innit?" says Steve.

Mickey Moody smiles. "You sound like a Londoner?"

"Steve," says Steve, wondering if it was supposed to be this difficult to breathe. "Bermondsey born and bred."

"Mickey," says Mickey Moody. "Billericay. You been playing?"

"Not a golfer, just love a sauna. Really opens up the pores," says Steve. He has just been googling saunas. "Had a walk round the course, got my ten thousand steps in, then straight in here."

"People don't normally wear T-shirts and shorts in the sauna," says Mickey.

"I hear ya," says Steve.

"Or shoes," adds Mickey.

Steve had suspected all this, but he wasn't comfortable with any form of nudity. Even feet.

"Saw you playing with that DJ. Rob whassisname?"

Mickey Moody looks at Steve more closely. "Rob Kenna? Did you?"

"I'm not a cop, I'm just nosy," says Steve. "What's he like?"

Mickey shrugs. "Don't care if you are a cop. Dunno, really, we just play golf. He seems all right. I've learned not to ask too many questions of people round here."

"Why's that?" Steve asks.

"What do you do, Steve? For a job?" Mickey asks.

"Scented candles," says Steve, taking himself by surprise.

Mickey nods. "I was in scrap, for years."

"You meet a few characters there," says Steve.

"You do, old son, you do," agrees Mickey. "And that's the point. I learned long ago not to ask anyone anything. Did my job, got paid, went home to the wife. People'd come into the yard trying to sell you all sorts, brand-new Ferraris, all stuff you wouldn't believe. Or they'd ask if you could leave the gate open at night and not look too closely at the crusher the next morning."

"Sounds a lot like the scented-candle business," says Steve. Both men laugh, and Steve follows this up with a hacking cough from the overpowering eucalyptus fumes.

"I always gave a polite no," says Mickey. "No offense given, no offense taken, but I'm not your man. And one by one these guys with the Ferraris and the dead bodies would get nicked or shot, or get coked up and die in their pool. And there was me, nice little business, nice little house, and now a nice little retirement, little villa by the golf course."

"Never tempted?"

"A couple of years we struggled," says Mickey. "And you start thinking, 'Maybe,' 'Should I?' You know? But it's not how I was born. I was raised by my grandmothers, and they'd have killed me. Where do you live now, Steve?"

"Ormskirk," says Steve. Where did that come from? Steve isn't even sure where Ormskirk is. Near Liverpool?

"Where's that?" Mickey asks. "Up north?"

Steve nods, hoping it is. "It's not exactly Dubai."

"Nowhere is," says Mickey. "This place reminds me of those days back in Essex, see? Everybody's at it all day long. Speedboats and hot tubs and God knows what. Money coming out of their arses, the lot of them. So I don't ask, you know? Maybe it's all legitimate."

"But Rob Kenna's just a DJ?" Steve says.

Mickey holds up his hands. "Who knows? None of my business. I like playing golf with the fella. But one day he won't be there anymore, I know that. We used to play with a lad called Big Frank, a fruit-and-veg importer; they found him dead in Colombia. Perhaps he was out there picking bananas? For a while there was a lad called Gomez, and he sold cars, until he ended up in the boot of one in a quarry in Kent. Not so long ago there was Davey: he got killed somewhere; they never found him. They come and go. Are you really in the scented-candle business?"

" 'Fraid so," says Steve, forcing himself to look at the naked Cockney, as if being in a sauna was the most natural thing in the world. And, just then, something rings a bell deep within him. What is it?

"Heroin on the side?" asks Mickey. "People trafficking?"

"Just candles," says Steve.

"You're one of the smart ones, then," says Mickey. "Take a good look around Dubai: there ain't many of us left."

Mickey would have made a good cop. Cops weren't allowed tattoos in Steve's day, though. Changed now—tattoos, beards, the lot.

How to finesse this? Steve needs to speak to Rob Kenna. And it has to be an "accidental" meeting, an introduction from an old friend. But is Mickey Moody too wily for all that? He needs a bit of peace and quiet so he can talk this whole thing through with Debbie.

"You okay there, fella?" Mickey asks.

"Sorry, miles away," says Steve. "Is your wife still alive, Mickey?"

"Died," says Mickey. "Cancer, five years back."

"Sorry," says Steve. "Same boat."

Mickey nods, then looks toward the door as if making sure no one is about to come in. "You ever talk to her?"

Steve also looks at the door, then back at Mickey. "All day, every day. You?"

"I was talking to her when you walked in," says Mickey. "I was telling her about the putt I made on the eighteenth."

Steve smiles. "Sorry to have interrupted you."

Mickey smiles too. "She don't mind. She loved a scented candle. Don't believe in them myself, no offense."

"What does she make of Rob Kenna?"

"Thinks he's a wide boy," says Mickey. "Tells me to steer well clear. Jabbers away."

You see, Debbie, Steve thinks, it's not just me. I'm not the only mad one.

And then he realizes what the ringing bell is.

"You're talking to your wife now," says Mickey. "I can see it."

Steve nods.

"She telling you to whip your shoes off?"

Steve laughs. That's exactly what Debbie would say. But what Debs is actually saying, right this very second, is *You clever bugger, Steve. You know who François Loubet is, don't you?*

Steve closes his eyes and smiles because, yes, he does know. He'll need a bit more evidence, sure, but at least he knows exactly what's happened now. He can't wait to tell Rosie and Amy, and work out what on earth they're going to do next.

Steve kicks off his shoes and peels off his socks. Feet as naked as the day he was born. Let no one say he doesn't know how to celebrate.

"That's the stuff," says Mickey.

91

I can call the police," says Susan to Jeff. "Or you might prefer to deal with this yourself?"

Amy wishes she was back in that car boot, curled up. What's her play here? She goes through Jeff's checklist. Point One: Assess the situation. Point Two: Assess your strengths. Point Thr—

Jeff pulls a gun from his jacket and points it at Amy. So much for the checklist. Amy immediately does the same.

Susan Knox eyes them both.

"Okay, children," she says. "I'm calling the police."

"No," say both Amy and Jeff, guns trained on each other.

Get out of this one, Amy.

"Put the gun down, Amy," says Susan.

Amy thinks about how nice it would be for Steve to come through the door right now. He would know what to do. Amy is at a loss, because Jeff's training is her training; they each cancel the other out. So what would Steve do?

"Put it down, Amy," says Jeff. "And let's talk. Persuade me it wasn't you."

Amy shakes her head.

"Someone was helping Max Highfield," says Jeff.

"Please let me call the police," says Susan. "I'm sure they'd happily ask Amy all of these questions."

"No," say Jeff and Amy again.

"It's all there in the files, Amy," says Jeff. "I should have seen it before. You worked with Highfield, you worked with Loubet."

"So did you," says Amy.

"I'm not going through all that again," says Jeff.

If Steve was in the room, what would he do? What would he notice? What's *wrong* here?

"But why didn't you notice thirty-five separate payments to Max Highfield, Jeff?" asks Amy.

"None of my business," says Jeff. "Why would I even look? That's what Susan's for."

"Don't drag me into this," says Susan.

Amy is making no progress here. So perhaps the time for "What would Steve do" is over. Sure, Jeff trained her, but hasn't she learned a few things of her own? Perhaps it's actually time for "What would *Amy* do?"

Here goes nothing.

"You recruited those clients yourself, Jeff," says Amy. "That's what I think. You set Max Highfield up to cover your own tracks. You set up those payments to him, in case somebody came snooping. You set up a deal with Vivid Viral, because you always take care of the little details. And, of course, you were in contact with François Loubet all along."

"You think I sent emails to myself?" says Jeff. "You think I paid someone to drive a car through the windows of Bruno's?"

"That's exactly what I think," says Amy, then speaks to Susan without turning away from Jeff. "Susan, if we looked at those files, could we tell if all those payments to Max Highfield were authorized personally by Jeff?"

"We could," says Susan. "But it would take half an hour or so. Why don't you both put the guns down, and I can—"

"No time," says Amy. She lowers her gun to the floor, then raises it a notch and shoots Jeff Nolan in the leg. Jeff fires back as he falls, but the bullet misses wildly. Amy is on him in an instant, and cable-ties his hands as he thrashes on the floor.

"Get up," says Amy, gun pointed at his head. "We're going for a drive. Susan, if I hear a police siren at any point, I kill him—understand? I need you to look at the files again."

"Amy," says Jeff through clenched teeth, "you're wrong."

"Too late, Jeff," says Amy. "Let's go."

Jeff's checklist came good in the end. Point Six: Act decisively.

The next ten minutes will tell her everything she needs to know.

92

Rob Kenna reaches the ninth tee.

"You got any isotonic water?" he asks his caddy. "I've only got normal, and I can't drink that because of all the estrogen in it."

Of course Rob's caddy has isotonic water. She hands a bottle to him.

Rob hits his tee shot right, flirting with the deep rough that lines the fairway. He gives a sigh of relief as it pulls up short of a thick line of trees. He's avoided some trouble there.

Rob prefers playing with other people, but there's not always the option, is there? Nelson Nunez will be here tomorrow, and he plays, so that'll be nice. Bit of golf, bit of business.

And it's nice to be able to think from time to time. He needs to cut ties with Loubet. He understands that Loubet has to stay under the radar, but, really, if you're doing business with someone, you have to be able to look them in the eye once in a while. You have to protect yourself.

Rob reaches his ball and asks his caddy for a nine-iron. That should do it. No breeze today, so just float it up there. He can see it in his mind's eye, landing dead center on the green, curling down a little toward the hole. Doesn't always work that way, but lovely when it does. Makes everything else worthwhile.

His caddy starts whistling. Rob gives her a glare. When has she ever whistled before?

"You bored?"

"Sorry, boss," she says, long red ponytail swinging in the light breeze.

She probably is bored, to be fair. She came to him via Mickey, and via Davey before that. She was just a caddy, but Rob has given her more responsibilities. She's been around the world a fair bit recently. She's the only person Rob trusts to meet and greet his targets. She knows his business. He's even asked her if she'd fancy turning her hand to the actual killing at some point, but it's not for her.

She whistles again. Rob raises his palms to her in objection, then settles behind the ball.

There is a rustle in the trees on his backswing, so Rob begins his setup again. Lots of stray cats living in these woods.

He has started his backswing when the first shot rings out. It hits him full in the chest. He drops his club and staggers backward. There's someone in the trees. Okay, yeah, there's smoke too. Rob falls to his knees. Someone is screaming. He thinks it must be his caddy, but he can see her running in the distance, red hair flowing behind her, so it must be him. More gunshots.

A figure emerges from the bushes and, pointing a shotgun, looks down at him. And so it is that, just before the final gunshot, Rob Kenna finally gets to look François Loubet in the eye.

93

osie had thought it was the boy from room service. She hadn't actually ordered anything from room service, but she had winked at him in the hotel lobby earlier, so when she'd heard the knock at the door, she just assumed.

She had forgotten, however, that she has recently entered a world where knocks at hotel doors are not always lovers. Sometimes they are assassins.

Rosie invites Eddie Flood in, because what other option does she have? Perhaps she can talk him round? And, if not, well, what a story. She doesn't know where Steve is, but he'll piece together what's happened here.

"I'm sorry to disturb you, Rosie," says Eddie.

"Bit late for that, Eddie," says Rosie.

"I wanted to be ready," says Eddie. "Before we met."

Eddie reaches into his bag for a gun. Rosie reasons that her time may be up. Not for the first time today.

"You'll answer one question, I hope?" says Rosie.

"A question," says Eddie. "Of course."

"Who hired you to kill me?"

"Kill you?" says Eddie, hand in his bag, looking genuinely perplexed.

"You're a hitman?"

"No," says Eddie. "Well, I mean, yes, but define 'hitman,' you know?"

"You tried to shoot my friend Amy," says Rosie. "You were working for Rob Kenna?"

"Rob?" says Eddie. "I mean, I suppose so. I took his money."

"And you kill people?" says Rosie, not unreasonably, in her view.

"Used to," says Eddie. "Even then only once or twice, and only if they deserved it."

"So if you're not a hitman," says Rosie, "what are you?"

Eddie looks embarrassed.

"You've been following us around the world, so you must have a reason," says Rosie.

"I wanted to talk to you, you see," says Eddie. "As soon as I heard your name, I knew it was my chance to meet you."

"So you're a crazed fan?" Rosie asks.

"I'm not a hitman, and I'm not a crazed fan." Eddie pulls his laptop out of his bag. "I'm so sorry I worried you. I'm a writer."

Rosie stares at him.

"I've used the last couple of days, you know, on the planes and what have you, to finish a book I've been working on."

"Uh huh," says Rosie.

"So it's all good," says Eddie, smiling. "I'm not here to kill you. I just want you to read my book."

"Oh, God, Eddie," says Rosie, putting her hand on his arm, "that's *so* much worse."

94

Steve is in a contemplative mood, as he walks along the quayside of Dubai Marina. Here he is, 3,000 miles from home, from the sofa that's been molded into the shape of his backside, from the creak on the third step of the stairs, and the picture of Debbie that smiles at him from the bedside table.

He yearns for all this, physically aches. To be able to shut his own front door, to shut out the world. To get out of the sun.

The Irish Pub is up ahead. It will have British sport and British beer, but it won't be The Brass Monkey with Tony and Jyoti and John. There probably won't even be a quiz.

It's a small life, Steve realizes, that he has wrapped himself up in. Small, and getting smaller.

A man in a suit on a yacht shouts at a woman in a dress on a night out.

Has he enjoyed himself, wonders Steve, as he enters the Irish Pub? Enjoyed this race across the world?

The pub is very noisy, but then everywhere seems to be noisy now. He supposes that Axley is noisy too, but it's his noise, so he doesn't notice it. What Steve doesn't like, increasingly as he gets older, is the noise of other people.

So has he enjoyed himself? Answer the question, Steve. Has he enjoyed seeing new things, meeting new people, buying new shorts?

"Enjoy" is the wrong word. Steve scans the busy bar. There are large flashing signs everywhere saying ENJOY THE CRAIC and IRISH EYES ARE SMILING. Steve has very recently been in a couple of actual Irish pubs, and he doesn't remember any neon signs. He doesn't remember a barman rolling a diamond-encrusted, golden bottle of vodka up his arm and across his shoulder either.

There are huge television screens hanging from the ceiling, all showing sport, the commentators and the graphics competing with each other. There's an awful lot of basketball; again, Steve doesn't ever recall a lot of basketball talk in actual Ireland. Try as he might, though, Steve cannot find any screen showing the snooker. There's some Premier League football, and Steve sees that it is raining in England. He really can't wait to get back.

Yes, "enjoy" is the wrong word. Steve hasn't enjoyed himself since Debbie died. Enjoyment is not how he measures his life anymore, so the question is unfair.

Is he glad? That's a better question. He's glad to have spent time with Amy, that's certain. Glad to have protected her, and to have been protected by her. It's not every daughter-in-law who will high-five you when you've shot a drug dealer in a Coldplay T-shirt, is it?

He's glad to have met Rosie, Steve has to admit that to himself, and he wonders if he will see her again when this is over? Where will she go? Back to her island? He hopes not; she is wasted on an island.

He is glad, he supposes, to have done *something*. To have made his world bigger, if only for a week. He is glad that he has remembered that he's pretty good at his job. That he can do more than find lost dogs and look at CCTV. Though he is very much looking forward to getting back to doing both.

But, yes, he's not bad at this. That's why he's here in this pub. And that's why he's thinking about what will happen next. Because the end is now in clear sight.

Although Steve feels the magnet of Axley beginning to pull him back, he is surprised to feel there's also a part of him resisting this. And at the very moment he sees the person he's been looking for, drinking a pint and talking on his phone, Steve realizes what these conflicting forces are.

The thing that is pulling him back to Axley is that groove in the sofa. The place that is the very shape of him. The place he has settled into so thoroughly over the years that it fits him exactly.

And the thing resisting that pull is remembering that, not so long ago, there were two grooves in that sofa. And one has vanished, as if it was never there.

It is not Axley that Steve wants to go back to; it is Debbie. But it is interesting to Steve that, wherever he's traveled, she has been right there with him. It's been nice to show her a bit of the world.

She's here now, Steve knows that, as he pulls up a chair and sits down next to François Loubet.

95

Amy has taken a lemon sweatshirt from around her waist and tied it around Jeff's thigh as a tourniquet.

Despite the extraordinary pain he must be feeling, Jeff is not screaming. Firstly, because he has too much self-respect, and secondly, because Amy told him she will shoot him if he makes any loud noises.

Also thirdly, because, after marching Jeff out of the boardroom, rather than bundling him into a car, she doubled back and put him in Henk's private den, behind the boardroom mirror. So Amy assumes that Jeff is starting to understand that everything is not as it seems.

They can see Susan Knox as she is looking through the personnel files on her computer.

"She won't find anything," says Jeff, voice getting quieter as Amy's gun presses closer to his temple.

"I know," says Amy. "She's not looking at the files. She's deleting the files."

Jeff looks over at her. In the boardroom, Susan is making a phone call.

Amy says to Jeff, "If I put the gun down, do you promise to stay quiet for one minute?"

Jeff nods, then gestures down to the tourniquet. Amy pulls it tighter, as the sound of Susan's call comes through the speakers.

"It's me . . . I know . . . I know . . . but it *is* an emergency . . . yeah, are you in a bar? Can you hear me? François? . . . They know it's not Max . . . no . . . no, it's all good, nothing for you to worry . . . Amy thinks it's Jeff . . . yep, Jeff . . . she shot him . . . I know, that's Amy . . . well, I'm going to confirm it for her . . . we don't have to kill him . . . I'll explain it all, he'll understand . . . we can't, François . . . me or him? . . . Jesus, Jeff's my friend . . . I'll sort it, François . . . but I said no more killing . . . I'll need more money . . . another hundred thousand . . . and this is the last one . . . the father-in-law? I don't know . . . Take care, take care."

Jeff looks at Amy. "You knew it was Susan?"

"No," says Amy. "I just knew it wasn't me and it wasn't Max. Which left you and Susan."

"So you shot me? It could still have been Henk."

"Yeah, I suppose so, but it turns out it wasn't, doesn't it?" says Amy. "Point Six, Jeff: Act decisively. I wanted to see what she would do. If she had called the police, I'd have known it was you, and if she had called Loubet, I'd have known it was her."

Jeff grimaces in pain. "You could have just punched me."

"A bit of logic and a bit of chaos," says Amy. "Seems to have done the trick."

"A bit of Steve and a bit of you," says Jeff.

"Shall we go and chat with Susan?" says Amy. "Then maybe get you to a hospital?"

Jeff nods. "I've got a guy on Harley Street who does all my gunshot stuff."

"I didn't hit anything important," says Amy.

"But why Susan?" Jeff asks.

"How long has Susan worked for you, Jeff?" Amy asks.

"Thirty years or so?" guesses Jeff.

"How much does she get paid?"

"Sixty grand," says Jeff.

"And where does she live?" Amy asks.

"Hampstead," says Jeff.

"How many people do you know who live in Hampstead on sixty grand a year? She must have been fleecing you for years."

"I thought maybe her parents left her the house?"

"Her parents are alive, Jeff," says Amy. "She brought them to the staff picnic last year."

"I left early," says Jeff. "You know me and people."

"When's her birthday?"

Jeff shrugs. "How would I know that?"

"Yours is the twenty-fifth of February," says Amy. "What did you buy her for Christmas?"

"For Christmas?" Jeff asks. "Nothing. She didn't ask for anything."

Amy nods. "And how did she score on your Psychopath Test?"

"Ninety-six," says Jeff. "Same as me. That's why she's head of HR."

Amy nods. "What did Henk score?"

"Like twelve or something," says Jeff. "He's surprisingly sane."

"That's why you were a good team," says Amy.

Amy's phone starts to buzz. Looking into the boardroom, she sees that Susan is ringing her. She answers, quietly.

"Tell me the worst," says Amy.

"It's Jeff," says Susan. "All of those payments were authorized from his personal laptop, and the emails from Loubet were from his own laptop too. He put the whole thing together. Amy, I'm so sorry I didn't see it sooner."

"Okay," says Amy. "What should I do? Police?"

"After everything he's done?" Susan says. "I don't know. He killed people, Amy. And for what? Money. Doesn't he have enough?"

"Money does unusual things to people," says Amy.

"And he was happy to see you die," says Susan. "Happy to set you up, happy to set Max Highfield up. I think there's only one thing you can do."

"Report him to HR?"

"Kill him," says Susan. "You'll have my full support."

Amy puts down the phone and looks at Jeff. "You know the odd Christ-mas present might have made all the difference? You have to make people feel appreciated—even I know that."

"You know one day I'm going to have to shoot you back?" says Jeff.

"I know, skipper," says Amy, and she and Jeff share a hug.

96

So you were François Loubet all along?" Steve says to Mickey Moody, plonking two honest pints of British bitter on the table. Steve has just let Mickey finish a phone call.

"Who's François Loubet?" asks Mickey, raising his pint an inch in thanks.

"The world's greatest money-smuggler," says Steve. "It's you, eh?"

"How do you work that out, then?" laughs Mickey. "Taking a bit of a leap?"

"So you're just a good, old-fashioned scrap-metal dealer from Billericay?" says Steve.

"Until anyone can prove otherwise," says Mickey. "Which they can't. You fancy watching the Man City match?"

"You're sure no one can prove anything?" Steve asks.

"Deadly sure," says Mickey. "And I'd be very careful if I was you."

"Oh, Mickey, I've been careful for years now," says Steve. "Hasn't got me anywhere. You need to take a risk or two in life, don't you?"

Mickey laughs and sups his pint. "Amen to that, Steve."

"You heard Rob Kenna was killed," says Steve.

"Another one gone," says Mickey. "I'm running out of mates."

"You are," says Steve. "Who have you got to talk to now except your wife?"

"That's enough for me," says Mickey.

"Why don't we talk to each other for a bit?" says Steve. "Couple of old men?"

"Nah, you're all right," says Mickey. "Let's just watch the match."

"They're not going to catch you, Mickey," says Steve. "You're too good."

"Nothing to catch me for," says Mickey.

Steve smiles. "Why don't you just tell me something about yourself that's true?"

"Something that's true?"

"No comebacks, no recordings, just you and me. Would be a relief after so many years of lying, no?"

The corner of Mickey's mouth goes up. Every criminal wants to tell the truth eventually. Enough of the truth to be seen but not enough of the truth to be convicted.

"Okay," Mickey begins. "You asked for it. At the age of fourteen I started to follow the milk carts around, on an old bicycle."

"I remember the milk carts," says Steve.

"Different cart, different route each day. I'd steal the pints of milk from Bethnal Green doorsteps, and then sell them on later to all the people furious their milk hadn't arrived."

"Enterprising," says Steve.

"After two weeks or so, and a nice bit of cash, which went straight into the building society, I got nicked by an off-duty police officer who was coming home from banging someone or other. Five in the morning, shirt flapping out of his flies. Anyway, I get away with a caution that time, and I took it seriously. I swore I'd never be arrested again and, fifty-four years later, I'm pleased to say I never have been. Never even had a speeding ticket, and that's the God's honest. Who else can say that?"

"Me," says Steve.

Mickey laughs. "The thing is with the police, you know they have a radar, and your only job is to stay under it. It's not rocket science."

"And you've stayed under the radar?" Steve asks.

Mickey shrugs. "I've known an awful lot of criminals, some very successful ones too. But one by one they make mistakes and get arrested, or they make different mistakes, and somebody kills them."

"Like you killed Rob Kenna," says Steve. "Things were closing in on you a bit?"

"Careful, Steve," says Mickey. "We're just two old fellas having a chat. Don't spoil it."

"You had to do it yourself, though, didn't you?" says Steve. "Usually when you have people killed you get Rob to do it for you. But you couldn't hire him to kill himself."

"You're a very interesting man, Mr. Steven Wheeler of Axley, Hampshire," says Mickey. "You're wasted in the scented-candle business."

"So you know who I am?" says Steve.

"Of course," says Mickey. "I've had people looking into you. But you won't find out a thing about me that I don't want you to know."

Steve smiles now. "You're one of the richest criminals in the world, Mickey. And I'm just a private eye from a sleepy village. You know I can't prove anything."

"Got that right," says Mickey.

"But I do *know* that you're François Loubet," says Steve.

"You don't know a thing, Steve Wheeler," says Mickey. "God bless you for even trying."

"François Loubet ordered the deaths of six people," says Steve. "And he ordered the death of my daughter-in-law. And I believe he shot Rob Kenna around three hours ago."

"Sounds like a wrong 'un," says Mickey. "But he's not me."

"You think your grandmothers would be proud of you?"

"Excuse me?" Steve sees Mickey's hackles rise.

"You think they'd be proud of how you make a living?"

"You don't talk about them," says Mickey. "Now let's enjoy the football before I have to make another phone call and have you dealt with."

"Well, you can't ring Rob Kenna anymore," says Steve.

"What are you?" says Mickey, staring at Steve. "Arsenal fan?"

"Millwall," says Steve. "You think your two grans would be proud that you walked out of your front door this afternoon, walked across a sandy track into a copse by the golf course, big bag in your hand, lay in wait for Rob Kenna, and then shot him dead?"

"You're delusional," says Mickey. "It's the sun."

"And then ran back to the safety of your house before the first siren even sounded? Without even zipping the bag back up? They'd be proud of that, would they?"

"You know nothing about my nans," says Mickey. "Don't try to wind me up. It won't work."

"I know something about them," says Steve. "I know their names."

Mickey looks at Steve over his pint.

"Their names are tattooed on your shoulder blades," says Steve. "Elizabeth and Louisa."

Mickey shakes his head and smiles to himself.

"God rest 'em both," says Mickey.

"Lou and Bet," says Steve.

"Lou and Bet," repeats Mickey. He thinks for a long while, then smiles. "That's all you got?"

Steve shrugs. "It's just good to know I'm right, that's all. I'm happy I worked it out. And that's why you should always wear a T-shirt in the sauna."

"I'll buy the next round," says Mickey. "There's your reward."

"I don't want a drink from you," says Steve.

Mickey nods. "Let me tell you something, Steve Wheeler. I was raised, back and forth, between my two grans. My mum died; my dad disappeared. I never asked why, and no one ever told me. But those two women were the making of me."

"Lou and Bet," says Steve.

"Lou and Bet. They taught me to work hard, to save what you earn, to look after your friends and family, and, most of all, never be flash. No one likes a show pony. So I live a quiet life. My villa's got everything I need. Little pool, thirty seconds to the golf course, spare bedrooms for the kids and grandkids to visit. No one is ever going to be knocking at the door, asking how I can afford it. The police have looked into me from time to time. Inevitable with the company I've had to keep over the years. But if you have the choice of investigating a man with a Lamborghini or a man who drives a Volvo estate, who do you investigate?"

"So why do it?" says Steve.

"How long have I got left on the planet? Twenty years or so? When I die my son and daughter are going to be very surprised. They'll be expecting to be left a bit, for sure. The villa's worth a few bob, but they won't be expecting two point six billion."

"Billion?" says Steve, smiling. "Family. You'd do anything for them, eh?"

"I'd do anything for them," says Mickey.

"Me too," says Steve. "That's why you picked on the wrong person this time."

Mickey laughs. "I'll need to keep an eye on you and Amy from now on. But if you leave me be, I'll leave you be."

"Afraid not," says Steve. "You've killed innocent people. And you've tried to kill my daughter-in-law."

"It's all business," says Mickey.

"Mickey," says Steve, "your family is not more important than my family. I promise I'll leave you alone when you're in prison. Probably Al-Awir, where you had Courtney Lewis killed."

"If you say so, old son," says Mickey. "But I'm not sure my tattoos are the killer evidence you think they are."

"No, the tattoos just helped me piece it all together," says Steve. "That's how I knew you were Loubet. And that's why I was able to get the video evidence."

"No one's been videoing me," says Mickey. "No one even photographs me. I'm just a boring old man. No one's watching."

"And yet I know you left your house at 2:05 with that long canvas bag, and that you returned home a little faster at 2:31, one minute after Rob Kenna was shot, canvas bag unzipped, shotgun on show."

"Impossible," says Mickey. "I'd have seen if you were hanging around filming me. You're not that good."

"No one was hanging around, Mickey," says Steve. "Though a bodyguard called Abby's been busy this afternoon."

"Riddles, Steve," says Mickey. "No one ever got convicted on riddles."

"Well," says Steve. "My final question should clear it up for you."

"Go on," says Mickey. "What's your final question?"

Steve drains the last of his pint and places it, carefully, back down on the table. "What sort of doorbell do you have, Mickey?"

97

You have to change your angle sometimes, if you want to see what's right in front of you.

On that hot wet pavement, with his life slowly leaving his body, Archer can finally see it all.

There are pools of light from gas lamps, but they're useless against the dark, useless against the shadows that haunt these black streets. Shine as many lights as you want, but Soho, that dirty old town, always has a way of staying hidden.

Archer thought he'd had him this time, could taste it like iron and gunmetal. After all those years hunting, there he was. The man people swore was a ghost, right in front of him. This whisper of a man, spiriting himself through the Soho underground of jazz clubs and dive bars, no two people ever seeing the same thing.

"I've seen the cat, sure, electric-blue suit, three women on his arm."

"I met the dude once, I'm sure. Taller than a doorway, cane tipped with gold."

"If you ever see him, make sure you unsee him fast."

"Now that Archer had finally seen him, seen the flesh and blood, he finally understood."

"SHOULD I go on?" asks Eddie. "Are you bored? Is it bad?"

Rosie D'Antonio drapes an arm across Eddie's naked chest. "I'm not bored yet, and it isn't too bad yet. You have me where you want me."

"You're sure?" asks Eddie.

"You'd better hook me quickly, though," says Rosie. "So far you're a better lover than writer."

Eddie looks disappointed.

"Buck up, soldier," says Rosie. "You're a very, very good lover."

Eddie returns to reading.

THERE are sirens in the distance, normal as birdsong around here. But it's all too late. A woman is kneeling to help him, red dress, kind voice. If Archer could have told her what he finally knew, he would. But, cheek on pavement, and the neon lights of the Soho sex shops reflected in the plum-black pool of his own blood, he has already spoken his last words.

When he first hit the ground, Archer had seen the man walk away, nice and slow, his whistle echoing along the high alley walls. He saw the man's knife slip from his sleeve and clatter down a storm drain. That's when Archer noticed it. The sole of the man's left shoe. Archer knew, finally, who he was. And knew, finally, why they'd never been able to catch him.

"No way?" says Rosie. "The sole of his shoe?"

She motions for Eddie to continue.

WOULD anybody ever catch him? This cool-cat killer? Archer's son, Eric Junior, is two years into his Met career. Archer knows how this will go. His son or his killer: only one of them will survive what's to come.

The sole of the left shoe. It was all there. And now Archer's son must spend a lifetime finding out what Archer knows but can no longer say.

EDDIE closes his laptop. "That's just the prologue, really, just rough."

"What does Archer see, Eddie?" Rosie asks. "On the sole of the guy's shoe?"

"You want me to tell you?" Eddie asks. "I think you'll be surprised."

"No," says Rosie. "I want to read it. The whole thing. And I want Archer's son to kill him, and to tell him why while he's doing it."

"You'll have to wait and see," says Eddie. "I didn't think I'd ever finish it, but then I've been sitting on private planes to South Carolina, to Hawaii—"

"Sorry about Hawaii," says Rosie.

"Nah," says Eddie. "Got a lot of work done, and at least it wasn't Alaska."

"You clever thing," says Rosie.

"Then Ireland, then England, then Dubai, nothing else to do but write."

"And then you caught me," says Rosie.

"Do you think anyone will read it?" says Eddie.

"I think lots of people will read it," says Rosie. "And I'm very lucky to be the first. After that it's going straight to my agent. What's it called?"

"It doesn't have a title yet," says Eddie. "I'm no good at titles. I want to name it after the guy with the shoe."

"The killer?" says Rosie. "Causes havoc wherever he goes?"

"And then some," says Eddie.

"Then I've got a title for you," says Rosie.

"Go on," says Eddie.

"Write this down," says Rosie. "*A Cat Called Trouble*."

98

From Heathrow, Bonnie went straight back to her mum's. Told her the job was canceled. The look on her mum's face was awful, but imagine what that look might have been instead?

Now, three days later, she, Felicity, and Tony are in Felicity's office.

The holdall is gaping open on the floor between them, padlock cut open by the bolt cutters Tony bought from the B&Q just off Junction 18 of the M25. The money they'd found inside is piled up on Felicity's desk. Just over a million pounds.

"I just . . ." starts Felicity. "And hear me out here. I just wonder what use it would be, Bonnie, handing it over to the police?"

Bonnie looks at the money again.

"That's your children's future sorted," says Tony.

"But I didn't earn it," says Bonnie.

"It's your bag," says Felicity. "They gave it to you."

"We have to report it, though," says Bonnie. "I'm sorry. It's illegal."

"I don't think money can be illegal," says Felicity. "Not all by itself."

Tony nods. "It's not like it's a bag full of drugs. That's illegal."

"That's illegal," confirms Felicity.

"But it belongs to someone?" says Bonnie.

"A man called Mickey Moody, in fact," says Tony. "Currently under arrest for murder."

"Yes," says Felicity. "And now it belongs to you. He couriered it over to your house, didn't he? And there's no note asking you to return it?"

"And Mickey Moody was happy to see you risk going to jail in Brazil for the next ten years," says Tony.

"Precisely," says Felicity. "He has other things on his mind. I don't suppose he'll miss this."

"But what would I do with it?" Bonnie asks. "I don't want it. I want to work."

"Then work," says Felicity. "Fly around the world with your mum and your kids, build your brand, spread some happiness."

"But I don't know how," says Bonnie.

"Then I'll be your agent," says Felicity.

"You'll be my agent?"

"We can learn together, and earn together, can't we? And I can funnel this money through my accounts while we do?"

"Won't someone notice?"

"Well, I've had a good year," says Felicity. "The taxman won't bat an eyelid."

Bonnie looks at them both. "But it's wrong."

Tony nods in understanding. "But there's an old saying, Bonnie. Two wrongs make a right."

"I think . . ." starts Felicity, looking at Tony, then lets it go.

"Okay," says Bonnie. "Okay, then. But I'll be working for it?"

"You will," says Felicity. "And I'll charge you ten percent, every penny of which will go to the families of Andrew Fairbanks, Bella Sanchez, and Mark Gooch."

"So you'll end up with nothing?" Bonnie asks.

"I was stupid," says Felicity. "I should have known something was going on. And people died because I didn't want to look too closely. That's on me, I'm afraid. It's like when I didn't check Sue Lawley's contract properly in 1983 and she read the news for free for the first year."

"What will I tell my mum?" says Bonnie. "And my kids?"

"You're going to work hard for the next few years," says Felicity. "And you'll get paid for it. Just a little more than the going rate, that's all. No one will ever know. And when the money runs out, we'll see where we are. If you make it, you make it, and if you don't make it, at least you tried."

"It just . . ." says Bonnie. "It just doesn't seem right."

"Bonnie," says Felicity, "show business is full of people with rich parents. They can afford to struggle for a few years, knowing they have money behind them. Now, you don't have rich parents, but you *have* just been given a bag containing one million pounds."

"And tax-free," adds Tony. "The best money of all."

"Bonnie," says Felicity, "I've been in this business a long time. I've seen talented people fail, I've seen morons become millionaires. There's no rhyme or reason to it. You need hard work, you need self-belief, and you need luck. You work hard, don't you?"

"So hard," says Bonnie. "But I don't have self-belief."

"You got on the train to come to see me, didn't you?"

"Well . . ."

"*That's* self-belief."

"And then," says Tony, "you were handed a bag containing a million pounds in untraceable bills belonging to a man who will never ask for it back."

"And that," says Felicity, "is luck."

Bonnie nods. "Okay, okay."

She looks at Felicity and Tony.

"Thank you."

"Thank you, Bonnie," says Felicity. "It's going to be fun."

"But you two have got nothing out of this whole thing?"

Felicity and Tony look at each other, with a shrug from him and a giggle from her.

99

A light red, I think," says Jeff. "With monkfish."

"No, white," says Henk. "A rich white with monkfish."

"Red would be more usual," says Jeff, running his finger down the list of red wines in the restaurant of The Wilberforce.

"With monkfish?" says Henk. "Goodness me, Jeff, what a muddle you are getting yourself into."

"Red, red, red," says Jeff, reading down the menu.

"Tell me when you get to the whites," says Henk.

"Red," says Jeff.

"White," says Henk.

"Red," says Jeff.

"I will give you gentlemen a moment to discuss," says the porter, waiting patiently. He then looks at Max's feet. "And I see that sir has invested in some shoes."

"Calfskin," says Max. "You see many calfskin shoes?"

"Oh, plenty, sir," says the porter. "Most people just say 'leather,' though."

The porter leaves the three men alone.

"You two back together, then?" says Max.

"I don't see why not," says Henk. "Our suspicions got the better of us."

Max nods. "And then I caught Susan Knox for you."

"Well, she used your name to cover up what she was doing," says Jeff, his nose wrinkling.

"Come now, Jeff," says Henk, putting his hand on Jeff's arm. "Let Max speak."

"Yep, she messed with the wrong dude," says Max. "You shoot for Max Highfield, you'd best not miss."

"It was Amy Wheeler who caught her, rea—" starts Henk.

"Come now, Henk," says Jeff. "Let Max speak."

"It was fine work, Max," says Henk. "Fine work."

"And she used the name 'Joe Blow' too," says Max. "From *The Rose of Sarasota*. People love that movie."

"Although chosen for its obscurity, I think," says Jeff.

"Did I tell you I'm going to be in a movie about money-smuggling?" Max says.

"Rosie D'Antonio's movie?" Jeff asks.

"Yep," says Max. "So weird, it's just like what happened."

Jeff and Henk look at each other. Let the man speak.

"The last mystery to solve is why someone has been sending me death threats," says Max.

"Henk always used to do that with new clients," says Jeff. "So he could up the price when they were nice and terrified."

"Yeah," says Max. "In this case a mystery, though."

"And one we may never solve," says Henk. "Any recently?"

"None," says Max.

Henk shrugs at Jeff, and Jeff smiles. The team is back.

The porter returns with a bottle of wine. "I took the liberty of bringing a rosé."

"Oh, lovely," say Jeff and Henk together.

100

All right, Susan? Don't know if you'll get this, but I read your name in the papers, and thought I'd give it a whirl. No ChatGPT when you write in pen and ink, is there? What you see is what you get now: Mickey Moody, large as life and twice as ugly!!!

I'm banged up, as you'll know, and fair enough too. I was stupid, and some other geezer was cleverer. That's the game, innit, Susan? Pissed me off, though, thought I had it all worked out. Now I'm crapping in a bucket. Takes me back to my childhood!

Sorry if I killed anyone you liked, and sorry they caught you too. I hoped you'd get away with it, to be honest. Pictured you dipping your toes in the Med or whatever. Still, Downview's not a bad prison. I had an aunt who did a ten-stretch there in the nineties, and she only said nice things.

If I can give you some advice from one prison cell to another, it is this. No regrets. We live our lives forward, not backward. So always make the best of what's in front of you.

You don't have to tell me, but I've got time on my hands. No telly, no golf. What's your story?

Cheers,

Mickey

Dear Mickey,

I'm glad I didn't "get away with it." I'm exactly where I belong.

As for my story, it's the same as yours. The same as so many people's now. Money.

I worked for Jeff Nolan, the man you tried to kill. And, in the end, the man I tried to kill too.

I had been "topping up" my salary for years and years from a few of Jeff's accounts. He gave me access to them over the years, so I could take care of things that bored him. Eventually everything bored him. It was just a few thousand here and there at first, and I invested wisely. I sometimes even invested in things that Jeff told me to, actually, though he didn't realize it was his money I was using. I bought a few properties. But I always paid back what I'd taken from any profit that I made, and no harm was done to anyone.

Recently, though, I'd started losing bits here and there—you know how interest rates have been, the global economy and suchlike. I had thought I was something of a financial genius, but I had merely been investing at a time when a fool could make money.

And I am a fool.

I started chasing my losses, and suddenly the money I could access from Jeff wasn't enough to cover what I was doing. And so I turned to you with my proposition, which I hoped would be lucrative and trouble-free. I'm not from a world of murder, Mickey, but I was desperate, and I accept that I walked through that door of my own free will. It was a mess, and it was a mess of my own making, so I have got everything I deserve. They have locked me up and I hope they throw away the key.

I will never forgive you for resorting to murder, Mickey, but that pales into insignificance against the fact that I will never forgive myself.

Money does the funniest things to people, doesn't it? I know your job is to wash it clean, but, Mickey, how on earth do you wash yourself clean afterward?

I now have a long time to ponder that question. Sin in haste, repent at leisure.

I have no interest in beginning a correspondence with you, so I shall bid you farewell, and hope we both find some form of forgiveness.

Yours sincerely,

Susan Knox

101

It is three a.m., and the village of Axley is gray-blue under a low moon. A lone pony stoops his head to drink from the village pond, and Steve Wheeler sits on his favorite bench. How many times has he sat here since Debbie died? Talking to his wife, sharing his day, trying to hear the faint echo of a reply?

"It's nice to be home," he says.

The pony looks up. He knows Steve, of course, but who are the other two?

"I think Debbie would be proud of you," says Amy, her head resting on Steve's shoulder. "I'm proud of you."

"I'm proud of you too, Amy," says Steve.

To Steve's left, Rosie D'Antonio mimes being sick, then downs the rest of a can of Red Stripe. "Has anyone ever told you two that you're too sentimental?"

"Says the woman who just had a half-hour conversation with her boyfriend," says Amy.

"Eddie is not my boyfriend," says Rosie. "I'm mentoring him."

"We've all heard you mentoring him," says Amy. "Through the hotel walls."

"Where to next, Amy?" Steve asks.

"How do you mean?"

"Mickey Moody and Susan Knox both under arrest. You're in the clear. So where are you headed? What's the next job?"

Amy shrugs. "I think I'm done."

Rosie cracks open another can.

"Done?" asks Steve.

"Jeff and Henk told me to take a couple of weeks off," says Amy. "But I think I fancy a change."

"Assassin?" suggests Rosie.

Steve looks at Rosie. "You're going to put those cans in the recycling when you're done, aren't you?"

Rosie raises her current can in cheers. "I'm not going to be done for a while yet, Stevie."

"What will you do instead?" Steve asks. "Maybe something over here? I could see a bit more of you?"

"Detective agency," says Amy. "Investigations."

"Competition, eh?" Steve laughs. "You'd be bored rigid! Sitting in a car all day outside the Tesco Express in Lyndhurst."

"I've got a different sort of agency in mind," says Amy. "Not so much investigating insurance fraud, more, you know, murders, stuff like that?"

"You're going to investigate murders?" Steve says. "You know there's not a lot of call for it? I think the police have covered that market."

"Not those murders," says Amy. "I mean the ones people can't solve, the ones people don't care about. The ones people give up on."

"People who can't protect themselves?" says Steve, and Amy looks at the ground and nods.

"Love it," says Rosie.

"And to pay for it all, we'll investigate a few murders on islands, murders in planes, that sort of thing too," says Amy. "Skyscraper murders."

"Good name for a boo—" starts Rosie.

"You'd need money," says Steve. "Offices, advertising. And you should see what I spend on photocopying."

"I have a rich friend," says Amy. "Offered to put up half a million for a third of the company."

Rosie snorts. "You're setting up a detective agency and you didn't ask me first? I'll give you three quarters of a million, for twenty percent."

"The other backer is a very close friend," says Amy.

"I'm a very close friend," says Rosie.

"But I shook hands," says Amy.

"Anything in writing?" Rosie asks.

"Well, no," says Amy. "But I don't like to go back on my word."

"That's business, baby," says Rosie. "Final offer, a million dollars for fifteen percent. We shake on it now."

"Deal," says Amy, and shakes Rosie's hand. "One million for fifteen percent."

"I should think so," says Rosie. "Who was the other offer from?"

"It was from you after I told you the idea on the flight home from St. Lucia," says Amy. "I don't think I realized how high you were, but thank you for your counteroffer."

Rosie shakes her head. "Well played, Amy. Serves me right for mixing marijuana and tequila."

The pony ambles past, nodding to Steve as he goes. Steve nods back.

"If you ever need advice, you can always ask me," says Steve. "I'll be at the bar of The Brass Monkey eating a microwaved shepherd's pie."

"You'll be doing more than giving advice," says Amy, rubbing her finger over Debbie's plaque. "You're my business partner."

Steve gives Amy's shoulder a squeeze. "God bless you for trying, Amy, but we both know that's not going to happen. I've had more than enough adventure lately, thank you."

"You looked like you were enjoying yourself," says Rosie. "If you want an observation?"

"I enjoyed spending time with Amy," says Steve. "I didn't enjoy having to shoot people."

"Yes, you did," says Rosie.

"You did," agrees Amy.

"And I enjoyed watching you wearing shorts," says Rosie. "And I own fifteen percent of this company, so I should have a say. Come on, you'd love it."

"I think I'm the best judge of what makes me happy," says Steve.

"You know that's not true," says Rosie.

"Says the woman who lives on a private island," says Steve. "You know you should buy a place over here, don't you? Have a bit of fun with actual friends?"

"I have a place over here already," says Rosie. "I'm almost certain."

"Where is it?" Amy asks.

"I want to say Shaftesbury?" says Rosie. "Is that nearby?"

"A337, A31, B3081," says Steve. "Forty-five minutes with no traffic."

Amy looks at the plaque on the bench.

"Go on," says Amy. "Dictaphone out. Ask her."

Steve takes his Dictaphone from his pocket.

"You know you can record messages on your phone now?" says Rosie.

"Have a chat," says Amy. "Rosie and I will go for a little wander while you do."

"See the sights," says Rosie.

"Talk about her new boyfriend," says Amy, and gets a punch from Rosie for her troubles.

Amy and Rosie stagger off, arm in arm. Steve is alone on his bench. It is a very familiar feeling. As they walk away, Rosie has clearly just told a dirty joke, probably about Eddie Flood, and his daughter-in-law is giggling. He presses "play" and starts to talk.

"Hey, doll, ridiculous one this evening. Amy wants me to go into business with her. Murder cases, you know, flying round the world, chasing bad guys. She told me to talk to you, but you'll know it's ridiculous too. I've got a business already, haven't I? I had a message about a lost cat only this morning. Who's going to find him if I'm in Monte Carlo or Finland or something? It's been nice spending time with Ames, but she'll come and visit. I've got the quiz every Wednesday, and I'd miss the gang at lunch if I was here, there, and everywhere. Not to mention Trouble. Who'd look after him when I went away? Well, Margaret, I know, those two are in love with each other. But, really, I've got so much going on here. They're showing a film next week in the Village Hall, *Men in Black II*, I think. That's the sort of thing I mean. And I like to sit here, Debs, that's the truth. I like to sit here and talk to you. And I know you've been with me, and we've seen a bit of the world . . ."

Steve can hear more laughter from Amy and Rosie, as a ginger cat rolls around on the pavement in front of them.

"But it's crazy, Debs. Murders? Come on. Been there, done that. I'll stay here. With you. Amy will understand."

Steve is always hoping to hear Debbie reply. And this time he does. He is certain of it. He reaches out his arm and feels her there.

"I understand," he says. "I don't like it, but I understand."

Rosie and Amy are making their way back to the bench. Rosie is carrying the ginger cat, who is purring very contentedly in her arms. Even the ginger cat is not immune to Rosie's fame. Steve realizes, later than he should, that Rosie is not irresistible to people because she is famous. She is famous because she is irresistible to people. Amy and Rosie sit down on either side of him. The ginger cat gives Steve the eye, as if to say, "Oh it's *you*."

"What did Debbie say?" Amy asks.

"Say?" laughs Steve. "She didn't say anything. I haven't lost my marbles."

Rosie puts a hand on his arm. "Don't lie to us, Stevie. What did she say?"

Steve bows his head, smiling. "Well, she swore at me for a while."

"I'll bet," says Rosie.

"And she told me to live," says Steve. "Because she doesn't have that choice anymore. So you've got yourself a business partner."

"Thanks, Debbie," says Amy.

"Thanks, Beautiful," agrees Steve. "But I can work from home a lot, right?"

"Sure," says Amy. "As and when."

"And it'll take a while to drum up business?" says Steve. "I'll have a few weeks to potter around? They're showing a film next week at the Village Hall. It's *Men in*—"

"I got a text from Henk this morning," says Amy. "A news presenter's been killed, and he's worried it's being covered up."

"Nearby?" Steve asks.

"Fairly nearby," says Amy. "Turkmenistan."

"I'll prepare the jet," says Rosie.

"Exciting," says Amy. "The first case for Maverick Steel International Investigations."

Steve shakes his head. "We're not going to be called Maverick Steel International Investigations."

"It's bold," says Amy. "It tells people who we are, what we represent, what they can expect."

"Amy," says Steve, "you're so great at punching people, and shooting people, and roundhouse kicks . . ."

"But you're very bad at naming companies," says Rosie.

"We're not going to call a multimillion-pound company 'Steve and Amy Investigate,'" says Amy.

"Course not," says Steve. "But the name of the company should tell people what we do."

"Which is?" Amy asks.

Steve spreads his hands, encompassing this team of three.

"We Solve Murders."

"We Solve Murders?"

"Well, we do," says Steve. "Don't we?"

Amy opens her mouth to complain but thinks better of it. The pony is making his way up the high street, while the ginger cat snores lightly. Axley is still and quiet. She nods at Steve.

"Okay, okay, We Solve Murders it is."

Owls hoot their greetings from the trees.

"*We Solve Murders*," says Rosie, nodding. "Great name for a book."

Acknowledgments

Well, here we are again, folks, I do hope you enjoyed the ride. So scary to write a brand-new book with these brand-new characters, but the fact you're reading this means that, at the very least, you made it through to the end. Unless you are one of those people who reads the acknowledgments first, in which case I honestly believe you are a dangerous sociopath.

I have so many people to thank for their wisdom, support, advice, and, in one particular case, almost constant meowing during the process of writing *We Solve Murders*.

But, before all of that, thanks first and foremost to all of you wonderful readers. Characters and stories don't exist without readers, so thank you so much for joining me in this new world.

I hope it was a relief that I hadn't suddenly written a seven-hundred-page meditation on the capriciousness of memory set among the asparagus farmers of fourteenth-century Italy. I'm not saying that such a book would be bad, far from it, I'm just saying that it would be bad if I had written it.

You will have spotted in *We Solve Murders* that, although the world is new, my brain remains the same. I think I mentioned "Twix," "Greggs," and "Lee Child" within the first fifteen pages or so. Which I imagine was a relief to us all.

I hope there was something in Amy, Steve, and Rosie that you could take into your hearts. They will be returning soon, I promise, and I guarantee that Steve will be flying around the world against his will, and Amy will probably jump out of a helicopter, while Rosie arches an eyebrow and mixes the perfect martini. Incidentally, I don't know about the rest of you, but the book I'm really dying to read next is Rosie D'Antonio's *Death Pulls the Trigger*. I do wish it existed.

There are also lots of other characters in this book I can't wait to return to. For example, I very much feel that we haven't heard the last of our US Customs and Border Protection officer, Carlos Moss. Quite how I'll get him involved next time, I don't know, but, rest assured, I will. I also feel like I don't want to leave Max Highfield behind. I know we are all eagerly anticipating *Rampage 8*.

I did feel, as I began to write *We Solve Murders*, that I was somehow cheating on my other characters. You know the ones I mean. But I was soon certain that they are all happily living in the same world as each other. In fact, if Steve were ever to jump in his Corsa, he could reach Coopers Chase in just over two hours. Various possible routes, but I think Tony Taylor would recommend A337, A31, M27, A27, B2192. Depending on the traffic, of course.

That's enough directions, time for more thanks.

Thank you once again to all the wonderful booksellers and librarians out there. Every time you hand over a book you are handing over magic, from Belfast to Brazil, from Crickhowell to Canberra. I hope to meet even more of you this year, so get your book recommendations and tote bags ready. And, yes, please, I would love a cup of tea, I'm absolutely parched.

Books don't get published without publishers—the clue is in the name—and I am lucky to have the very best of the very best.

Special thanks to my editor Harriet Bourton at Viking for being so brilliant, and for pretending to be super chill every time the word "deadline" was mentioned. You hide your terror very well, Harriet.

I am so beyond blessed that the entire Thursday Murder Club team at

Viking also joined me on this new journey. Thank you once again to the fabulous Amy Davies, press and PR supremo Olivia Mead, Rose Poole, Meredith Benson at Penguin Audio, Rosie Safaty, and Roseanna Battle (note to self: *Roseanna Battle* would be a good name for a Max Highfield movie).

Thank you to the awesome UK sales team, Ruth Johnstone, Autumn Evans, Lucy Keeler, Caitlin Knight, Emily Cornell, Chris Wyatt, Grace Dellar, and Jessica Sacco; and in Ireland, Carrie Anderson—all led by the incomparably brilliant Sam Fanaken. And thanks also to the international sales team, Jessica Adams, Nadia Patel, and Laura Ricchetti.

I am deeply grateful once again to the production genius of Natalie Wall and Annie Underwood, and the exemplary copyediting of Donna Poppy.

Thank you to Richard Bravery for another storming front-cover design. A cat sitting on a gun, how well you know me. Incidentally "Richard Bravery" could be the name of Max Highfield's character in *Roseanna Battle*.

And my final Viking thanks to the two big bosses, Preena Gadher and Tom Weldon. Even if they hadn't been helpful, I would have thanked them, because I am nothing if not a corporate suck-up, but, thankfully, they are both kind, wise, super-talented people.

Five novels in now, and my constant guide has been my wonderful agent, Juliet Mushens (with the help of Seth, of course). Thank you to the whole amazing, and amazingly patient, Mushens gang: Emma Dawson, Kiya Evans, Alba Arnau Prado, Catriona Fida, and Liza DeBlock (and welcome, baby Theo!). Thank you also to my wonderful American agent, Jenny Bent.

I am so grateful to my lovely publishers from around the world; I am really trying to tick the territories off one by one as I can. Special thanks to Jess Malpass for shepherding me through Australia so entertainingly.

My American publishers continue to dazzle and delight. Thank you so much to Pamela Dorman, and Jeramie Orton, what a joy to meet you and your whole team in New York this year. Further thanks, from the land of the New Forest to the land of South Carolina, to Brian Tart, Andrea Schulz, Patrick Nolan, Natalie Grant, Kate Stark, Rebecca Marsh, Kristina

Fazzalaro, Magdalena Deniz, Mary Stone, and Alex Cruz-Jimenez. Further thanks to Tricia Conley, Tess Espinoza, Mike Brown, Diandra Alvarado, Jason Ramirez, Colin Webber, and Andy Dudley, and the amazing Viking Penguin sales team. I'm certain I'll be seeing you all again very soon!

Thank you, on two particular points of order, to Olly Smith (apparently a lovely Pink Padel rosé is just the ticket with monkfish) and Tom Lidstrom for naming The Wilberforce. And a special thank-you to the people and the ponies of the beautiful New Forest. As a child we used to go camping every year at Hollands Wood (just on the right as you leave Brockenhurst), and I apologize to the campsite owners for all the bloodshed (in the book, not on the family holidays).

Thank you, also, to Jn Pierre, who really is a St. Lucian taxi driver/politician, but definitely isn't involved in any of the nefarious things that Ferdy knows about in the book. Neither, to my knowledge, has he ever crashed. If you're at the airport in St. Lucia, do ask for him and tell him I sent you.

Thank you, as always, to my mum, Brenda. I just emailed her to say that a newspaper would like to take a photo of her with Dame Helen Mirren on the set of the *Thursday Murder Club* film, and I assumed that was okay with her?

Her three-word reply was "You assume correctly." That's my mum for you.

Thank you to the rest of my awesome family: Mat and Anissa, Jo, Richard and Salomé, Matt and Nicola. Hola, from Uncle Richard, to Mika, Leo, and Neni, and love, as always, to my grandparents Fred and Jessie.

This book is dedicated to Jan Wright, my late, greatly loved Auntie Jan. Jan died the day after her birthday, having just spoken to everyone who loved her (that was a lot of people) and looking forward to a trip to the café at M&S. Not bad going, Jan. We love you and miss you.

Readers often ask me if any of my characters are based on people I know, and they very rarely are. But I can confirm that Trouble is based, in very large part, on my constant writing companion, Liesl Von Cat. Liesl actually managed to delete an entire paragraph of the story for the first time ever this year. Can't wait to see what she has in store next time.

Thank you to my children, Ruby and Sonny, for growing up to be such funny, smart, kind adults. It is a great privilege that you still enjoy hanging out with me.

And, finally, at the heart of everything, all my love and thanks to my wife, Ingrid. What a dream it is to go through life by your side, Ingrid. Here's to many more adventures ahead, your hand in mine.

See you all same time next year, for the further adventures of a gang of friends called Joyce, Elizabeth, Ibrahim, and Ron. I do hope they've enjoyed their year off and are ready for a few more murders.

Until next time, you lovely people.